Flowers of Cardhon Nimloth

S.M Fox

S.M Fox

Contents

Chapter 1

The oldest of their clan was dead.

Nesterin had finally croaked at one-hundred and sixty-five. It was a long life by clan standards. But with her passing came a thrashing uncertainty within the hearts of the Runda Nor. The old, grumpy female might have been the last of their clan to be blessed with long life. Radelia always thought it their god's way of punishing the clan for their ineptitude. Nesterin's passing was a reminder that the clan's former glory was never coming back.

Radelia stepped out of her hut, and the dewy forest air greeted her skin. There was no sky above her, only a green canopy. Their homes were wrapped around the trees and camouflaged with moss and branches. Her hut, like all the others, was little more than a child's treehouse with a spacious circular balcony. And even from her hut, she heard the growing murmurs from the accumulating crowd.

Whatever was going on, it wasn't typical. Perhaps the old woman hadn't kicked it after all and gave the healers a few whacks with her cane to prove the point.

Grabbing hold of a rope, Radelia unfurled it from the post. The zipping of rope against wood was the only warning she had before her feet left the bridge. Hurtling upward, the wind pelted her face and whipped her hair. She closed her eyes and smiled.

Letting go of the rope, she landed on a bridge three levels higher with a woody thud. The onlookers paid no mind. The Runda Nor wasn't a clan that bowed or fawned over their future empress. They'd leave that to the High Elves.

"We found Nesterin this morning," she said as the crowd gave way. "Why are you all standing around?"

"The healers won't touch her," Jonik said, motioning to the exposed doorway. "It's their job, but they won't do it."

That was strange. The surrounding elves were arguing about the situation since no one wanted to enter a dead elf's hut uncleansed.

"There's no accountability!" someone behind her complained. "The healers can do whatever they want, and no one reigns them in."

"Perhaps you miss the kingship?" another taunted.

"I'm just saying some oversight would be nice. If Kieran were in charge—"

"If I wanted a king, I'd go to the castle."

If she didn't say something, they would argue themselves in circles. She tilted her head and made light of the situation. "Nesterin and that resin cane are Elpharae's problem now."

In the sprawling treetop village, only the healers could touch the dead. Everyone knew that except the healers, evidently. Mutters of curses trickled from ear to pointed ear. Radelia shook her head. Few things frightened the Runda Nor. They would face charging boars and scale mountains, but when it came to the dead, terror paralyzed them.

Her father said it was because death wasn't natural to elves. They lived and endured the ages with grace and wisdom, and... Well, she'd stopped listening by then. But the point was, her clan were descendants of a race that rarely died, so death was scary.

Not that she couldn't relate. Death scared the shit out of her too, but someone had to deal with the body, or it would stink up the entire village. Nesterin's final petty revenge.

"Is there a healer here?" Radelia asked, her eyes scanning the crowd.

One emerged from Nesterin's hut, wiping her hands on her apron as she whispered a prayer. Radelia smiled. Katar may have been a healer, but her best friend wasn't the holier than thou type that caused scenes like the one Radelia was currently dealing with.

Katar nodded for Radelia to join her inside. She hesitated for a moment—hanging out with a dead body gave her the creepy crawlies—but she entered anyway. "Why are they refusing to do their job this time?"

"Many of the healers claim they can hear Elpharae no longer," Katar said. Her brown, chin-length hair was poking out of her healer's cap. "They think our god has forsaken us and they won't have Elpharae's protection if they touch the body."

"Is that it? I thought perhaps she left a curse on the hut."

"She did," Katar said with a mischievous grin. "I burned it before anyone saw it."

So the healers weren't protesting because Nesterin threatened to haunt them from the grave for giving her daughters her cups or something. At least, not to their knowledge. They'd found some other reason to shirk their duties.

"It's always something with the healers," Radelia grumbled, glancing at the lump still in the bed. She looked so small despite the piles of fur she had accumulated. The hag outlived all six of her husbands and had the furs to prove it.

"Yes, but this time, I fear they're right. Another babe was born last night…"

Radelia put a finger to her mouth and shushed Katar. She glanced at the doorway to make sure none of the others had heard; her father had been trying to keep the problem under wraps.

"Rounded ears?" she whispered.

Katar nodded. Moisture accumulated along her lash line. When Katar felt scared—which wasn't often—her eyes instantly teared up.

Maybe it was true. If Elpharae had forsaken the Runda Nor, what would become of her clan? After everything they'd sacrificed to worship them, for them to just abandon the clan was…well, it was unbelievably fucked up.

"Maybe it's not their fault," Radelia offered, hoping it would ease Katar's fears. "Something might be blocking their voice, their power."

Katar cracked a smile and brushed Radelia's cheek with a warm hand. "How is it your skin never dries even in the winter air?"

Any conversation that veered away from the things Radelia could not control were welcome. The future empress wanted to be a strong leader for her people. To be a graceful and otherworldly elf, like in the stories her father regaled them with as children. She wanted to lead with the wisdom of ages and the spirit of Elpharae.

But refinement was not a trait used to describe Radelia Bellas.

"A good beauty regimen," Radelia teased. "One that involves fresh air, lack of food, the occasional bath, and no small amount of dirt."

"Ah ha," Katar said in a mocking tone. "Well, I don't suppose you'd take a break from such a rigorous schedule to help me with the remains."

Something inside Radelia squirmed. She didn't want to be anywhere near the body, but she wasn't about to let Katar do everything herself. High Elf kings sat on thrones while their people did the dirty work. It was why her people left Cardhon Nimloth. Her father helped the clan in any way he could, and so would she.

"I didn't come to watch," she said, reaching for the apron hanging on an uncut branch. "How can I help?"

Using an old cart delegated to ferrying the dead to the mountain, Katar and Radelia each grabbed a handle and pulled it through the forest. When her mother had died, there was scarcely a trail. But in the twenty years since, her people had carved a path to the mountain, and the dirt underfoot was smooth and hard.

Before they left with the body, Katar placed a series of prayers along the door. Painted rocks with symbols of their god to ward off ill-intent or any misgivings Nesterin's spirit undoubtedly had.

"I just hope I found all the curses," Katar said. "How bitter can one elf be?"

Radelia pulled the cart the way a mule would have, except even the mules wouldn't go up the mountain of the dead. It was like they knew on some instinctual level that massive birds waited to feast on anything that remained in their territory.

"The longer you live, the more sticks you have to sharpen, I suppose."

She could relate. After only being alive for three decades, Radelia had a few sharpened sticks of her own. One for the High Elf king who drove her people to such a meager and shitty existence. Another for Kieran for dropping her like a hot coal on the burner without explanation. The last would have been for Nesterin, but she already got hers. Radelia had been on the receiving end of that cane far too many times.

"Would you rather deal with a latrine blockage or eat snails alive?" Katar asked. It was a game they played when tasked with mundane work.

Straining to pull the cart through a wet patch, Radelia grunted and cursed something crude enough that even Katar's brows raised. The cart finally gave, but the sudden lack of tension caused her to trip. If she wasn't an elf, she'd be ass over face in the mud.

She considered her friend's question. Radelia had done both things at one point or another, and she wasn't sure that she had a preference either way. They were both shitty options that left her cringing on the inside. The hollowed bamboo pipes that carried sewage from the treetop huts to the latrine pits below were notoriously unreliable, but it was that or nearly two-thousand asses hanging over windows.

When shit hit the ground from that height, did it splatter into nothing? Game was the clan's food staple, so she imagined the hunters would still need to watch their step.

Her lips twisted on her face before she said, "Live snails, I guess."

Katar's mouth opened as if she were about to heave the dried meat they had for breakfast. "But they are wriggling and slimy."

"So is the shit."

Too far?

As a healer, Katar seldom did manual labor. She had a trade and had apprenticed for years with some of the most skilled healers in the clan. They'd joined the apprenticeship together, but it wasn't long before her father sat her down and explained that it did not suit her.

In other words, the healers ran to her father and complained so much that they kicked her out.

After a brief stint in the military and a traumatizing afternoon in the nursery, they'd decided Radelia was best suited for tasks that required a brawny arm and problem-solving skills. Unburdened by others.

Katar's eyes screwed shut. "Ah! I wish you hadn't told me that!"

Radelia grinned. Her friend's reaction was worth it. "They're not so bad once you get used to them."

The healer gave her an incredulous look and cried out, "Why?"

"If I'm hunting, I don't always have time to stop and set up a fire. I'd rather eat raw snails than lose the beast and have a village of hungry elves to contend with."

Katar was quiet then. As if Radelia had said something thoughtful for once.

Air is nice today...

Radelia glanced up at the tree with an amused expression. They never had much to say, but it was always hilarious when they piped up.

"What did it say?" Katar asked as she scanned the trees.

"They said the air was nice."

Katar looked up at the wide-bodied tree and considered its wisdom. "Should we say hello?"

Radelia shook her head. "Nah. I can understand what they're saying, but I don't speak their language."

It took her a while to work that out. For the longest time, the other hunters would give her strange looks as she tried to converse with the trees. The elders in the clan eventually explained to her that while some Runda Nor could understand tree, that wasn't the same as speaking it.

The forest air was sweet and piney. Birds called to one another across the canopy and the ferns rustled with the occasional breeze that shifted through the woody maze. The forest was home. It was where Radelia's soul drank from a well of fortifying peace.

Her pointed ears pricked. She let go of the splintered rail.

Katar said nothing, but she too stopped. Not that they'd heard something. It was the opposite that gave them pause.

Searching the clusters of branches and leaves in the canopy, she noted the birds had gone quiet. A silent threat stifled the air, yet the trees themselves said nothing of the trespasser. Radelia's mind instantly went to the worst-case scenario: High Elves.

If it was a hunter from the Runda Nor, the birds wouldn't notice. Only an elf unfamiliar with the forest could alarm the birds. Trees were never the most observant beings. To them, all elves looked the same. Just so long as they didn't hold axes, the trees didn't care what the elves did.

Daggers materialized in Katar's hands, and it poised her for an attack. Radelia almost felt sorry for the High Elf, except she didn't. Not a stone's throw away from where they stood was where the hunters had found her mother's body. Her leg was broken beyond repair, and her throat slit. Radelia had no intention of turning it into a family tradition.

Her mother had broken her leg on a hunt when the High Elves found her. Rather than waste their magic healing her, they'd killed her the way one puts down a lame horse. Such a typical High Elf move. Just because they still had magic didn't mean they got to decide who was or wasn't worthy of it. Her mother deserved it. Damn them for thinking otherwise.

The only warning they got was the break of an errant breeze. Someone was behind them. Radelia and Katar spun around at the same time. Notching her arrow, Radelia followed the movement, ready to strike. Dagger after dagger materialized before flying from the healer's hands in a rapid succession. Twelve in all pierced the bark several inches deep. Where did she keep them?

There was a cry of surprise from a recognizable voice.

In a blur of movement that even Radelia struggled to register, Katar had pinned someone to a tree with her daggers. It was General Kieran, and he was scowling at the healer as if she had pissed in his shoes.

Radelia folded her arms and laughed. "High and mighty General Kieran," she said with a mocking bow. "What are you doing out here?"

The general had the dark brown skin of his mother but the most unusual hair color. It was a burnished red and reminded her of a wood stain, not like her bright copper curls. No one else had hair like it. Some said he used henna dye, but if that were true, he had been using it since they were children.

His voice was slow and deliberate, as if it took every bit of willpower to keep from throttling the healer. "I came to help."

"Then why not actually help rather than trail behind us for half the journey?" Katar asked. Her grip on the daggers did not lessen in the slightest.

Radelia's eyes shifted between the two. Had he really been following them the entire time? General Kieran was a busy elf. For him to take time out of his day for anyone was unusual.

Her cheeks flushed. Out of the three, she knew the forest best, yet the general could trail them without her detection. Katar had somehow known all along. So much for being good at something.

"Couldn't live without me?" Radelia asked with a grin and a wink.

Kieran sighed and rolled his eyes. "Just get me down from here."

Once they freed the general from the staggering number of blades, Radelia watched as Katar put each of them back. It was captivating! Pockets hid in the healer's flowing sleeves, in her apron pockets, inside the apron—she even had a few in her cap. At some point, the small blades were being tucked into a garter strapped to her thigh.

Radelia leaned over and said, "I didn't even see you lift your skirt."

Katar laughed. "I'll never give away my secrets."

"No," Kieran said, his back turned to them, "but you give everything else away."

Radelia turned to give him a piece of her mind, but Katar was always quicker.

"Remind me to visit your first lieutenant tonight. I haven't gotten her yet."

They always bickered like that. It was probably why Kieran didn't want to make himself known and why Katar was happy to ignore him for a time. "What is it with you two?"

"You keep poor friends," Kieran said. "She will lead you astray from duty."

"Says the elf who is shirking his duties to stalk us doing ours!" Katar flared back at him like a child unjustly scolded.

"No, we are all friends. At least we used to be," Radelia said.

She was so tired of it. Bickering was a favorite pastime for Runda Nor, and her friends were no exception. Everyone had an arrowhead to sharpen when they needed to be working together. How could she rally an entire clan when she couldn't even get her friends to be cordial?

Winter after winter, they starved and died in droves. They spoke of accountability and yet blamed their neighbors for not sharing. As empress, she couldn't make her clan work together without issuing a divine order, but then they would name her a tyrant.

There was no winning, and her friends arguing while Nesterin's body rotted in the middle of a wolf-infested forest proved that.

Her throat was raw and tight. The air was too muggy. Crowded and surrounded by too much, Radelia broke from the cart. She took off, running into the forest while Kieran and Katar called and pleaded for her to come back. They could push that damn cart up the mountains and feed the beast birds themselves.

Slowing only when she came to the edge of the forest, she scaled up a branchy tree and perched at the top. The horizon was something they seldom saw, living among the trees, so Radelia squinted against the unrelenting light.

The world was so big from up there.

She felt overwhelmingly small. Helpless. The lands of man were green rolling hills, and planted in the middle of it all was a massive living castle. Birthplace of all elf-kind and the source of their magic, dwindling as it may be. The only hope for the Runda Nor was to reclaim it, just as her father said, but they still had to convince General Kieran. How could Radelia do that when she couldn't even resolve a squabble?

Chapter 2

A soft whisper roused her from sleep. As her eyes focused on the dawning light, Kieran came into focus. She barely recognized the mud-caked general. It was his rigid posture that gave him away.

Why was he there? She had half a mind to lift her fur blanket to invite him in, but she knew how that would end. After being bitten several times, she was wary of the wolf.

"What?" she asked.

His mouth did that thing where it twitched as he tried to figure out what to say before the words came out. "I wanted to apologize for yesterday."

Ah, that was why.

Radelia sat up, still clutching her furs in the icy morning air. "Did you just get back?"

"I didn't mean for that to happen," he said. "I just wanted to make sure you were safe. Katar knows how to bring out the worst in me."

Still sleepy and more than a little cranky from being woken so early, Radelia sneered at him. Yes, it was always someone else's fault, wasn't it? "At least she doesn't hold decade long grudges."

"It's more than that," he growled. "She's one of those people who gets away with everything. She scoffs in the face of our traditions and hides behind your friendship for protection."

That wasn't true. Katar was more faithful to their god than most, more so than Radelia herself even, and she was about to rule the Runda Nor. Everyone skirted the rules in Runda Nor, especially where faith was concerned. What else could they do when their god didn't answer?

"Everyone cheats the healer initiation," Radelia said with a tired sigh. "They just don't tell you because you'll judge them."

"...that can't be true."

Daylight had come on quickly, expanding the hut to its true size. Which wasn't much to look at, but it was home. Their vegetable garden grew along the wall opposite her bed, and a rough-cut table with two empty chairs awaited the mornings she spent with her father.

"They can't hear Elpharae anymore," Radelia whispered. "I don't know how long it's been going on, but it's far more serious than you realize."

His pause told her everything. Kieran hadn't come to tell her he still cared for her. That his feelings were too strong to live without her. He came for some other reason. Radelia would have kicked him if the blanket hadn't trapped her legs.

"I need to ask you a favor."

"It can't wait?"

Kieran lowered his head. "Your father has requested a meeting first thing in the morning. He plans on asking me to launch an attack on Cardhon Nimloth."

Asking her to support him must have been an act of desperation. He knew where she stood on the matter. They had every reason to attack the High Elves.

"Another babe was born a man," she said.

"The mother could have laid with a man."

That was bullshit, and they both knew it.

"Four babes in a row? That was one busy man. None of those mothers interacted with the humans, and it's not like men can traverse our village."

Kieran buckled under the weight of the fact. "Cardhon Nimloth is a living thing. If we attack, we risk killing the castle. If it dies, all elf-kind will suffer."

"We're already suffering, Kieran!" She threw back the furs and got out of bed to start the heating pot. Having a fireplace in a tree wasn't possible, but her people had learned long ago that if they lit a candle under a ceramic dome, they heated their homes without the risk of burning the hut down.

"Look at us," she said, gesturing at the empty hut. "Two more generations and we will be forced to live with the humans."

"Or, if we attack," Kieran countered, "we will sit victorious on a pile of rubble."

He was being ridiculous.

"We are the elves of the forest. If anyone can nurture Cardhon Nimloth to health, it's us. Not the High Elves who worship the stars."

Kieran chuckled at that. "If I've learned anything from my time on the Ruby Isle, it's that it doesn't matter which god you worship. None of them listen. We are alone with our actions."

Before she could argue the point, Kieran was striding toward the door. The chattering of birds muffled his footsteps. It wasn't his actions that left him alone, but his inaction. What use was a general when he refused to put his armies to use? What love could there have been between them if he flinched at the notion?

All these things, Radelia felt with a heart full of wisdom, but her mouth uttered, "Oh, fuck off."

She dressed and prepared some tea. The larder wasn't exactly plentiful, but she made toast with freshly cut tomatoes topped with herbs and salt. Radelia had barely set the cups and plates on the table when her father, the emperor, sat down, dressed in a white linen tunic that enveloped his body and sloping shoulders. His hair was whiter than a winter's morning, but old age had done nothing to the clarity of his green eyes.

"This looks wonderful," he said, motioning to the plate.

"Creativity comes from necessity," she said, repeating his own adage to him.

He smiled, revealing several missing teeth. "Indeed, it does."

They ate their breakfast in silence at first, but as their hunger was satiated, less important matters prevailed. "Was that our general I heard this morning?"

Radelia rolled her eyes and made a noise of disgust.

Her father nodded as if he understood her frustrations but didn't want to add to them. Like any father, he wanted to relieve her burden, not add to it. But she was the princess, and his troubles would be hers regardless of how he tried to ease them.

"It's a unique situation we find ourselves in. The Runda Nor has never had governing bodies. What started as a rag-tag group of fighters has grown into a full-fledged organization."

"One that only answers to him."

Radelia chewed her stale bread, felt every sharp crumb scratch at the gums and the roof of her mouth. They deserved better. She knew it, and her father knew it, but Kieran was content with brooding self-punishment.

"I know Kieran is difficult," her father said with a sigh. As much to her as himself. "But he cares deeply for those under him, and I can't fault him for being protective. If you were in the militia, I would be hesitant as well."

Anger boiled in an instant. She couldn't say where it came from, but Radelia slammed her fists on the table and felt the unyielding wood repel them.

"What is to become of us if we don't take back our home? The High Elves will leave us with less than nothing. Our home, our heritage, and now the very essence of what it is to be an elf."

Her father chewed thoughtfully at this. He swallowed, then spoke, "What is it to be an elf? Certainly, there are traits—our dexterity and grace to be sure. The longevity of our lives was once among them, but is that the whole of it? Pointed ears and a sharp aim? No. I think there is more to it than that."

Radelia had no idea what he was talking about, yet it strung her heart tight, yearning for an understanding that only he could provide. "What is it then?"

"Divinity," her father said at last. "Have you ever had a good look at humans? The webbing between their fingers and the acceleration with which their offspring learn things their forbearers could not? Man is self-perpetuating. Their species learns and grows, even in their anatomy. Knowledge passes through their children innately. Yet ours does not."

She shook her head, unable to grasp his words. What did he mean? That learned experience could pass from a human to their child by instinct?

As if sensing her confusion, her father explained, "They came from the oceans, you know. In great big boats, though they no longer have the skills to make them. Many were stranded on an island between here and the northern continent. With no food to be found, many swam to our shores rather than starve."

"And that's why their children have webbed hands and feet?"

He leaned back in his chair as if satisfied with her conclusion. "Not because of a single event. But man spent many a decade living off fish. They built settlements along the shores, and swimming became a necessity. Now, all their children have webbing between their fingers and toes. If Elves endured such a calamity, we couldn't adapt."

She was catching on. Like the small fibers of a larger thread, her thoughts wove into a single, cohesive string. "We are of divine origin. We cannot adapt as man can."

"Precisely," her father said. "Our gods made us in their image, and our existence depends on them. Man can adjust to new fields and horizons, but the elves must live in the way the gods intended us to live or we won't survive."

And what way was that? Radelia wondered. Their god did not intend for them to live as they did in the forest. Elpharae was the god of the earth, but their clan weakened in the forest because they did not belong there.

"We belong in Cardhon Nimloth."

"Precisely," her father said.

He stood and gestured for her to follow. They stepped outside and beheld the splendor of their treetop fortress. A labyrinth of bridges connected huts with thatched roofing. They'd tied ropes like the one she'd used to travel at every point to stabilize the bridges. No one else used them to travel like Radelia did, but they were useful in bringing things up from the forest floor.

"I need you to look with your third eye," her father said. "Not the ones you opened at birth but the other set given to you by Elpharae themselves."

A chill went up her spine. She hated using that ability. Whether a gift or a curse, it gave her insight that isolated her from the rest of the Runda Nor. A well reserved for the Bellas line she would rather leave untapped—and her father asked her to drink from it.

She looked at him with pleading eyes. Please don't make me.

"I know you fear it," he said. "But it is important for the days to come."

So she did.

Radelia closed her eyes to the splendor of their thriving community and opened the eye that told the future. At first, she saw nothing out of the ordinary. The interconnected bridges held steady, and the huts remained unchanged. But as she beheld the city, Radelia saw two wisps of children giving chase.

They were clumsy. Stumbling and causing the bridges to sway wildly, the boys without pointed ears plodded along at half the speed of a Runda Nor child until one lost their footing. Radelia gasped and cried out, reaching for the boy, but it was too late.

The child fell.

A strangled cry left her throat, and she wanted to wake up. She wanted to open her eyes and see the actual city before her. To smell the moist pine and stale wood once more. It was no use.

There were four in total. Four elf children who were not elves fell from the bridges at different stages of their lives.

When they fell, there were no more.

The Runa Nor were not there. As if the entire village had been abandoned, she saw no signs of life. Was this their future? Or rather, the lack of one?

She watched time lapse over decades or even centuries as the city she stood in became a dilapidated husk. Rotted ropes and collapsed roofs. She shook her head, unwilling to see more.

A gasp lurched from her throat, and Radelia turned to her father, who nodded as if he already knew.

"Yes," he said. "Those children will die if they remain here, and the Runda Nor will perish if we do not return to Cardhon Nimloth."

CHAPTER THREE

Chapter 3

Another night, another revelry.

Ettrian stood in his tower and watched as the High Elves danced and sang as though it were the last night of their lives. It never failed to amaze how an ever-enduring populace continued to do so when the dawn would bring much of the same as it had for centuries.

He placed a hand on the wall, and it gave beneath his palm. The decay within the castle had been trickling out for decades, if not longer. Did they ignore the castle softening around them, or were they too drunk to notice? Ettrian watched in revulsion as a drunk elf smeared the blood sap on his face. They did not know what it meant.

Time was ever shifting under their gaze. While the world changed around them, they were safe with the illusion that it didn't change for them. What was perilous to most meant little for the undying, so when the walls of their castle cracked and bled, they could not see the danger.

But King Ettrian knew it marked the end of their kind.

"You should join them," Balqen suggested with far too much cheer for an elf so advanced in years.

He sighed. "Nothing like a dark cloud to hang over their celebrations."

His vassal made a noise of disapproval. "They're your people. They will fear you less when they know you."

A couple lay on the lawn among the wildflowers and honeybees, making love as though no one were looking. Praying to Isilynor as they no doubt did every night for a child that would never come.

"They have their entire lives to know their king. What's left of it, at least."

His people's mistrust and hatred, he could endure. It was the blood on his hands that haunted the king. The treason he'd committed left an unhealing wound in his heart. And it was all for naught. Cardhon Nimloth remained unchanged.

The elves of the forest still live...

"Hmph." He failed to see how that tidbit from the spirits was useful. Their cousins had abandoned the castle long ago, and their scouts never could locate their village within the forest. Perhaps it was for the best.

"Pardon?" Balqen asked.

Ettrian winced. He'd forgotten the old elf was there when he responded to the unseen spirit. "Nothing."

Hearing voices was not normal, even for elves.

"Call the other vassals," Ettrian said. "We must go over the court's agenda for tomorrow."

He disliked being unprepared for court, though he failed to see why they even bothered the day after a revelry. Half the time, the High Elves were too sick with drink to show up to their own petitions, petty as they were. Someone took too much butter from the reserves or there was a family squabble to settle. Still, it was his place to respond as it was theirs to petition him.

If Ettrian couldn't save them, he could at least rule them for a time.

He turned away from the window, unable to bear the sights below. Wedging himself into a chair made for smaller elves and adjusting his feet over so post so his knees didn't hit the top of the glossy table, Ettrian read the histories of his people. There had to be something. A clue to why Cardhon Nimloth was dying and what would become of his people if it did. Though he had a good idea what the outcome would be.

His vassals shuffled into the room, all dressed to impress as they were likely pulled from the revel. Omaro wore a simple long tunic with a cord around the belt. Some might have perceived his attire as plain, but the silver that threaded the cuffs and slit of the neckline matched his belt. Weaving silver into thread was a painstaking and expensive endeavor.

The healer bowed politely and made way for Leaf and Aracaryn while Balqen took up the rear. Aracaryn was a vision in her sheer white gossamer gown. Her ebony skin reflected the gentle candlelight, giving her an ethereal appearance. The princess of the Ruby Isle held the highest station next to his own. She even stood to inherit the throne should any untimely demise befall Ettrian.

She hurts more today...

It was so subtle, but through the flowing skirts of her gown, Ettrian noticed the slightest of limps. He kicked out a chair. "Please, sit."

Aracaryn hesitated under the scrutiny. He didn't mean to make it so obvious. "All of you," he added.

Too young for formality, Leaf plopped sidelong across Ettrian's bed. The bed that was custom made to accommodate his size dwarfed the petite female. Only a doll at the edge of a bed. Her white pixie hair framed her little round face, and she wore a permanent scowl as if she thought it would make the other vassals take her more seriously.

"There is little to discuss," Aracaryn started. "The stables ask for more brushes, and there is a couple asking for a new room since theirs is too cold."

So, they were noticing.

Cardhon Nimloth's magic was evaporating like water on barren soil. The barrier that kept out the elements was weakening. But moving families around was not an issue. There were less than a thousand High Elves in a castle grown large enough to accommodate five times that number.

"I know whom you speak of," Ettrian said. "They live on one of the far branches of the castle."

"They take hours just to get to the dining hall," Balqen reflected. "I'm surprised they didn't move sooner."

Omaro and Leaf remained silent. They had no quarrel with such a basic request. It was tasks like these that made their job an easy one.

Aracaryn frowned at the next parchment. "There is an anonymous petition to change the laws surrounding divorce."

Ettrian leaned back in his chair, ignoring the squeak of protest. Why would anyone want to change their marriage laws? He waited to see if the spirits had any input, but they never seemed to have insight when he wanted it. Ettrian only heard what they said in passing; it wasn't like they were speaking to him directly or that they could read his mind. He could hear the things that piqued the curiosity of the dead and no more.

Omaro stretched out his hand. "May I see that?"

"This elf is requesting a divorce without parental consent. One initiated by a single party."

"Someone wants to dissolve their secret marriage without divvying up the family wealth," Leaf said with a slight smirk.

"So it seems," Aracaryn commented.

Ettrian had no expertise in such matters. Their parents hoped he and Aracaryn would wed to unite their kingdoms, but the attempt at matchmaking had thrilled neither. He had never actually been in a relationship. Being king meant he was forbidden to engage in acts that might sire a child out of wedlock.

And no High Elf wanted to marry him besides.

"I'm not opposed to it," Ettrian said. "I would not force a couple to remain together if they do not wish it so."

"Yeah, but what if one wants the divorce and the other does not?" Leaf asked.

Ettrian shrugged. "It's basically the same thing. If one wants out of a marriage, the other will eventually want the same."

Omaro cleared his throat. "I think the issue here is wealth. Families that have lived for thousands of years accumulate many precious items. When a couple separates, their wealth must separate as well. The longer they are together, the more entangled those finances become."

Balqen stared at the black velvet drapes and said, "Perhaps if we learned more about this, we could make an exception. Secret marriages do not remain secret for long in such a small community. So, this might be a recent event."

"I don't think we should change the law for one person," Leaf said. "They made a mistake. They should own it."

Aracaryn's upper lip curled into a sneer. "And should we make you own all the mistakes made in your brief life?"

"Hey, at least I didn't marry someone in secret and try to back out of it."

"Not everyone has a choice in marriage," Aracaryn countered. Ettrian suspected she was talking about herself more than anything. "We do not know if they made the joining under duress or intoxication. If the partner's intentions were noble or if there was some truth withheld."

Leaf rolled her eyes. "Right. Someone put a knife to their lover's throat and demanded a pact be made."

"Such things have happened on the Ruby Isle—"

"But we're not on the Ruby Isle, are we?" Leaf interrupted. "If we were, we'd be scheming and vying—"

"That's enough." Ettrian's voice engulfed the room. It was enough to jar his vassals' attention. "Omaro, reference the laws on annulment. If this pact was made recently and under false pretenses, it should fall under that category. All claims to wealth will be forfeit."

The healer's brow raised. "I wasn't even aware we had such laws."

Ettrian had spent enough time in the library researching the demise of Cardhon Nimloth that he had stumbled upon many curious and little-known things. He had never expected annulment to be used, but he was wrong.

"I think that is the right course of action," Balqen agreed with a fist knocked against the table. "We don't need to change the law if there is already one in place."

Aracaryn nodded. Her approval eased her shoulders and grim expression.

Tension was building between his temples. Ettrian pressed the bridge of his nose with his fingers and massaged the thin bones around his eyes. "If there's nothing else, return to the revel. I'm certain you're missed."

As his vassals filtered out of his room, Ettrian spotted Leaf glowering at Aracaryn when she thought no one was looking. They contrasted one another in every way possible, and it was grating on his nerves. He didn't pretend that Aracaryn was the easiest to get along with, but Leaf was intentionally baiting the princess without cause.

"Leaf," he called as she lingered in the doorway. "Come here."

The young elf did as she was told. "That was unworthy."

Green-blue eyes lowered under her dense lashes. She was a beautiful girl with agility and intelligence that surpassed her sires. Sometimes he forgot these things, but up close, there was no denying it. Leaf was a child of magic. Her eyes glowed as bright as stained glass on the longest day of summer.

The last child born to the High Elves sixty years ago was not born of natural means. He studied her face and wondered if she resented the method by which they'd brought her into the world. The way she was the last breath of magic as her clan suffocated.

"I'm sorry, my king. It's just that she always brings up her homeland when we all know she hasn't lived there in over a century."

That was true. When Aracaryn spoke of the Ruby Isle, it was often with a tone of supremacy. Their kingdom didn't trade with men. The Ruby Isles was rich in gems and silver. They had a fleet—not that the High Elves needed one in the middle of the continent. They had a long-standing royal line with heirs to spare.

"I understand," he said with a nod. "But perspective is important. It sets precedence for how other kingdoms rule, for better or worse."

Leaf's hands slapped at her sides. "Yeah, I get it, but there's a reason she's here and not there, so maybe she should just get over herself."

Ettrian raised his brows. That was not kind. Nor was it fair. "You are a vassal now," he reminded her. "I know you did not ask to be, but you are, and as such, you will deal with many unpleasant things."

Not wanting to appear the petulant child that she was, Leaf bowed and left.

Releasing the groan that had built in his chest, he went back to reading his books. If there was anything to be found, he would have found it already. The king suspected he would need to take his own advice and find an outside perspective. But who?

Who could give him the answers short of Isilynor herself?

A faint giggle echoed throughout his rooms. Ettrian closed his book and waited the way a father would wait for a child to finish their exciting story.

That tickles…

His eyes searched the room. Spirits didn't speak for his benefit. Sometimes they were repeated memories or random observations, but this voice was different. It droned with the sound of many. "Care to elaborate?"

They're back! Oh, look at them… They're so rugged. I missed them so…

Ettrian sat upright with a start. It seemed Cardhon Nimloth had visitors.

Chapter 4

"He did what?"

Radelia swayed with the news. She couldn't believe what she was hearing. That stubborn ass of a general had finally made a move, but she hadn't expected something so heroically stupid.

Her father was without explanation. "We had our meeting. As usual, I begged him to march his army, and he said he would only go to war after scouting the castle for himself."

She was pacing small circles around their hut. "So, he went to spy on them alone?"

"Well, not alone," the emperor said. "With a small group."

Who would have a pair of stones large enough...

Radelia stopped pacing. She looked at her father with a ferocity that had him sliding deeper into his seat.

"He said he needed her. Katar is a shadow when it pleases her—"

"That's my shadow!" Radelia's voice was straining in her throat. "That's my best friend he took. He hates her!"

"That does not mean he would let any harm befall her."

Kieran took Katar on a secret mission to spy on their enemies. The elves that practically chased them out of their home and banned the worship of their god. The creatures that murdered her mother. And he took her to them?

Emotions came crashing down on Radelia all at once. Slapping her hands over her face, she covered the tears leaking from her eyes. Katar was her best friend. Her only friend when Kieran had abandoned her. What if they didn't come back? If the High Elves took them from her? She didn't know what she would do.

"War is casualty, my dear."

"This wasn't supposed to be the price. Katar is a healer. She should have been safe from the fighting."

The emperor shook his head. "She would have gone wherever you went. We both know that."

Radelia plopped on her bed. Katar wouldn't have to fight. She was a healer and they traditionally avoided fighting, but everyone knew Radelia was shit at fighting. Shit at healing. There wasn't much that Radelia couldn't stumble with, but Katar never minded. "I should have known Katar would jump at the chance to do something so dangerous."

"She is a skilled healer, but it's too boring for her, I fear. She longs for adventure." Her father placed a hand on her shoulder. "Katar will be fine. She always is."

He was probably right, but it didn't stop the onset of fatigue after Kieran throttled her last nerve. Radelia crawled into bed and wrapped herself up in furs. Her father didn't console her. He understood she needed to rest and come to terms with what had happened.

Elpharae, I don't know if you can hear me, but please keep them safe.

Wails of devastation came from outside the hut. Her heart collapsed in on itself. Were they back already? The High Elves must have caught them in the forest. Kieran was slow in the forest, but Katar would have been fine. She would have pulled him to safety or remained by his side. Elpharae help him if they got caught.

Throwing off the furs, Radelia rushed to the door. Her father remained seated in his chair, drinking his tea as if he could not hear the cries of his people.

Bracing the railing, she watched a bizarre scene unfold. The militia, with their studded belts and high boots, were restraining an elf female, prying a newborn child from her hands. Her partner fought back, railing against four militia men as one of them stepped on a platform that lowered with two stomps of his foot.

"Father!" she cried.

But he did not move. The emperor of the Runda Nor did not stir from his chair, but his eyes fixated on his cup with contemptible intent.

Turning her full attention on him, she pointed an accusing finger at the situation outside. "Stop this!"

Kieran would never allow this. His militia was going rogue, and with the general gone, authority went to the emperor. So why wasn't he stopping them?

She didn't want to believe it, yet the truth was plainly set before her on their bare table.

"You saw the future," he breathed. "You know what fate awaits those human children if they remain here."

Her face contorted into one of utter disappointment and betrayal. With Kieran gone, her father used his temporary power over the militia to yank children from their parent's arms? How could he do such a thing?

He noted her distress and nodded. "You must learn it sooner than later. I seldom use my title, but I had to intervene."

"What are you doing with them?"

His eyes went wide as he gripped the mug. "I'm not heartless, Radelia. I'm sending the babes to a nearby village. Their clumsy feet will be safe on the ground, and they will be but a few miles from their parents."

Her heart ached, and her broken fingernails cut into her palms. She hated this. There had to be a better way, but she saw none. Radelia had seen the fate of the Runda Nor and of those children specifically. Something had to change. But this couldn't be the answer.

That night, she prayed in the shrine of Elpharae for the first time in years. It was a small hut no larger than a woodshed with a single, crudely carved stone in the likeness of their god. But she prayed like a healer who stared longingly at a phallic-shaped gourd.

On her hands and knees, she begged the stone for a sign. Her thoughts were on the children falling from the bridges and the empty, abandoned huts.

"Just give me something!" she raged at the stone. "For fuck's sake, anything. Even tell me to piss off, just speak."

The statue said nothing. It was just stone, after all. There was no more magic in that hit than there was in the entirety of the village. They had already lost their Elven grace, but Kieran wouldn't fight. He would spy on the High Elves, but by the time he got around to coordinating an attack, it would be too late.

She had failed in every endeavor in her life. The thought of leading her people to the end was unbearable. If only there was a way to reason with the High Elves. To share the magic that would restore her clan. It was a shameful act that her father would never subject himself to, but so much time had passed that perhaps they would listen.

It was well into the night when Radelia shook her father awake. Feverish from prolonged prayer in the cold and damp, she roused her father with a reckless urgency.

He mumbled as she shook him. "Wh... Wereshrew?"

"Father," she said.

The emperor rolled over and sat up. "Radelia, what is it?"

"What if we bargained with the High Elves?"

"What?"

How could he not see the answer staring them in the face? "We need to concede this useless war."

He was shaking his head. "No, we cannot do that. Cardhon Nimloth is ours. We are the elves of the earth—"

"Soon we won't even be that anymore," she said. "Let me talk to them. They must need things in that castle. Let me negotiate peace so that they may share their power with us once more."

"No."

If he'd slapped her in the face, it would have been less offensive than an outright no.

"We have seen the same fate, Father. This is the only way."

"No, it's not, and you know it."

He was alluding to Kieran rallying his militia. The emperor relied on Kieran deferring to his perspective, and they all knew the general saw himself as some noble warrior. "We both know Kieran withholds that power because he can. Because he fears losing."

"All the same," her father said, wrapping the furs around his shoulders to stave off the damp. "I'd rather have leverage in negotiations or no negotiations at all. It's ours and begging the High Elves for respect put us into this mess to begin with."

"That's not what Kieran says. He says that our people attempted to instigate a coup and lost."

At this, her father spun around, facing the mossy wall of the hut. "Kieran spent too much time in the Ruby Isle. Those blood sorcery elves only speak falsehoods. How would they know, anyway?"

That wasn't her point. If history diverged between clans, and no one in her clan was there, who knew what had actually transpired? And she understood where her father stood. It wasn't like she enjoyed the idea of waving that white flag. If anyone had cause to hate the High Elves, it was her—they killed her mother. Still, between asking the High Elves for help and going extinct, she would choose the former.

Walking around the edge of the bed, Radelia pulled the furs down, forcing her father upright to reclaim them. "We don't know what happened because we weren't there. Is your pride worth more than the future of our clan?"

His eyes were wide with shock and anger. "Yes! Our pride is who we are."

"Yours or theirs?" she asked, pointing to the village outside their hut.

"Both."

"Those elves who had their children ripped away. What do you think they would give to have them back?"

Her father was leaning toward her, scowling at her like she was the enemy. "What has gotten into you?"

The fate of the Runda Nor. The children without Elven features. Perhaps even Kieran had gotten under her skin. He had taken Katar from her. She had no one to debate or reason with because he took her best friend from her.

"I'm going," she said. "And you can't stop me."

"Radelia Bellas," her father said in a tone that shook the very roots of the trees themselves, "I issue a divine order. If you step foot inside Cardhon Nimloth, I will banish you."

A strange calm came over her then. Like the silence before a heavy storm or the warrior's prayer before a battle. Radelia took a deep breath, and without turning to face her father, she said, "You once told me that divine orders are tools of tyrants."

"Then I am a tyrant," he said simply. "But I will be a tyrant with an heir that can do better than I ever could."

CHAPTER FIVE

Chapter 5

I t was no wonder that the patrol didn't catch her. Ettrian barely glimpsed the shadow that scaled the towers of Cardhon Nimloth. So slight, he thought it to be a shift in the moonlight or a trick on his eyes, but when the patrol had vacated the area, several clumsier shadows followed.

The king watched them from a distance, attempting to understand their aim, but they were unfamiliar with the castle and kept circling back only to hide from another passing patrol. Ettrian suspected they were not looking for anything; they were scouting defenses.

There was no mystery who they were.

He navigated the eastern hallways that wrapped around the court-yard and went up a seldom used flight of stairs, stepping over the occasional rot and dead leaves that had blown in from a window no longer protected by the barrier.

While he preferred his halberd, the long pole was useless in the narrow rooms and halls, so he opted for a great sword. Few elves used two-handed weapons, and most did not know how to counter them. His size may have been troublesome for the furniture, but at least it was useful in combat.

Ettrian lurked in the shadows of the winding hallways and reliefs cut from the tree itself. He watched the intruders, waiting until they cornered themselves in the labyrinth he called home. They were not untrained, he noted. The forest elves used sign language, and the only sound he heard was of their calloused fingers rubbing together while making their gestures.

There were four of them. Three females and a male. He had them cornered in an unused room where their dry hands scratched words at an increasingly rapid pace. They were arguing over something, but what?

Perhaps they were trying to leave the castle to report their findings but couldn't find a way out, and the room they'd found themselves in had no window large enough to escape through. If he were them, he'd be equally concerned.

The whistle of steel being pulled from a sheath was the only warning Ettrian got before a sword lunged from the open door, missing his nose by an inch. The male charged toward Ettrian. Rather than parry, the king used the flat of his blade to deflect the blow. The wind gushed from the male's mouth. His charge broke so abruptly that his feet came out from under him, but trained as he was, the male caught recovered.

Ettrian knew he had no way of dodging any projectile weapons, and the shadow in the group no doubt had many, so he picked up the male by his leather vest and used him as a shield against his own companions.

The male gasped and kicked. His hands clawed for Ettrian's eyes and face, but the king's arms were longer. "Lay down your weapons and kick them toward me," Ettrian said with a gentleness one reserved for children caught with their fingers in the honey jar.

With the furious male cursing and the toes of his leather boots scratching on the floor, Ettrian noted the rest of the intruders. Two of the females were disarming, sliding a bow and arrows in his direction, but the shadow was nowhere in sight.

"Come with me," he said to the smallest female, who was visibly trembling as she stared up at him.

A point as sharp as a needle was at his throat. "You'll not lay a finger on her."

Ah, there she was. The shadow. She had been right beside him all along.

Enthralled by the threat, Ettrian smiled. "But you'll find that I can and will," the king said, staring at the petrified female.

In an instant, Ettrian turned, smashing the shadow with the male in his grasp. They went tumbling to the ground. A female tried to grab her bow, but Ettrian pushed her down like a bully in the courtyard before grabbing the frightened female by the wrist and yanking her out of the room. The king shut the door just as the shadow and the male slammed it and then turned the doorknob until it broke from the door.

"How could one so large be so quick?" the male said from behind the door. "Some freak experiment with breeding giants and elves?"

He had been called many things in his eighty-three years. Half-giant was far preferable than other terms whispered by the court when he stalked through the room. They would have to try harder than that to upset him. According to the books in the library, giants were rather kindly creatures. Good with children and pottery.

"I'm sorry, little shadow," Ettrian said, his voice low and smug. "I have ten fingers, and they have work to do."

The poor elf girl fainted then. The king scrambled to catch her before she cracked her head on the floor. He had plans for her, after all.

Scooping up the girl and slinging her over his shoulder, Ettrian glanced at the door once more. Little Shadow would not remain contained in that room for long, and she was still armed. That would complicate things. Armed hostages were not good company.

He walked through the main stairway. The guards bolted from chairs and ran in his direction. "We have guests in the upper east wing. Our dear cousins have finally paid us a visit," he advised. "Still armed but locked in a room without a doorknob. Guard them with caution."

"Should we kill them?" one asked as Ettrian walked by, the girl's feet dangling dangerously close to his groin. If she were not timid, a swift kick would be her freedom. Hopefully, she didn't wake up with any brave epiphanies.

"No," he said. "They are not to be harmed if you can help it."

He didn't commit high treason only to succeed with his father's wishes. The bastard could churn in his grave a little longer.

"Summon the council to my chambers," he said. "We have work to do."

As Ettrian made his way to the courtyard, an unseen spirit sighed as the wind rustled through leaves.

She's leaving…

The king turned around and regarded the occupied tower. The surrounding darkness remained unmoving. His prisoners had not escaped, but someone had. There must have been a lookout. Someone who was fleeing the castle to report back to the clan. Good.

His vassals were already outside his bedroom door when he reached the steps. Leaf moved toward him, but Ettrian stayed her with a gesture of his hand. "I'm unharmed, and so is she."

The king set the girl on an overstuffed armchair. "Search her for any weapons," he instructed Leaf. Aracaryn, the ever pragmatic one, came with a cord of rope and bound their prisoner's feet and arms.

His four vassals stared at the prone elf with varying expressions. It was Balqen's puzzlement that Ettrian found the most striking. "They don't look like us anymore," the oldest vassal said at long last.

The king tilted his head and observed the prisoner. He had noted the same nearly sixty years ago, but his vassals had not left Cardhon Nimloth in quite some time. They were fortunate enough to avoid his father's hunting trips.

While only the peaks of their ears appeared from long, usually silver hair, the forest elf's ears were longer and more exposed around her chestnut hair. "Their eyes are different too," the king added. "Larger and with multiple colors."

Balqen eyed the king and said, "The varying eye colors were always a trait, but that's the only thing I recognize in my kin, I fear."

Ettrian often forgot that the oldest among the castle was also Runda Nor, for his hair had become white from age, disguising his heritage. Balqen Bellas was the younger brother of the elf that led the forest elves into the woods nearly a millennium ago. The only one of his vassals alive in such times was Aracaryn, and she did not come to the castle until well after the forest elves left.

"Why do you think they have changed?" Aracaryn asked, still staring at the foreign elf like she was a waste of excellent wine.

"I couldn't say. Perhaps they've had to adapt in ways we do not," Balqen said.

"Men adapt," Ettrian said. "Elves are born of gods, so we cannot. Our fates are pre-ordained and unmovable."

"Clearly, something has changed," Omaro said. Being a healer, he took great interest in the elf and studied her the way one would if they were a medical dissection. Ettrian turned away from the healer then. "I wonder if they are experiencing similar hardships to ourselves."

The king suspected so. Their trespass was an act of desperation. Something must have happened to the forest elves for them to investigate the castle after a thousand years of avoidance.

"There are three more in a room," Ettrian said.

"How did they even get in?' Leaf asked, seating herself beside him. Her eyes never broke from the intruder.

"They scaled the walls," Ettrian said, with no small amount of amusement. "One led them. She's extraordinarily dangerous."

"Then why do we let her live?" Aracaryn asked. "She might escape and assassinate innocents."

He had weighed the odds already. The little shadow was deadly. She could easily kill most of the High Elves drunk on wine and passed out in their beds before anyone had an inkling something was amiss. But no, he doubted she would do that for one reason and one reason only.

"Not at the risk of her companions," he said. "She is fiercely protective. If she thinks this one is still alive somewhere, she won't."

"So, we let this one go," Aracaryn reasoned, picking up the logic. "She goes home, and our hold of the hostages strengthens both ways."

Ettrian nodded. This elf was harmless. He would send her home to tell a harrowing tale of the giant elf, and the little shadow would play the prisoner under the false pretense that the girl's life was in his hands.

"Why do they hate us so, Balqen?" Ettrian asked.

The old elf seated himself in a chair facing their captive. "Well," he said, "it was many things all welded into one, I suppose. My brother said the High Elves insulted us, treated us as second-class citizens. When your grandmother, the queen, banned the worship of their god, it all became too much."

Ettrian knew why Balqen had stayed. His wife, still fair and immortal, remained by his side even when he sacrificed his Elven grace. He envied Balqen in some ways. Imagine having such a noble wife. Her family's disdain for him was ever apparent, yet she was unmovable in her fidelity.

"What do we do with the others?" Omaro asked. "The longer we keep them, the more dangerous they will become."

Ettrian folded his arms and leaned back in his chair. "They are common elves of their clan," he said. "Two of them, at least. They are not without training. Intelligent even, and I'm willing to bet their clan will miss them."

The elf's eyes were fluttering and her breath quickening. She was waking.

"In the meantime," Ettrian said with a slight smirk, "we must get all the information we can out of this one."

Her eyes were wide as she looked about the room. Like an animal caught in a cage, she was searching for an escape, but there was none.

"By any means possible," Ettrian stressed.

CHAPTER SIX

Chapter 6

A new latrine ditch needed to be built, and it was her unfortunate job to dig it.

There were times, mainly while knee-deep in shit, that Radelia looked back on her brief stints in other occupations with fondness. Stories of the time she tried to be a teacher still served as a cautionary tale for those in training.

What happened with the pet squirrel was unfortunate.

So, with no formal training, she did other odd jobs around the forest villa. Radelia was an excellent hunter when allowed to go it alone, but more often, the hunters wanted to travel in groups. The others were quiet enough, using hand language, but they couldn't hear the trees and were often confused when she insisted on going in a different direction.

And so, the story always went down the same path. She'd abandon the party to follow an animal. They'd think they lost her and send a search party loud enough to scare every animal within miles. Anger and frustration ensued, followed by a long, patronizing talk from her father. Which was maddening since he didn't know the first thing about hunting.

There wasn't much skill associated with ditch digging, but it was independent work, and there was lots of it. With an uptick in population came the inevitable need for more houses. More houses meant more bamboo pipes that funneled waste into the latrine ditches.

Armed with a long, flat shovel, Radelia had been digging since dawn with a group of nine. For people who scarcely ate, they filled the ditches quick enough. Clawing her way out of the hole, she surveyed the forest grounds. They concealed the ditches and their odor with a top made of net moss so dense, her clan often used it for insulation and roofing. The only downside was that come summer, the heat in the upper canopy would kill it off.

But on the forest ground, net moss grew vast over the latrine covers. Not only did it keep the stench in, but it camouflaged the base of their village. An old human merchant that traded with their clan would pass right through their village without the faintest idea.

Her people would spot him with his rattling cart. If anyone had goods worth trading, they would pursue him, but it always appeared to the human that they were waiting a few miles away.

"Why do you keep doing that?" a digger asked, staring up from the pit.

She shook her head, not understanding the question.

"You keep looking north as though you're expecting something."

It wasn't like she could tell him. Kieran's operation was a secret to everyone apart from herself, her father, and a few high-ranking militia elves. It wasn't like they had spies to worry about, but all the same, it wasn't her place to speak of it.

She shrugged and gave a weak smile. "Just want to look at something that isn't dirt."

Radelia wouldn't have to look northward every five minutes if Kieran and Katar hadn't departed on a secret mission without her. She wouldn't have spent half the night tossing and turning in her furs. Of course, they would have said it was because she was the heir, but what did that matter when the clan was on the verge of ending?

"You going to get back to work or what?" another elf shouted from the pit.

Giving one last glance in the castle's direction, Radelia slid into the pit and resumed digging.

Why was her father so stubborn? She understood the clash between Kieran and her father. Perhaps the general had offered multiple solutions only to be countered with the same unyielding demand. She didn't imagine for a moment that Kieran offered the mission to appease the emperor; he did it for her.

But why did he have to take Katar?

"Easy there, Bellas."

She looked up from the dirt wall and realized she had carved too far. Her skin burned from exertion and cold. Wiping the sweat off her forehead with the back of her sleeve, Radelia shrugged. It was such a burden, knowing the things she knew. Without Katar, there was no one she could confide in. Radelia was certain she'd have an easier time breathing if the elves buried her in the pit.

When the digging was done and covered, Radelia went to the showers with the rest of the diggers. Hot water was a precious commodity so high in the canopy, but while they dug, someone had lit the makeshift boilers that relied on gravity to pour streams of heated water through bamboo pipes. The crew only had so much time before the water turned cold, so they wasted no time in washing.

Males and females stripped naked and showered together. They paid no mind to one another's bodies and scrubbed with squares of net moss and hard soap that left their skin stripped and tight.

"You're using that on your face?" a female asked as she watched Radelia.

"Yeah?" She had dirt on every inch of her body. What else was she supposed to do?

"If I did that, I'd have dry patches and red splotches."

Radelia observed the pockmarks that lined the female's face. She wasn't alone in that concern. Most of the Runda Nor had rough, leathered skin. Radelia's beauty was most apparent in the harsh elements. Katar often chided her for it.

Cold ice water pelted her chest; Radelia yelped and jumped back with a laugh. The shower was over.

Wrapping a linen towel around her body, she walked home barefoot. It would have been easier to use the ropes, but she didn't want the lecture from her father about sailing through the village naked again.

There were voices in the hut that were not her fathers. Radelia slipped in and dressed in his room since it had a drape over the entrance. His room smelled of incense and melted beeswax. In the corner was a miniature shrine dedicated to Elpharae, one of the few relics still preserved from a time when the Runda Nor lived within the castle. It was a wood carving of an elf without gender. Veins of silver ran throughout their body as they posed with their bow, shooting some unseen enemy with a silver-tipped arrow. It had two little diamond eyes that captured the candlelight. .

It put the stone statue in the hut to shame, but it wasn't like the Runda Nor could achieve such a level of craftsmanship in the wild. The statue before her

If the idol in the hut couldn't hear her, perhaps the one in her father's room could. Soaked in the magic from Cardhon Nimloth, if there was any channel to their god, this was it. She dressed before kneeling on the cushion and said a prayer.

"What do I do?" she whispered. "I need a sign. Anything."

But the idol only stared at her with their sparkling eyes.

"The village of man isn't just going to take a bunch of orphan infants for free," a voice breezed through the curtain. "They will want resources to help care for the infants."

"We don't have any to speak of," her father said. "We could spare some honey and perhaps some furs..."

"That won't be enough," the elf warned. "What's stopping them from selling the babes? We need to send the parents along. It's the right thing to do."

"We can't," her father said. "Those are skilled laborers. Smiths and linen weavers. One of them is the best midwife we've ever seen. She can pull breached children from their mothers. There are at least fifteen females due in the spring. She can't leave."

Her father was rustling through their belongings. Radelia winced, knowing full well that for which he was searching. "This is the last of our wealth," her father said.

The stash of emergency gold.

Whenever there was a surplus from a good harvest or a hunting season, her father would take coins instead of trade. It wasn't often, since gold was useless in the forest, but in times of crisis, the Runda Nor had learned long ago that men would trade their last loaf of bread for gold.

"You will go yourself?" the elf asked.

Her father hesitated. "I do not think that's wise."

Someone of high rank had to go. To ensure that the village would provide for the children and to negotiate the terms of gold distribution. With Kieran still gone, there was only one other choice.

"I'll do it."

The words slipped from Radelia's mouth before she could think of a reason. Drawing the curtain back, her father frowned as if he hadn't expected her to materialize from his bedroom.

"I'll see that the babes are safe and negotiate with the men on our behalf."

Her father didn't approve; she could tell by the way his lips went thin across his drawn face. But there was no other.

"Very well. Radelia shall go."

Dressed in her finest—which meant her newest leathers and the cloak her father wore at his coronation before she was born—Radelia climbed onto the rickety old cart while elves hitched up the mule. She absently touched the purse on her belt beside the unfamiliar sword. It would have been better to bring her bow—a weapon she actually knew how to use—but everyone assured her that the road would be safe.

"Even those High Elves respect the road," her father assured her. "We've never had trouble."

It hadn't occurred to her until then, but she would pass by Cardhon Nimloth.

Grabbing the reins, Radelia's fingers flexed in the leather gloves. Dressed in the emperor's garb, his sigil stamped on a silver broach on the neck of the cloak, any who saw her would know she was speaking on his behalf.

Sobs interrupted her thoughts. Radelia turned around and saw the militia herding the mothers away from the litter of babes in the sleeping cart. Her heart ached for them. It was cruelty but allowing them to remain would mean their deaths.

"Just tell us why!" one female wailed as she threw herself against the wall of militia.

Enough of this shit.

Radelia climbed down from the cart and approached the growing crowd. They stopped and stared at her expectantly. What was she going to say? The truth might have been too much to hear, but they deserved a reason.

She sucked in a deep breath. "You've heard stories," she said. "The powers that are said to reside within the Bellas line."

"It's true?" someone asked, though she couldn't tell who. "You can see the future?"

Radelia nodded. "We seldom use it. It's not right to look into the future. Not everything is as it seems. What we know is that man cannot walk the same paths as elves."

She tried her best to maintain a regal composure. One that did not tell too little or too much. But she felt herself ready to burst at the seams on formality.

"They'll die if they stay."

Wincing at her own bluntness, Radelia half expected the crowd to bowl over the militia in a riot, but they stopped.

As if all the Runda Nor could see the vision themselves, they turned to regard the bridges and ropes overhead. "They'll fall," a mother said.

"Please believe me when I say we don't do this out of ill omen or prejudice. We do it for the safety of the children. I have gold, and I will barter for their safety. You can visit them any time you like. When they are old enough to return, they will be welcome."

She wasn't certain how much solace that last sentence gave. If they were still immortal like the High Elves, the few years would be nothing. But for the Runda Nor, each season could be their last. Those parents would be strangers to their children's eyes and for no fault of their own.

Radelia climbed back on the cart and urged the mule forward. She did not look back.

Chapter Seven

Chapter 7

Another day, another court song and dance. Ettrian sat in his gilded chair. Crafted by the elves whose mastery reached its peak hundreds of years ago. The throne was elaborate perfection, not a single leaf misshapen. The clawed feet that outstretched were symmetrical in every measurement. The throne was no more a challenge to create than it was to sit in.

How utterly boring.

The High Elves stood on either side of the white carpet that led to the throne. They followed the unspoken rule that nobility stood to the left and everyone else stood to the right. Ettrian never understood the divide. It hardly mattered since their lines had consolidated over the centuries, but the craftsman and skilled labor had long since married into nobility and kept to their side, and the nobility that were forced to take up trades stood where they always had. Such was the way of Cardhon Nimloth.

The populace was small but even smaller in the early morning after a revelry. Hopefully that would mean a brief court. He needed to get back to his research, fruitless as it was.

"My king," Aracaryn started, "We have an anonymous petition regarding marriage laws."

She gave him the letter, and though they had read and discussed it the night before, they put on a song and dance for the benefit of the court. He skimmed the letter, noting the exceptional handwriting—an indication of longstanding nobility—and nodded.

"There are laws already in place regarding divorce and annulment. I shall help conduct research myself regarding this situation."

He searched the crowd for signs of interest. Not that it mattered who made the request, but curiosity was a brief reprieve from monotony. Some elves were squinting as if the daylight was too bright. Others were massaging their temples. Ettrian had to resist the chuckle forming in his chest. They always loved a good party.

"What is next?" he asked.

"The stable hands request more brushes," Leaf said with thinly veiled annoyance. He didn't blame her. At an age she should have been training and fooling around with her peers, Leaf was a vassal. She stood alone and without others near her age. It wasn't fair.

Ettrian wished he could dismiss her from the duty, but it was not in his power to do so. The vassals formed to keep him in check, after all.

A falling star...

A lover betrayed...

They fell so far...

In separation, they fade...

Oh, good. The spirits were singing. Because that wasn't at all distracting. Ettrian wasn't familiar with the song. He suspected it had something to do with the elf-kin locked away in the castle. "Now is not the time," he muttered, hoping the spirits would get the hint.

"My king?" she prompted.

"Now is not the time to bother me with such trifles," he said without hesitation. "Any requests such as these will go through trades or fellow crafters. No one needs my permission to get the tools they need."

Everyone was giving him that expression. The one that suggested they wanted to depart the room as quickly as possible. He was a frightful creature to his people. Their glassy, bloodshot eyes reflected his image back at him. A large, stooping monster with black hair hanging over his scarred face. Dressed all in black, as was the custom for mourning.

The murderous king was descending into madness before their eyes. He cast his eyes downward, sick of seeing himself.

"We have a more important matter to discuss," he said.

All four vassals stared at him then. Despite numerous debates, they always outvoted him when it came to discussing the decline of Cardhon Nimloth. He wished nothing more than to be transparent with the elves, but the vassals did not want fear to hasten the demise of their home.

"Last night, I caught intruders," he said.

Gasps blurted from the audience. "I handled the situation," he said with a wave of his hand. "Our cousins from the forest have returned. I wished to reveal this to you for the sake of transparency."

No doubt gossip had spread from the guards that took shifts guarding the door. It would only be a matter of time before someone was brave enough to ask. He might as well disclose it to the people. Not everything needed to be kept secret.

"Why are they here?" Someone asked from the nobility side.

"What do they want?"

Everyone was muttering amongst themselves. There was nothing more thrilling for a High Elf than gossip. Those in the gallery would seek the members of their family in the guard or the vassals themselves, searching for fruit that only their station could reach.

"We are questioning them," he said, coming to a stand. "That will be all for today."

There was no point in evading the vassals. They were furious. Even the ever-steady Omaro was wide-eyed and panicked as the elves all rushed them for more information. Ettrian had a head start at least.

His long strides took him through the courtyard and up the library steps. If he was careful, Ettrian might get a few hours of peace before they cornered him.

"What were you thinking?"

No, of course not.

The king closed his eyes for a moment. It was too late to evade her. Aracaryn had beaten him to the library. Her rooms were in the southwestern tower that mirrored his own. He turned to face her. "They should know."

"Know what, exactly?" She was so angry her fists balled as though she meant to strike him. "That our cousins plot war?"

"We don't know that."

"The shadow, as you call her, nearly chopped off their attendant's fingers this morning. Clearly, it's not a family reunion."

He laughed then. It was the wrong reaction, but Ettrian was rather fond of the murderous female. Aracaryn's nostrils flared, and for a moment, Ettrian braced himself for a fist in his face.

"Do you see the way they look at me?" he asked, gesturing toward the great hall. "They fear me. The only way to ease that mistrust is with honesty."

"Your need for love will be your downfall."

Something within him twinged. She had struck a nerve. Before he could reel it in, the words came out. Words he would probably regret. "And the lack of it will be yours."

She didn't argue further. Instead, Aracaryn whirled around in her silken blue gown and stormed out of the library.

That didn't go well.

Ettrian refocused his mind. Rummaging through books stacked on the floors and along old statues of former kings, he picked one up at random and frowned at its contents.

"Am I making stew?" he accused the empty room. "Is that what you think I plan on doing next?"

Grabbing the next book, he opened it to find jewelry designs from over a century ago. His eyes went to the ceiling. "Really?"

The library made no answer.

Reaching for a book at random, he opened it to find yet another bland food recipe. The king lowered himself to the nearest chair in defeat. The library had no intention of cooperating with him any more than his vassals.

It was going to be a long day.

Fidgeting underneath the cloak, Radelia chewed on a broken fingernail and shifted on the hard wooden bench. The mule plodded along at one pace, and that was a meander. She had tried to urge him to move faster, but he only stopped and looked back at her with his unimpressed gaze when she did.

"Get going, you old bastard!"

The mule trudged onward. He had one route and one task. Even without a rider, the mule would carry the cart back on its own. She now understood why their merchant was always an older elf who slept most of the journey.

Maybe she should just pull the cart herself. Time was of the essence. The precious cargo in the back was asleep, all bundled in furs, but if they cried, Radelia would have no idea how to stop it. Then again, she was trying to impress the village of man as a princess, not a beast of burden.

The road curved around the outside of the forest, revealing the splendid castle in the distance. She straightened at the sight and gasped. Cardhon Nimloth surpassed even her wildest dreams.

The exterior was a series of branches braiding into an impossibly high wall. The windows were round gaps in the braids that spiraled into towers and ledges. Legends said that it was her people that shaped the tree into a fortress by carefully managing its never-ending growth. Rather than hack and chop like a man, her ancestors carefully placed obstructions for the tree to grow around, resulting in windows and doors. It was the High Elves that carved the statues of their god into the tree, the fools they were.

What did a goddess of the stars care for trees anyhow? If anything, the High Elves should have lived in a stone castle, allowing them to stand on the rooftops to stare upward at the night sky. It was a matter of pride and status. The High Elves were snobs who loved to look down on everyone else, and Cardhon Nimloth provided the tallest vantage point.

She spotted a few guarding the top of the walls. The distance made them small and undistinguishable. There were so few. The militia's numbers swelled somewhere in the thousands, but she counted just half a dozen along the walls. They had grown lax in their arrogance. It gave her some comfort knowing that.

Somewhere, Katar and Kieran were nearby, taking count and watching the rotation of guards. For all Radelia knew, they were within the fortress itself, disguised as High Elf sentries, learning everything they could.

Once the castle was far from her sights, Radelia sunk back into the bench. She closed her eyes and allowed herself to drift in and out of sleep.

Images of the castle were still strong in her mind. She dreamed she was standing before the great doors staring up. She wanted to knock, but her hands were too stiff to form a fist. Probably because her leather gloves didn't allow for it, but in her dream, she wasn't wearing gloves and was only vaguely aware of it.

The doors opened to her, but when they did, gooey red sap greeted her. It trickled along the walls and dried along the polished floors. Something was wrong. Radelia stepped back from the entrance, only to find the exterior was worse. Blood oozed from rotted knots like open wounds. Cardhon Nimloth was dying.

"Hello?" she cried out, but there was no one. No guards, just the wind pulling at her cloak.

A chorus of whispers sang from within the castle. It was a song she had never heard before. Yet her heart recognized it. A song of the Runda Nor was beckoning her inside. The fortress was calling to her.

Just as she was about to step inside, her body lurched to a stop. Echoes of raspy newborn wails echoed in the barren halls.

Radelia opened her eyes. Men and women surrounded her. Thick-bodied, with gangly earlobes. They were muscular, and most were much taller than her. She was short, even by elf standards. Some humans were staring at her like she had dirt on her face, others peering into the cart with confusion. One man was making solid eye contact while he had a finger wriggling around in his nose. A babe was squalling in the arms of their mother, signaling the newborns in the cart to do the same.

Kieran always said she had a lot in common with men. She never realized it was an insult. If she ever saw him again, she would stuff him into an elk carcass and sew it shut.

"Hello," she said, clearing the phlegm from her throat. "I am the heir to the forest clan. I have a bargain to make."

Sitting on a long bench in their hall, she explained the situation over an ale. Why they liked to drink from horns, she'd never know. The Runda Nor sometimes bought ale from the village. It came in large barrels, and many loved it, but it was never to her taste.

"Times are going to be tough come winter," the elder said, his long brows hung over his heavy-lidded eyes. "I don't know if we can feed more mouths."

"We will compensate you, of course. And we will continue to do so in payments."

One woman turned to the apparent leader. "Children are one thing," she said. "They could do chores and would do well here, but these are newborns."

"We needed to take them from the parents before they became too attached," she said. The ale soured in her gut, but she drank even more to drown her own words. "And we need the parents for work come winter."

Another man, much younger than the others, frowned. "What will you do if this keeps happening?"

She had no idea. It was a question Radelia had asked herself many times and her father only once. His response was to smash his cup against the wall and curse their god for inaction. "I don't know."

"We know things are tense... with your cousins," the leader said. "But perhaps in light of the situation, make amends."

The ale had gone to her head at that point. Her tongue was numb and without consequence. "Things will change when I'm empress."

She couldn't believe she said that. Radelia fully expected the leaders to frown on such treason, but they nodded, and one even laughed.

"I'm sorry," the oldest one said, struggling to restrain his laughter. "It's just that I once said the same."

There was a wisdom in men. Her people did not give them enough credit. Their homes were sturdy and their livestock healthy. They had things her people did not. Security, a bountiful harvest, and when the winters were too long or too harsh, they found other ways to survive. All without magic.

She felt like a beast living in squaller compared to them. Their great hall had many candles and a roaring fire. Simple things that her people refused to accept to live in the forest among the trees.

When her people first left Cardhon Nimloth, they feared the High Elves would retaliate. They built huts in the treetops for protection, but when no one came, the Runda Nor remained. Rather than find more accommodating lands, they built on what they had and insisted it was Elpharae's will.

"Perhaps we will build a settlement somewhere nearby," she said. "We may have to."

"Your clan would be most welcome as neighbors," a younger man said. "We've been allies a long time. We will keep the children for now, under the agreement that this is only temporary."

It was a relief that they agreed. She half expected amid the tough questions and lacking answers, they would decline. Her ride home would be a hard one, and it would be harder still trying to convince her father to act. All his hopes were pinned on Kieran's return and the decision to declare war on the High Elves.

They were running out of time.

She gave the young leader a gold coin. His brow raised as he held it between his fingers. "There will be more next time I visit."

"This will be a good start," he said. "My wife and I have no children. I can't burden her with four newborns at once, but with this I can hire several nursemaids."

Radelia nodded. That was good. He and his wife would see to the children personally.

She departed the village with a slightly less heavy cart. That didn't make the mule's pace quicken any, but Radelia no longer minded. Returning to the Runda Nor was something she did not look forward to.

Nothing like a warm welcome of resentful scowls from her people and aimless justifications from her father. The only thing she looked forward to was a second glimpse of a castle. She wondered if her dream had meaning. Maybe Elpharae was responding to her prayers in a roundabout way. Though the blood could only mean war was coming.

Something was moving toward the forest. Radelia squinted against the summer sun. It was an elf. "Move," she urged the mule, who honked in response to the slap of the reins.

It wasn't a High Elf. They had long white hair and wore dresses. This was one of her own. One of Kieran's scouts. Why was she just walking away in plain daylight? Radelia's heart lurched. Where were the others?

She stood, unable to wait for the mule to quicken his pace. "Hey!" she shouted.

The elf spotted her and ran, stumbling, in her direction. She hoped it was Katar. Maybe she killed everyone and took the castle for herself.

It was wishful thinking, but that was the hope that kept her going in those agonizing moments before the elf came into view.

Radelia slumped to the bench. It was not Katar but one of Kieran's new recruits.

"Where are the others?" she asked when the elf came closer. Larriel was her name. Extending her hand, she pulled the recruit onto the slow-moving wagon. The elf's eyes were red and bloodshot. She tripped and fell into the seat. A strong odor was emanating from her mouth. Something fermented, or perhaps poison.

"Are you okay?" Radelia asked.

"They caught us," she said with an awful slurring. "They gave me something. Radelia, I don't think I have long... but I don't care."

"Tell me everything."

Larriel's account of events made little sense, but amid the tales of a giant elf and the fact that she lived to tell the tale suggested the others were still alive. Some kind of beast had captured them and locked them away in a tower while the High Elves interrogated Larriel, using some kind of tonic to coax the truth from her.

"What did you tell them?" Radelia asked.

"Everything!" the recruit said.

Well, it was a good thing the recruit did not know everything. Though, even the blind in their clan knew something was amiss. It was a little kept secret, but few knew the extent of their troubles.

"I told them about the babies and the healers being twats. About how the emperor wants to go to war, but Kieran doesn't want to go to war!"

No, the recruit told them damn near everything.

"Do they know they have Kieran in their grasp?"

Larriel was slumping on the bench. She gave a lazy shrug that suggested she couldn't recall just how much she had told the High Elves.

This was bad. So bad. The High Elves knew the emperor's plans and the inner conflict between military and leadership.

Those were weaknesses easily exploited.

"They said I looked weird," the recruit said, staring into the sun as though it didn't belong in the sky. "We don't look like them, but we used to."

Whatever fiendish poison they gave the scout made her lose track of any single path of thought. Perhaps she was delirious. Poor girl, how much time did she have left?

A calm came over Radelia then. If they could get information out of Larriel about the Runda Nor, what stopped her from getting information about them?

"How so?"

"Well, their ears and eyes are smaller. They're taller too. Not as tall as the elf with black hair. He was so big. His shoulders barely fit through the doorways, and he had a massive sword but swung it around like it was a willow switch."

Black elves were not strangers to them. The Runda Nor had many varying shades of skin, hair, and eyes. The Black elves ruled the island known for its wealth in the soil. Their hair was still white like the High Elves, though. Radelia was pretty sure no one mentioned their size either. Whoever this elf was, he was certainly not of any clan she knew of.

"Did he hurt you?" she asked slowly, fearing the answer.

Larriel shook her head for far too long. "No. They gave me a drink and talked to me for a while. One of them said he was a Bellas and that he was the brother of the first emperor."

It was a startling revelation. A Runda Nor still lived in the castle? He must have been thousands of years old. They clearly still held on to immortality, which suggested they still held a firm grip on all Elven magic as well.

"He was nice but sad. They were all sad."

Radelia scowled at Larriel. She actually felt sorry for the High Elves? "Why do you think they were sad?"

"I don't know. It felt like the time I got lost in the forest by myself."

She didn't know what to make of that. Before she could ask, Larriel leaned over and vomited before falling asleep. There was nothing more Radelia could get from her.

It was reassuring that her friends were still alive, but a greater concern came over her.

When her father learned they captured Kieran, what would he do? Based on what he had done, she was certain he'd abandon them and attempt to install a new, more pliable general with less experience and hope the militia remained intact.

But that could take months, even a year. By then, more than a dozen infants would be born, and her father wouldn't be able to send them all to the same village. They would have to abandon the children when their purse emptied.

The thought of going back to her people as a failure was unbearable. How could she continue to lie to them? Taking the children away from their parents was a terrible necessity, and it only promised even more nauseating choices in the future.

Never again would she be a responsible party to such cruelty.

It was a break from her father's reign. Her people seldom agreed on anything, but when it mattered, they all rallied together. Even when the emperor yanked babies from their parent's hands, the Runda Nor supported him for the greater good of the clan.

But for how long? Her father was equally aware of the time they didn't have, but she feared what he might try to do. She supported the war right up until the point where her dearest friends were certain casualties. Something had to be done.

Chapter 8

E ttrian tried to hide his laughter in his hands, but it was of no use.

Aracaryn was staring at him with total disdain. "I fail to see why any of this is funny."

The other vassals were uneasy as well. He shouldn't have been laughing, but one could only contain themselves for so long. Balqen was staring down at his lap, the smirk twitching across his lips.

"The *interrogation*," he emphasized the word, and Balqen burst into a fit of laughter. "Was a success."

"They are plotting war," Aracaryn reminded. "I see nothing funny about that."

"No," the king straightened. "Of course not. I'm only laughing because the poor girl was so intoxicated by the wine."

They only poured her half a glass. She took three, maybe four sips. It was only after they all heard the slur of her speech that the healer had the most devious of ideas.

"Omaro, telling her it was truth tonic was genius," Aracaryn admitted, a smile rippling across her lips.

The healer bowed. "I aim to please."

Indeed. The poor girl was stumbling her way home. He assumed she would sober soon enough and that her travel would be safe. It would be a shame if a wild boar skewered their drunken peace offering.

A grisly image came to mind. The forest elf being impaled by a massive tusk. He shook off the vision. She would be fine. What happened to the female hunter all those years ago was his father's doing. That elf would have never fallen from the tree otherwise. Their cousins had adapted and could navigate the forest better than anyone.

Ettrian would never forget her face.

He tried to banish her from his mind. Her green eyes closed, but when they opened again, someone else had taken her place. She was similar in appearance. Same lips and tanned skin, but her hair was the color of burned copper. He didn't know who she was, but the king suspected he'd soon find out.

"I expect we won't need to hold these visitors long," Ettrian said, stretching out of his chair. It had been a long night. The warmth of daylight was being absorbed by his black curtains, radiating a warmth that was ideal for napping.

"Why do you say that?" Omaro asked.

How could he explain?

Something, or rather someone, was coming to the castle. He disliked spouting such cryptic things because he could never explain them. And if he was wrong, no one would ever let him forget. And ever was a long time for an elf.

"They are important to someone," he said. "It's clear the way our guest revered the male. He has status among their people."

"We know nothing about them," Leaf said. "So, he's special, but what if he's just respected and not needed? I hate not knowing."

"Indeed," Ettrian agreed.

They knew so little of the Runda Nor culture. Did they have nobility or ranking among them? Would they go to war over a perceived slight, or would they send envoys like civilized nations? Even Balqen was without ideas. So far removed from his kin, he didn't recognize them anymore.

"Perhaps we need scouts of our own," Aracaryn suggested.

Ettrian raised his thick brows and nodded. It wasn't a bad idea, but it would be difficult for a High Elf to blend in. That, and they didn't know where the village was. The forest was vast, and the road ended several miles in.

"How would we find their village?" Balqen asked. "The men say it's hidden by some kind of magic."

"Even more reason to find it," Aracaryn insisted. "What if they're hoarding the magic?"

That was ridiculous.

"It was apparent from that girl that they haven't any," Ettrian said. Not at all interested in revitalizing his father's ill-founded paranoia. "The village is hidden, but not through magic. More likely, it's well concealed."

After the meeting, everyone left but Balqen, who nodded at Leaf, suggesting he'd catch up with her later. Ettrian sighed and prepared himself for the lecture.

"Might as well sit down," the king gestured.

"Oh, I think I will," the old elf said. "Creaking bones and all."

They sat in the quiet for a few moments, sipping wine and pretending everything was a mess before he started.

"You guard the Runda Nor as though they're our own."

It wasn't the angle he expected. As the oldest, Balqen and Aracaryn were allies of sorts. Elves often banded together by age groups. Not that generations differed, but history had a way of leaving its mark.

"Cardhon Nimloth is the birthplace of all four races of elves, yet only two reside within its walls."

"Three," Balqen countered. "Well, sort of. It can't be helped that the Ice Elves are extinct."

Little was known about the Ice Elves—if that was even their proper name. The race that had fled in the second age left little mark on Cardhon Nimloth. "Still, they left. The Dark Elves left for the Ruby Isle. The Runda Nor left for the forest. How is it that none of them wish to remain here?"

Balqen shrugged. "I can't speak for the Dark Elves. Certainly not for the Ice Elves, but I was there when your grandmother made life hard for the Runda Nor."

"Precisely," Ettrian leaned in. "My predecessors wanted them to leave. I think that's why we've grown weak."

"A king that thinks we're stronger when united," Balqen muttered under his breath. "Those are strong currents you're fighting."

Yes, and his beliefs cost him dearly.

"Just be sure that you're not alienating the allies you want so badly."

Ettrian laughed. "Ah, I was waiting for it. Aracaryn came to you about our little tiff."

The old elf looked up through his wiry brows. "She's not your enemy, Ettrian."

They had different impressions of the princess. He remembered the way she followed at his father's heels. Aracaryn gave him none of the courtesy she bestowed on the former king. Ettrian respected and valued her insightful council, but there was no love between them.

It wasn't fair, really. Entitled to speak her harshest criticism, but he could not strike back. He was king, yet he did not rule without the vassal's approval. The conditions in which he ascended the throne were based on old precedent, one that he instituted himself, but Ettrian was growing weary of the restraints.

"I am tired," he said. "Perhaps we can continue this conversation another time."

Balqen wasn't finished. He could tell by the disapproving shake of his jowls, but the vassal stood and moved to bow.

"We need to do something about our guests," he said before leaving. "They won't eat the food."

He imagined they thought it was poison. Or perhaps it was so far removed from what they ate in the forest that they feared it.

"There's a book in the library about Runda Nor cuisine," he said. "Give it to the cooks."

"Where is it?"

"The book?"

Balqen nodded. He had lived in Cardhon Nimloth for so long, and yet he was unaware of the secrets within the library. The spirits were rather insistent on cookbooks that day. They had their reasons, even if he didn't understand.

Ettrian gave a pursed smile. "Any book will do."

The vassal had a worried expression. No doubt the vassal thought he was mad. Balqen must have wondered if the burden of kingship was too much or if the guilt was too racking. They would learn to trust him eventually. Or they'd have him executed. One or the other.

Before Balqen could reach the door, it opened. There was no knock, which suggested Leaf was in an agitated state.

She froze in the doorway as if she had forgotten that she had just walked into his bedroom unannounced. "Sorry," she blurted. "We have a guest."

"I told you we would."

"Yeah, but..."

She didn't finish that sentence, and he understood why. They didn't believe him. He gave Balqen a knowing smile. One that suggested he knew what they thought of him and that he didn't care. "Find the book and meet me in the great hall."

It was the stupidest idea she had ever come up with. But there she was, knocking on the doors of Cardhon Nimloth. She didn't expect to make it that far. The guards at their posts stared at her as she approached. At any moment, they could have reached for their bows, but they didn't.

As she got closer, their expressions came into focus. Tilted heads and passive expressions. They didn't consider her a threat at all? Their two clans were locked in a cold war for a millennium, yet the High Elves were nodding as she reached the door.

It was like they were curious about her or didn't know what she was. Fair enough. She didn't get them either. Larriel said the High Elves looked different, but Radelia didn't understand until she saw them for herself.

They looked almost human. Men in fancy armor strutted about the top of what should have been her father's castle with their tall, beautiful bows. Who would she have to kill to get a bow like that?

They saw her and didn't shoot. She knocked, and nothing happened. Tapping her foot errantly on the steps, she considered making a break for it. Her father was going to be furious. She was defying a divine order. That wasn't something to play around with. Once it was spoken, it couldn't be unspoken.

Then again, if she went home with magic and the beloved general, she would restore her people. Happily ever after and all that shit. It would force the emperor to accept and be grateful for her heroic efforts.

Maybe there would be a yearly potluck between the Runda Nor and the High Elves. Who knew? Anything could happen. She scratched at the hair behind her ear and pulled the cloak together, straightening the symbol on the collar.

Anything could happen.

Like being poisoned or flayed alive. Maybe they sacrificed other elf races to their star god. It was a terrible mistake, but before Radelia could run away, the doors opened, and a tall, thin Dark Elf in a shiny blue gown greeted her with a smile full of super white teeth.

The elf before her disrupted every panicked thought, and they all came rushing down to one impression. She was beautiful. Wow, just look at those cheekbones and perfect brows. Radelia felt so awkward and inferior in her father's oversized cloak, her hair clumped and tangled.

Everything from her dress to her arms and the way the light reflected off her black skin and the locks that coiled and fell well past her shoulders. Those otherworldly eyes matched the morning sky. If that was an elf, what did that make Radelia?

"We've been expecting you," the elf said slowly, placing a hand at her heart. "I am Aracaryn."

They were expecting her? Radelia had every opportunity to greet the elf with formality. First contact in over a millennium between estranged races. This was a monumental occasion that the High Elves were apparently expecting.

Of all the things she could have said, the introductions she could make, she said, "What?"

"My name," the Dark Elf said louder and slower than the first time. "Aracaryn."

Yes, she got that part. Radelia nodded. Perhaps it was their custom. She didn't follow their own social rituals half the time, but it was probably important to mimic theirs.

"My name," Radelia shouted up at the elf. "Is... Rada—"

She stopped short of her full name. If they knew she was the heir of Runda Nor, they might hold her captive. Best to keep that information to herself.

The Dark Elf raised her white brows with surprise. "You speak our language? I didn't mean to offend."

What else was spoken on the continent? It occurred to her then that she had just shouted at the poor female who was trying her best to be nice. "No offense taken," Radelia said with a wince. "I thought it was a custom your people held."

"Please," the elf opened the door wider. "Come in."

Radelia's legs wobbled as she took that first step. Still not sure if she should or not, but Kieran and Katar were somewhere, rotting in a dungeon. Maybe being tortured in the same way poor Larriel was. She needed to see inside the castle and find out if her dream was just that or if it was a sign from Elpharae.

"You said you were expecting me?"

"Our king suspected you would come," Aracaryn said as they walked into a large, open room.

How would he know? They were holding her friends captive. Maybe they just assumed someone would come for them. Whatever the case... Radelia stepped into the castle and lost her trail of thoughts.

She gasped as she beheld the heights of the entryway. The archways were a series of entwined vine-like branches and the floors smooth with a mirror shine. Tapestries with intricate designs hung on the walls, mesmerizing her with their colors.

The beauty of it all flooded her eyes with colors and sizes. Wood was worked in shapes and curves she didn't think possible. A grand staircase worked its way around a magnificent room toward unseen rooms. Birds flew across the sky above. How was this possible?

"You don't get rained on?" she asked, unable to contain the dumbest questions to herself. Typical Radelia move.

"There is a barrier that protects us and our gardens from the elements. Food grows year-round here. We have no winters."

Must have been nice. Radelia bit her tongue before saying as much. What her people wouldn't give to have a warm home and a constant harvest. Why were they denied such gifts? Her people worshiped their god just as she assumed the High Elves worshiped theirs, and yet, they had nothing while the High Elves had everything.

"The king was expecting me?"

"He caught your scouts," Aracaryn said, her eyes sharpened at the word scouts. "He assumed someone would come to negotiate on their behalf."

The Runda Nor didn't keep captives. Not that they ever had the opportunity, but they also didn't have the food and means to keep prisoners. Had it been her people that found the scouts, they wouldn't have been sent home like Larriel.

Radelia shook off the grisly thought. Her people didn't have that luxury, but hopefully, she could change that.

"They didn't hurt anyone?"

"Not at all. The king found them and locked them in a guest bedroom."

The tight feeling in her chest eased. They were still alive. She was right to arrive when she did. The High Elves didn't suspect she was the princess. They thought she was an ambassador of sorts. Which wasn't wrong. She did just negotiate with the men after all.

"What can you tell me about your king?" Radelia asked.

The Dark Elf paused at that. She didn't know what to say. In the Runda Nor, people openly criticized her father, but Radelia got the impression that it wasn't the same Cardhon Nimloth.

"Be cautious, Rada. He will not be what you expect."

A shiver ran down her spine. That was an ominous warning if she ever heard one.

Turning around, Radelia took a new glance at the doorway.

Apart from the blood. It was exactly what she saw in her dream. The same room, same floors. Even the potted lemon trees on each side. What she had seen was not just a dream. It was a warning.

Chapter Nine

Chapter 9

It was the most excitement his people had seen since Leaf was born over sixty years ago. Everyone was pooling into the great hall with total disregard for what side belonged to who. Blacksmiths rubbed shoulders with his cousins while bakers chatted with Balqen over the book now clutched firmly in their flour-coated hands.

The king sat on his throne, and for the first time, he looked forward to it. When his father died, Ettrian had his father cremated with his crown. It was a tall, pointed thing encrusted with diamonds. He always hated it and assumed his father wore it to make himself appear as tall as the queen.

Ettrian's crown was a simple laurel made from silver. He needed no additional height or more attention to his status. No one was proud of how he took the throne, himself least of all.

This was a chance to reunite their two clans. He welcomed it, and he was curious about the state of the Runda Nor. Perhaps learning of their hardships would bring insights into their own. The room buzzed with promise and renewed interest in their mundane lives. Ettrian laughed as he noted the way his fingers trembled.

Silence fell as Aracaryn entered the room. Beside her was indeed a Runda Nor elf. She was painfully small and frail. Her brassy hair was wild, freeing itself from a loose braid at every plait. Her cloak was far too large for her and hung over her shoulders as it dragged dirt and leaves along the floors.

"My king," Aracaryn said, "May I present Ambassador Rada."

The spirits were snickering. Of all the times to start their mischief!

"Shh," he whispered under his breath, though it was loud enough for those nearest him to hear. Leaf's eyes shifted toward him, but she said nothing.

"Welcome to my court," he greeted.

Aracaryn gave a formal bow, and the ambassador watched before mimicking the same behavior. He gave his best attempt at a smile, but the little elf was so startled that she nearly tripped on the runner. He shouldn't have smiled.

"Please, come. You are welcome here."

Omaro was smiling so hard that Ettrian thought his face might crack. "Stop it," Ettrian muttered. "You're scaring her."

"I'm scaring her?"

"He's not scaring her," Leaf said under her breath. "You are."

Ettrian sighed. She was right. Aracaryn sensed the mounting tension around the throne, and she darted her eyes not once but twice to Balqen. Of course, the Runda Nor would be more comfortable if she knew one of her own was among them.

"Balqen," he said with a gesture. "Is the younger brother of your emperor."

The ambassador frowned as though he had said something strange. She regarded the vassal before saying, "The emperor has no brother. Only a sister."

Of course, their emperor must have passed on, and a successor had taken their place. "Apologies," he said. "We are no longer familiar with your current emperor. When Roquinal Bellas left with his people, his brother remained."

She nodded. "I see. You are the brother of the first emperor."

"How many emperors have you had since?" Ettrian asked with growing concern.

Something within the ambassador flared then. Her hazel eyes narrowed, and he noticed she had a smattering of freckles across her tan skin. "How should I know?"

His own temper rose. What kind of impudence was this? Such an uncordial little ambassador. She was angry at them for not knowing anything about a clan that remained hidden for a millennium?

"Ambassador Rada," Aracaryn started. "Our people have had no contact for a long time. We know nothing of your people. Our king only wishes to learn."

The elf looked at him again. Her frown was apparent. Her voice was weak with a profound sadness that struck his heart. "Then you have no idea what our people have endured. The misery your people have inflicted on ours?"

He sat mute. His mouth slacked, and his mind went blank with accusation.

Everything he did was to ensure the safety of his people. Not just High Elves, but Runda Nor as well. He risked his own life to spare theirs. Ettrian had killed his king, his own father, all to shield the forest elves from a foul plot, and yet, they blamed him for whatever ills had befallen them.

"I guess that is my job," he said, feigning amusement. "Making everyone suffer."

The vassals attempted to thwart the building tension in the room. Balqen stepped forward to speak reassuring words to the spiteful little ambassador, and Aracaryn nodded softly to support whatever he said.

The High Elves didn't know whether to lower their heads or mutter amongst themselves. Omaro gave him an uncertain look before clapping his hands to gain everyone's attention and announce the only solution High Elves had for any occasion.

"We're going to throw a revelry to celebrate our guest!"

There was applause, but it was the kind people made when they paid for a show, only for it to be cut short without a refund. Averse and without joy. Ettrian let out a groan of frustration at the thought of another revelry and rubbed the bridge of his nose to soothe the oncoming headache.

He made his escape while Aracaryn and Balqen showed the ambassador to her room. Fleeing the throne through the courtyard, he tossed his crown into a blueberry bush as he stormed to the safety of his room.

Only it wouldn't be safe for long. His vassals would come knocking. Demanding. Critical of his every word. No one truly understood his actions, but if he tried to explain them, would it matter? Aracaryn would sit quite comfortably on the throne, instantly uniting two of the elf kingdoms while he pandered to that loathsome ambassador in the great hall for all eternity.

Slamming his hands on his vanity, Ettrian stared at the long-faced stranger, scowling back. The only thing he recognized was the scar along his temple, a memento from the day he killed his mother. Self-pity didn't make him any more appealing, so he left the mirror and picked up a book.

The ink on the pages faded on the parchment only to be reborn. Illustrations of jewelry broke apart and emerged as a tale about the marriage of Elpharae and Isilynor. The Elven gods were once bound together in the stars, but they'd separated, leaving his kingdom fractured.

New illustrations formed, depicting a double star with two Elven lovers entwined. Ettrian looked out his balcony window. The stars were dimming as usual for the time of year, with the exception of one. Isilynor's star remained bright until the *Dú ú- elena*, the starless night.

There was a soft knock at the door before it opened.

Aracaryn stepped inside, quiet with a sympathetic expression. Did she pity him?

"I thought you'd be furious with me," he said.

She shook her head. "The fault is mine, my king. We didn't know what we were getting into. To introduce her so quickly... I don't think any of us were prepared for that."

He should have been. It wasn't like the Runda Nor left because they were brimming with a sense of adventure. Their clans parted on bad terms. He put his own excitement on the ambassador and expected her to play along. She came because she had no alternative.

Ettrian shook his head. "I hoped it would go well. I should have known better."

"Hope is a lovely sentiment," Aracaryn said. "But I'm old, and I've found that hope is for the young."

"I'm young, but already I'm beginning to understand."

Aracaryn lowered her gaze to the floor. She wanted to say something, to comfort him perhaps, but there was nothing to say. It would be a long, arduous task to make peace with the Runda Nor. It would start with the ambassador and the guests, but it would be several lifetimes before their people could trust one another. Time that Cardhon Nimloth didn't have.

"Whose attending her?" he asked.

"Balqen's grandchildren, Yinren and Miabelle."

Oh, no. Ettrian's eyes went wide with the thought. He shook his head. "Not those two. Anyone but them."

Aracaryn's face formed a wince. "No one else wanted to attend to her."

A matter so delicate was handed to a set of wild boars. He respected Balqen, even loved him, but his grandchildren were the epitome of what was wrong with High Elf culture. Lowering his face into his hands, he shook his head and laughed.

"You have a habit of laughing at the worst times," Aracaryn said.

"Cardhon Nimloth is dying, our people are barren, magic is fading, and the Runda Nor are on the verge of declaring war," his words muted behind his massive hands. "Miabelle and Yinren will be the snowflakes that create the avalanche."

"They're not that bad," she said.

He looked at her between his fingers, and she rolled her eyes. "I'll speak to Balqen to see if he can control them."

Ettrian was laughing then. Aracaryn shook her head, but she laughed as well. There was humor in the darkness. Detached from watchful eyes and possibility. If elf-kind fell, it might well be at the hands of the notorious fraternal twins. Who else would so thoroughly stoke those fires other than himself?

"No, I need to speak to the king," she insisted.

"Yes, yes, of course, but your journey has been so long," the female servant urged. Practically herding her up the stairs into a room.

It was a mistake.

She should have never stepped foot in Cardhon Nimloth. She needed to go back to tell her father about the dream. Katar and Kieran were somewhere in the castle, but Katar would find a way to escape. She had to trust that. They would be furious if they learned of her rash rescue mission.

Radelia turned to go back down the stairs only to find a male elf with short, strawberry-blond hair with a long braid at the bang. There was something oddly familiar about him, but she couldn't place it.

"We won't force you to stay," he said. "But at least rest first. Have some food, a nice hot bath, perhaps?"

To her, a bath was a bucket large enough to stand in while she scrubbed herself as quickly as she could before freezing. Not at all something she wanted to do in a castle full of enemies.

"I only came to free my friends," she said. "If the king will not let them go, then my time here is at an end."

"The king let Larriel go," the female said. "I'm sure he would release the others if you asked."

Radelia turned to face the female. Her hair was ashen brown and curly, unlike most of the other High Elves. The servant filled out her pale green gown in ways that made Radelia stare when she shouldn't.

But something else struck her then. As strange as their king was, the High Elves were different. They actually seemed quite nice. The thought made the bile rise in her throat, but the fact was immutable.

"You learned her name?"

The pretty servant stared blankly. There wasn't a single thought in her head. Radelia was certain of it. "Well, yes?"

"We were Larriel's attendants. That's why Miabelle and I asked to be your attendants," the male said, gesturing to himself with a delicately posed hand.

"Well, we asked," Miabelle said with a grin.

"More like begged," the male corrected.

She felt like she was in some parallel universe where High Elves were not the bane of her clan's existence. Were they truly so unaware of everything outside the castle? Her mind went back to the moment she walked up to the castle and the guards waved at her.

Kieran had these people all wrong. They were not calculated soldiers who could defend the castle from a raid. Cardhon Nimloth, the source of all Elven magic, was being ruled by a handful of beautiful morons.

In that moment, Radelia came to the startling conclusion that her people didn't need to go to war to claim Cardhon Nimloth. They didn't need to shed a single drop of blood. The only thing that stood between her people and the castle was the king.

"I am a little hungry," she relented, placing a hand on her stomach.

Miabelle clasped her hand and urged her up the stairs with a giddy laugh. "You're going to love the revelry! I hope we have a dress that fits you..."

The cool-bellied feeling of regret promised she would not enjoy whatever the servant had in mind. Radelia glanced back at the male, who gave an apologetic shrug.

"I'll get the bath started," the male called.

After the hike up the winding staircase, Miabelle opened an arched door, and with a sweep of her hand, she announced, "This is your room!"

It needed no introduction. The room was the size of at least four huts, but there was nothing like it back home. The floors kept the same glossy finish that reflected the light, but there were squares of woolen fabrics arranged with the furniture. Even the villages of man didn't have fabrics so vivid. Bluer than the deepest of rivers, panels of fabric created a canopy over a bed adorned with four pillars.

The bedding was so inviting. Fluffy and tufted, promising a sweet sleep without chill or the light of dawn if she closed the curtains. There was a seating area made with the softest leathers and a desk all set for correspondence.

Against the wall, there was a stand-up curtain, a wardrobe, and a large copper tub balancing on four tiny feet. There was a door just off to the side of a pitcher and washbowl that she suspected was to be a private latrine. Imagine using the latrine inside and alone!

It was incredible. A testament to the world her people had lost so long ago. The Runda Nor helped build Cardhon Nimloth, shaping the very roots of its foundation. It was only fair that they take it back. Of all the words to describe her amazement, Radelia went with just the one.

"Shit..."

"Does that mean you like it?" Miabelle asked. "Larriel made the same face, but she didn't use that word."

She turned to the servant, who was setting a silver platter piled high with food on the table. "Are my friends in a similar room?"

Miabelle smiled. "Their room isn't as nice, but seeing how they try to kill us every time we open the door, we can't exactly move them."

"I can help with that," she said. "Maybe if they know I'm here and negotiating for their release, they will relax."

The servant's smile was no longer the carefree smile of a young maiden but someone who was trying to hold in a fart. It seemed they had no intention of telling her where her friends were. How much of their discussion was an attempt to handle her? To avert her gaze from the unpolished aspects of their lives. Outwardly and with a single glance, everything was magical and beautiful, but how long before she saw the real Cardhon Nimloth?

"I'll leave that decision between you and the king," she said. "It's my job to feed and dress you and help you navigate the High Elf court."

Those were all things Radelia would need to free her friends and get closer to the king. It didn't take an expert in High Elf life to understand how things worked. There was a hierarchy. She knew that much from the stories her father told her. While the Runda Nor had changed over the years, it didn't look like much had changed in Cardhon Nimloth.

Miabelle was nothing but a servant. She did as she was told by her supposed betters. That would change when Radelia became queen. Sitting on one of the sofas, Radelia stared at the bounty on the tray. Some she recognized like fruit and bread: apples, oranges, and berries fully ripe regardless of the season.

There were other things she wasn't too sure about. Some kind of pale-yellow preserves, she could tell by the seeds. A round white pudding. Salad with nuts and berries. Radelia opted to start with the orange. She hadn't had one since she was a child. A merchant happened by with crates full of the fruit, and the Runda Nor bartered for some.

Peeling back the rind, it hit her with the sweet citrus scent. She closed her eyes and allowed it to take her back to the days when her mother was still alive.

"My mother loved oranges," she said. "She used to dry the peels and keep them just for the smell."

"My mother is gone too."

Radelia opened her eyes. Something had drawn those memories from her, and it wasn't a sweet nostalgia. Before she could ask, Miabelle stood and said, "I'm going to see about that bath."

Still munching on her orange, Radelia watched as the servant raced from the room. Was it something she said? Perhaps Miabelle lost her mother recently. It was still raw in her heart. There was no telling what recent meant to people who lived forever, but she imagined they would be more sentimental since death was a rare thing. Yet another mental note to make.

Don't mention mothers. Don't use foul language. Don't eat the blue cheese.

She'd probably put that stationary to use. By the end of the day alone, Radelia would have a page full of don'ts.

There was a knock at the door. Radelia stared at it, wondering what would happen next.

"Um, Lady Rada?" The male servant said behind the door. "May I come in?"

"Yeah," she said with a mouth full of fresh bread. It was so soft and delightful. Yeasty, and the crust was coated with something rich and delectable.

The door opened, and the servant picked up the bucket once more and hauled it toward the copper tub. He could have just asked her to open the door, but for some reason, he knocked as though it were the front door to someone's house.

"I brought your water," he explained as six other High Elf servants followed him in. It must have been tough carrying it up all those stairs.

"Did you bring water all the way from the kitchens?" she asked.

"We have a pulley device to avoid the steps, but yes, I'm afraid so."

"My people have learned to use gravity to siphon water. Perhaps one of our engineers could show your people how to do it."

His brows raised in surprise. "That would be really nice."

Imagine it. The Runda Nor teaching the mighty High Elves how to siphon water. Something about that made her greasy lips form a smile. "What is this?" she asked, holding up the pale-yellow spread.

"It's butter. You don't have it back home?"

She shook her head. He made it sound so simple, like it was something everyone had.

"It's churned cow's milk," he explained. "I'm surprised the villages of men never traded it."

Radelia imagined it was a luxury that was traded to better customers. The Runda Nor had little to offer apart from furs and some Elven crafting. "When do I get to speak with the king?"

"Oh, probably at the revelry tonight. He rarely attends, but I think his vassals will lock him out of his room for this one."

She cringed a little. The king didn't seem to be the partying type for good reason. "Is... is he part giant?"

The servant laughed for a moment before realizing she was serious. "No. His mother and father were both High Elves. He inherited nearly all his mother's traits, however."

"His mother was that tall?"

The servant nodded. "She had the black hair too. Only the royal line does."

Did she have that moody disposition as well? So many were referred to in past tense. Best stick to her notes. "What can you tell me about him?"

His face made the same ass-puckering expression as Miabelle, right down to the crinkle of their lips. Maybe they were married or related...perhaps both? It was a small community, after all.

"He..." the servant struggled. "Well, he keeps to himself. He was only crowned recently, so the king is in mourning."

"Is that why he dresses all in black?"

The male nodded.

Dyes blacker than coal must have been hard to come by. It was an expensive way to mourn. But money clearly was no object for the High Elves. "Anything that might help me," she chose her words as thoughtfully as she could muster. "Negotiate with him?"

The poor servant was tapping his fingers on his legs while he searched that smooth little brain of his for answers. "If he talks to himself, just ignore it."

"Oh."

The servant nodded and said, "Yeah. Um, I'm going to get Miabelle. She will help you with the bath."

He left her with more questions than answers. It explained the moment when he shushed the dead silence in the throne room. The king must have hoped she didn't notice, but her ears were as keen as any. If she could hear the trees talking about acorns, she could hear him from across a dead silent room.

The Runda Nor were not the only ones who needed saving.

Chapter Ten

Chapter 10

Radelia considered the possibility that the servants were not servants at all but rather assassins. Leaning over the tub half full of steaming hot water, she tried to come up with excuses to avoid it. "I don't think that's necessary."

Miabelle looked her over and said, "Oh, trust me. It is."

She opened a little jar and poured something else into the water. The surface became waxy and reflected the rainbow. Something to ensure her death?

"It's scented oil," the servant said. "Smell it?"

Bending over the water, Radelia inhaled. It was a pleasant, floral scent. Maybe it wasn't an attempt on her life, just more extravagant High Elf nonsense. At Miabelle's insistence, she unlaced her vest and shrugged off the shift underneath before stepping into the water.

It was warm and inviting. If this was how she died, it wasn't a bad way to go.

Sinking shoulder-deep into the tub, she swore every muscle in her body went lax. She closed her eyes, but not before catching Miabelle's pleased expression. "You don't take baths in Runda Nor?"

She promised herself that she wouldn't give anything about her village away, but the water was so soothing. Anyway, it wasn't like the High Elves would attack them. One of them would break a nail, and they'd call it off.

"We live in the treetops," she explained. "Can't really get tubs up there."

"You mean, you live in the trees?"

"Houses built into the trees. We have showers and means to wash, but nothing like this," she said, moving her arms in the water. Pressing back against the weightlessness.

"What are your house colors?" she asked.

"House colors?"

Miabelle's voice traveled about the room. The sound of wood sliding against wood, the wardrobe. "We wear certain colors during formal events to indicate what house we're from, or the rare occasion when a revelry isn't themed."

She'd just told the servant about how they didn't have bathtubs; what would make her think the Runda Nor wore bright colors in the forest? They really didn't know anything about her people. Evading predators and High Elves alike was the reason for building their homes at such heights.

It made her wonder if the stories about High Elves trying to steal hunters in the woods were just a myth. True, they were tales they told in the dark to frighten the young and old alike. Nesterin swore that in her youth that she was nearly caught by High Elf hunters. But that might have been for dramatics.

"Do your people go into the woods at all?" she asked.

"No, not really. King Ettrian the First did, but they never caught anything. I think he was just trying to bond with his son."

"The current Ettrian?"

She made a noise of agreement. "Blush, I think. It will compliment your beautiful skin."

Opening one eye, she spotted Miabelle. She had a pile of pale pink fabric in her hands, and she was whirling it about the room. The servant was going to put her in that. Clearly, her intent was to make it impossible for Radelia to move freely or escape. Gritting her teeth, she sunk deeper into the water and gave her head a good scrub.

"There are things you must know before the revelry," the servant said, spreading the gown across the bed. "You should always bow to nobility and address the king formally. You don't have to call him your king, but he deserves respect as one."

"What do I call him then?"

"Your grace."

Fair enough. "And how do I tell the nobility apart from the servants?"

There was no response, but she felt the prickle along her neck that alerted her when she was being watched. Radelia sat up in the tub. Miabelle's face was working through a range of emotions. She must have said something offensive.

"I didn't mean to be rude," she said. "My clan doesn't have nobility."

"Not even your emperor?"

She shook her head. The water pulled her down as if urging her to return to its consolation.

"Well, everyone has a job in Cardhon Nimloth,"

"Even nobility?"

The servant nodded. "There are skilled labor jobs, you have those, but nobility also have jobs."

"Such as?"

Miabelle's fingers were twisting in her lap. "We see to guests and plan the revelries."

Shit. She stepped in it again. Why didn't she realize it sooner? With all the fuss and new faces, Radelia had totally forgotten that one of the vassals had introduced the servants as his grandchildren. "So, you're not servants, you're nobility."

"Attendants," she corrected. "Yinren and I attend and assist, not serve. No one has servants in Cardhon Nimloth. We did once, but the population is too small for that now."

No wonder Miabelle was acting like she stole her last ration. They didn't have servants, and it was rude to assume so. But still, even her father had Katar helping around the hut from time to time. "Not even the king?"

"Especially not the king."

"And the old guy, he's your grandfather."

Miabelle gave a nod up and down. Radelia half expected the attendant to throw that bath oil in her face. "That means you have some Runda Nor linage."

"One of the reasons they wanted us to attend to you."

"So, how do I know who's noble and who isn't?"

"Well, that can be a little tricky. You don't bow to us while we serve as your attendants, but you bow to the vassals, the king, any of the king's relatives...better yet, if I introduce them formally, just bow."

"That works."

Miabelle nodded and stood, appearing satisfied with herself. She said, "Okay, time to get dressed and tame that hair. I'll get Yinren."

The dread of attending the revelry had built all afternoon as Ettrian watched the High Elves set up décor in the gardens. Hastened with excitement, they wheeled out barrels of wine from the cellars and pulled up the massive tents. Did they not grow tired of it? He was tired just watching them.

If the ambassador was forced into attendance, it was only fair he attended. Ettrian suspected she had no interest in parties either, but after that disastrous introduction, neither of them had a choice. Gods only knew what sort of things Miabelle and Yinren had put in the ambassador's head.

"Would it be too much to ask for the spirits to remain silent tonight?" he asked out loud.

He glanced around the room as if waiting for a reply. There was none because spirits did not heed the words of the living. Not even a king's.

With the brightest star emerging from the darkening sky, the anticipated knock sounded on his door. No one came in, which meant either Balqen or Omaro were there to summon him.

"Enter."

"Sorry to disturb you, my king, but it's about to begin," Omaro said with the practiced gentleness of his occupation.

Ettrian gave a soft chuckle. "Did you draw the short stick?"

"Coin flip, actually."

He turned to face the once-disgraced healer. The smile on his face suggested he understood the joke. So few got Ettrian's humor, but unlike the others, Omaro knew what it was to take life into his hands. To make the choice despite the direst of consequences.

"Let's not keep them waiting."

They walked along the eastern wall, possibly the longest and most roundabout route—all he needed to do was walk down a flight of stairs. He stopped at the edge of a balcony and surveyed the revelry from the heights.

"Balqen has been in constant contact with his grandchildren," Omaro said. "It seems the Runda Nor are barely surviving in the forest. They have little to offer in terms of trade and don't even have the essentials. Rada thought Miabelle was trying to drown her in the bath and asked Yinren what butter was."

He could only imagine how they appeared to the ambassador: decadent, spoiled, and weak. She wouldn't be wrong in that assessment, but it must have been upsetting to see all the High Elves' wealth when her people had none.

"We need to do more," the king said. "I'll speak to her tonight and find ways to arrange for goods to be sent to the Runda Nor."

"How will we do that?" Omaro asked. "They're hostile, and we don't know where their village is."

"They trade, even if it isn't much," Ettrian said. "Ask the trader in the nearest village to stop by. There will be extra coin for his trouble."

Omaro bowed.

Winter must have been a matter of life or death for the forest elves, and it was but a few months until the snows fell outside Cardhon Nimloth. Provisions that appeared to be a windfall from the generosity of humans wouldn't be denied.

"Oh," he said as an afterthought. "And make certain the trader understands that under no circumstances are the Runda Nor to know it came from us."

"Of course."

Candles were being lit in the gardens below. That was his cue. Rather than delay any further, the king took the nearest stairway, a steep, circular staircase made of iron rather than wood. An homage to a time when the population grew faster than the tree and additions needed to be made. Most avoided such stairways as if they didn't want to be reminded of how far the elves had fallen. Ettrian rather liked them. They weren't nearly as slick and were wider and more comfortable for his massive feet.

He rounded the third loop when the stairs beneath him shifted. Gripping the cool railing, Ettrian held his breath. One slow step was enough to cause the stairway to shift to the left. The rot must have loosened the stairway. If he wasn't careful, it would collapse with him in the center.

Stepping more toward the center and what he hoped was the strongest point, the king eased down another step. Why hadn't anyone marked the staircase unsafe? Perhaps no one knew. He was several stones heavier than the average elf, and few had reason to linger along the eastern wall.

Aracaryn was right. He did laugh at the worst times, but he couldn't help it. Imagining the High Elves finding their notorious king dead by a rogue stairwell. Biting his lip until a metallic tang lingered in his mouth, Ettrian hurried down the stairs, only inhaling a breath once he reached the bottom.

He looked upward at the stairway, deeming it a hazard he did not want any drunken elf to stumble upon. The king gripped the base of the railing and used his legs to lift. The wood groaned in protest as Ettrian twisted and tugged, straining under the resistance.

Finally, the splintering of wood sent a shower of debris from above as the stairway crashed to one side. The stairway was far more stable for anyone determined to use it.

Stepping into the gardens, the king dusted wood fragments off his shoulders and walked into the candlelit gardens.

Unable to deny the beauty of it, he stood quiet for a time, taking in the spectacle. From his room, it was all so distant and pretentious. Being in the thick of it was something else. The purple night flowers were opening in the warmth of candlelight. What was bright and green in the day was shadow and obscurity in the night.

The tents, with their lavish setup of ornate carpets, were softer somehow. Less harsh with their lines and curls. A long table was set up by the main hall laden with little star-shaped pastries with a spot of red jam in the center. That struck Ettrian as ironic since the castle was oozing red sap in the corners no one cared to look. Perhaps the decay of Cardhon Nimloth was manifesting in their minds in ways the king didn't expect.

The rustle of tulle gowns and flowing tunics muffled the footfalls of the elves around him. They paid no mind to the king that lurked in the shadows. He made no attempt to hide himself, but Ettrian wasn't exactly someone that could be hidden.

An attendant walked past him with a silver tray of goblets. If she noticed the shift in the weight, she said nothing and readjusted her grip. Ettrian downed the full cup of wine in a few swallows, only to have it refilled immediately by the next attendant.

"Thank you."

"My king," he said with a nod, not stopping to bow.

The vassals must have given the elves instructions to not fawn or crowd him. Which was nice. If this was how everyone was going to be, he might attend the revelries more often. Drinks were not nearly as prompt when he sulked in his room.

Scanning the tents, he noted they were all empty. Eyed but ignored by those passing by. Were they reserved? He wasn't certain if he should claim one for himself. It would make things awkward if he camped under a tent that wasn't intended for him.

Somewhere in his fretting, his cup was filled again. He looked around, but the attendant was already gone. Smiling, he drank the contents. His anxieties were absurd; he was king, for gods' sake. Annoyed with his own uncertainty, Ettrian bent his head to step inside the nearest tent and settled himself on a pile of pillows arranged on the ground.

What he saw next was nothing short of comical. The moment he claimed a spot for his own uses, the elves in their finest gowns rushed for the surrounding tents. He watched as one elf garbed in teal dove for the carpeted space like she was trying to swim away from shark-infested waters.

He laughed under his breath, whirling around and trying to take it all in. There was a game children played where they had to sit on a chair before the music stopped. Only an adult would remove one seat after each song. It was like the adult version of that.

Oh, look, his cup had mysteriously filled yet again!

Just when the king had decided that revels weren't so bad, Leaf came marching toward his tent. She was the only female not wearing a gown.

"My king," she said with a bit of practiced formality. Curious.

"Join me."

She sat with her legs folded before her. He offered her wine, but she shrugged it off. She kept her back straight and was surveying the grounds like she expected some unwelcome intruder. "The Runda Nor are not our only guests tonight," she said. "Three messengers from The Ruby Isles are here as well."

That wasn't unusual, given that their clans were longtime allies.

"How fairs their king?"

There was an uncertainty on the young elf's face. As if she wanted to say something was wrong but had no basis to do so. "I hate that feeling," he said, sipping his wine a bit more slowly.

"What?"

"When you feel like something is amiss, but you don't have the proof."

Leaf looked around the tent before she spoke. "Aracaryn was acting strange after they left her chamber."

Given that they were her people, the princess usually handled anything in regard to The Ruby Isles. They had vastly different customs that could be easily misunderstood. For that reason, he counted himself fortunate that Aracaryn was on their side. Well, as much as she could be on anyone's side.

"And where is our Runda Nor ambassador?"

"Word has it there was a situation with the gown—"

"Understood," he said before he could learn anything more. There were things that even kings did not need to know.

A group of elves began to sing a bawdy song about illicit love affairs from the next tent over, and others were laughing, whispering in one another's ears. For once, he didn't feel entirely apart from them, but in many ways, he still was.

They packed into tents by the dozen, whereas his tent only held two. Before he could decide it was a good thing, a trio of elves entered his tent.

Ambassador Rada approached, wearing a pale pink gown that bloomed with tulle at the bottom. The loose, sheer cutouts around the neckline and arms revealed just how thin the elf was. The bodice was laced fully closed, but the fabric still drooped. There was no doubt some padding around the bust area, but it did little to accentuate her feminine features.

Her hair was free of the tangled little braid and flowed in a cascade of wild curls. Which he found rather charming.

"Welcome," he said. "I was just asking for you."

"Your grace," she said with a bow.

"Would you like something to drink?" Not waiting for an answer, he said up and gestured to the nearest attendant. "Please, come in."

CHAPTER ELEVEN

Chapter 11

She fell to the cushions, not because it was expected but because of the overwhelming odor emanating from the king. It was like fermented juice. He was sprawled out along the carpet, propped up on one swaying elbow, the cup gripped tight in his fist.

His black hair was swept back, revealing a thick scar that went from temple to cheek. Radelia didn't mean to stare; it was just that no other High Elf had scars. Her people had lots of them, but apart from the old elf and the king, the elves in Cardhon Nimloth were perfect.

Soft moans of a couple shagging away just a few feet away. Why didn't they keep that business to the tents, or better yet, their rooms? It was distracting.

"I wanted to discuss the prisoners," she started, ignoring the heat rising to her face. There was a nudge from behind. Miabelle was warning her, but Radelia didn't care. Katar and Kieran were her primary concern. Once they were free, she would be able to do what needed to be done.

"The guests, you mean."

"Guests are not held against their will," she said between gritted teeth.

He was smiling. Did he take nothing seriously?

"I would let them go, but they've tried to kill anyone who opens the door."

Miabelle had told her as much. "I will speak with them." There was another nudge against her back. "With your permission, of course."

His thick brows fell as he was no longer smiling. "I wonder, why were they sent here in the first place?"

She had practiced a response for that question. Even a people as daft as the High Elves would want that answer. "We heard rumors that the castle was declining. We wanted to see for ourselves."

He threw his head back and laughed. Sucking her lips to her teeth, her fingers searched the carpet before finding an errant pillow. Before Miabelle could stop her, Radelia launched it at the king's fat head.

Whatever came next would be worth it. The round pillow bounced against his cup, spilling the drink in his face. The little blonde elf was quick. She had a dagger to Radelia's throat, threatening to bleed her dry if she so much as took a breath.

"Leaf," the king said, giggling like a maiden. "Stop. It's fine. I deserved that."

The vassal's blade vanished, but the girl called Leaf remained uncomfortably close.

"Forgive me," he said. "I don't normally drink wine."

It must have been a type of ale. That explained the condition she found Larriel in. "So, the scout you released wasn't poisoned; she was drunk."

"I imagine the rest of them are, too," the king said, glancing at a tower. His eyes gave away their location; they must have been in the northeastern tower. Once everyone passed out, she'd go there and free them.

A trio in the tent across from theirs stood up. The males followed the female to an unoccupied spot on the lawn where they began...She had to tear her eyes away from the spectral. If the king noticed, he said nothing of it.

Focus, dammit!

"We have a deep connection to Cardhon Nimloth," Radelia lied. "We can feel something is amiss."

"Then you're more insightful than most that reside within its walls."

Was he admitting his reign was weak, or was he calling her a liar? He was far too jovial for it to be the former, but maybe that was the drink. She exhaled, allowing the frustration to seethe from her chest. She'd get no answers from a drunk.

Moving to get up, Miabelle's unseen hand pulled her back down. She turned to glare at the attendant but stopped at how pale both were. Was he truly so frightening to them? Yes, he was intimidating, but no more so than the little vassal that wanted to slit her throat.

"Will you free my people or not?" she asked.

"I would, but I fear it's not my decision."

"Of course it is! You're king, are you not?"

He shrugged and reached for a new goblet. "I often ask that same question."

Leaf was no longer staring at her but at the king. Radelia was beginning to see. The king had a council, and they were the ones who decided Kieran and Katar's fate. If she wanted to see her friends released, she had to convince the king's vassals.

"But you support their release?"

"I want them to stay, but not against their will." His words were becoming increasingly slurred. It was an opportunity for her to understand his motives so long as he didn't pass out.

Think, Radelia, think. Who were all the vassals? There was Leaf and Balqen. Aracaryn, perhaps. That tall one that announced the revelry would take place. There might have been more. Leaf would be a lost cause after throwing the pillow, but perhaps she could persuade the others.

"I rather like that you heed your council," she said. "My people do not believe a leader should have unbridled power."

"It's nice to know you approve of something."

She slumped in her cushions. Talking to him about anything of importance would get her nowhere. He set the cup aside, and an attendant spirited it away, so there was that. "Leaf, be a dear and get me something to eat."

Leaf's eyes went to her and then back to the king.

"Go," he said slowly.

Radelia turned to her own attendants and nodded for them to leave as well. It took less prompting for the twins to leave. They couldn't wait to get away from the king. Looking around the gardens, it was clear that he was not popular.

"We got off to a bad start," she said. "My name is Rada, ambassador to the Runda Nor."

"And I'm Ettrian. The High Elf king, etcetera."

He was so dismissive about his own title. It was oddly refreshing after bowing to half the elves she had encountered thus far. "What are your favorite foods?"

The king laughed, but it was one of appreciation, and he nodded. "I enjoy pies filled with savory vegetables and buttered green beans."

"I have those growing in my garden," she said, not feeling at all easy with the small talk. The more she got to know him, the harder her task would be.

He pointed and said, "They're growing on a trellis back there somewhere."

It was followed by an awkward silence. Her eyes lingered on his scar. It was fleeting, but the king caught it. "A memento from a terrible day."

"I didn't mean to stare. It's just that…"

"No other High Elf has scars?" He was so blunt. A trait the Runda Nor praised, but she imagined the High Elves didn't appreciate it. The way they danced around uncomfortable topics was confusing, but the king said exactly what they were afraid to.

"And Balqen," she added, emboldened by his honesty. "He is old when the rest of you are so youthful."

"Unlike most scars, this," he said, tapping at his temple, "is the mark of a sin so great that no magic can undo it."

She leaned forward, eager to hear a tale of magic and sin. What did he do that was so impossibly evil that a scar must remain? Ettrian didn't elaborate further, but his face was close to hers. Radelia's mind was blank in the face of what happened next.

He took her by the wrist and gently extended her arm as if it were a priceless relic as he traced along the various scars she had accumulated over her three decades of life.

"I suppose you'd know all about scars," he said, tracing the marks. Each brush of his finger summoned a ripple of feelings. All of them conflicting.

Then, all at once, he pulled away, leaving her hungry but grateful he stopped because she couldn't. "You're mortal."

She was confused. Not just by the statement or what had transpired between them, but because…

"You didn't know?"

He shook his head. "Are all the Runda Nor mortal?"

The king's tone took on a seriousness then. There was a sense of urgency in his voice. All her life, she was told that the High Elf goddess, the bestower of immortality, took it from her people as punishment. But his people had no idea.

"All of us," she said. "Your goddess cursed us when we left."

He gasped, sitting up as though he had woken from a nightmare. "No, I don't think that's what happened. There's more to this. More than any of us realize."

Before she could ask what that was, Ettrian was on his feet and marching away. Radelia could only sit there, dumbfounded.

Miabelle and Yinren came running. Falling to their knees, they chattered at her wanting to know what she had said, if she had offended him. Too many questions, and she couldn't answer them all at once.

"I don't know," she tried to say, searching for him amid the crowd.

Someone cleared their throat, and the twins went silent. Radelia looked up at him with relief. "Why don't you two go off and enjoy yourselves," the old elf said. "I'll see to the ambassador."

Balqen slowly seated himself on the table. "Hope you don't mind if I don't join you down there. I may never be able to get back up."

"I think I might have pissed off the king," she blurted out.

The old man chuckled. "What were you discussing? For a moment, I thought things were rather friendly."

Her cheeks burned. Was everyone watching them? It was strange how, in the moment, the whole party fell away. She wasn't aware of any other person except him. "He learned that the Runda Nor are mortal."

The old man blinked. His reaction confirmed that even the oldest among them didn't know. "That's troublesome indeed."

"Why? It's not like it affects you."

"Not directly," Balqen said. His gaze was distant in that moment. "Then again, not much would affect me these days."

"Why did he get so upset?"

The old elf sighed. "It's a long story, but all you need to know is that the king took a big gamble, and you just confirmed that he was right to do so."

She rolled her eyes. High elves always spoke in riddles. Couldn't they be direct just once? Balqen wasn't unsympathetic or oblivious to this fact. "I know it's not the answer you want, but when he's ready, the king will tell you."

Unlike the High Elves, time was something she didn't have. At the rate they were going, she'd have the full story in a decade, and her people would be in shambles. Twelve babes were to be born come spring, and the village of man couldn't take them all. The best thing to do was to free her friends and do what had to be done.

She hated the idea. Hated it right down to the marrow, but assassinating the king was the only way to save them all.

Chapter Twelve

Chapter 12

ortal.

He couldn't begin to fathom how it came to that. Did leaving Runda Nor have such consequences? Ettrian shook his head. That couldn't be right. The Dark Elves left ages ago and were still immortal. Elven grace had been taken from the forest elves, and they believed the High Elves were at fault.

Pacing his low-lit room, the king deliberated the Elven lore of their gods, and none of it made sense. The Dark Elves didn't even know their god's name. Lost to some battle or another, they didn't pray to idols or throw revelries, and yet they appeared just fine.

She doesn't want them talking to the king...

That's because they have nothing good to say.

He had heard the spirits for as long as he could remember, but it had never stopped him from searching for the speaker with his eyes. Stepping out of his room, Ettrian found Aracaryn with her back facing him and the Dark Elf envoys clustered in the hallway.

"If I didn't know better, I'd say you were preventing them from coming at my summons."

Aracaryn's shoulder blades smoothed as she straightened. "My lord, these are no ordinary envoys; they are Basilla."

"Then all four of you come in."

Aracaryn stood apart from the three envoys—not that he'd have trouble differentiating them. The envoys wore identical masks and gowns. The fabric had printed lines and sewn in pearls and gold ribbons. He wasn't one to comment on what females wore, but the garments were rather tacky.

"Thank you for coming," he said before glancing at Aracaryn. The brushed silver likenesses were disturbing in their enduring serenity. "I wished to ask about our cousins who rule the isles."

"Of what?" the center elf asked.

"What is the state of magic for your people?"

"It thrives," the left said.

"It declines," said the right.

And the center replied with, "It's middling."

He was beginning to understand why Aracaryn didn't want them to meet with him. He looked to his vassal, and she gave an apologetic shrug. "Only those who figure it out for themselves will have answers from the Basilla."

Ah, and she wasn't allowed to explain the riddle. Ettrian wasn't in the mood for games, but it was his one chance to learn more about the Dark Elves without Aracaryn's lenses.

"And how fairs the king?"

"Beloved of the nameless god," the middle said.

"By none," said the left.

The elf on the right followed up with, "By all."

"My lord..." Aracaryn softly warned.

He motioned for her to remain silent. She called them the Basilla. For them to come, it must have meant something important had happened. Two of the envoys spoke lies, and one spoke the truth. He had no idea which did what at any given time.

"Who rules the isles?"

"Queen Ellyn," the left said.

The right said, "King Rhys."

But the middle said, "Queen Aeson."

Aracaryn's father was King Rhys, and her grandmother was Ellyn. He had met the king only once upon his coronation. There, his father and the newly appointed king of the isles spoke of loss and mourning. Ettrian understood the riddle.

"I'm so sorry, Aracaryn," he said. "If you wish to return to the isles for a time, I will understand."

Her face was awash with so many emotions. He understood how that felt. The loss of a parent was a strange sort of grief for royalty. It was a time when a child was supposed to mourn the loss of their parent and the life they had before the weight of responsibility, and yet they were expected to be happy to accept the crown.

To grieve or celebrate too much was frowned upon, but one was supposed to know just how much was appropriate. In his case, the fact that he didn't celebrate at all was just as confusing to the populace as his mourning.

"I do not know," Aracaryn said. "My younger sister and I are not exactly cordial. I'm afraid my presence is not only unwelcome but seen as a threat."

"Of course," he said. "Whatever you need."

He felt for Aracaryn. She was close to her father. His reign was short, but he was known for being a merciful and joyful ruler like his mother before him. But there was something in the Basilla's riddle that revealed itself to him then.

The magic that once thrived was declining, and the Dark Elves feared it would fade entirely.

Whatever was befalling the elves, it was happening to all their clans but in different ways. The Runda Nor were no longer immortal, and the High Elves had lost their fertility.

"How is magic declining for the Dark Elves?" he asked.

He had solved their riddle, and the Basilla no longer felt the need to keep up with the game.

"We are mighty with the name of our god," said the left.

"Our magic doesn't come unless there is blood sacrifice. We are barren," the middle said.

"We are dust," concluded the elves on the right.

The clans shared similar struggles. Only, the High Elves had never attempted sacrifice—not intentionally, at least. He'd see to it that such ideas were not explored. Dark Elves always had a firmer grasp on magic. They had chartered its depths and understood the balance that must be kept. If the High Elves got wind that blood sacrifice was an option, there would be elves with various levels of self-inflicted wounds scattered about the gardens.

"Thank you, Basilla," Ettrian said. "You may leave."

Aracaryn wrapped her naked arms around her chest. He offered her a blanket folded on a nearby chair. To his surprise, she accepted it.

"Vulnerability looks strange on you," he said.

"My people are taught that vulnerability is a bad thing."

He nodded and sat at his table. His father held similar sentiments despite being a High Elf. "Is that why you and my father got along so well?"

"No," she said, joining him at the table. "In truth, I think he just enjoyed flaunting me to your mother."

He was taken aback by that. Never once had she spoken an ill word about his father. As far as Ettrian knew, she was his steadfast ally and perhaps something more. It seemed he was wrong. "I thought the two of you..."

She laughed. "I'm not attracted to men at all, actually. It was something he accepted when my people could not."

It seemed a strange thing to worry about. High Elves cared about the gender of their partner about as much as the color of the wine they drank. "Such thing matter on the Isles?"

"Indeed. Especially for the next in line to the throne."

That wasn't totally unlike High Elves. He was forbidden to lay with a female until marriage for the sake of lineage. Should he wish to marry a man, an official female concubine with an heir would need to come first.

"Is that why you were sent here?" he asked. "To keep the royal line uncomplicated?"

And the reason why she couldn't return.

"Yes."

If she did, her people would assume she was the rightful queen. Aracaryn would be expected to marry a male and reproduce an heir. She would be living a lie. He leaned his head back and sighed. There were so many expectations for royalty.

"The Runda Nor are mortal," he said as if confessing some horrid truth. "They think we're responsible. Perhaps we are."

"It was good that you acted when you did," she said. "We were about to make a horrid mistake."

Had he not acted, Aracaryn would have as much blood on her hands as his father; they all would. Instead, Ettrian bore that weight alone.

His eyes focused on a crack in the wall. Reflected in the flames was a wet, shining substance. Blood sap. The lifeforce of Cardhon Nimloth was seeping from the dark corners where no one cared to look. The decay had made its way to his rooms. It would only be a matter of time before it was visible to all.

#

It was the early hours of the morning when Radelia slipped out of her room. She lifted what was the simplest garment she could find in the wardrobe, revealing her soft leather boots. Yinren had insisted her clothes be washed and the leathers conditioned, but he'd spared the boots.

"No amount of conditioning can help those," he said, leaving her rooms with the rest of her garments.

She wore a white silken shift with a blue linen bodice with two slashes around the skirt. As far as dresses went, she rather liked it. If a patrol were to pass by, they wouldn't wonder why she was dressed as though she were on a stealth mission.

Katar and Kieran were somewhere to the northeast in a tall tower. She felt like a field mouse navigating the wheat stocks, scurrying all about the castle.

Somewhere along the line, she had gone too far, and the all too familiar cold crept along her arms. The High Elves claimed their magic formed a barrier about the castle to keep out the cold, but it was clearly weak along the outskirts.

Rounding back to the warmth, she took several wrong turns before finding a stairway. Only it was dislodged from the posts.

What had happened? She touched the splintered wood. Something warm and wet was on her fingers. Holding her hand up to the window, Radelia gasped. It was blood. What evil wretch would nail iron rods into a living being? She already knew who tore them away. There was only one elf strong enough.

"I'm sorry," she whispered to the walls. "This should have never happened to you."

Fuming, she lost all interest in stealth and stumbled on something.

There was a groan. Leaning down, she realized she had tripped on a someone. In the corner of the corridor, a High Elf male was curled into a ball. "Are you dying?" she asked.

"Yeah..."

If he was injured, she couldn't just leave him. Whatever he did, he probably deserved it, but she kneeled and rolled him over.

"What are you doing?" he whined.

"I'm helping you."

He squinted up at her. "With what?"

She didn't understand. She was trying to find the wound. "You said you were dying."

"Not literally," the elf said with a laugh. "I drank too much."

"So, you're not dying?"

He shook his head and winced from whatever pain ailed him. Once when her people got a barrel of ale, it made some feel sick. They vomited over the railings of the village and complained of headaches the next day. It must have been the same thing. "So, should I just leave you here, or do you want me to help you get back to your room?"

Extending his arm upward, Radelia pulled the High Elf to his feet. "Lead the way," she grunted under his weight. High Elves were thicker than her people. Probably from all the food and drink.

Please let his room be close by.

The elf staggered, but he pointed the way without hesitation. If he could navigate his way to his room in such a state, perhaps he could tell her where Kieran and Katar were. "How do I get to the northeast tower?"

Plopping him onto a bed that she sincerely hoped was his, the elf wrapped a blanket around himself, boots and all, and said, "Take a left...stairs, more stairs..."

She supposed that would have to do.

While the directions were not the most specific— the first left was much further than she had anticipated—Radelia did find the stairs. Gazing up at the seemingly endless spiral, she was suddenly struck with the fear of falling.

It didn't happen as often anymore, but when she first began traveling by ropes, there was this sort of warning. Her body would scream at her, threatening to lock up at the absolute worst moment. Eventually, Radelia learned that would never actually happen, but she never imagined the sensation would occur when her feet were so firmly planted.

She lost count of how many steps were taken, but when the stairs were fully behind her, Radelia was panting, and the muscle above her knee was weak.

At the end of the short hallway were a set of guards. She froze, not wanting to alert them. Freeing her friends would be impossible without sounding the alarm.

Well, shit.

They hadn't spotted her. She could go back down the stairs and go back to her room without incident. But Kieran and Katar were right there! Just behind a door and two guards. If she could get it open, her friends could make quick work of the guards, and they'd all be free. But losing the trust of the High Elves would make it nearly impossible to get close enough to do what had to be done.

That's when a loud snore had her jumping out of her skin.

It came from the guard. Her eyes narrowed as she approached the pair. She was still several feet away when she smelled it. The guards smelled nearly as bad as the High Elf she found on the floor. Radelia got closer. Toe to toe with one guard, she poked him in the chest, and he didn't so much as stir.

Stepping around the guard, Radelia leaned against the door and closed her eyes. She wanted nothing more than to open it. But to do so would jeopardize everything. "Katar? Katar, are you in there?"

There was a soft rustling from the other side. "Radelia?"

She choked on a sob. "It's me."

"What are you doing?"

"Shhh," Radelia urged. "The guards are asleep."

Katar lowered her voice but repeated the question.

"I came here to save you," she said. "But you're not the only ones that need saving."

"The High Elves...they're not what we thought," Katar said.

She wiped the tears from her eyes, laughing at the words that came next. "They sent Kieran's scout home unharmed and want to send you home as well. They're harmless."

"Not all of them."

"Then you understand."

"I do." A shaky sigh came from her chest. Pressing a hand to the door, she imagined Katar's hand mirrored her own.

"In the meantime, cooperate," she urged. "Don't attack them when they bring you meals. Most of them are untrained. They don't even realize the castle is dying."

"Understood."

She wanted to say more. She wanted to tell Katar that she loved her and that she would do anything to free them. The High Elf sentimentality must have been rubbing off on her.

It was a long walk back to her room, and not because she got lost. Her feet knew the way and led her to the door. Almost too tired to open it, Radelia pushed against it with her weary body and collapsed into the impossibly soft bed.

Her last fleeting thoughts were of the lonely king with his sad eyes hiding behind the wicked smile.

Chapter Thirteen

Chapter 13

Do you think they'll stay?

I hope they do. Forever and ever…

Ettrian rolled his eyes. It was too early in the morning for so much chatter. His head throbbed from the drink of the previous night, and the last thing he wanted was invisible commentary.

"Something vexes you, my king?" Leaf asked.

"Always," he grumbled, poking at the soft-boiled egg.

The other vassals remained quiet, but he could sense the exchange of concerned glances. He knew what they were thinking. They took a chance on him for the sake of the royal line and his mother but had instilled a madman on the throne.

He could just tell them.

It was a thought that occurred to him many times, but the king always hesitated. Something in his throat stopped him, and his brain went blank as he opened his mouth. His gift was like a curse in that he couldn't speak of it.

Then again, if they thought him mad, telling the truth likely wouldn't change that.

The king took a good, hard look at his vassals. In the three years of his reign, they had become something like friends.

"Did my mother possess any unusual abilities?" he asked.

Leaf dismissed the question, knowing it wasn't for her, but the other three took the question seriously.

"It was said her connection to the stars was unlike any other," Omaro said. "She could predict what shapes they would take and knew the precise moment the stars went black."

Balqen nodded thoughtfully in agreement.

"The king once said that her connection to the stars was powered by those she had lost," Aracaryn added.

That made sense. Their people worshiped the stars not only in the name of their goddess but of the High Elves who were no longer with them. It was said a new star formed when one of their own was lost, but no one truly believed that. It was more akin to the phrase men said when their loved ones passed; Everything happens for a reason.

His mother was old. Ettrian knew that much about her. She had fought in the wars of the first ages and lost many loved ones, including several children before him.

"Why do you ask, my king?" Balqen asked.

Should he say it? He couldn't begin to fathom how he'd go about it. Yet perhaps if they knew...

A guard came rushing into the great hall. "My king," he said. "You must see this."

All too eager to escape his quandary, Ettrian was on his feet and following the guard to the front door.

"We sent for the merchant and prepared the goods for delivery," the guard explained. "Only, this is how he arrived."

Was he shot upon arrival? Were the forest elves attacking caravans? Bandits?

Of all the things he anticipated, nothing could have prepared him for what came next.

An old, weathered man stood before his cart, hat in his hands. "Pardon, my king, but we just don't know what else to do."

Ettrian didn't see what the problem was. The man had an empty cart ready to take to the forest elves. "What is it?"

"The Runda Nor gave us good coin, but there are just too many of them now. We got no room to keep them."

"Keep who?"

Peering over the wall of the cart, Ettrian was stunned. Four small bundles wrapped in furs peering up at him with little blue eyes. One turned his head to nuzzle the blanket, exposing a rounded ear.

"Orphans?"

"No, my king," the merchant said. "These are elf babes."

His stomach flipped. Bracing the cart, he listened to the explanation. The Runda Nor had no trouble producing children, but more and more were born as men. The treetops were not safe for such children. The strength it must have taken to let go of something so precious.

"We have to take them back," the merchant said. "It's hard to turn down the coin, but winter is coming, and we just have no way to keep them. One wet nurse can't feed them all."

Ettrian didn't have a wet nurse, and neither did Leaf. They drank milk from goats or cows. Surely the men knew this, but with resources being what they were, even that could not be spared.

"Keep your coin," he said to the merchant. "We shall take the babes and any more they bring you."

He motioned for the guards to take the babies, but they stopped short of picking them up.

"What are you waiting for?"

His guards trembled at such small things. "I'm sorry, my king, it's just that we don't know how."

Exasperated, he pushed them aside. "Like this," he said, scooping one of the babies up. "Make sure you support the neck."

There was a similar reaction when Leaf was born. The royal family took great interest in the triumph that was her birth. They took turns holding her as if she were a sacred deer. His arms ached as if recalling the hours he sat holding her for a painting.

He helped the guards one by one until each of them had a child. He took the last.

"What is this?" Aracaryn said.

All four vassals were wide-eyed and peering into the little bundles of fur. "They are elves, though they may not look it. They are to be raised no differently than anyone else.

Balqen was laughing with sheer delight as he took a child from a nervous guard and began talking to the baby. Aracaryn cringed as a guard offered one to her. "No, no," she said. "You hang on to that."

"Best not mention this to the Runda Nor," he said to the merchant. "And don't tell them where the goods come from either. They're liable to set your cart on fire."

The merchant nodded, visibly relieved to be free of the cargo.

"Take the children to the kitchens where it's warmest and the closest to foods and linens. If Leaf is any indication, they will go through many cloths. For now, we must keep this quiet."

They nodded in understanding. The last thing anyone needed was for the ambassador to think they were stealing Runda Nor children. He didn't imagine she would react well, but it was the safest place for the young. They didn't have elf characteristics, but at least they would have their elf heritage.

"Vassals," he said. "With me."

Closing the door to his room, the vassals all coped in their various ways. Aracaryn was furiously pacing the room. Leaf found a nail that needed chewing. Omaro was in a state of silent bewilderment. It took great effort to pry the babe from Balqen's hands, but his smile remained unchanged.

"Are we certain they're elves?" Aracaryn asked.

"Why else would the merchant try and take them back to the forest?" Omaro said.

Ettrian knew it to be true. The Runda Nor were declining faster than their people. "The ambassador confirmed that their people are born mortal. They have no connection to magic, so it's not possible that they're the cause of our troubles."

"Yet the fact remains that all of this started around the same time the Runda Nor left," Omaro reminded him.

"It's related," he agreed. "I just don't know how. But if we don't restore Cardhon Nimloth's health, we might follow the Runda Nor into extinction."

They sat with that horrid truth for a long moment.

Elf-kind was dying, and there wasn't any one clan to blame. His father thought that by culling one group, there would be more magic for the others, but he was wrong not only in morality but theory as well.

"How do we stop it then?" Aracaryn asked.

He didn't know, and that was an answer the princess would not accept. She stood in front of the king, inches from her face. The subtle scent of rosewater emanated from her chest. "You said that you would find a way to save Cardhon Nimloth. That's the whole reason we backed you."

"I saved you all from making the worst mistake of your eternal lives," he flared. "If that's not proof enough that I can resolve this, I don't know what is."

The Runda Nor were the key to their salvation. That was the only thing Ettrian was certain of. If his father had gone through with his plan, there would have been no hope at all.

"If they have no magic," Leaf said with unusual quietness. "How will they make us stronger?"

He turned to face her. The closest thing he had to an ally said what all the vassals were thinking. Cardhon Nimloth needed its magic bolstered, not drained faster by an influx of weaker elves. She might as well have said she lost all faith in him.

They wanted to send the forest elves back. Bar them from entering Cardhon Nimloth forever and live with their eyes and hearts closed to the crumbling walls around them. All he truly had to go on was the fact that the spirits wanted the Runda Nor to return.

If there was ever a time for the spirits to speak, it would have been in that moment. A meager hint or a fragment of history for him to find a foothold. "What is the solution?" he asked, not to his vassals but rather to the spirits. "How can we save Cardhon Nimloth?"

No one provided an answer. Not his vassals. Nor the spirits.

Aracaryn scoffed at his plea, shaking her head. "I petition the vassals," she said. "If no improvement is made in three months' time, we vote on the king's abdication."

His vassals were uneasy. Fearful. All of them with expressions that suggested they were asked to dine on raw entrails. Aracaryn wanted to force them to declare their loyalties, but Ettrian would rather not know.

So, he took yet another burden from their shoulders. "I agree."

#

In the light of day, the gardens were a utopia.

Miabelle had a private matter she needed to attend to, so Yinren was tasked with giving Radelia a proper tour of the gardens. Larger than the village of men, the gardens were the source of High Elf foods and, evidently, the drink they loved so much.

Low fences wrapped in grape vines created walkways through plowed patches of earth. Pristine rows of leafy greens gave way to a modest orchard where Radelia plucked a red, shiny apple for a snack.

"It's arranged by the three seasons," Yinren explained. "Our fall harvests, followed by spring. The summer menagerie is on the side that gets the most sun. Even we can't control that."

In the center of the gardens, her attendant gestured to a great pool of water. "And this is the heart of Cardhon Nimloth!"

She suspected it was a source of great pride or something meaningful, but to her, it was nothing more than the core of what was once a tree, carved into the likeness of a giant elf. She held a pitcher, but water only trickled from it into a series of other bowls, creating a piddle of a waterfall.

"It's nice."

"Once, the water spilled out. It was an amazing display," he said, staring up at the likeness. "These days, we have to add water to make it work."

"What other things do you do now that you didn't do a thousand years ago?" she asked.

Yinren shrugged. Together they walked the grassy areas where the party was held the night before. "Grandfather says that the harvest grew faster and that in the winter, they used to watch as the snow slid off the barrier."

"What does it do now?"

"If it's heavy enough, the snow piles on and blots out the sun. We light the braziers along the walls to keep that from happening."

They ate lunch in the great hall with the other High Elves. A leafy salad with tomatoes and cucumbers coated in seasoned oil. There was a soup with vegetables and bread for dipping. While wine was available, most chose water.

Yinren gossiped idly about various High Elves. He told her about the vassals. The one that initially greeted her was a princess of the Dark Elves. Glancing around the room, there were many Black elves intermingling with High Elves.

"Is there a lot of difference between the two clans?"

"Maybe," he said. "The ones that remain are the families that never left. Aracaryn is the only one who returned from the isles." His eyes flittered around before he added in a low voice, "Rumor has it she was unfit to rule her kingdom, so she was sent here in hopes that she'd marry our king."

What did the princess do that made her people reject her? Perhaps she went against her father's wishes and disobeyed a divine order. It was unsettling to know that even in places where royalty meant something, they could still be considered unworthy.

"What about your grandfather? Why is he so old?"

Yinren cast his eyes to his salad. "You've met Leaf."

She could still feel the blade at her throat. Radelia nodded.

"Her mother was the last to carry an elf child. When she began to miscarry, my grandfather and a few others attempted a magical ritual. Leaf was born, but all the elves who performed the ritual died except my grandfather. He lost his immortality and now ages like a man."

Time slowed in the room then. She gazed at the stillness and saw what wasn't there. Children. Not a single child existed in Cardhon Nimloth. How could she miss something so obvious? Radelia couldn't unsee it. In every corner of the hall and every patch of lush grass, no child laughed or played.

"You have no children."

Yinren shook his head, yet his face remained passive as though it didn't matter. That was why their numbers were so few. Why room upon room was empty when she explored the night before. "Doesn't that worry you?"

"I can't exactly make children," he explained. "While many of the High Elves can go either way, the door only opens one way for me."

"What?"

He worked to conceal the smile. "I only enjoy the company of men."

Well, that was a roundabout way of saying it. High Elves loved their innuendos. "Oh."

"And with the way things are going with Miabelle, I don't know if she wants children."

They were circling back to Miabelle's personal matter. The way she stammered and excused herself that morning left Radelia wondering just what was going on. There was no need to prod Yinren. Given enough silence, he'd spill the details.

"She's married, you see. Only she knew Grandfather wouldn't approve, so she married him in secret. A mistake she's trying to rectify."

There it was. She struggled to appear surprised. Not that Miabelle was married, but because she knew Yinren would tell her everything. In truth, she couldn't muster any sympathy for Miabelle. Their whole world was crashing down on them while the High Elves fussed over bad marriages and gossip.

"In the Runda Nor, we only marry before death," she explained before biting into a little tomato. "That way, when an elf passes, their partner gets all their stuff."

"That's why Grandfather wouldn't approve. I told her, he's only after the nobility and wealth, but did she listen? It would do him in if he learned that all his wealth and status would be shared with a field hand."

Distributing wealth to lesser High Elves—how sad indeed. Their numbers dwindled, and their barrier weakened. Their beautiful well was running dry while their king talked to himself...but Miabelle had married a coin collector. "The tragedy."

Yinren gave an empathetic nod. "I know. It's so sad." Apparently, sarcasm wasn't something the High Elves were familiar with.

After lunch, Radelia changed into a different gown. One that revealed more skin than she was comfortable with. Yinren had pointed to the king's tower in passing while they traversed the gardens. Tucking a small blade into her low bodice, Radelia made sure the garment concealed it. Someone had to set a better course for the elves. Who else, if not her?

CHAPTER FOURTEEN

Chapter 14

It was a gentle knock on his door. Ettrian assumed it was Aracaryn or Omaro.

"Come in."

When the ambassador crept in, he found himself unable to recall just who he had expected or even their names. She was wearing a gown with a sheer skirt that only concealed her legs with numerous folds. The corseted bodice was so low that even her small bosom threatened dissent. It was a gown intended to be worn at night. In the dark. And only for a brief time until her lover took it off.

He returned his gaze to the book in his lap. She might not have known the dress was inappropriate. After last night, she no doubt saw many females in such gowns and thought it was normal.

"It's good to see you, Ambassador," he said, not removing his gaze from the page. "Please, sit and join me."

"I wanted to talk with you about what I've seen since arriving."

"I imagine so."

"You have no children."

He shook his head. "No, I have none."

She was silent for a moment before reiterating. "The High Elves have no children."

He winced at the slip of his own words. Trying to keep focus on the words, the book's letters betrayed him. They fell away from histories and reassembled themselves into pictures.

"Elven immortality is said to be granted at birth," he explained. "Our goddess, for whatever reason, no longer deems us worthy of her gifts."

"My people believe something similar," she said, getting up from her chair. His eyes followed the sway of her skirts. Try as he might, Ettrian couldn't help but follow the outline of her legs. "We assumed that Elpharae no longer hears us because we are unworthy. What if our gods cannot hear us for a different reason?"

She turned to face him then. Her skin was flushed, and her hands fidgeted slightly at her sides. Rada was fully aware of the gown's exposure. What were her intentions? Perhaps he had given her the wrong impression the night before. It was a moment of weakness in his lonely existence. He had forgotten himself, and it shouldn't have happened.

Swallowing the lump in his throat, he said, "I'd love to hear your theories."

Confliction worked along her face. As if she didn't know whether to believe his interest was genuine or because what she said was far-fetched. Did she come to seduce him or speak of gods? Ettrian got the feeling that even she didn't know.

"Something is indeed amiss," he said. "Not just our clans, but the Ruby Isles are having difficulties of their own. Magic is waning for everyone, not just us."

"Shit."

Indeed. He couldn't help but crack a smile but returned his gaze to the book only to find lewd depictions of lovemaking.

"What are you reading?"

She moved closer, forcing Ettrian to slam the book shut. "King stuff," he said with a forced smile, ignoring the sweat that formed above his brow. "Marital laws, mostly."

Rada was standing a few inches away from his knees. He strained to keep his excitement concealed with the book held fast in his lap. "We had a request for research into marriage annulment."

"You see to that yourself?"

"Well," he said, shifting in his seat. "I do a great deal of research. Anything that could provide insight into our combined dilemma, but—"

She leaned down, bracing the arms of the chair to prevent his escape. When Ettrian murdered his father, he did so with the understanding that no female would ever want him. King or otherwise. He had accepted that fate and had long given up hope for romance. But her lips were partly opened, so close to his.

If she knew the truth, she would change her mind. How could anyone want him after what he did? Still, he was powerless to deny the allure of a beautiful woman.

Something fell from her and landed heavily on the book. She gasped and straightened, backing away as though she finally saw the monster he was.

Ettrian looked down to find a letter opener in the fashion of a sword.

"It was just a precaution," the ambassador stammered. "I didn't know it was there. Please don't harm them."

Of all the things to do in that situation, what he did was probably the worst thing. He threw his head back and laughed.

How stupid was he to think she wanted him? Rada spent most of her time with the gossip monger of Cardhon Nimloth. She knew what he did, and she found him just as vile as the rest of them. She didn't come to seduce him. She came to put him out of his misery.

"I'm sorry," he said, gasping for air. "If you mean to kill me, you'll have to try a bit harder than that."

The ambassador's face soured at his mockery. No one ever saw the humor of life's little events the way he did, and she was no exception. A flurry of black tulle fabric was marching toward the door. "Oh, come on," he said. "I don't hold it against you."

She whirled around and stared at him with utter bewilderment. "Why are you like this? You don't care that I..."

"Want to kill me?" he finished. "I'm holding your people hostage, you blame me for your clan's demise, and I can't imagine what my own people have told you. I'm just surprised you came in that."

As if suddenly aware of how exposed she was, Rada attempted to cover her chest with her hands. If anything, he was grateful the moment was cut short. Had she taken it any further, he might have broken his royal vows.

He stood and reached for a blanket. The ambassador flinched, but he unfolded the blanket and offered it to her. Still stifling his laugh, he said, "You can keep the letter opener if it makes you feel more at ease."

Snatching the blanket from his outstretched hand, she wasted no time in covering herself. "So, you've seen for yourself that my people are also in trouble. Have you noticed the cracks in the walls? The blood sap?"

She nodded but eyed him skeptically as he returned to his seat. "Yes, I suppose you would notice, even if my people don't."

For whatever reason, that got her attention. "Why are they so blind to it?"

Ettrian had no explanation. "I wish I knew. I devote every spare moment in search of answers, but the books refuse to show me answers."

She slowly joined him. Leaning over the table, she nodded to the book that had opened, revealing two elves in a compromising position. "Perhaps you're looking at the wrong books."

His skin burned as he hid his face in his hands. "It wasn't like that until your failed assassination attempt, or whatever it was."

"Uh-huh."

Of course she didn't believe him. His own people didn't understand the magic of the books half the time. Did they think themselves such excellent librarians that they instantly found the books of their desire? Perhaps his thoughts shifted with such a polarity that the ink only changed for him.

"We must appear to be such fools to you," he lamented.

Rada smiled and shrugged, knowing better than to answer.

"And I am the king of fools."

He closed the book, still hoping for redemption if they stayed on topic. "Our revelries are unheard and unseen by Isilynor, and your prayers are unheeded by Elpharae. When did your people first start noticing this?"

"Immortality was lost to the first generation born in the forest," she said, pulling the blanket closer. "Some lived for hundreds of years and others less than eighty. In the last fifty, most could no longer hear them, but the healers could."

"Your god, you mean?"

She nodded. "The healers are the most devoted and have the strongest connection to Elpharae, but even they no longer hear them."

"What led the healers to believe your god no longer answered?"

He already knew. It was the birth of the children, but he wanted to hear it from her mouth. Confirmation that the babes were indeed elves. Her eyes glistened as she looked away. "Our babes were born different. They resemble man, not elf.

"At first, we thought one of our females was with a man, but we live in the treetops, you see. It would be difficult for a man to travel among us unnoticed. And when several more babes were born the same way, we knew it wasn't an issue of mixed breeding."

"Both parents were elves, yet the babes were not."

She nodded. "I had to take them to the human village myself."

It explained her sour mood the day she arrived. Nothing set the tone for reunification like ripping infants from their parent's arms.

"Why send them away?" he asked.

"We travel by ropes and unrailed bridges; humans struggle with such things as adults, let alone young children. It wasn't safe for them."

There was more. He saw it in her face. The tears she shed told him that there was an experience there. An accident, perhaps. "They could adapt..."

Rada shook her head. "The royal line has abilities. Remainders of magic. They possess foresight. The princess saw their death in a vision. She also saw the village empty and the halls of Cardhon Nimloth awash in blood."

So, there was some magic left to the Runda Nor. If that was true and not some political farce used to control their people, perhaps they could use it. "The gift of foresight is a great gift indeed. If you could convince your princess to come to Cardhon Nimloth, maybe she can see something we cannot."

"Her father would never allow it. They believe High Elves are the enemy and won't be convinced otherwise."

He sighed. So much for that. "That's a shame. If we could just see what the castle needs, we might be able to restore what was lost."

"We're on our own. Asses in the wind."

Such colorful language. It was no wonder the royal family sent her to negotiate with the humans. "Do they know you're here?"

Her eyes went wide, and she shook her head. He was beginning to understand what had transpired.

The Runda Nor were desperate after realizing all their babies were being born human. The ambassador was sent to the human village to give the babes to men for safekeeping. Along the way, she must have encountered Larriel, learned of the failed scouting, and taken matters into her own hands. If she didn't, Emperor Bellas and his heir would have left them to rot.

"I'll make a deal with you," he said. "Let's work together. Help me search the libraries. Give me the Runda Nor context I'm lacking."

"And what do I get in return?"

He didn't understand. "My deal is a win for both of us."

She raised one brow. "For our people, yes, but what about me?"

"Help me, and I won't tell my vassals about your assassination attempt."

If they learned of what happened, Ettrian half expected Aracaryn would provide a sharper blade and a reason to use it. Rada didn't have the gumption to kill anyone. She didn't know it, but her heart was too strong for such a desperate act.

She sighed and uttered something crude before agreeing. "Fine, but let the scouts go."

"As I said, it's not in my power, but I will try to persuade the vassals."

Satisfied with the arrangement, Ettrian showed her to the door. "Keep the blanket," he said as she tried to give it back. "And take this corridor. It's the long way to your room but seldom used."

He didn't want anyone to see her in that gown. It wasn't for concealing a potential scandal, nor was it because she was self-conscious.

The image of her running across the lawn in a blanket would have been hilarious. But there were feelings attached to the idea of her body being on display for others.

What a lurking, possessive monster he was. If he couldn't have her, he wanted no one else to either. Not that she would have been interested. Rada was repulsed by his people for the same reasons he was. They were so vain and selfish. Blind to all others as they looked from their high walls, ignoring the cracks. She cared deeply about their people and was willing to risk her station to make things right, and in that, they were alike.

When Ettrian closed his bedroom door, he leaned against it. Only in the low light of his room could the king admit to the feelings she stirred within him. She must have been aware of it, that gnawing, thrashing beast that stirred within him. It was only a matter of time before she learned the truth and flinched, just like all the others.

Chapter Fifteen

Chapter 15

Miabelle's voice was the first Radelia heard the next morning. "Morning!"

The curtains were flung open, and the daylight blasted her in the face. Wincing, she rolled over, pulling the blankets over her head with a groan.

"The breakfast this morning is buttered toast with cheese spread, your favorite."

Radelia ignored the attendant with all her heart. She didn't sleep well after her failed visit to the king. Sickness came over her just thinking about it. That image played in her head over and over. The way the blade fell out of her bodice right in his lap. She told him the knife wasn't hers! Ugh, even she was tired of her own shit.

The one shot she had, and Radelia blew it. There'd be no second attempt. She and everyone else was stuck with him as king.

Though, the idea didn't strike dread in her heart as it once had. He knew magic was fading, and unlike everyone else, the king was actually doing something about it.

"Oh, tell me you didn't wear this while I was gone," Miabelle said.

She didn't need the reminder. The most dangerous part of the night before wasn't the blade's delicate location or the assassination of the enemy king. The real danger was a nipple breaching the surface of her bodice. Though she supposed the king would have been rather joyful.

"And this blanket...Radelia, you didn't!"

"And what if I did?"

Miabelle grabbed her rather forcefully and pulled her upright. "You cannot seduce the king," she said.

"Why? Surely even he engages in the revelries from time to time."

"He doesn't. He can't. Royalty mustn't have a partner before marriage. Otherwise, anyone can step forward and claim they carry the next in line."

Radelia didn't see what the fuss was all about. Everyone took partners, whether long-term or just for the night. Judging by the activities all about the lawn, the High Elves were not so discriminating.

Miabelle gasped with frustration. "Tell me you didn't."

"Nothing happened."

She nodded and only then released Radelia from her manicured grasp. "I know you don't understand, but if the king were to lay—with a female at least—they would force you into a marriage with him."

Radelia frowned at the way she said it. Like he was some troll waiting to ensnare the fair princess. Ettrian wasn't all bad once she got past his eccentricities. "Why do you hate him so?"

"I don't hate him; I fear him, and so should you."

"Why?"

Miabelle wouldn't say. She laid a gown across the bed and said, "I'll see you in the great hall."

Unlike her brother, Miabelle kept much hidden. She must have learned that secrets were necessary after marrying the wrong elf. Radelia washed her face with cold water and dressed for breakfast. Lacing up the slack bodice, she ignored the itchy chest pads sitting beside the garment.

If she was to work side by side with the king, she would need to have more information. Why were his people so reluctant to be near him? Her father was well-loved. His station didn't isolate him in the ways it did Ettrian. Then again, her father helped build the huts and shared his meals while the king remained cloistered in his room or in the library.

Yinren would be far more willing to share gossip.

As she descended the staircase, Radelia sensed the fear that enveloped the massive room. The strange, muffled cries reminded her of when the healers wouldn't see to the dead. Something was happening. She quickened her pace down the steps.

The High Elves were staring up at a tapestry. The long, white, flowing linen embroidered with gold thread in the likeness of their goddess was soaked with blood. A horrid dripping echoed throughout the room.

Radelia approached the tapestry and peered behind it. Holding her breath as she prepared for the worst. A hanging body or a disgusting prank. But behind the beautiful, hand-made design was a great split in the wood. The blood was coming from the castle itself.

Who knew how long it had been there. Rather than panic the High Elves, someone covered it with a tapestry and hoped it wouldn't get worse. Well, it got worse, and the High Elves didn't understand.

"It's because you're here," someone uttered. "Isilynor is angry with us for allowing you to soil our home."

They were all staring at her. Their eyes accusing and expressions grim. The High Elves had ignored the cracks and decay until faced with it, then linked it to her arrival. She was facing down an angry mob, bracing herself for the worst when a stranger stood beside her.

"That crack had been there for some time," he said, gazing up at the tapestry. "I was ordered to cover it by the vassals."

The High Elves saw something they could not unsee. Their eyes fell to various blemishes and pools of blood sap leaking from the corners previously dismissed. Radelia scoffed. They knew it wasn't her, and yet they were eager to point the finger.

Balqen emerged from the crowd. He stared at the tapestry and then at her. "Let's get this cleaned up," he told the stranger, who was probably a worker of some kind.

The vassal led her away from the hall and into the gardens. Tension from the moment eased with the fresh air. "I apologize," he said. "We have been trying our best to shield them from the truth."

"Why?" She stopped short, knowing the answer. Just as her father tried to keep the babes a secret. A panicked crowd never led to anything good.

The old elf nodded. "There's no hiding it from them now. I fear our revelries won't hold the same enthusiasm."

"Oh, but what will you ever do without parties?"

The sarcasm was lost on Balqen. He stared at her blankly.

"What I mean is why do the revelries matter so much? Elf magic is dying, yet your people insist on them."

As if suddenly aware of how frivolous it appeared, the vassal gave a surprised chuckle. "It must look rather contradictory. The revelries have purpose. We don't just throw them because we're bored."

"A distraction then?"

He shook his head. "It's how High Elves communicate with their goddess. They lay together under the starlight and pray for conception."

She thought back to the party. The way the elves left the tents to couple in the grass. As lascivious and kinky as it was, there was a reason the High Elves were so sexually active. She was suddenly ashamed then. What Radelia had witnessed a few nights prior was not promiscuity but rather desperation.

"They're trying to procreate."

"Yes, and sadly, it won't work. It hasn't in a very long time. Even Leaf's conception was aided by magic that we no longer possess."

She wrapped her arms around herself then. More aware than ever of the consequences should they fail. "Why does everyone fear the king?"

The question made the old elf even wearier. His shoulders slumped, and his eyes were tired. "It's a story best heard from the king himself. I'm not proud of the role I played. I was so lost in my own grief," his voice wavered before he hurried away. "Excuse me."

Well, shit.

Standing alone on the lawn, Radelia didn't know what to think. She had no idea that her question would strike such a nerve. Balqen wanted her to ask the king, but he was too self-loathing and cryptic to give her the straightforward answer she needed. Piss on that.

"Yinren," she called. "Has anyone seen Yinren?"

\#

Every meeting with his vassals was like a little reminder of what waited for Ettrian when they finally buried his unmoving corpse. It wasn't that he was ungrateful for their help, he couldn't imagine doing it all alone, but the squabbling grated on his last nerve. The youngest and the oldest, the lowliest and the most noble, were gathered to give

Ettrian an insight from all walks of life within Cardhon Nimloth. The intent was pure and noble, but between the generation gaps and social disparities, there was lots and lots of bickering.

"My apologies for being late," Balqen said as he entered Ettrian's room.

"You didn't miss much," the king said flatly.

Aracaryn gave him one of her famous scowls. "Actually, this is rather important."

The old vassal hurried to the chair and sighed with relief as he sat.

Ettrian indulged Aracaryn's concerns. "It seems the Runda Nor have been busy as of late."

"Oh?" Balqen said.

Leaf chimed in. "She's asking the Dark Elves to ally with them."

Aracaryn nodded at the unrolled parchment on the table. "My sister's second sent this to me."

Ettrian had read the letter twice and found it suspiciously lacking.

Dearest venerable sister,

The clan of Runda Nor seeks our aid in attempt to thwart the High Elves from their seat of power within Cardhon Nimloth. Their claim is that they are the rightful owners of the castle and that they alone can restore the fading magic which we're all experiencing.

It is the queen's wish that you resolve the matter between the two clans. Should you fail, the queen will be forced to take matters into her own hands.

Sincerely,

Second to the queen,

Her most royal majesty Aeson

Long may she reign

Nothing like a declaration of war to brighten one's afternoon.

Balqen gazed up at Aracaryn with utter horror. "Do you think your sister will side with Runda Nor?"

"If for nothing more than to spite me, yes."

In the first age, when war was most frequent, there were four elf clans. There had been a few skirmishes and bruised egos since then, but not full clan versus clan battles. Their people either lost their appetite for blood after the extinction of the Ice Elves, or the cause of all the wars was eliminated. Of course, with their history being exclusively from the High Elf perspective, no one would know the truth for certain.

"I hate to add to our burdens, but our people had quite the morning. One of the tapestries was soaked in blood sap. They blamed the ambassador. The director and I tried to debunk such ideas, but I fear many still believe it to be true."

"The decay is becoming impossible to hide," Leaf agreed. "They're scared."

No furniture arrangement or tapestry could hide the truth from the elves. If the infertility of the last thousand years hadn't clued them in, the rotting castle would.

"The ambassador has agreed to help me search for answers," he said.

"What if there are none?" Balqen asked softly. "We keep blaming others. Pointing a finger at one clan or another. What if there is nothing to be done because the time of elves has simply come to an end?"

The thought had occurred to Ettrian. Usually in the dead of night when he woke in a cold sweat from a nightmare he couldn't recall.

What if it was all for nothing? Studying his vassals, he could tell they were lost in similar thoughts. Their worst nightmare spoken out loud.

It was easy for him to succumb to the darkness. For Ettrian had always dwelled in shadows and in the footsteps of his parents. Reality was his burden, but hope belonged to the elves that prayed under the stars. It wasn't fair.

"No," he said. "I refuse to accept that."

"Then you still hope—"

"Hope is for children," he said, cutting Balqen off. "And for starry-eyed elves. For as long as I reign, I will continue to do whatever I can to make things right."

In the corner of his eye, Ettrian thought he saw an approving nod from Aracaryn.

"I will write to my sister," she said. "Inform them that we are in talks with a Runda Nor ambassador to resolve the situation."

"I have elves cleaning up the mess in the great hall," Balqen added.

"I'll check on the babes," Omaro said. He was so silent that Ettrian nearly forgot the healer was there.

"And Leaf will help prepare for the starless night festival," he said with a smirk. She had hoped he'd forget, but he was not a kind king.

She rolled her eyes but didn't argue.

"I'll help as well," Aracaryn assured the young elf.

"I'm still looking into that annulment law," Ettrian added. Memories of the night prior came on suddenly. "There's also the matter of the scouts. The ambassador is asking for their release."

"Absolutely not," Aracaryn said. "We don't know their importance. Especially considering the news from the isles."

"I'm afraid I agree," Omaro said from the corner. "We know they are of some importance to the Runda Nor. Otherwise, why send the ambassador?"

But they didn't send her. Ettrian didn't dare say otherwise. They might vote to send her home.

"Nope," Leaf said. "They stay."

Balqen nodded in agreement.

At least he could tell Rada he tried. He doubted that would be sufficient, but it would have to do until they had more leverage. "I'll tell her myself."

With nothing else on the agenda, the meeting was concluded. His vassals bowed and moved to leave.

"Omaro, a moment."

The healer waited until the others left before joining the king at his table. "You were quiet."

"Apologies, the babes have been rather demanding."

That would explain much of his lethargy. Omaro's room was near the kitchens. When he was appointed to vassal, he was given the opportunity to resume his old room, but the healer refused, claiming that his old room suited him fine.

"Are they well?"

"Quite well," he said, smiling with his glassy eyes. "But there are four of them. When one cries, they all start crying. But I do love it."

This he had to hear. "You love the sound of crying babes?"

"No, just, it's been so long since we've had young ones. Everything is so new to them. Life still holds excitement. I remember how excited everyone was for you and Leaf."

He nodded in understanding. "I was a consolation."

"You were a gift," the healer said with surprising sharpness. "I couldn't save your mother, but I know she would have been proud."

Ettrian had about enough of the conversation. "I am to meet the ambassador in the library," he said as he stood.

"Of course," the vassal bowed and left without another word.

Alone in his room, the king looked in his mirror and traced the scar. Omaro wasn't to blame for the death of the queen, yet he accepted responsibility and the banishment to the kitchens nonetheless.

In one horrid night, the famed healer was all but banished from Cardhon Nimloth. Not for being unable to save the queen but because of the scar that refused to fade.

Of all the spirits that remained within the castle, Ettrian was fortunate his father was not among them. He disappointed his father so much in life he could only imagine how much the deceased king would have hated Ettrian's reign.

A little smile crept along the corner of his mouth. It was always the little things that kept him going.

Chapter 16

She didn't find Yinren. Instead, Leaf found her as she wandered the gardens in search of the gossipy attendant.

"Hello," Radelia greeted her with a bow. "Have you seen my attendants?"

The female was a head shorter than even Radelia, making her the smallest elf she had ever seen. Perhaps High Elves continued to grow as they got older, but by that logic, Balqen would have been as tall as Ettrian.

She shook her head. "We have larger concerns."

What had she done this time?

They walked the summer harvest. Saying nothing of the withered berries or the drooping cucumbers and half-rotten tomatoes. "You probably heard about this morning," Radelia started.

"Have you been keeping correspondence with your king?"

No, not at all. Though he must have realized something was amiss. The trip to the village and back was a day's travel. Asking for forgiveness rather than permission was something her father loved about her, but Radelia feared this would be the exception. "I've only been here for a few days."

Leaf slashed at a wheat stock with her thin blade. "I'm sure no one has told you, but the Runda Nor have contacted the Dark Elves. Your people claim the castle is rightfully theirs."

She had to bite her lip to keep from saying something she'd regret. "The emperor isn't fond of the Dark Elves. He insisted they were the same as High Elves but with sorcery."

"Fondness or not. They're asking for the Dark Elves to support their claim."

That was news to her. The only one with any connection to the isles was Kieran, and he was locked away in a tower. Radelia shook her head. "That's strange indeed."

Leaf spun on her heel, stopping short of a few inches from her chin. "I need you to write to your king. Tell them the truth."

"What part?" Radelia asked, crossing her arms. "That Cardhon Nimloth is dying under the High Elves' control? That you have the scouts held captive with no signs of release? Any news I send will be fuel to the emperor's flames for war."

"Then it is true," Leaf gasped. "The emperor wishes to wage war on us."

She hadn't meant to reveal that. There was no point in trying to hide it if her father was reaching out to the other Elven clan. "He has been trying for some time," Radelia said. "But the Runda Nor don't just blindly follow orders. We think for ourselves. The general of our army runs independently of the emperor."

"Like the vassals," Leaf said with some reservations.

"Yeah, sort of. The emperor leads the people, the general leads the militia. Both must consent to any attacks."

"What's to stop your king from killing the general and appointing a new one?"

That, Radelia didn't know. "He wouldn't do that. He loves the general like a son."

Even if he was a stubborn bastard. She'd rather jump off the nearest wall than admit it, but Kieran was right. The High Elves couldn't defend Cardhon Nimloth, but they would try, and laying siege to the castle would cause more damage to the already distressed tree. An all-around bloody mess. Runda Nor would be the elves sitting on a pile of rubble with nothing to show for it.

"So, what do you intend to do, exactly?" Leaf asked.

"King Ettrian and I will work together in finding answers," she explained. "I'm to meet him in the library. If we find answers, a plan, anything, I will send word that hope is not lost and that the best course is a peaceful one."

Leaf nodded. As pacified as the little vassal could ever be, she walked away without so much as a goodbye.

Radelia bristled at the rough exchange. Ignoring the watchful eyes of the High Elves working in the gardens, she made her way to the library to find Ettrian sitting on the ground. Pillars of books circled around him.

It wasn't what she imagined. They had books at home, of course, but not many. And they weren't piled in heaps and wobbly stacks amid wood pillars in the likeness of their goddess. Had these people ever heard of a bookshelf? The only room in the castle with windows, they arched at the tops like the doors of the rooms. The yellow stained glass gave the lighting a soft warmth.

"What's with the glass?" she asked.

"It's said to be easier on the eyes of the readers," the king said without looking up from his book.

She wouldn't know. The only time she had to read was on solstice nights when work was canceled in observance. "So, where do I start?"

His eyes locked on hers, and for a moment, she recalled the night before. She burned under his gaze before he cut her loose. "Think about what you want to know and pick up a book."

There was no one else in the library but them. Was it really so easy? Just pick up a book? Any book? Snatching one off the nearest pillar, she sat on the hard floor. "Okay, but maybe invest in some chairs."

"Noted."

The book had no title. None of them did. Not on the covers or the spines. That explained why the High Elves struggled to find anything. Maybe that was why they didn't bother to arrange them. Or that they didn't care. They probably didn't find books as fascinating as their king. Not when they could get drunk and rut on the lawn.

She opened the book and frowned. The pages were blank. "Is this a joke?"

"What information do you seek?" he reminded her.

Radelia spent her morning being accused, suspected, and offended. She probably did a bit of offending herself. The king's games were not something she was in the mood for. "I thought you took this seriously—"

"Focus," he interrupted.

Fine. Radelia closed her eyes and thought about the Runda Nor. Her people claimed that they were the ones who made Cardhon Nimloth. Was that true, or was it her father's excuse to seize control before the High Elves killed it?

Opening her eyes, she watched as the ink-stained the blank pages. Blobs at first, but then they took shape. There were words and pictures. He wasn't bullshitting! "It's magic!"

The king made a soft noise of agreement but nothing more.

She read the pages as fast as they could form. The images depicted a plane of inhospitable lands before two gods conspired to change the fate of the continent. Elpharae planted the seed that would become the great tree while Isilynor shielded it from the harsh winters. Once it became large enough, they summoned their two clans to build and shape the castle together.

"The Runda Nor didn't do it alone," she said. "Both our clans were here in the beginning. They called their elves from the forest, and she called the elves from the mountain to tend the magic and help it grow."

"Why is your god a they?" he asked. "It's not how High Elves depict Elpharae."

"They are the god of fertility. They are the bird and the bee."

He didn't get it. The tables had turned, and she was suddenly the one using innuendos. "Reproduction requires two—or more, according to some of your people."

The king's brow knitted. "So, you're saying your god is both male...and female."

Was it so hard to believe? A god, creator of worlds and races, transcending through time and space, didn't require the old twig and berries?

Ettrian scooted closer. He smelled clean and sort of minty. The king took a bath before meeting her. "Look at this," he said.

His book was all about Elpharae and Isilynor as well, only his book referred to her god as a he. "Why is your book saying something different?" she asked.

"I don't know. I suspected this was the reason I couldn't find the answers we needed. When the scouts refused to eat, the books showed Runda Nor recipes, but when the cook went to use the book, the recipes changed."

The books gave different versions of events depending on who read them. "I didn't realize books were so bent on self-preservation."

Laughter erupted from the king, but for once, it was the right time to laugh. Side by side, they might find a way to bridge the knowledge between their clans. Radelia had to force her eyes back on the book.

"So, both clans built Cardhon Nimloth, which means both have equal claim to it."

"What happens when you ask why magic is fading?"

Why was magic fading? Why were her people being born as humans? Why weren't they immortal? The questions came on so furious that the ink vanished and reappeared several times. "Looks like we've assumed all the problems are caused by the same thing."

"And that's not the case?"

"Why are my people mortal?" she shouted at the book.

"Yelling at it won't help."

The ink resurfaced. It was lore related to Isilynor.

"Goddess of the stars, hope eternal, gives the gift of immortality to those she deems worthy.... So, your goddess thinks my people are not worthy."

It was just as her people feared. Elven grace was bestowed on those who remained loyal to the star goddess.

"Ask about why my people cannot reproduce," the king urged.

The magic of the books had lost its enchantment on Radelia. Some bitch up there didn't think her people were worthy. Why? Because they didn't pray to her? Balqen was Runda Nor once, and he prayed to Isilynor, but he lost his immortality too.

"No," she said, trying to sit up. "I think I'm done."

Grabbing her wrist, he said, "Please. I only get the kind of answers that would've made my father happy."

Something about the way he begged. Ettrian really was trying to fix things. And from what she'd gathered, his father was sort of awful.

Here's to spitting fathers.

"Why can't High Elves reproduce?"

The page took the shape of Elpharae, the Runda Nor version sans twig and berries. "Elpharae is the god of fertility...blah blah blah."

"So then your god is the reason my people cannot make children."

Radelia could only stare at the king. It never occurred to her that her god held sway against his people. It was always poor Runda Nor, forsaken and discarded. But it made sense! "It's like when partners break up and they divvy up the kids and belongings."

Ettrian nodded. "You once said it's like Elpharae can't hear you. Maybe it's because we're asking the wrong gods."

It all made sense in her head, but how were they going to find out if it was right. She didn't imagine the High Elves would be willing to call out Elpharae's name while doing the dirty on the lawn. "Do you know anyone who's open-minded enough to try asking my god for a baby?"

"Perhaps." The king's face betrayed him. His lips did that thing where they wriggled around, knowing if they opened, the truth would come out. "Do you have a symbol for your god? Something inconspicuous?"

There were the stone idols, but he probably had something smaller in mind.

"Show me the symbols for Elpharae."

The ink took shape, depicting several signs from a crescent moon, a triangle, and a leaf.

"Leaf," the king uttered, his fingers touching the picture. "That was why Balqen named her Leaf."

Radelia wondered about that. It wasn't exactly a High Elf name.

"I know what to do."

Following the king through the gardens and the halls, she had to run to keep up with his stride. The elves watched as they passed by, stopping whatever work they were doing to gander. The topic of gossip for the night.

She was amazed at how Ettrian navigated the halls. Amid the rows of identical doors, he knocked on one with utmost confidence. The door was opened by a familiar High Elf. His hair was braided away from his face and knotted into a tail that ran down his back. She'd know those bloodshot eyes anywhere.

"Hey," she said. "I know you!"

It was the drunk elf she helped home the other night.

"My king," he said. "And you."

"Her name is Ambassador Rada," Ettrian corrected. "And I have a task for you."

Chapter 17

In the weeks leading up to the starless night festival, Ettrian's step was lighter. And while his days were not much different, his smiles came easier. When he woke, the king held his morning meeting with his vassals, dodged court unless necessary, and spent his afternoons with the ambassador pouring over books.

His people were busy crafting masks and décor for the biggest celebration of the year, but from time to time, he spotted the occasional elf at a standstill. Staring at a newly formed crack along the wall or flinching at a new puddle of blood sap. While his mood was improving, the castle was not.

"You finally got seating in here!"

She was wearing the blue bodice and white linen shift again. These days, her hair remained loose and free-flowing rather than braided back. The movement fascinated him. Her hair bounced and reflected light in a mass of spirals unlike any in the castle. Her attendant, Miabelle, had some curl and must have known a thing or two about how to style and care for it.

"I'm ashamed it took me as long as it did," he said, seated on one of the leather sofas. "I'm sure you noticed, but new things in Cardhon Nimloth are hard to come by."

Wasting no time, Rada sat on the loveseat opposite him and grabbed a book. "We've learned that asking direct questions gives non-direct answers. So, what was life like before the Runda Nor left?"

Focusing on the same question, something they found useful, the ink told two different tales as they'd come to expect. Information was a curious thing, as it turned out. The books might have told two different versions of the same events, but the story wasn't inherently different. If anything, what he and Rada took away from the books was fascinating.

When Ettrian read the poem written by one of his grandmother's poets, it told the tale of a Runda Nor rabble-rouser. Almar the Unhappy, the poet named him. The illustrations depicted a brown-haired elf with a notch in his left ear complaining at the queen high on her throne.

Almar the Unhappy disliked the way his shoes were made but refused to craft his own.

Almar the Unhappy complained about how loud the children were who trampled through his orchards but offered no safe place for the children to play.

Almar the Unhappy had so many grievances but offered no solutions. For he did not want to be happy, he simply wanted others to be unhappy with him.

"Have you reached the poem of Almar yet?" Ettrian asked.

"Almar the Accountable?"

Just as he suspected. Her eyes found his, and she understood right away that their stories conflicted. "This is one we tell the Runda Nor children still," she explained, straightening as he joined her on the sofa.

While Rada leaned over to read the High Elf poem, he caught the soft scent of lilacs in the oils combed through her hair. He closed his eyes and inhaled before reading the book in her hands.

Almar the Accountable warned that shoes would fall apart after months of wear, but the court ignored him.

Almar the Accountable warned that the children trampled the gardens of the Runda Nor so carefully tended to, but the High Elf children were allowed to run amok.

Almar the Accountable only wanted what was best for the elves, but the only opinions that mattered were those of the High Elves.

So, there they had it. Two different accounts of the same events. Rather than give preference to one version or another, he waited to see what Rada made of it.

She was frowning. Confliction and doubt were working across her freckled face, and he wished there was a way to soothe her discontent. He'd had hundreds of years to learn that there was something not quite right about the way their clans viewed one another; she'd had less than fifty.

"They both make valid points," he said at last. "I think the biggest takeaway is that the Runda Nor felt their voices were unheard."

The events leading up to the clan's departure were rationalized by poets and scholars, but up until he worked with Radelia, it was all one-sided.

"We know this already," she said, setting the book down. "This tells us nothing about how they used magic and why it isn't working."

Rada was frustrated with the books just as he was before he learned their secrets. He imagined she was also grieving on some level. Of all the things they had learned in the last few weeks, it was that the High Elves always held a position of power.

The royal family line held small portraits of each member dating all the way back to the first king and queen of Cardhon Nimloth, and all of them were High Elves. The idea of rectifying that oversight was a pleasant one, but Ettrian suspected that his vassals would insist on him marrying the princess and not an ambassador. So, he kept his musings to himself.

"Come," he said, taking her hand. "Let's go for a walk."

Her hand slipped from his grasp the moment they stepped out of the library. A dull pain twisted in his heart. Did she not want to be seen holding hands with the king? He imagined it would make her appear less legitimate as an ambassador, more biased, perhaps. Or was it because the rumors finally made their way to her?

"They're really going all out," she said.

Elves were on massive stilts walking along the walls, hanging up decorations. Even the most dexterous of races struggled on such contraptions. Every time one swayed or staggered, Ettrian's whole body lurched with panic. "I don't think I can keep watching," he said with a laugh. "If one of them falls, it will be my undoing."

"My king," an elf called for him from across the gardens.

He gave Rada a slight grin. "Let's see what they've done this time."

The ambassador kept glancing up at his face while they walked. Just when he was about to call her out on it, she said, "They're so childlike sometimes. I forget some are thousands of years old."

"They are thousands of years old, but their experiences are limited to the confines of the castle. Some of them have never left the safety of its walls."

"Explains why they gossip so much."

Ettrian raised one eyebrow.

"Shit," she cursed under her breath. "I'm not trying to insult them, but anyone who has had to hunt their own dinner could care less about who wore what."

"What about the rumors surrounding me?" He lowered his head to catch her eyes.

"They're too afraid to speak of you." Her expression had lost all playfulness. "Why is that?"

Before he could answer, the elf that called to him earlier approached. "My king, Aracaryn wanted us to cover the chandelier, but we can't reach."

What did he care of chandeliers? He was about to say as much, but her words echoed in his mind. They're too afraid to speak of you. This was an opportunity to be seen solving a problem without his vassals as a buffer.

"We don't usually cover the chandelier," he said, mindful of his tone and the height of his shoulders. "Is there a special reason Aracaryn requested it?"

"I think she wants to make this a very special event, given the recent troubles."

Ettrian gazed up at the great chandelier. Thousands of precious stones were cut and arranged precisely to reflect the light of the day throughout the hall. It was a magnificent piece and something his people cherished. No chain suspended it; the chandelier defied gravity by the will of Isilynor herself so that the High Elves could see the stars even on the darkest of days. "The chandelier is held in place by the barrier itself."

"I never realized until you mentioned it."

"It must be too high for the stilts," he said. "I'll explain to Aracaryn that it cannot be done. No need to worry."

"I can do it," Rada said.

He turned to face her. She wasn't serious, was she? Before he could question her, the ambassador was making her way up the stairs. She meant to leap from one of the upper stories of the great hall and land on the thing.

Ettrian chased after her and reached out his hand in hopes she would take it once more, "Perhaps it would be best if we leave it be."

"It's not a problem. I make jumps like that for breakfast back in Runda Nor."

She was so small and quick. Darting from his grasp, Rada was already two stories up. Eager to fling herself from a massive height. Ettrian was leaning against the stair railing for support. Despite his size, Ettrian was not fond of heights. In fact, he loathed them. Avoiding his balcony as though it were infested with fleas, he never walked along the top of the walls unless it was necessary.

And the female he admired most was eager to fling herself from nine stories. For what? Aracaryn's aesthetic? The world spiraled around him as images filled his mind of Rada splatting to the ground over and over.

"It's really not necessary," the king said as a bout of vertigo washed over him. "Please..."

"What's going on?"

He turned to face Balqen. Never in his life was he so happy to see the old elf. "Balqen, you must stop her. She's trying to jump to the chandelier."

The vassal craned his head to get a better look. "Oh, yes, well, it was only a matter of time."

He didn't understand. Why was it only a matter of time?

"Her people live among the trees, remember?" the old elf said. "We might be content to swim in our little pond, but Rada is a bird. She must fly from time to time."

But she wasn't a bird. She had no wings, and gravity was not a friend to any elf that high up. Ettrian watched helplessly in the center of the gathering crowd. If he couldn't stop her, perhaps if he stood directly underneath it, he might catch her if she fell.

Rada leaned over the railing. She smiled and waved while the elves cheered. He shook his head, silently begging her to change her mind.

There was silence, then the soft padding of bare feet striking wood. Like a leaf in the wind, Rada launched from the hall, and in slow motion, he watched as she soared through the open space before clinging to the floating chandelier.

Everyone burst into cheers except Ettrian, who was more likely to vomit if he opened his mouth. She had wrapped the cover around her waist prior to jumping. Untying it, she flicked the fabric out before draping the top of the chandelier. The crowd cheered, and she gave them a dramatic bow.

When she finished, Rada peered down at him with a grin. She did it. Yes, it was amazing, but just how did she intend to get down? As if thinking the same thing, the ambassador gripped the golden bars and hung by her hands. "Are you ready?"

"Ready?"

She took his response as confirmation and let go.

The ambassador fell. That terrible moment was a lifetime and mere moments as she came crashing down. Ettrian gasped and outstretched his long arms, praying to every god in existence that he'd catch her. A weight hit him. The king clung tight and shifted his balance.

Rada was in his arms. He squeezed her tight as everyone around him cheered. Why would they encourage such reckless behavior? The urge to lash out at the elves was culled only because Rada was pressed tight against his chest.

"I can't believe they are cheering for that stunt," he said.

"They're not," she said. "They're cheering because you caught me."

It was true. They were commending him. One even dared to give him a pat on the back. Balqen emerged from the crowd. "My dear, that was incredible," he told Rada. "But you should know the king is afraid of heights."

"I'm not afraid of heights; I just think it should be up there, and we should be down here."

Rada was slipping from his grasp. Ettrian was reluctant to let her go, but the heights of the moment had passed. If he held her any longer, it would have sent the castle into a frenzy. There would be lectures about his royal vows.

"My king," she whispered. Ettrian's knees went weak as she sauntered away.

"We have some preparations to go through," Balqen said, redirecting the king's gaze.

He gave her one more lingering look as she joined Miabelle and Yinren before trailing after the old vassal.

CHAPTER EIGHTEEN

Chapter 18

"That was incredible!" Yinren said as the three of them went bounding up the stairs.

Radelia was still panting. She really needed to eat less and take a few more laps around the castle. She thought the stairs would've kept her active enough, but it would take a bit more effort on her part to maintain the fitness required for home. Whenever that would be.

A needling guilt scratched at her heart. What was she doing, exactly? Other than flirting with the enemy. She'd visited her friends only once, and since then, they remained locked up with no release in sight.

The vassals voted against the king because Larriel let it slip that one of the scouts was of some importance. The High Elves didn't know Kieran was the sole factor when it came to war and the militia's movements, but they knew letting him go was unwise.

"What's wrong?" Miabelle asked as they made their way to her door.

"I just feel guilty," she confessed. "My friends are prisoners while I'm enjoying all the castle has to offer."

"And then some," Yinren quipped.

Miabelle gave him a sour look for the briefest of moments. "You're doing everything you can."

"No," she said. "I'm not, and we all know it."

"If it bothers you so, perhaps send word to your people that the scouts are safe and that the king himself is researching the problems your people face."

"It's not just our problem. It's yours too."

Miabelle shied away from any topic that made her uncomfortable. "I'm going to get a bath ready."

Yinren remained silent for a few moments before saying, "So, how are things with the king?"

"There's nothing to tell. He and I research together and nothing more."

"You didn't see his face when you jumped. You have that male so wrapped up in your hair it's a wonder he gets anything done."

She didn't know how to respond to that. Her feelings for the king were so marred by guilt. Radelia had told him the truth as much as she possibly could, but what would happen when he learned who she really was? His vassals would likely throw her into the room with the scouts.

Shuddering at the thought of being locked in a room with Kieran and Katar constantly bickering, Radelia pivoted the conversation.

"Why does he have those vassals anyway? From what I hear, Ettrian the First didn't have advisers."

Even Yinren appeared uncomfortable with that level of gossip. "It was the condition that allowed him to be king."

"But he was next in line."

Yinren's head bobbed back and forth. "Yeah, well, he's really young by High Elf standards. Youth tends to be full of bad decisions."

High Elves had a knack for avoiding uncomfortable conversations. There was a lot of pain running through this community. She recalled the conversation with Balqen. He bore a monumental weight on his slumping shoulders. Something about making bad decisions because he was grieving. "How did your parents pass?"

It was personal and against the notes scrawled on the notepad that sat unheeded on the writing desk, but it was related somehow. She knew it was.

"They were killed," Yinren said softly. "By Runda Nor."

Radelia was crying. She didn't know when she had started. Her face was so hot that she didn't feel the tears until they dripped on her chest. "I'm so sorry."

Yinren sighed. "It was a long time ago, and we don't know what exactly happened. They were devout to our goddess and thought they could convert Runda Nor elves. Then, one day their bodies were carted home."

"How long ago?"

"Three, maybe four hundred years ago? So nobody you know was responsible. Miabelle and I both decided that we were never going to place blame. Ettrian the first told them not to go—even issued a divine order—but they wouldn't listen. Our grandfather was so angry for a long time, but he's past that now. Ever since he became a vassal to our king, he's changed for the better."

It amazed her that they could endure such loss and not harbor resentment toward her people. The pain of losing her own mother was felt whenever she read those conflicting books that downgraded the Runda Nor, making them sound less than they were.

"I don't know how you do it," she said.

"We've had a long time to think about it. It's either make peace with it or live angry forever."

She nodded, seeing the practicality in that. Immortality didn't diminish grief; the elf had to set it aside before it became all-consuming. Not all that different from her mortal existence. "I'm very sorry," Radelia said again. "I lost my mother. I know how it feels."

"To one of ours?"

"We think she fell and broke her leg. Rather than let her suffer, one of yours slit her throat. I didn't understand why they didn't heal her with magic, but I know now it's because you don't have any."

Yinren collapsed into the chair. His face was whiter than usual. "That is precisely why."

He promised to be faithful once they were married. So much for that.

Ettrian listened to the spirits gossip about the living. He supposed there wasn't much else for the dead to do. Normally, he tried his best to ignore the random musings, but he wondered...

"Does this have anything to do with the annulment request?"

He's trying to talk to us again...

Alone in his room, the king often tried to communicate with the spirits. They knew he could hear them, and clearly, they could hear him, but for whatever reason, they never responded. It was irritating. Like, someone speaking loudly at a party, and when you asked them to lower their voice, they just kept on like nothing you said mattered.

His door burst open. It was so sudden that the king jumped. "Leaf!" he gasped. "One of these days, you're going to walk in here while I'm getting dressed."

She stopped and sort of looked him over with a frown. "I didn't know you even changed."

"Of course I change my clothes. And I bathe."

"All your clothes look the same, I guess."

He looked down at the standard uniform he had worn since the death of his father. Black tunic, black leather pants, black boots. Etrian supposed she had a point. "Anyway, why are you here?"

She flopped a letter onto the table before him. "You have to see this. The others are coming as well."

The wax seal was a crudely shaped B in undyed beeswax already broken. He narrowed his eyes and opened the rough parchment.

To whom this may concern,

The Runda Nor have no ambassador. We do not recognize anyone by the name of Rada. Should such an elf attempt to return to us, she will be shot on sight.

The rightful ruler,
Emperor Bellas

By this point, the rest of his vassals had funneled into his room. He extended the parchment to Aracaryn, who then read it out loud.

"I knew something wasn't right," Leaf said with a flare of her nostrils. "She hadn't sent a single word to them in the weeks she's been here."

"An imposter?" Omaro asked. "What would anyone have to gain by such a façade?"

"One who took matters into her own hands," Ettrian said. "She revealed to me that she came here without permission. An attempt to free the scouts because the emperor wouldn't."

"But it says they don't know her at all," Aracaryn said. "Yet if she were to return...which implies they do know her?"

It was a cryptic message, and its intent was not aimed at them. "Bring her here."

Escorted by two guards, the ambassador was led through his open door. To her credit, Rada was unshaken by the way she was summoned. Her face was hard and posture rigid as though she were expecting a blow to the back of her knees.

"What do you make of this?" he asked, handing the letter to Leaf, who took far too much satisfaction in giving her the letter.

He gauged her reaction as she read the letter. She was never good at hiding her feelings. Every wince and catch of breath told him that Rada was an elf rejected by the ones she loved most.

Still clutching the paper, she dropped her gaze to the floor.

"You were never supposed to come here," Leaf accused. "Their emperor doesn't even know you."

"He does," she said with a wet voice before smothering the sob in her throat.

Ettrian leaned back in his chair. He would have liked to say he felt sorry for her, but the truth of it was that he didn't. She had kept things from him. Lied to him. And he wanted to punish her for it.

"He claims to not know your name," Aracaryn said. "What does that mean?"

"This is pointless," Balqen said. "Who she is doesn't matter. What we do know is that she's useless in brokering peace with the Runda Nor."

That was a sharp stone to throw. The ambassador winced at the word useless. What manner of king watches elves hurl insults only to wish they'd throw bigger ones. It served nothing but his cruel satisfaction as she wilted before them.

But then, his mood changed like the passing of a storm. He didn't want her to suffer. All he wanted was her trust, and he wanted it still. If he let them continue, she would be lost to him forever.

"Enough," he said, with a gesture of his hand. "Rada, sit down."

She did as he commanded but refused to meet his eyes. There was guilt. He craned his head to the left until her eyes were forced to meet his. "They don't know your name yet say you cannot return. Who are you?"

"My name is Radelia Bellas," she said with a pride and clarity that set the vassals on their heels.

Balqen laughed in surprise. "Another Bellas..."

Omaro was less impressed but remained silent. Leaf looked the princess up and down before saying, "You? A princess?"

He couldn't say that he was shocked by it. As far as reasons went for not revealing one's true self, that was a worthy excuse. She didn't want them to know she was a princess who had come without her father's permission.

"From our time researching together," he said for the benefit of the vassals. "I've learned that royalty in the Runda Nor isn't the same as it is here."

She nodded.

"While she is the heir to the line of Bellas, Radelia is a figurehead for the most part. She doesn't own the forest; she merely lives in it. She nor her father hold the militia, but they can ask for its strength. Stop me if I'm wrong, but you lied because you did not wish to give us false hope."

Radelia nodded, rubbing the sleeves of her gown. "I thought if I could bring the scouts home, my father would see that there were alternatives to war."

"But instead, you're banished," Omaro said, "and we are where we started."

Has no one noticed the flowers the lady wears?

Ettrian had to stop himself from asking out loud. What flowers did the spirits refer to and which lady? Then again, he supposed there was only ever one lady. Pushing back his curtains, the king opened the doors to the balcony and edged along the wall. He ignored the thumping of his heart and the difficulty of breathing.

"In the Isles—"

"Oh, come off it, Aracaryn," Leaf growled. "This isn't the Isles!"

"I realize you're too young to understand empathy or experience, but it is relevant."

Ettrian squinted in the daylight as he inched closer to the patio overlooking the gardens. In the center of it all, Isilynor's pool dribbled with all the enthusiasm of an old man taking a piss. He laughed at the analogy. Clearly, he spent too much time with the princess, and it was influencing him.

At first, the king didn't see any flowers near Isilynor's statue. Perhaps the spirits were referring to something else entirely. But there was just a hint of green.

"We have a princess, banished or not, that is grounds for war," Omaro warned.

His heart stopped, and for a moment, the king forgot all about his fear of heights. Pale little buds were camouflaged against the white pine of the statue. Flowers were sprouting from the core of Cardhon Nimloth and forging a crown around Isilynor's head.

"You think they're using this as a way to sway the Isles?" Balqen asked.

A half cry, half laugh escaped his throat. Something they had been doing was working. The core of the tree was blooming once more. He didn't dare call it hope, but it was the right direction. It must have been.

"My king," Omaro said. "What are we to do?"

"With what?"

"The imposter? Our little princess and declaration of war?"

"They can't gruff about Radelia being here if they banished her," Balqen said.

Ettrian turned to regard his vassals with new eyes. Their squabbles, what were once his own, felt so small and petty in comparison to what the spirits had shown him. Radelia was the key to the castle's survival, and he wouldn't allow her to leave.

"She stays," he said.

Omaro's eyes went wide. "You can't be serious."

"He's got a thing for her," Leaf said. "Didn't you know?"

"I am king, and you will watch your tone," Ettrian said with a resounding sharpness that made all the vassals flinch.

He approached them then. They shrank in his shadow as if fearing he'd do to them what he did to his parents. Very well, then. If they wouldn't grow to love him, he would use terror as a means of herding the elves into safety like cattle from a storm.

"Sending her back means sending her to interrogation and death. Is this what you want? Her knowledge of the castle, our numbers, all in the hands of those who wish to attack us?"

"As I was trying to say earlier," Aracaryn shot a glance at Leaf. "I know what it is to be discarded by my own people, but this puts us in an awkward position. We're just fortunate that they didn't accuse us of stealing their princess."

He decided that he wouldn't speak of the flowers. They would see for themselves soon enough.

"Radelia," Ettrian asked, softening his voice. "What do you want?"

Through trembling lips and a tear-streaked face, she looked up at him and said, "I just want to help my people."

"And you are," he promised. "More than you know."

She nodded, wiping her eyes. The vassals were eyeing him with various levels of skepticism, but they would know the truth of his words.

"Tonight, we celebrate the Runda Nor princess."

"But we're still preparing for the starless night," Balqen said.

"It's customary to have a revel before the holiday. Why not?"

He had never met a High Elf that could say no to tradition or a party. Word would spread that Rada the ambassador had lied and was actually a princess. Rather than let the gossip trickle out, he would control the narrative.

"The princess disguised herself as a commoner to learn of our people, found us worthy, and revealed her noble birth," he explained.

Leaf, who no doubt wrote the letter to the emperor, stormed out of the room. He had no pity for her. She had taken it upon herself to send the letter without his leave. He suspected her motives were driven by jealousy more than anything.

"I will agree on the condition that the princess remains under careful watch," Omaro said. "We can't have her fleeing Cardhon Nimloth or delivering any correspondence."

"I don't think that's necessary," Ettrian said.

"She lied to us once," Balqen said. "A little precaution wouldn't hurt."

Aracaryn shifted her weight to her good leg. "Besides, we don't know how the elves will react. You recall how quick they were to blame her for the tapestry."

By leaving, Leaf forfeited her vote on the matter, but even if she was there, he would still be outvoted. "Fine," the king said. "Post guards outside her doors when her attendants are not with her."

He hoped that was enough to satisfy them. More than anything, he wanted to speak with Radelia alone. To show her the flowers and see her face light up. Only that wasn't what occurred.

"If there's nothing else," she said flatly, "I will return to my room."

Ettrian watched her walk away. He wanted her to come back, to talk with him, or even yell at him. But the nature of their relationship was clear. She had slipped from his grasp many times, and now he finally understood why.

Radelia didn't want him. She indulged him to further her mission, nothing more.

CHAPTER NINETEEN

Chapter 19

Radelia was a prisoner.

On some level, she had been from the day she stepped foot through the doors. It wasn't like she could leave before. If she had tried, the High Elves would have stopped her one way or another. Plopping on the sofa, she tried to keep from thinking about the guards outside her door but in the deafening silence, she heard their armor as they shifted and moved about.

For her own safety. Utter bullshit.

Half of them thought she was a spy, and the other half thought her own people would kill her. The worst part was that she didn't know if either were true. If her father took her back on the condition that she tell them everything, she might have. Would they kill her outright? Radelia didn't like to think so, but they might.

The Runda Nor didn't hold much sacred, but defying a Divine Order was up there with pissing on Elpharae's idol. Which only happened once. And that was only because a pipe broke, and there wasn't anyone to blame directly.

Of all the things running through her mind at that moment, the king's face shouldn't have mattered, but she couldn't stop seeing it.

She huffed with frustration. Hating herself for feeling guilty about keeping up the charade. It was like she was lying to her friends.

Only, they weren't her friends after all. When those vassals argued about what to do with her, he appeared happy. Like he was relieved to know she had been lying all along. He was pleased as a child with a honeycomb while her neck was on the chopping block.

He didn't vote for the guards, so that was something. But he got all pouty looking at the end, like he was sad she didn't want to stick around.

She wanted to run into the forest and forget both clans ever existed. Set up her own little hut somewhere deep in the woods where no one could find her and stuff her into a dress or be caught between other people's squabbles.

There was a soft knock at the door before Miabelle stepped in. The attendant said nothing and averted Radelia's gaze with fierce determination. Guess Miabelle thought her a traitor too.

"Your grandfather told you?"

The attendant went to the wardrobe and pulled out a light green bodice embroidered with gold. "I am to dress you for the revelry."

"So, we're not going to talk about it?"

Miabelle stopped and lowered her head. "Maybe everything isn't about you."

That struck hard. Like a wounded animal, she struck with her claws and teeth bared. "I'm trying to bring magic back to our people, stop a war, and keep myself from getting killed. So, sorry if I'm not focused on your failed marriage."

Dropping the gown, Miabelle made for the door. She lifted her head with as much defiance as any pampered elf could, "Your life might have been harder, but that doesn't make it any more meaningful than mine."

As the weight of her words sunk in, Radelia closed her eyes to block out the light. Claws retracted and tail firmly tucked. If there was a dark, smelly place to hide, it would have been too good for the likes of her. Miabelle was right. She did think she was better than the High Elves. Despite everything she had learned thus far, Radelia really did think her ever-shifting moral ground was higher than theirs.

In the time she had been there, Radelia had been met with kindness and respect. She had learned about grief, beauty, and sacrifice. Her own father disowned her for something that Ettrian would have simply laughed at. She grew up believing her people were the truly free elves, but Radelia was no longer certain of that.

There were two facts that remained. First, she was a shit ambassador. If her father hadn't sent that letter, it would have been found out eventually. Second, her friends were still locked away. If she couldn't free them the diplomatic way, she'd go about it the other way.

The revelry to kick off the other revelry was to be held that night. Based on what Radelia knew of parties and High Elves, they'd all incapacitate themselves with wine, allowing her the run of the castle. There was only the matter of the door.

Radelia paced her room, trying to recall just how it was locked. There were no locks in the castle from what she could tell. Why openly steal when you can just dupe a noble? She winced. Miabelle's words echoed as if reminding her of what an ass she was.

Fine. So, no locks, but there was no door either.

Rubbing her chin, Radelia surmised that someone had taken the doorknob off as a makeshift lock, but it had to be around. Otherwise, how did the High Elves send meals into the room? Her best guess was the kitchens. All she would have to do is get the doorknob and put it back in the door. Kieran and Katar would be free, and for all the High Elves knew, the kitchen attendants simply forgot to take the doorknob.

Grinning, Radelia went to the wardrobe and sifted through the ever-accumulating gowns. Miabelle had set one out, but it was green. Not that green was a bad color, but she wanted something a bit stealthier than the piles of fabric abandoned on the floor.

She picked it up, her excitement deflating in her chest. If her father had any idea she was contemplating an apology to a High Elf, he'd wish she was never born. It wasn't integral to freeing Kieran and Katar. It was something she needed to do for her own sake.

Radelia dressed and went downstairs for some supper before the party.

Picking up a plate, she helped herself to the spread of breads and cheeses. She got some butter, of course; that stuff was magic. There were some fruits and some kind of vegetable salad with a citrus scent, so she picked up some of that as well.

She sat alone, but it wasn't long until other elves joined her table. A trio of Dark Elves with long, silky silver hair approached. "May we join you?"

"Sure."

"It must be so exciting," the elf on the left said. Her eyes were just as blue as the High Elves underneath her thin silver brow.

At first, Radelia wasn't certain they were speaking to her at all, but the one on the right followed up with, "You finally get to reveal who you truly are."

"Oh, I love old-fashioned High Elf theatrics," the middle said. Unlike the other two, her eyes were as red as the blood sap that tear-dropped from the castle. "They're so quaint."

Ettrian said he would announce her formally at the revel. Explain that the deception was necessary or some bullshit. But these three already knew. Radelia sort of felt like a mouse being cornered by three purring cats.

She wasn't certain how to act or just what to say, but whenever people spoke that way to the king, he had a particularly effective way of dealing with it.

Radelia laughed. It rang false between her ears, and her face strained, but the Dark Elves at her table were no longer smiling. Whatever she was doing, it was working. "It's just a bit of fun," she said in her best Ettrian impersonation.

"The poor emperor," the elf on the left said with a sigh. "No wonder he's so sad and angry. All the humor in Runda Nor left with you, Princess."

"I could have told you that," Radelia said with as much bravado as a dead branch. Strong and secure on the outside but rotting inside. "If you think the emperor is cranky, the general is even worse."

"But no one has seen the general in quite some time," the elf on the left said. "I wonder where he could be—"

"Elves of the court," a booming voice sounded from the throne. The trio departed her table with a curtsey before moving to the front. Radelia could have wept with joy. She was in a sticky situation with those Dark Elves. Come to think of it, she didn't recall seeing them before.

"Before the starless night, I wish to share a truth," Ettrian said. He was still wearing all black, and there was no crown on his head. "Our ambassador is none other than Princess Radelia Bellas."

Gasps and cheers went around the room. Some were giggling and others applauding. They weren't upset by the deception. The High Elves were pleased? She didn't understand how being lied to was an exciting thing, but they were happy, so Radelia stood up and bowed, and the crowd cheered even louder.

Ettrian motioned for her to approach the throne. Radelia sighed but played along. She parted the crowd and joined the king at his throne. "There will be an honorary throne placed beside mine," he announced with a sweeping gesture of his massive arm. "And tonight, we celebrate not only the efforts made for such a special celebration but for our princess as well."

Ettrian dismissed the elves with a nod at Balqen. The old elf stepped forward and said, "To the festivities!"

The High Elves funneled out of the great hall as though they had somewhere important to be. "It really doesn't get old for them," Radelia said, more to herself than to the king.

"Oh, it does," he mused. "But now they get to tell each other how they knew you were a princess all along."

She regarded him then. He seemed tired, his long face more drawn than usual, but the mischievousness in his eyes lingered still. "How fares the king?"

Ettrian feigned surprise. "You're concerned for me?"

Radelia scoffed and rolled her eyes. "We don't have to talk if you don't want to."

"Oh, but I do."

Ettrian paid no mind to the stares or gossip as he walked Radelia to his tent. There, he poured wine for two. The way her nose crinkled over the lip of the cup was adorable. She sipped anyway but not before making a face.

"No to your liking?"

"The humans sometimes throw a barrel of ale into a deal," she said. "This is sweeter and nowhere near as potent."

An honorable male would have suggested otherwise. Elvish wine was twice as strong as the wine made in the village of man but tasted far better. After a second sip, Radelia had lost all sense of caution and tipped the goblet back.

Oh no. He moved to take the cup from her, but Radelia was quicker. She had managed to drink a full cup within a few minutes. He took the pitcher away before any more damage could be done. "How about some water?"

"Are you happy now?" she asked. "Now that you know the truth?"

She looked so small in the fullness of the dress threatening to consume her. Perhaps he could ask someone to make gowns that fit. Radelia couldn't safely go back to the Runda Nor anytime soon. "Happy?" he asked. "I'm not certain that a king in my position is allowed such things."

"You were smiling," she said with an accusing finger. "When your vassals read the letter, talking about killing me. And not the creepy smile. It was the good kind."

Radelia's words were so badly slurred that he suspected she'd have no memory of anything said come morning. "Look at the statue."

She had to crawl, but peeking out from the corner of the tent, Radelia saw what he saw. Her eyes went wide, and she gasped. "Flowers."

"Not just any flowers," Ettrian explained. "Long ago, the white flowers of Cardhon Nimloth were said to have miraculous healing properties. It's a sign. The castle is coming back to life."

She looked at him with glassy eyes and scarlet cheeks. On all fours, Radelia had no idea how she appeared to him then. Ettrian had to tear his gaze from her. Thrusting a glass of water at her, he said, "Drink."

"What do you think is making them bloom?"

Ettrian had no way of knowing for certain. "At night, when I'm alone in my room, I delude myself into thinking it's because of us."

"Us?"

He drank the wine to ease the pain of what he was about to say. "I know little of love and—"

She was on him then. Not hugging and clinging like a silly drunk. Rather like a predator, straddling him at the hips with her hands pinning his chest. The slight weight of her body sitting on his groin was somehow more debilitating than if someone were to drop a boulder on him.

"I can remedy that." Her voice was low and seductive, but the lingering slur of her words told him everything he needed to know. "Just let my friends go."

His heart sank. It was nothing more than a drunken barter. The heat that scorched him inside and out had died, leaving him empty. Ettrian took in a deep breath and regarded the elf pressing against him with the intensity of the magnet on a compass. It occurred to him that he held some power in that exchange.

While he wasn't an expert on females, it didn't take one to know that Radelia was sexually attracted to him. It seemed to him that there was a disconnect between love and sex for her. One could ultimately lead to another; he simply lacked the context.

"You know I can't," he said softly, tugging at her hair with his fingers.

Lowering herself, Radelia's face was so close to his own that he could taste the wine that still coated her lips. "You're their king. They will forgive you. Besides, Kieran will be of more use to you if he returns to the clan."

He had to bite his lip to keep from grinning. Radelia was giving away more than she realized. Smoothing his hands up her thighs, she squeezed his hips and bucked slightly. One perk about his chastity was that he didn't know what he was missing out on. Though, Ettrian had a fairly solid idea.

Working his way to her hips, his thumbs pressed lightly into the shallow pockets along the pelvic bone, and she let out a cry loud enough that nearby elves were beginning to take notice. "We should go somewhere more private to discuss this."

She nodded and wasted no time in making her way to his room. Grabbing her, he pulled her close and nuzzled her neck before whispering, "Not my room, yours."

He guided her through the western walls. There was no point in hiding, but he hoped that in the darkness with only his hand as a guide, Radelia might be more inclined to speak on Kieran's usefulness. "Perhaps I should send him away," the king whispered, pulling her in close as he guided her over a wide crack in the floor. "You have far too much respect for him."

"He was right," she muttered. "I hate it when he's right."

"I'll be certain not to tell him then."

She stumbled, bouncing into him. At the rate she was going, he'd have to carry her to bed. "Good."

So Kieran was the reason the Runda Nor hadn't marched on Cardhon Nimloth. It painted a different picture of the male that was currently locked away in the tower. Why would someone of such importance risk getting close to the enemy?

They stopped in the doorway of the great hall. Pressing against her, Radelia made it clear she was ready for anything. Her hands snaked their way to the ties of his pants, but he pinned them above her head before crushing his mouth against hers.

Slowly pulling his lips away, she chased his mouth hungrily, nipping at his lips. "What else do you hate about him?"

Playing the jealous lover was an easy task. There was clearly something between them. Rather than deny it, he fostered the resentment for his own gain.

"He's cold and calculated. He cares more about his precious militia than what I need." Kieran was the leader of the militia. A group of warriors not associated with the emperor. In his absence, the group could be persuaded to go to war.

"I don't know if I should reward him or execute him for leaving you in my hands in such a desperate state."

"You'd have nearly fifteen hundred angry Runda Nor warriors on your hands," she teased, nipping at his nose.

That was a notion so harrowing, he nearly dropped the charade. Their militia alone outnumbered the entire High Elf population. If they did attack in such numbers, it would be like a swarm of wasps consuming a wayward critter. Even the high walls could only defend from so much when there was no one to guard them, and most High Elves were next to useless when it came to battle.

"No more games," he said, pulling her along. She hesitated at how sharp his voice was, but as they headed up the stairs, she giggled and looked around to make sure no one was watching. They were, of course; she just didn't see them.

High Elves volunteered to be attendants for a single reason. It allowed them the excuse to lurk in places where they could eavesdrop and spy on one another. In their inebriated state, most were unaware of the shoes poking out of the bottom of a tapestry like the pair they'd just passed.

It wasn't just the High Elves who were curious. The spirits were as well.

This is getting good...

Ettrian grinned.

They were just outside her door when Radelia could take it no longer. Colliding into him, she quite literally climbed him, wrapping her legs around his hips. Ettrian allowed his lust to emerge, and he worked the errant fabric of her gown away until he could feel the heat between her legs. She was moaning and biting his neck. For a moment, he thought he might not be able to do what had to be done, but groping for the doorknob, he stepped back into the room.

Radelia was tearing at his tunic, trying to pull it off. He staggered to the bed. Closing his eyes, the king begged his goddess for strength before pushing Radelia off. She landed on the bed with a bounce. Undeterred, she was yanking at the laces behind her back, her hands only slowing as he started out of the room.

"What are you doing?"

"It's a good thing you're not an ambassador," he said, marching out before second thoughts could take hold. "You'd trade your entire clan for one night of passion."

Slamming the door shut behind him, Ettrian winced at the frustrated scream from within the room. There was a collective groan of disappointment from the spirits, and the attendant who was spying behind the tapestry stomped away.

Disappointment was the cornerstone of his reign, it seemed.

CHAPTER TWENTY

Chapter 20

"**S**hould we plan a wedding?"

Aracaryn's shadow was looming over his tent. He drank a cup of wine to celebrate his newfound information. As he lay there alone, watching the other High Elves tumble one another on the lawn, Ettrian drank another to drown out their sounds of pleasure. By the third cup, he found he could do nothing but stew in his regret.

"I don't know," he said, honestly flummoxed. "She lusts for me, but I want more."

Seating herself on a chair, she said, "Do you recall the urn?"

He flushed. "I still cringe at every teapot."

When Aracaryn's father came for a visit, he offered Ettrian an urn without explanation. He was still just a young prince then and didn't know what to make of it. It was only after drinking what was probably the worst tea of his life that he found out.

"Drinking the ashes of my mother wasn't one of your finer moments," she said.

"Give me a few more centuries and I'm sure I can top it."

Aracaryn shook her head. "That's not my point. You were given a marriage proposal so different from your own customs that you did not understand what it was."

He eyed his vassal, hoping he finally understood something that came from her mouth.

"Our customs are so different she doesn't understand my feelings."

"Even if she does share them, I imagine Radelia is going through a lot at the moment."

Ettrian understood that much. She needed friendship and security, not a lovesick male pining for her. "Perhaps I'll have a chat with our guests in the tower."

Aracaryn's arched brows raised. "You think that wise?"

"They don't know she was banished for their sake," he explained. "Perhaps if I tell them, they will tell me of her."

He traveled to the northeast wing amid the throngs of elves doing all the things he vowed to not partake in until marriage. Biting his cheek as he kept his eyes fixed on the great hall. Others were drinking and singing songs. In the great hall, there was an obligatory hush. A male had brought out his lute and played while everyone remained polite and listened. Some aspects of revelries never changed.

He approached the guards and held out his hand. One provided him the doorknob without so much as a blink. They were still armed, and there was a good chance the Runda Nor would attack him, but perhaps they could be reasoned with.

Taking in a deep breath, the king turned the doorknob and walked into the room.

The shadow was watching through the slit that served as her only view of the outside world. To her right was the male, presumably doing push-ups before pausing to stare at the king. The last female was curled up on the bed. It had been nearly a month since any of them had bathed or changed their clothing. The word ripe came to mind.

"Accommodations being what they are, I hope you are well otherwise."

Two out of the three stood. He frowned when the third did not get up. "Is she well?"

"She's homesick," the shadow said.

"We were never properly introduced. I am King Ettrian."

"You're the king," the male said, his wide green eyes unblinking. There was a distinct demarcation along his hair. Two different colors, as though his hair had been stained and grown out. Some sort of Runda Nor beauty ritual, perhaps.

"I am," he said. "And we mean you no harm."

"Then let us go," the shadow said. Her brown hair was cropped short at the chin. She was small like Radelia.

"I'm afraid I can't," he explained. "Your emperor has all but declared war and is now allying with other clans. You should know that he banished Radelia."

"No," the shadow whispered, clamping a hand over her mouth. The male remained silent.

"I was hoping to gain some insight on the matter. Would he truly banish his own daughter?"

"If he thinks she's in league with you, yes," the male said.

Ettrian bowed his head. The Runda Nor hated them so much that they would disown their loved ones. He shook his head. Unable to empathize with such revulsion toward his fellow elves. "Then it's not safe to send her back."

"You care about her?" the shadow said.

He looked up. Just as he hoped, she would see into him. "Yes, but I don't know if she feels the same."

The male scoffed. "Keeping her closest friends prisoner isn't a romantic gesture."

"I realize that," he said. "My vassals do not think it safe for you to leave either."

Something in the male shifted. He was defeated all of a sudden. "Radelia loves her father. It blinds her to his shortcomings. The emperor is paranoid. He sees High Elves lurking in every corner and is convinced you plot against him."

"It's not entirely unfounded. My father did plot against the Runda Nor, but I hold no such animosity."

"Why should we trust you?" the shadow asked.

He grinned. "I don't expect you to. Radelia held the same beliefs for a few days. If you didn't try to kill the attendants at every turn, I suspect you'd see the same."

Or perhaps if she had a larger window to look out. It really was unfortunate that they trapped themselves in the tower. If they felt shame, the scouts did not show it. They remained defiant and willful with no inclination to give a second pause.

"If you'd permit it," the king said, gesturing to the female on the bed. "I might be able to see to that one's release. I can also provide more suitable living arrangements."

"Can we see Radelia?" the shadow asked.

"Turn over your weapons, and I'll see to it."

The shadow and the male exchanged a glance before the male, clearly the higher ranked between them, said, "Agreed."

Easing the tensions with the guests and sending one home would send a message to the emperor that things in Cardhon Nimloth had changed. It was likely that the emperor still assumed his father ruled and still intended to cull their whole clan. Ettrian was intentional with his information, but that didn't guarantee the scouts interpretation would be an accurate one.

"Let's get started," he said, grabbing a laundry basket. "They will check you a second time before departing this room."

The male dropped his sheathed sword and a bow into the basket while the shadow began withdrawing dagger after dagger from various pockets in her garments. When she lifted her long tunic, exposing the length of her thigh, Ettrian averted his gaze.

One by one, they clinked and clanked into the basket. He counted seventeen, but they kept coming. At some point, he gave the male an incredulous stare. The male shrugged and kept his eyes wisely on the basket.

"If that's all," Ettrian truly hoped that it was. "I'll notify my vassals and see to better accommodations. I imagine you'll both want baths."

"That would be a treat," the shadow said.

"And whenever the princess awakes, I'll notify her of the new rooms and permissions."

He was just about to leave with his basket full of daggers when the shadow said, "We share private meals with our mates."

He stopped in the doorway. So that was the way of it. High Elves ate their meals in the great hall as far away from their spouses as they could. Living for as long as they did, most craved new conversations except for Balqen, whose wife never knew what meal would be their last together. The last time Ettrian tried to eat in the great hall, no one joined his table. Nor the tables near him. A silence as irritating as a rash left him with no appetite. That was the last time he tried to eat among the others.

It was something so simple. So obvious. All the time they had spent together was working in the library or at the mercy of his vassals. To

High Elves, simply spending time in approximation with one another was courtship, but for the Runda Nor, that wasn't the case.

"What are your names?" he asked. Though he already knew, he wanted them to give an introduction themselves. Would Kieran boast of his power? Ettrian didn't suspect he would.

"I'm Kieran," the male said. "That is Katar."

"Thank you. I'll give that a try."

He could feel the stares pelting against his back as he left. They didn't trust him. Not for a moment, but they also didn't lie. There was integrity, but to what extent? There was only so much he could do. It seemed Radelia would be an ambassador after all.

Aracaryn had not moved from where he left her, though she did arrange herself more comfortably on the pillows, careful to conceal her deformed foot.

"You're unharmed. Was there a breakthrough?"

He glanced at the space where Radelia once lay. The softness of her skin still lingered on his. All the scouts had rough skin. From the tips of their noses to the span of their cheeks and foreheads. All but Radelia, whose skin remained unaffected by the rigors of living in the wilds.

"They are her friends," he said. "She came here against her father's wishes because they are dear to her."

"But is she dear to them?"

"Oh, yes," he said, sitting on an empty wine barrel. "They are much more cooperative knowing she's here. What's more, the male is the sole leader of a militia that could swallow Cardhon Nimloth whole. Thankfully, he is entirely against the idea of attacking."

Aracaryn remained with the unspoken implication. As long as Radelia remained with them, the scouts wouldn't misbehave. He made his intentions clear, but there was no trust between them. Ettrian had their dearest friend and princess in his grasp. In their minds, she was the true hostage. Any misstep they took could endanger her.

"What bargain did you make?"

"One of them is a sickly thing. I want her sent home before we have a dead Runda Nor on our hands. The others are to be moved to a better room. One with a nice, large window that overlooks the gardens."

She smiled. "You would have fared well in the courts of the Ruby Isles."

Ettrian didn't feel it was a compliment, but Aracaryn's admiration was clear. "How so?"

"As noble as they are, you mask your intentions with the guise of manipulation."

Was that the way of it with her? He found it hard to believe Aracaryn did anything out of altruism. "The truth is that my intentions are not noble. It's self-interest."

In the absence of any true affection, Ettrian grappled with possessive urges. He wanted to ensnare her. Pull every advantage like spider's thread until she was so wrapped in his machinations that she had no other choice but to remain by his side. That was not love, but it was no easy thing being wrought by desire.

He was his father's son, after all.

The thought ached like poison in his marrow. A choice was set at his feet. Ettrian could tell her the truth of how he came to his throne as well as the death of her mother, or he could say nothing. He could explain that it was for the sake of her people and trust her to understand, or he could let her find out after leading her down the aisle.

Both were acts of mercy, but would she understand? In the cold light of morning, forgiveness could lose its luster as his acts of mercy piled before her.

"I don't want her to know about my father," he said. "Not about what he intended to do, nor what I did."

"My king," Aracaryn hesitated. "It's a small community. Better she hear—"

He jerked his head in her direction, his glare so fierce that the vassal went silent. "Anyone who tells her will answer to me."

Not wanting to stir his ire further, she nodded. "I'll have the scouts moved to one of the west gate rooms and see to it that there are bars on the window."

He didn't answer. Ettrian stared up at the fountain. Isilynor's crown remained healthy in the bedding of decay. If the flowers of Cardhon Nimloth could thrive in the rot, so could Radelia.

A roaring, pounding noise woke Radelia. Opening her eyes, the blare of daylight stung like hundreds of quills burrowing through her eyeballs. She squinted, searching for the horrid noise that threatened to shatter the thin bones of her temple, but there was no drum banging beside her. It was the sound of her own blood pumping through her skull.

She sat up with a groan. Why would anyone subject themselves to such torture? Her stomach felt as though it were inside out, and everything ached.

"Morning!"

Savory smells wafted from the bowl of broth set before her. It was plain broth, but there were little specks of something green floating in it. Some kind of herb. Radelia's mouth and throat were so parched that she ignored the spoon and drank from the bowl. As she drank, Radelia swore she could feel her body absorbing each drop. There was a minty taste to it that also washed away the mossy coating on her teeth.

It was only after she consumed the broth that she had a look around. When did she go to bed? Rubbing her head, the last thing Radelia could recall was Ettrian urging her to drink water.

She regarded her savior with utmost appreciation. "Thank you, Miabelle."

Her attendant's quirky smile suggested she understood all too well. Radelia's aches and pains abated slightly. Enough that she no longer felt utterly debilitated.

"Is it a potion? Some kind of magic?"

"It's just broth with a small amount of white wine and mint."

Whatever it was, Radelia was emerging from the wine sickness. The previous night's events came in sparse pieces without context. He said something that pissed her off, and she got the feeling she said too much. She cringed, and Miabelle extended a bucket.

"No, I'm not going to throw up."

Miabelle's bare shoulders bumped. "Just in case. I saw you with the king..."

She didn't remember that part. There was some recollection of an explanation. Radelia had accused him of being happy when her true identity was revealed, and it wasn't what she expected. What was it? The dull throb behind her eyes returned when she tried to remember.

"Does that mean I'm his betrothed or something?"

"If he were any other High Elf, no. But he is the king."

"Right, he's celibate until marriage or some shit."

"Ah, no...not exactly. He can't be intimate with a woman in a way that produces a child. Not that anyone here would venture to try."

Again, Miabelle spoke with a cryptic worry. Sure, he was weird. He laughed at the wrong times and sometimes talked to himself. Sometimes Ettrian's eyes searched the room like he was expecting someone, but he wasn't bad. Moody, but not mean-spirited.

"What is it with you High Elves? You treat your own king like a leper."

Miabelle bowed her head. "We're not allowed to speak of it."

Why? Why weren't they allowed to talk about it? She imagined her father was on the receiving end of all sorts of ire after sending the babes away. Radelia frowned and scratched at her arm. He never did anything that merited criticism until recently.

Did her clan know he banished her? Maybe he was right to do so.

"If the princess is done regretting the previous night, perhaps she would like another bowl of broth?"

The princess did want that, among many other things. "Miabelle, I owe you an apology for the other day."

The attendant said nothing, but she was clearly waiting for more.

"You were right. I told myself that my clan deserved better because of our hardships, but it's clear the High Elves have suffered in your own ways. Since coming here, I've learned a great deal about enduring sorrow. Being immortal means that you're stuck with the consequences of your choices forever."

Miabelle extended her hand to Radelia. "You're forgiven."

She hesitated. Was it really so simple? It was a humbling apology, but surely there were lingering resentments. If someone insulted the entirety of her clan, they'd need to do a lot more than that. "I'll do your chores or—"

"Get up, silly." Miabelle took her hand and pulled her up. "If High Elves clung to every wrong, we'd be unable to stand the sight of one another a century from now."

Radelia walked beside Miabelle to the great hall, where elves swarmed the buffet table. The High Elves forgave easily because they had to. There was a startling lightness to that realization. Whereas the Runda Nor still held grudges over an event that none were witness to.

Being immortal meant rearranging one's priorities. Otherwise, they'd burn with resentment for all eternity.

Radelia slurped down another bowl while Miabelle politely sipped from her spoon. The way the attendant's eyes kept shifting to the entryway every few minutes roused her suspicion.

"Are you waiting for something?"

"Hm?" Miabelle's tone was high and false.

"Out with it."

"I don't have the faintest idea as to what you're talking about."

Bullshit.

Radelia stared with an intensity that had Miabelle squirming. Just when she was certain her attendant would crack, she nodded to the stairway. A trio was descending. Radelia stood without realizing it. Behind two guards was one of Kieran's scouts. She didn't know her name, but there was no mistaking it.

The scout was dressed in the same leathers, but her tunic was clean, as was the brown hair tied at the nape of her neck. Her eyes shifted around the room like a caged animal, but her hands were free.

She wasn't certain when she moved, but Radelia was at the base of the stairs and face to face with the scout. "You're going home?"

"I am," the scout said, her large eyes watering. It had been nearly a month since Radelia had seen another Runda Nor. In the sea of small-pointed ears and small eyes, her own people appeared so strange.

"Send my love to them." Her throat dried as she spoke. They may not want to hear anything from a traitor.

She accompanied the scout out of the door, where an old human waited on a full cart. There was a canvas over the top, and it took every ounce of willpower to not ask about the contents. The merchant might have been making another stop, but he'd never come to the Runda Nor with so many goods before. Radelia suspected they were baskets her people wove and attempted to sell being returned to them. They were struggling, and winter was hurtling toward them.

Come winter, elf magic meant little to the empty bellies. They would be hungry, and there would be nothing she could do. There she was, fat and happy, drinking wine and wearing fine gowns while her people bartered woven baskets for stale bread.

Too ashamed to look the scout in the eyes, she heard the merchant tell a guard that another special delivery would be coming along shortly before the whip was cracked and the wheels churned in the dirt.

She didn't ask about the special delivery or why the vassals agreed to send the scout home. Ettrian had somehow convinced them. It was a gesture of goodwill that would be ignored, but at least one more Runda Nor was home. She should have been overjoyed, but guilt and an unshakable wine sickness squashed her merriment.

Not wanting to face Miabelle or anyone else, Radelia moped up the stairs and back to her room. She wanted a bath but didn't want to ask for help. So, she stripped down and washed herself Runda Nor style in the tub with the water from a pitcher.

She was just about to climb under the covers when Miabelle came in. "I thought you'd be happy to see she's going home."

Radelia pulled the blanket over her face. "What am I even doing here? My people need me, and I'm here. Doing nothing."

"That's not true." The bed sunk in one spot as Miabelle sat beside her. "My grandfather says that the king is more hopeful that the castle can be saved."

A little pang ached in her heart then, but Radelia shook it off. "All we've learned is that history has two versions of events. We've found nothing to explain why the castle is dying or why the gods can't speak to us. Nothing."

"I admit, I'm no scholar, but it seems to me that these things are linked. Magic began to wane when our people parted ways. The last king feared that your people were multiplying too fast and draining the magic but—" Miabelle stopped cold.

Flipping the cover down, Radelia looked at her attendant. She was pale. As though she had seen her own death.

"But what?"

Miabelle shook her head. "But Ettrian doesn't believe that," she said with far more evenness than Radelia liked. She was hiding something, but what?

"In any case, it seems both gods have forsaken us."

Miabelle frowned as she stared out the window. "It's not like that."

"What is it like then?"

"I don't know, but my grandparents are from different clans, yet they need each other. Maybe the gods are lost without one another."

Something occurred to Radelia then. She sat up and stared at the attendant. Miabelle and Yinren were unique in that they were the only two descended from both clans. High Elf and Runda Nor combined.

"Miabelle, you're a genius!" She threw back the blankets and grabbed the attendant's hand. "Come with me."

Chapter 21

Ettrian had been pacing the summer garden for the last half hour. Somewhere amid the lush red berries and the tall wheat, his royal highness was lumbering around while High Elves tried their best to ignore his presence. For once, his mutters were not in response to spirits.

No doubt the Runda Nor spy, Katar was watching him with amusement as he rehearsed how he'd ask Radelia for dinner at the starless night. Shame and embarrassment were hallmarks of his existence thus far, so he didn't mind being the butt of the Runda Nor jokes. What seized the voice in his throat and drew the moisture from his skin was the possibility that Radelia would say no.

He had never courted anyone before, and the king was keenly aware of the consequences should she be offended.

Never in a century did he expect this. He prided himself on being a peaceful, level-headed king that would never instigate war with anyone. Yet, if things went wrong with Radelia, Ettrian might go down in history as a king who led his armies into battle because of his penis. And there were already too many of those.

No. The king shook his head. He doubted she'd be so offended as to return home and declare war. At the very worst, things would be awkward.

He focused on his surroundings and discovered a High Elf female was staring at him as she slowly plucked one raspberry after another from the vines along the castle wall.

"I'm sorry," he said with a sigh. "I don't mean to interrupt your work."

She relaxed slightly, but the hesitation was apparent in every deliberate movement. "Are you debating someone?"

He suppressed the smile. Isilynor knew what she was thinking. "Myself. I wish to court a certain elf, and her culture is very different from ours."

"You mean the princess?"

From the kitchens to the royal tower, everyone knew the gossip in Cardhon Nimloth. He didn't so much as use the lavatory without someone knowing about it. Ettrian nodded.

"She loves butter," the female said. "And she looks at the roses a great deal."

In an odd moment of vulnerability, Ettrian realized that his people's gossip was also his gain. Like the spirits, only visible to everyone else. And they spoke back, which was nice. "Do you like her?"

The female smiled and nodded. "She speaks more like the humans do. Upfront and sometimes crude, but the way she jumped on the chandelier...I'll never forget it. She didn't have to, but it was important to us, so she did it."

They saw so much, his people.

"She'd never let any harm come to us."

"I always thought the starless night was romantic. I think she will too."

He fully agreed. Ettrian assured himself that he would ask when the moment was right but was constantly battling the urge to control the conditions. If he asked too late, she might be grumpy. Too early, and she'd be distracted. It was ridiculous, and he was embarrassed by his own fretting, but he couldn't help it.

"Thank you," he said. "Your kindness humbles me."

She bowed, and Ettrian made his way into the spring garden to give her some peace while she worked. He inspected the roses and decided the red and white splattered petals were the most beautiful.

The starless night was unlike any other revelry. There were no tents in the gardens. All along the walls were thick round candles caged in glass. A lot less wine was served as the elves were expected to dance while wearing black gowns. For once, he would be properly dressed for the occasion.

During the morning meeting, it was Balqen of all elves who broached the topic of gowns. " Radelia does not have a black gown. We hadn't anticipated her staying this long."

"I've already seen to it," the king said. "Send Miabelle to the royal tailor. The gown should have been properly altered by now."

Aracaryn gave him a curious look before saying, "You had one made on such short notice?"

"Not exactly. Black is a difficult color and takes months to prepare. However, my mother's gowns were kept in pristine condition—"

Leaf gasped. "You're putting her in that gown?"

Omaro jerked slightly, and Leaf was bumped from under the table. Interrupting the king was a punishable offense, after all. He didn't mind, but there was a reason he avoided telling the vassals until the day of the event.

"My king," Balqen said, "that gown is so lavish...Radelia may not fully appreciate it."

"Not to mention the late queen's sheer size. You could make two dresses, and both would still cause Radelia to trip on the fabric," Aracaryn said.

He had considered this as well. The tailor had a few ideas, and besides, he needed the statement of the gown.

"It's more than that," Balqen said, understanding the implication. "He means to make her queen and wants all to know it."

The room went silent.

Aracaryn's sour expression said it all. She didn't approve. Never one to keep silent, she said, "And does Radelia understand this?"

"She will," he said, shifting in his chair.

"A Runda Nor queen," Omaro breathed. "Has such a thing ever been done?"

No, in fact. Never in the history of Cardhon Nimloth had a Runda Nor been linked to the royal line. Their status remained that of cooks and cleaners. Their chambers were always relegated to the ground floor.

Marrying Radelia was not only his heart's desire, but it would send a message to all Runda Nor that they were welcome in the castle. Her father banished her, but he was too old to sire another heir. She was their only option when the emperor passed away.

"Never," Balqen said with a glint in his eyes. "In one gesture, the king unites two clans once more."

"If she says yes," Aracaryn'sr tone was full of doubt. "Their ways are not our ways, and she was banished. According to Radelia herself, her title is just that. When their emperor dies, they may simply follow another."

That much was true, but at least he'd have Radelia.

"It's a gamble," Ettrian conceded. "But one I dearly wish to make."

"And what if two months from now," Omaro asked. "The vassals convene and vote to revoke your kingship? Do you think Radelia will remain by your side?"

He grinned. With the days growing shorter, it was understandable that the vassals didn't see the crown of little white flowers. It was too delicious to share just yet, so the king withheld the information just a bit longer.

"What a better match than a pair of defunct royals?" he countered.

No one could argue with that logic, and in truth, Ettrian knew the vassals did not have the gumption to see their threat through. It was unprecedented. Only one king was overthrown in the history of Cardhon Nimloth, and that was because he was beyond cruel and truly insane. That king also happened to have a brother, which made the choice an easier one. Ettrian had no siblings, so the vassals would employ Aracaryn as regent until his heir came of age.

Being the last of his line did have some perks.

His morning meeting with the vassals ended with discontent and threats, just as it always had. The most sacred night of the year was fast approaching, and Ettrian felt woefully unprepared.

Turning to a nearby worker, he asked for a knife and went to cut some roses when the worker paused and said, "If you cut those, they're liable to wither within a day or so."

Ettrian regarded the male. A gardener with a leather apron and rough hands. This was the second time today that a High Elf had ventured to converse with him. Was it because he seldom ventured from his tower, or was there another change? Perhaps seeing him at the revelries made him appear more approachable and not the horrid ogre that sat upon the throne.

"What do you recommend?"

"The partially opened ones would serve you better," the gardener explained. "In a few hours, they will finish opening and will stay fresh longer."

"What if they open and they're not as beautiful as the others?" Ettrian asked. "What if they open and the petals are all deformed or riddled with bugs?"

"No one can say for sure what lies in the heart of a rosebud, but given a chance, I'd wager there's some good in there."

Ettrian got the distinct notion they were not speaking of roses. Was this his people's subtle way of giving their approval? He hoped it was. The last thing he wanted was a riot over a Runda Nor in the queen's gown. "I'll do as you say. Thank you for your expertise."

Roses in hand, with specific directions on how to keep them fresh for several days, Ettrian went to his room and put the roses in water. If he had planned for it, the king would have asked for a vase, but he settled for the pitcher of water to wash his face instead.

Stepping out onto his balcony as far as he dared, Ettrian watched his subjects and considered the possibility that they didn't fear and mistrust him as much as he thought. And that, perhaps, he mistook his own self-loathing as theirs.

There was another matter nagging his mind. One that had nothing to do with Radelia. His people had reminded him that they saw to him whether he realized it or not, so he should do the same. Returning to his table, Ettrian opened a book with the desire to review any and all marriage laws.

"Focus, Miabelle!"

"I'm trying," the attendant whined. "It's just that we have so much to do to prepare for tonight."

Radelia had dragged her to the library and practically pushed her into the loveseat with a book. Only when instructed to focus on why Isilynor and Elpharae parted ways, the histories of the starless night wrote themselves on the blank pages. Miabelle had one thing on her mind, and that was yet another revelry. Reeling in the urge to tell the attendant her stupid parties meant nothing in the face of destruction, Radelia reminded herself that this was a sacred holiday to them.

To be fair, she knew nothing of the event. So she might as well learn about it. Falling into the chaise, she said, "Okay, tell me about the starless night."

"Every year, all the stars are reborn. They fade into the night sky and then reignite all at once brighter than ever. Isilynor's star will shine the brightest on this night. Her power will be at its peak. Honestly, have you never seen it?"

Radelia shrugged. Runda Nor lived in the dense forest and seldom saw the sky. It wasn't that they were oblivious to the anomaly; they just didn't give a shit. "It doesn't mean much to us."

The attendant glanced at her with what could only be described as judgment, but she said nothing and kept reading. "The phenomenon first occurred nearly fifteen hundred years ago, shortly after the Great Catastrophe. The High Elves have taken it as a sign of Isilynor's love and support despite the event that nearly destroyed the continent."

"Great Catastrophe?"

"You don't know about that either?" Miabelle was openly scoffing at her. "Do your people not teach history at all?"

"About as much as your people actually read it."

The attendant glanced around the empty library where their only company were the statues of dead royals and flushed. "A rock no larger than an apple came crashing down from the stars. It wiped out a whole settlement of elves. If it weren't for the mountains, a great wave would have wiped us all out."

A great wave...

Radelia stroked her chin. "My people tell a story of a great wave that shook the mountains. Some thought it was Elpharae's wrath, but others said the humans were somehow to blame."

"They did start arriving around that time. Some explored and went back to their continent on their massive boats, but others stayed and colonized."

Was the Great Catastrophe linked to the separation of the gods? According to the ever-changing books, Elpharae and Isilynor were married and existed in the sky as twin stars until one day, they called it quits. A rock hurtled to the earth. Not long after that, Isilynor began the light show from the sky, partnered with the steady decline in Elven magic.

"It feels like they want to end us," Radelia said quietly. "Like when throwing rocks didn't work, they cut us off."

Miabelle shook her head with a vengeance. "It's not like that. I don't know why, but it makes me sad."

It probably made her sad that their gods hated them and regretted ever making them in their image. She was sad about it too, but also angry. So what if they weren't everything the gods hoped they would be? That didn't mean they didn't deserve to exist at all.

"The day is growing late," Miabelle said, closing the book. "We have to get you ready for tonight."

Radelia wanted to attend another High Elf revelry about as much as she wanted to grapple with a porcupine. Just the thought of wine had her stomach threatening to revolt, and she was convinced that the headache never truly went away. It was still in her skull just waiting to bludgeon her once more.

But she followed Miabelle to her room all the same. When she entered her room, there was a black-gowned figure standing beside the wardrobe. Radelia hesitated but laughed when she realized it was a sewing form wearing a beautiful black gown.

Black gems were embedded in the black gossamer layers of the skirt that was shorter in the front before trailing the floor in the back. The bodice was a corset with gleaming sapphires for the grommets. Up close, she could see the intricate work of gold threads woven into the sheer material in a lace effect that carried its way to the sleeves and high neckline.

Far more modest than many of the gowns in her closet, Radelia found herself unsure of it. It must have been a borrowed gown, but it was on a form that mirrored her own size. It was delicate and un-yielding at the same time. Whoever owned the dress must have been a formidable woman.

"Did Aracaryn have a spare?" she asked, lightly grazing the neckline with her fingertips.

"It's not her gown," Miabelle said. "It once belonged to the queen."

Radelia shot her a look, and the attendant nodded. The queen's gown? She couldn't imagine how that would make Ettrian feel. From what she gathered, the queen died giving birth to him. And the gown was hers. It wasn't like it would stir painful memories of his late mother. But parading around in his dead mother's gown while he still mourned just didn't feel right.

"I can't wear this," she said, stepping away from the garment. "He never even got the chance to meet her."

"It was the king's idea," Miabelle said, placing a gentle hand on her shoulder. "Radelia, I think he's in love with you."

The notion had been floating around in her mind for some time. Ever since the first revelry when they were far too close to mistake it as anything else. He had kept a respectful distance while they worked together in the library, so she thought perhaps the flirtation was only a symptom of the wine. After her father sent word that she was banished, Radelia's focus returned with a vengeance.

But something had happened last night. More than a raging embarrassment, but she got the distinct feeling she had turned a corner of some kind. That damned wine was worse than any truth potion.

"Radelia, say something."

Miabelle was bracing the bedpost as if she were about to be sick. "If you don't want to be with him, just say the word, and I'll get you out."

She could only stare with a slack jaw. Her attendant was willing to risk her future to defy her king and help her escape if need be. That wasn't what she wanted at all. "Miabelle..."

"Let's just say I know what it's like to be married to someone I don't want to be married to, and I wouldn't wish it on anyone."

Radelia hugged her then. Not the graceful, High Elf gesture of barely touching. She full-on bear hugged Miabelle, lifting her off her feet. "You're a true friend, but you don't need to worry. He's not the monster you think he is."

Miabelle wriggled free and wiped her eyes. "If you were queen...it would make me so happy. All of us."

"Well, let's not go that far," she joked. "He hasn't even asked me out on a date yet."

At least, she didn't think so.

"I think he means to tonight. The gardener helped him pick roses."

High Elves moved at such a slow and yet fast pace at the same time. He hadn't asked her on a date, but there was talk of marriage. Back home, elves courted, bedded, moved in together, had children, and only married in the twilight of their years. Sure, she liked him, but getting married first was like trying to navigate a cavern without a torch.

What if they weren't compatible after all? They'd be stuck together, like it or not, in the same way her parents once were. Some of the rules surrounding kingship made sense, she supposed, but what a hefty gamble.

Miabelle helped slip into the dress. She squeezed the bedpost while the garment was laced in the back. She liked how the front was higher; that way, she wouldn't have to hold it while she walked. And despite all the material, it was rather comfortable.

"What happens if he breaks his celibacy vow?" Radelia asked.

The lacing paused. "I don't know, but probably nothing good."

She just wanted to sample the goods before making a lifetime commitment. "Well, it's not like any harm can come of it. The High Elves are infertile."

There was a firm tug around her waist. "Whatever you're thinking of doing, don't. He's on thin ice as it is."

Radelia looked back at a blanched Miabelle. "The vassals might force him to abdicate."

"Why?"

"I can't—"

She was being ridiculous. "A moment ago, you swore to break all the laws to help me escape if need be. Why can't you speak of this thing?"

"I just can't!"

Miabelle was on the verge of a meltdown. That was the last thing Radelia wanted, so she eased back. Though between the mutterings and hints, Radelia had suspected the worst. Had Ettrian killed his own father? He wouldn't have done such a thing for power. There was a good reason, she just needed someone to explain it.

"Okay, I'm sorry. I just don't understand why they would make him abdicate."

"Ettrian swore he could bring the magic back. If he can't, his crown is forfeit."

She didn't give a shit about him being king. He would be happier if he abdicated. Ettrian was more at ease in the library with his big nose in a book than he was sitting on the throne. "If he's no longer king, does that celibacy rule still apply?"

"He still needs to produce trueborn heirs."

She clicked her tongue. No getting around that one. "I don't care if he's king, but he'd never forgive himself if the castle died."

His potential unemployment wasn't a problem in her mind, but she would need to get to the bottom of the whole voices thing. Jonik heard voices in his head, but they never told him to kill anyone. They scared the shit out of him—rightly so. The healers gave him a medicinal tea to drink every morning, and it diminished the voices. However, if Ettrian's voices were anything like her third eye, no medicine would help.

"Did the queen hear voices?"

Miabelle shrugged. "I don't know. She was very tall, like Ettrian, and she had long black hair. She was beautiful but in a terrifying way."

Perhaps she too heard voices, but unlike Ettrian, she had guidance on how to handle it. Radelia's own magic was something taught and cultivated by her father. Had he not been there to help her use it, discovering it on her own would have been a horrendous experience.

"It is a gift passed down our line from Elpharae themselves," her father once said. "For Bellas are said to be made in their image."

She always assumed that was his puffed-up way of clinging to Run-da Nor heritage, but perhaps there was something more to it.

"It's true," Miabelle agreed as if it wasn't the most arrogant statement ever. "That's why Ettrian looks so different from us. He is a descendant of Isilynor herself. The Dark Elves lost the name of their god long ago, but they believe the same."

Having direct lineage to a god was a lot to casually embrace when Radelia couldn't even put stockings on without focusing on her balance.

Fully dressed, Miabelle applied a special oil the way Yinren had taught them. Small amounts worked into her curls with a scrunching motion. The bristle brush was banished from her room, and a wide-tooth comb had taken its place.

"Well, you're ready. Are you sure about this?"

Oh, Radelia was certain. "Just as certain as I was when I jumped on the chandelier."

"That's comforting." Miabelle deadpanned.

The sun was low in the sky when they emerged from her room, and Radelia couldn't wait to get the king alone.

CHAPTER TWENTY-TWO

Chapter 22

P er the custom, Ettrian's place was on the balcony.

It was lined with a carpet and overstuffed pillows. A cask of reserved wine was brought along with a spread of fruits and cheeses. There were slices of imported cured meat cut so thin they curled. High Elves didn't generally eat meat. Keeping livestock in the gardens wasn't exactly possible without a great deal of mess.

When the humans first came to their shores, they brought their techniques for preserving meats with them. Ettrian was rather fond of the cured meats. He plucked a slice from the platter and dropped it into his mouth. Smokey and salty, he closed his eyes and savored the taste and blessed those round-eared geniuses.

One of the attendants found a blue glass vase for the roses. Staring at the mountain of bread beside a soup bowl filled with butter, he said, "There will only be the two of us."

The attendant shifted with visible discomfort. "Princess Radelia has a healthy appetite, my king."

He knew this to be a trap.

Never should a male ever comment on a woman's food intake. It was right up there with the rule about saying only nice things about a gown, even if she had grown out of it. "Very good. Thank you for considering her needs."

After his third glass of wine, Ettrian was able to grip the railing of the balcony and look out at the gardens below. There was still no sign of Radelia. She would have been impossible to miss in that gown. His nerves were so frayed. She had him drinking like a true High Elf! Wouldn't his father be proud? He just hoped she wouldn't refuse to wear the gown. No doubt Balqen's granddaughter let the origin of the dress slip.

Oh, look at her! She's a vision!

She needs a golden crown to match...

"I'm working on it!" Ettrian said to the wind.

...he's talking to himself again...

The king rolled his eyes and muttered about the stupidity of the spirits while he sipped more wine. He knew nothing about how the Runda Nor courted, but it certainly wasn't how the High Elves did things. He should have asked her friends what to expect, but the arrival of more babies and the size of the militia told him all he needed to know.

Since they took in the first few infants, another arrived two days ago. The merchant informed his guards that they should expect three more within the next few weeks. All were round-eared but otherwise healthy babes. Fertility was not a problem; he just hoped commitment wasn't either.

At long last, Radelia descended the wide staircase that led to the gardens. He held his breath as she took the first few steps. Everyone was staring at her. He could hear the gasps as she passed. She wasn't surprised by the reaction and appeared to take it in stride. Miabelle had told her who the dress belonged to.

Anger gave way to relief. If she understood the meaning behind the dress and still wore it, that was a good sign. He had drunk too much but realized it too late. His tongue was thick in his mouth, and his mind swam in maroon thoughts. Unlatching from the railing, he sat on the carpet and ate several slices of bread, hoping to fill his stomach with something other than wine.

After what felt like hours, a soft knock echoed on his chamber door at last.

The door opened, and the attendant announced, "Princess Radelia, my king."

He extended his arms and said, "Welcome!"

Radelia's expression said it all. She knew he was drunk. Unfortunately, not drunk enough to be oblivious to his own awkwardness. "Celebrating a bit early, I see."

Brushing his hair back from his face, he couldn't help but laugh. "I dislike heights," he explained. "Wine gives me the courage to be out here."

The king didn't dare try and stand. Especially not on the balcony. So, he didn't get up to greet her, but she came to him and seated herself. The train of her gown was so long it trailed around the doors and into his bedroom.

"Do you like the gown?"

"I do," she said, absently smoothing the fabric. "It's the most beautiful gown I've ever seen. Thank you."

There was an unusual softness in her tone. Shy almost. Her gaze averted his, but she was smiling. "Please," he said, gesturing to all the food. "Help yourself. Have you tried cured meats before?"

"We eat nothing but dried meat," she said but eyed the rolls curiously.

"Not like this," he promised. "The humans cure their pork with salt and time and then slice it so thinly it's near transparent."

Before she could reach for it, Ettrian selected his favorite variety and reached to place it in her mouth.

Don't just shove food in her mouth, you dolt! She's not a horse!

He cringed at the criticism. The spirits were always the loudest during the starless night. Radelia didn't take offense. She leaned in and took a bite. Closing her eyes, she chewed before nodding. "That is divine."

"I would never make an enemy of the humans for this reason alone."

"My people are indebted to them as well," she said. "But not for preserved meats."

She must have been speaking about the infants. There was no way for her to know that the humans had tried to return them. Should he tell her? He didn't want to brag, and there was a fear that she would misinterpret his reasoning.

"I must confess something."

Radelia reached for his hand and nodded with an expression that made him feel like he could say anything in that moment. Confessing to killing the elf he was certain was her mother and both his parents just wasn't what the mood called for, even if it was everything he wanted to say.

"I care very much for your people. For you above all."

He did it. Ettrian had admitted his feelings for her. Gauging the soft furrow of her brow, though, it was not the confession she wanted to hear. She must have learned something about his father or perhaps her mother. Did she hear the babes all the way from the kitchens and assume the worst or that he had been funneling supplies under the false pretense that the humans were sharing a windfall of goods.

Lies stacked upon lies. All his decisions were made with the best intentions, but he was so scared to lose her. He would tell her, and soon, just not tonight. Let them have a peaceful, romantic night where she and him were all that mattered.

"I must know before we go any further," she said, taking his hand in hers. "You hear voices. I know you do. Where do they come from?"

Of course she'd noticed. He lowered his head. Yet another lie he had somehow managed to forget. That much he could not deny her. "I've heard them for as long as I can remember. They're spirits of departed elves."

Her face was unreadable. "You speak to the dead."

"Not exactly. I speak to them the way old elves yell at clouds. I can hear them, but they are either unaware of it, or they choose to ignore me."

The truth was out. Might as well wrap up the feast and send her on her way. He should have known he didn't stand a chance with her. He was too strange, too dark to be with anyone, let alone Radelia.

"I can see the future."

The nausea turned to lead, and the world stopped spinning around him.

"I hate it, but my father says it's a gift bestowed on the direct descendants of Elpharae."

"What have you seen, Radelia?"

She was fighting back the tears. "Our village was empty. The children fell from the bridges, and I don't know what happened to them. I think they're all dead..."

Radelia Bellas had far more reason to come to Cardhon Nimloth than he realized. It wasn't just to save her friends or help her people. She was driven by visions of the future. "Did your father know this?"

She nodded. He was wrought with sympathy for her. He tried to wipe away the tears, but there were too many. "I don't understand. He knew and yet banished you for trying to change their fates?"

"My father has the gift too. I can't help but feel like he saw something I didn't. What if I'm the reason my clan perishes?"

He shook his head, swallowing the hard ball in his throat. "No. Radelia, you are not the reason. I can promise you that."

Helping her up, Ettrian's legs trembled as they reached the balcony railing. He was holding her so close he could feel her breath through his tunic. It wasn't out of romance, it was out of terror, but she embraced him all the same.

"Look," he pointed to the statue of Isilynor.

It was already dark. The stars were waning by the moment, but Radelia's eyes were keener than his own from her time in the wild. She gasped and wiped the errant tears away herself. "Flowers?"

He had shown her as much the other night, but she must have been too intoxicated to remember. Unlike him, Radelia couldn't have known just how strong the wine was or how it would affect her.

"Whatever we're doing, it's working."

She remained in his arms as they watched the stars dissolve in the black skies. All was not lost. Not yet at least. In the darkness, his people lit the candles along the walls. The soft glow emanated around the castle. What did it look like from the stars? Could Isilynor see it from her fixed position from above? The stars moved and changed, but she always remained constant.

"Watch now," he said, pointing at the goddesses' location.

The star blinked three times and went dark. His people cheered, encouraging her to shine her light once more. There was another set of blinks and more cheers.

"You see," Ettrian whispered in her hair. "She's acknowledging us."

There was another set of blinks.

"No," Radelia said, leaning heavily into his arms. "That's not it."

He craned his neck to look at her face. What did she mean?

"It's what we do to find our missing hunters at night."

After another succession of blinks, the star ignited. Brighter than before, Isilynor lit the stars around her. The light spread to every star in the sky. How could they have been so stupid? Isilynor wasn't trying to say hello; she was searching for her beloved. The gods never parted ways. They were separated by force. Isilynor was lighting a signal to find Elpharae.

He looked to the crown. The buds had opened under the starlight. Their petals reached upward as if trying to grow high enough to reach her.

"Do you know what this means? The rock that caused the Great Catastrophe must have knocked Elpharae from the sky. Our people thought it was a sign that our clans were meant to part ways, but that was never the gods' intentions."

Ettrian nodded. The ramifications were sobering. His people took it as a sign of supremacy. That their goddess cast off the Runda Nor god, but she needed them. That was why magic was failing.

"But how do we right the stars?" he asked. Hopelessness ached in every fiber of his being.

She didn't have an answer because there was none. It wasn't like they could find a god and launch them back into the sky. Elpharae was the god of earth, and the Runda Nor took that to be literal. They were a part of every stone and clump of dirt.

"We can't," Radelia said. "But there is a link between our clans and the health of the castle. If we can focus on that, maybe not all is lost."

Ettrian looked at the lonely star. "Might as well start working on a giant catapult then."

Radelia laughed. "Oh, it won't be that bad."

She woefully underestimated just how much her clan hated his. "Maybe if we throw rocks up there, one might stick."

Throwing her head back in a fit of laughter, Ettrian grinned. He seldom made people laugh. Cupping her head, his fingers tangled in her hair, the king leaned down and kissed the princess. Ettrian meant for it to be a light and gentle thing, but Radelia returned it tenfold. His still-trembling knees straightened as he forgot they were standing on the balcony.

The hands that were wrapped around him began running along the top of his pants, searching for the ties. He stepped back out of surprise. "I can't..."

She growled in frustration but was willing to resume kissing for the time being.

"Marry me," he said between kisses.

Radelia raised one eyebrow. "Just like that?"

"Why not?"

"Hold on, big guy," she said with a laugh.

Ettrian grinned. It wasn't a yes, but it also wasn't a no.

CHAPTER TWENTY-THREE

Chapter 23

They remained together long after the last reveler curled up on the lawn. Radelia didn't learn anything about Ettrian she didn't already know or at least suspected. He was hiding things from her, but she couldn't very well change the subject after he asked her to marry him.

Instead, she shared some insight on the Runda Nor way of partnership, and the king's jaw fell to the carpet.

He sat with his long legs crossed while she laid her head on his thigh. Towering over her, even from that position, his hair was swept to one side to keep from dangling in her face. His scar was fully exposed. It was a long, straight cut. Like someone took a sharp blade and dragged it across his temple only to lose sight of its victim at the slope of his cheekbones.

"You just..." He joined hands as if too embarrassed to say it.

"If we like one another, we shag. If we keep shagging, we move in together."

Ettrian's face went through a series of emotions. Every time he moved his lips to speak a question, he stopped as if he thought better of it. "And as princess, you're not expected to remain celibate until marriage?"

She shook her head. Deflated by the high standards that only he had to keep, Ettrian rolled his eyes. "Well, that confirms it. All the elf clans think it's a stupid, archaic rule except mine."

"Especially given that you guys can't have children, I don't see why it matters."

"It's a matter of precedence," he explained. "As king, I have more privilege and therefore more rules. If I were to argue that the law is no longer relevant, it could be argued that the ancient law I used to become king is also no longer relevant."

The talk of celibacy and precedence did nothing for the romantic mood she was trying so hard to cultivate. Old and useless, she couldn't deny that Ettrian took these laws and his vows seriously. He was like Kieran in that he had a sense of duty, only he was better at explaining his reasons. That might've been because he was raised to rule. Unlike Kieran, who sort of fell into it.

"So, we can't do anything."

Something shifted in his expression then. "Well, I didn't say that..."

His hand smoothed across her neck and over the lace of her gown. She craved the touch of his skin and regretted the high neck of the gown. It was sheer, but not sheer enough at that moment. Ettrian's other hand felt at her back until she arched, allowing him to pull her further into his lap. The heat of his breath brushed the top of her head, she became keenly aware of where his free hand was going.

Her breath quickened as his fingers traced along her chest and down the front of her corset. Of all nights to be wearing a bone-reinforced garment! She didn't know what he had in mind, but when Radelia sat up to pull at the laces, he stopped her.

"There's no need for that," he whispered in her ear.

She looked at him, wondering just how anything was going to happen if she was caged up in that dress, but he held her fast with one arm, grabbed a pillow with his other, and plopped it a few feet in front of them.

Thinking he meant to lay back so she could play with him, Radelia laughed with surprise when he lifted her from his lap and laid her head gently on the pillow. He was on top of her then. His mouth crushed against her lips as his tongue sought hers. Ettrian supported enough of his own weight to keep her comfortable, but she was otherwise pinned against the floor.

Radelia didn't want to reach for his pants since that was a firm line he couldn't cross, but that didn't stop her from wrapping her bare legs around his hips to grind against him. More than anything, she wanted to know just what she was working with. He was a giant of an elf…was everything proportionate?

Supporting his weight with one arm, his other hand found the small of her back and pulled her to him as tight as the corset would allow. She bit his bottom lip. If he would just let her take the damned thing off, they could have some real fun.

His mouth broke away from hers, leaving her gasping as he trailed down her neck. Slipping out of the leglock, he worked his way down, kissing the sheer parts of her gown. Where was he going? Radelia opened her eyes as he worked the layers of her skirts upward.

Ettrian might have been a virgin, but in that moment, it was Radelia who felt woefully inexperienced. He was nibbling the inside of her thigh, pressing the other flat with the palm of his hand. She had a feeling she knew where he was going, but why?

Sensing her pause, Ettrian looked up from between her legs. "I thought you were experienced."

"High Elves must do things differently." It was no wonder they couldn't get pregnant. She had seen plenty of them in action but never watched closely enough.

"I see," he said with an evil grin.

Using his tongue, Ettrian licked her mound, undergarment and all. A zap of excitement made her twitch. Not waiting for a response, he pulled the protective linen down. Her legs cooperated awkwardly as the ties loosened around her knees before falling loosely at her ankles.

Kicking her knickers off to the side, Ettrian resumed doing whatever it was he was doing. The heat rose to her face as he nibbled and kissed his way up her thigh and in the hollow spot where her thigh connected with her pelvis. Her breasts swelled, and her nipples pressed into the bodice of her gown, erect and sensitive against the firm fabric.

Gently brushing her lips with his tongue, her opening ached as she tried to guide his tongue there with her hands. He obliged teasingly, not enough to satisfy her but enough to make her buck. When he moved to the top of her mound, something new happened altogether.

She cried out, half with excitement and half shock. Nothing she had done with Kieran or that tracker when she was young felt half as good as Ettrian's tongue. He made small, gentle circles with enough pressure to make her legs tremble.

Relenting to his desire, Radelia pressed herself against him. Handfuls of black hair in her grasp, she pulled at him, moaning and writhing as her body went tense. His groans were distant, but the tongue lapping at her was erratic and desperate.

Just when she didn't know if she could take anymore, something released within her. Waves of pleasure wracked her body, rendering her helpless as she jolted as though she were struck by lightning.

All too soon, it was over.

There were no thoughts. No cares in the world could reach her. Ettrian's cheek was pressed against her propped-up thigh. "What do you think?"

Radelia blinked. She stared at him, trying to form the words, but she was just too relaxed to care. "I needed that."

He snickered and patted her thigh. "I'm surprised you've never had an orgasm before. Those Runda Nor boys need a lesson or two."

She couldn't agree more.

The boy she'd fooled around with in her youth was just as clumsy and inexperienced as she was. He told her she was pretty, and they decided to have a go at it the way adults did. It wasn't pleasant, and she bled so much that the boy became convinced he had somehow caused internal bleeding. That was one of the more embarrassing trips to the healers.

Kieran didn't know any more than she did. He was shy, and she had always instigated their encounters. Radelia had always wanted to feel the throes of passion that Katar described, but it never happened for her that way. She was beginning to understand why.

"What about you?" she said, propping herself up on her elbows. "Can I do something like that for you?"

"Not at the moment, I'm afraid," he said. "Your pleasure became my own."

That was a nice way of saying he came too soon.

All of a sudde,n the bedroom door was open, and Leaf was running into the room. "My king—" She finished her sentence with a yelp and turned around.

Radelia couldn't see it happen as it was all behind her. That might have been why she was too startled to move or react. She just laid there, legs wide open, with Ettrian camping between them, his eyes fixed on Leaf.

"I warned you," he said. "I told you that one day, you were going to barge into my room at the wrong time."

"I'll leave."

Leaning her head back, she observed the vassal from upside down with curiosity. High Elves were always rutting in public; why was she so embarrassed? Leaf had her back turned, her hands on her hips, and the back of her neck was as red as a tomato.

"No, no," Ettrian said. "You must have something important to tell me."

Leaf hesitated. "The female scout... She escaped."

Lifting her head, she locked eyes with Ettrian. "I'll find her."

"What if she left the castle?"

Radelia didn't think so. As much as she hated him, Katar wouldn't leave Kieran behind. "They're not on the best of terms," she explained. "Katar probably just wanted to get away from him and didn't think anyone would notice."

"Leaf, how did you learn she was missing?" Ettrian asked.

Still with her back turned, the vassal said, "A guard spotted an intruder. We checked the room, and she was missing. The male refused to say where she went."

Something didn't add up. Katar wouldn't have been caught on her own unless it was intentional. "The only person to ever catch her was Kieran, and they've been at one another's throats ever since."

Ettrian scoffed. "I caught her."

From what she understood, he held Kieran over his body like a shield before throwing him at Katar. It wasn't the same. "You caught the others, so Katar relented. She wouldn't abandon them."

"Do you want me to go with you?" he asked.

She did, but Ettrian's face was leaning heavily on her thigh for support. He was exhausted after their little celebration. The last thing she needed was a sleepy giant following her around the castle with his guard down. "I got this," she said. "Why don't you go to bed?"

"Leaf will accompany you," he said, drudging to a stand. Ettrian frowned, then said. "Perhaps you'd like to change out of the gown first."

There was no time to return to her room to change. She borrowed one of Ettrian's tunics and fastened a belt he claimed he wore as a child. Being barefoot wasn't a problem in a castle, so she left her fine slippers with him. All the while, Leaf remained fixed in the same spot.

"I'm dressed; you don't have to do that anymore."

The vassal didn't turn or nod or anything. She just walked out the door. What was her problem? Ettrian was no help. He was already climbing into bed, throwing his black covers over his body. "Good night, Radelia," he muttered. "Return to me when you can."

He appeared so sweet when he slept. If he meant for her to return the same night, she could climb in bed and snuggle up to him and...

"Are you coming?"

Radelia rolled her eyes. Leaf was not her favorite person. It seemed the feeling was mutual. She'd have to be wary of that one. "Yeah, I'm coming."

#

They had been roaming the halls for what felt like hours. Armed with a candle she borrowed from Ettrian's room, Radelia hoped Katar had snuck back into her room. The entire time, Leaf hadn't uttered a single word to her.

"How did she get out anyway?" Radelia asked. "I thought there were guards."

"The king decided they were no longer a threat," Leaf said between gritted teeth. "He had them moved to a grand room with a big window overlooking the garden."

She had no idea they had moved. "Why doesn't he ever tell me when he does something nice?"

"Probably because he knew it would blow up in his face."

"Katar won't blow up anything," Radelia assured. "She left for a reason."

"If you say so."

They scaled some stairs and emerged on the outer wall. Even in the dark, she sensed the staggering height. No wonder Ettrian didn't like heights. She was content in the trees and sailing through the air by a rope in nothing but a bath towel. Even for her, the height of the walls was dizzying.

"No sign of her," Leaf said with a sigh. She leaned against the wall and stared down into the gardens. "What if she did leave? To report back to your king and raise an army—"

"I told you. Katar wouldn't do that. She couldn't even if she wanted to."

Leaf's disgust was magnified by the low candlelight. "Yeah, I know, the general won't go to war, but what if she convinces him?"

What was her problem? The Runda Nor had yet to do anything to her or any of the High Elves, for that matter. "Kieran might not tell you where she went, but he'd tell me."

"Fine."

Radelia had had enough. Ever since the day she arrived, Leaf had been a little shit. "What is your issue with me?"

The vassal whirled around. "My issue is that you're lying about something, and I don't know what it is."

"That's it?"

Leaf nodded.

"Okay, fine, you want to know the secret? The only thing I've been withholding to my knowledge, and you'll stop being a bitch?"

"I never make promises."

The heat was rising to Radelia's head. She wanted to throttle the little pixie. Even if she could get her hands on Leaf, she was the one with the weapons and the training. Not to mention, Ettrian was in a delicate situation with the vassals. If she attacked one, Radelia couldn't imagine it would go over well with the rest.

It wasn't even a big deal. Even if they knew they were holding the general hostage, it wouldn't change anything. He would still refuse to go to war for the sole reason that Runda Nor would die in droves. And as she explained countless times, no general, no war. The militia just wouldn't follow anyone else.

"Don't you get it?" Radelia was shouting. Her voice was echoing in the walkway. "Kieran is the general. Katar can't leave to tell the general because she's stuck with him day and night. Neither of them wants to go to war; they just don't want to die."

Leaf was staring at her with wide eyes. Her anger deflated, but then the vassal reached for her dagger. "Don't move."

Radelia sensed it too late. Someone was standing behind her. She dove out of the way only to be caught by another stranger. Tangled in their arms, she kicked out, but they caught themselves easily. They were elves.

The petite vassal charged, blade drawn and gleaming in the low light. She could hear them cut through the air and clash against metal. Even in the dark, she could sense the attackers withdrawing. But that didn't stop Leaf. She pursued the intruders soundlessly into the tower. Radelia grabbed the candle and raced after them, wishing she had a bow.

Chapter 24

E ttrian was having the most pleasant dream. One where he was either already married or no one cared that he was intimate with a woman. Just when things were getting good, he was woken by something. He didn't stir, and his eyes remained closed, but the king was conscious and acutely aware that he was not the only person in the room.

"She's not here," a voice whispered.

"But he is."

Two males were around the balcony. He distinctly heard a smacking noise. They were eating the food from his feast! He couldn't decide if they were idiots that thought they could kill him so easily or if they were dangerous enough that they had no need for stealth. He had to suppress the laughter. The sheer irony of being murdered in the same room he killed his father in...it was just too good. The world had a funny way of returning actions.

Ettrian had no intention of dying. Not at the hands of those fools and not until he saved the castle and married the princess. He didn't keep his halberd in his room. The thing was too long for the low ceilings. Ettrian would need to improvise.

With clarity that only a life-threatening situation could provide, Ettrian's mind searched the room for anything that could be used as a weapon. The candelabra on the table, books, the chairs, and perhaps the table itself. Why was his room so sparse? He could feel their approach as the hairs raised on the back of his neck and their breathing became more rapid. Ettrian would not reach the table, and there was only one option he could think of.

Kicking out with both feet as hard as he could, the bedpost splintered, taking all the drapery with it. The intruders let out a cry of alarm as Ettrian scampered out of bed and went for the nearest chair. Lifting it over his head with one arm, the king sent it crashing down on one intruder, shattering the chair.

Not wasting any time, he reached for the next chair and smashed it against the person trying to escape the drapes. There was something so liberating about protecting himself in such a way. He was trained with an exotic weapon meant to keep his enemies at a distance. In their arrogance, the High Elves assumed no one would ever be so bold as to attack the king in his own chamber. This made the second time they were wrong.

Metal clashed on metal in the hallway. Ettrian's heart lunged. It wasn't him they were looking for after all. "Radelia!"

In his rush to reach her, the king clipped his head on the top of the doorframe. A blinding pain was followed by a rush of wetness rolling down his head, covering his eye. Holding the wound, he kept going. Of all the elves for Radelia to be with, he was thankful it was Leaf.

No one else was more skilled than their young child of magic, but who knew how many there were. But who were they, and why did they want to kill Radelia?

Was it possible her own father sent them? It was absurd. She always spoke so fondly of her father, but perhaps it wasn't as she thought. Kieran did warn him that the princess was blind to the emperor's shortcomings, but this went beyond a shortcoming; this was assassination.

Rounding the curve of the hallway, he came upon four elves. Radelia stood behind Leaf, who was fending off both intruders. One broke through Leaf's defenses and lashed at the princess, but she kicked his slashing arm with a well-aimed foot, sending the short sword flying. Even unarmed Radelia was formidable in her own right. He suspected if she truly wanted to kill him that night, she would have found a way.

The king grabbed one of the intruders by the back of his neck and smashed him into the wall. Bones shattered and cracked before the body slumped to the ground. The other intruder yelped and flailed to get away from the king, giving Leaf the opportunity to stab him in the kidneys.

He stepped into the dim light of the candle Radelia held, and both females eased at the sight of him. Radelia rushed to him, her hands searching his forehead for the wound. "It's fine," he said, embracing her. "I hit my head on the doorframe."

"You emerged from the dark like a shadow," she said. "I didn't see or hear you!"

"It seems I'm an elf after all.

"Leaf, sound the alarm. There are two more in my bedroom. Who knows how many there are in the castle. You and I," he said to Radelia, "need to get to the armory."

Cardhon Nimloth was under attack. They had less than a hundred full-time guards and another two hundred that took guard training but were only reserved for special situations.

This was an assassination attempt. A small group with a limited purpose. The guards would be enough for the time being. Next time, they may not be so fortunate.

"What is going on?" Radelia asked as they moved as quickly and quietly as they could through his own home like thieves in the night.

"They came for you," he said. Not knowing how else to say it. "I was a secondary target, but you were the goal. They meant to kill you."

"Me? Why?"

Because, banished or not, Radelia was still the Runda Nor heir. Because her father likely wanted to name someone else heir, but his people wouldn't accept it. Because the best way to wage war without damaging the castle itself was by destabilizing from within. All those reasons wrapped in one, but saying as much would start an argument.

"I don't know," he said. "We need to keep moving."

Why did the spirits not speak? Perhaps they didn't realize they were dead and remained silent out of fear? Most likely, they were asleep. Contrary to what most assumed, ghosts, wraiths, and other unliving souls slept quite a bit. Sometimes they kept him awake at night with their snoring.

The armory was a long chamber that spanned multiple rooms. It was nearly as large as the great hall. Walls were lined with busts donning armor, and racks occupied the center of the room with thousands of swords. Armor and weaponry from a time when High Elves numbered in the tens of thousands. Their army would file in, and when they marched to battle, only an empty husk remained.

These days they barely had enough people to clean and polish the armor to keep it from rusting.

Radelia made herself familiar with the bows mounted on the wall. The way she inspected each one before posing with it was rather adorable. "What?" she asked without looking up from the longbow in her hands.

"Nothing."

Ettrian had his own area of custom-made armor and weapons. His halberd, of course, was designed by the master weaponsmiths of the Ruby Isles. With their vast wealth of gems and alloys, the metal workers had learned to forge the most intricate of items. It also helped that the Isles owned the largest mine on the continent.

His light chainmail was forged by the strongest metals, though he did not know the name for it. Some secret formula kept by armor masters on the isles. It was a gift from his father for his sixtieth birthday to celebrate the end of his formal training.

Taking the slinky mail off the hooks, Ettrian held it in his hand. Those were happier days, before his eyes saw the flaws in his father. He supposed all grown males someday look at their sires and see them for who they truly are, but in his case, Ettrian saw someone with an unchecked bloodlust.

The former king wanted to punish the Runda Nor for fleeing during his mother's reign. An event Ettrian could only imagine left a strong impression. There were deaths that followed. Balqen's children were intent on converting the wayward elves, which led to their demise. But that was so long ago, those perpetrators were long dead.

If Ettrian hadn't killed his father, he would have doomed all elf-kind. The proof was in the flowers and the books themselves. By strengthening the bond between Runda Nor and the High Elves, they could rebuild Cardhon Nimloth. And perhaps that would be enough for Elpharae to reach Isilynor once again.

He slipped the mail on and straightened it around the short sleeves. Belting a short sword at his hip, Ettrian still went for the halberd. It was useless within the confines of the castle, but should the intruders find themselves in the gardens, they would be in for a horrid surprise.

Radelia had settled on a short bow with a variety of arrows. He suspected she didn't know which did what but had every intention of finding out. He knew some were laced with poison for sleep and others for death. Some were blunt for intense pain, among other things.

"Find what you need?" he asked.

Radelia looked him up and down and bit her bottom lip. "Yeah, I'd say so."

"Not until you bind yourself to me," he teased.

She rolled her eyes. "One battle at a time."

Marriage wasn't a battle, but she had a point.

They departed the barracks, Ettrian going first since he had more armor and a sword. Leaf had moved quickly since then. Guards were stationed along the walls, and he heard their march echoing along the corridors.

As Katar and Kieran had already proved, getting into the castle was a simple thing, but he still wondered how the intruders found their way in when everyone was attending the starless night. Yes, they were preoccupied, but with all the High Elves roaming throughout the night, someone would have noticed the strangers.

Radelia followed him to the gardens, her eyes scanning every direction. She was paying special attention to windows, but he didn't suspect they would be there. The garden view was coveted by the High Elves, and all of them were occupied.

The only reason they were able to move Kieran and Katar into one of those rooms was because Miabelle demanded to vacate her room.

She claimed it was because she wanted to be closer to Radelia to better attend to her needs.

"Kieran should be in that room," Ettrian said, hoping that was what she sought.

Sure enough, the male was standing at the window. Radelia waved, but Kieran only nodded. He made a series of hand gestures to which she replied in rapid succession.

"What does he say?"

"Katar saw the intruders and went to deal with them," she explained. "They spotted at least six coming from the great hall an hour ago."

Ettrian looked at Radelia and then at Kieran. All of that was said with hand gestures. It was remarkable. It also confirmed to him that the little shadow had her reasons for escaping. She sensed Radelia was in danger and left.

"Do they know the intruders? What did they look like?"

Radelia signed to her comrade. While Ettrian didn't know the language, it was plain on Kieran's face that they knew all too well.

"They're Runda Nor," she said quietly.

Her own people were trying to kill her. Ettrian feared that would be the case, but he didn't want to be the one to say so. He wanted to hold her, to comfort her, but Kieran was still signing. "They were born to our clan but not of our clan."

"What does that mean?"

"Many of our people leave the clan for various reasons," she explained. "Some meet human females and settle in the human villages, others travel to the Ruby Isles to train like Kieran has, and some leave seeking work we don't offer."

At least they weren't from her clan. Hopefully that meant they were not taking orders from her father. It couldn't be ruled out entirely, but at least it wasn't as likely.

While Radelia and Kieran conversed, a whistling hurtled in their direction. In a panic, Ettrian wrapped himself around the princess and braced himself for the arrow's impact when a sharp clink sounded.

There was a groan of pain followed by someone falling off one of the ramparts used to stabilize the weakened wall.

Someone was on the move. Fluid and easily, they slunk down the ramparts and slid down the ladder before landing in the summer gardens. He had his suspicions, but they were confirmed when Katar emerged from the rows of wheat.

"Your security leaves much to be desired," she said with a low, teasing tone.

Radelia broke from him and rushed to her friend. There was something unnerving about a woman so dangerous being so close to her. Reeling in his protective urges, Ettrian reminded himself that they had a strong bond and trusted one another. They were friends, and he trusted Radelia's judgment.

Ettrian signaled to a nearby guard, wide-eyed and disturbed by what he had seen. "Should I escort her?"

The guard clearly didn't want to take Katar anywhere. Ettrian didn't blame him. "No, I want you to bring the male to my room. We need to figure out just who these elves were and what they wanted."

With Kieran and Katar by her side, Radelia felt as though everything was as it should be. It was only when she opened Ettrian's door that they hesitated.

"Everyone convenes in the king's bedroom?" Kieran asked with a frown.

"Unorthodox," Aracaryn said from inside the room. "But the most secure area of the castle."

Radelia went first, leading the others. She gasped at the scene. The bed was broken, as were two of the chairs. The room was half ransacked. They must have attacked him while he slept. She looked to Ettrian who said, "Apologies for the mess."

She didn't care that it was a mess! He could have been killed. Radelia was about to say as much, but the vassals were already talking. "Who were these intruders?" Balqen asked. "They look like Runda Nor, and yet not."

"They are renegades," Kieran explained. "Elves who left the clan."

"Mercenaries?" Aracaryn asked.

"Most likely," Kieran agreed.

Ettrian was leaning against the wall, still wearing the chainmail. "I heard them speaking in my room. Radelia was the target; I was just a bonus target."

"I got this off one of the bodies," Katar said, unfolding a small parchment. It was a list of names and titles.

Radila Belles

Leaf

The king

General

"They couldn't even get my name right," she complained.

"Literacy isn't a requirement for hired killers," Katar said. "It seems someone wants both sides to take losses."

"Who is the general?" Balqen asked.

Before anyone could explain, Leaf countered with, "You're looking at him."

Radelia's cheeks flushed. It was a secret she had planned on telling Ettrian at some point, but not like that. Though, no one appeared concerned or surprised.

"Someone wanted them dead while in our care," Omaro said.

"I think you mean while we were held hostage, but yes," Kieran fired back.

"Can you blame us?" Aracaryn asked. "What would you have done in our situation?"

Kieran scowled at the princess. He didn't need to say it out loud; they all knew Runda Nor took no prisoners.

"We don't incarcerate," Radelia spoke up and eased the tensions. "We don't have the means. Death is a last resort. Typically, we banish offenders."

"I see," Aracaryn said, though she didn't take her eyes off Kieran.

"So, these mercenaries," Balqen steered the conversation back on course. "They're Runda Nor outcasts looking to destabilize both clans. Who has the most to gain?"

"And why me?" Leaf asked, leaning over the list.

"You're a child of magic," Ettrian said. "Our youngest and most precious. Killing you would enrage the High Elves beyond reason."

Radelia was pacing the room. Her arms folded over her chest. Someone wanted both clans to be without heirs. Without Kieran, the militia would disband. If Leaf was assassinated, the High Elves would likely use all their wealth and power to cut the Runda Nor off from what little trade they had. It would be the death of them.

It was calculated. Not a list that could be composed without an informant. "We have a spy."

Radelia noted how everyone in the room looked at Aracaryn at that moment. Something in that soured her belly. All her life, she had been taught that someone else was the enemy. Someone who looked and acted differently from her. Only when she arrived in the castle, Radelia realized that wasn't the case at all.

"Runda Nor are taught that High Elves are the cause of all their problems," she said. "Never mind that we insist on living in a hostile environment or that we could seek out the truth. It's always someone else attacking us while we claim to be the more deserving clan."

Katar and Kieran both looked startled for a moment, but it was true, and they knew it.

"Spoken like a High Elf," Aracaryn quipped. "They have every right to suspect me. I stand to gain the most."

"In my experience, the best spies are the ones who don't know they are spying," Katar said. "Someone writing a letter to their loved ones could be interceded, visitors might be bribed with ale to speak about their time in the castle... It's not always so plain as a spy."

"In any case, we're all alive and must forge ahead," Ettrian said. "It's no secret there are tensions between our clans, and any number of people might see profit in that. What are we going to do to ensure it doesn't happen again?"

"We need to send them away," Omaro said. "All three of them. Just until we can figure out who's behind all of this."

"It would be easier to protect the king that way," Leaf agreed.

That was utter bullshit. "I'm not leaving," Radelia said, looking to Ettrian for backup.

Only, he didn't say anything. He looked at her, sad and defeated in the corner of his own room. She took a step back, shaking her head. He wanted to send her away too.

"I'm afraid I must agree," Balqen said. "I don't want any harm to come to Radelia or her friends."

"Hang on," she said, fists ready for a fight. "Where would we go? I can't go back, you know that."

"Someone needs to tell the emperor what is happening," Kieran said. "I'll go back to the Runda Nor and tell them all I've seen. If they won't take Radelia back, I'll threaten to leave with the militia."

"And go where?" Katar said. "You don't have a way to feed an army that size."

"Radelia has nowhere else to go for the time being," Aracaryn said. "Before we start shipping princesses off, we need to—"

"You should go too if you care so much," Leaf shot back. "That way, we know you're not the spy."

A bitter spat broke out among them. Kieran and Katar were doing what they did best while the vassals argued amongst themselves. Intermingling their own agendas into the matter at hand. Radelia's future was on the line, and Ettrian was drowning in self-doubt. How could they marry if he couldn't defend her from his own vassals?

So much for getting hitched.

Everyone was fighting except her and Ettrian. They locked eyes from across the room. She couldn't stand arguing and bickering. It was all her parents did growing up. That was why Radelia preferred the forests. Old elves warned them to not get married too soon, but they did it anyway, and she was stuck with it.

She couldn't believe she was stupid enough to fall into the same trap. Shaking her head, Radelia shoved past everyone between her and the door. Everyone went silent, and in the distance, she could hear Katar call out, "Wait, Radelia, I'm sorry…"

Radelia tore through the castle and didn't stop running until her legs threatened to quit. Besides, she had no idea where she was. Somewhere far below the ground level. She took some circular stairs and kept going thinking she'd end up near the gardens, but the stairs kept on going.

The air was damp, and the ceiling narrow and low. She was in a cellar of some kind. Feeling her way around, Radelia stumbled into a wooden thing. Her hands discovered a wooden crate and a candle beside some tools that had to be flint and steel. After several misguided sparks and burning her finger on the heated steel, she finally managed to light the candle.

With the space around her illuminated, Radelia quickly found that there was a candelabra on the ground beside the crate. Candles were scattered around it. She must have knocked it over by accident. She let out a breath only after all the candles were set and lit. Going back was probably the wiser choice, but Radelia wasn't exactly a wise elf.

She walked toward what was probably the gardens for a long while before the channel gave way to an open cavern with twisted and gnarled roots creating a single massive column down the center. How far down did the roots go? Radelia held up the candelabra to find the ceiling was dirt, and those were most certainly roots.

It must have been the center of Cardhon Nimloth.

The living tree, shaped into a castle. The source of all elf magic rooted to unimaginable depths, and she was standing at the heart.

What should have been a momentous occasion wasn't at all what she expected. Perhaps all the fighting had soured her mood, but she had expected more. Placing a palm against the roots, Radelia gasped at how cold they were.

Something had always bothered her about Cardhon Nimloth. It was a living tree yet never spoke like the trees in the forest did. She assumed it was because there were no other trees to speak to, but that wasn't it at all.

Ettrian heard voices. What if it wasn't the dead he was hearing, but Cardhon Nimloth itself? She'd need to ask him about it more if she got the chance. Radelia winced at the thought of being forced to leave. She'd rather eat live snails and clean the latrine pipes than leave.

Pressing both hands against the roots, she closed her eyes and focused. Using what little magic passed down from the Bellas lineage, she opened her third eye. The eye to the future.

Clasping her hands over her mouth to stifle the scream. Radelia sagged to her knees. The roots were blackened and decaying. Only held in place by dead fibers. Cardhon Nimloth was dead.

She fell back, her third eye shuttering closed before sinking back into the pits of her subconscious. Laying on the cold ground, Radelia wept.

Chapter 25

Keeping Radelia safe was all that mattered. Why must it hurt so much? Hatred never changed truth, and he hated this truth to its core. He could not keep Radelia safe. Cardhon Nimloth lacked the military or infrastructure to keep a princess safe. They barely had enough of a population to keep the castle functional. All around him, the vassals and the scouts bowed their heads, ashamed of squabbling the way they had.

She made them all realize how foolish they were being. The way they leapt at the opportunity to go for one another's throats during a crisis. It was pathetic. The Runda Nor elves didn't argue so much as they questioned one another's logic. And High Elves were supposed to be the more elegant clan.

Worst of all was the expression on Radelia's face. She felt betrayed. He understood that, but he'd rather her be alive than anything. It was a temporary solution, and they were merely discussing it, not banishing her.

"Sending her away isn't the right thing to do," Katar said at last.

"What else can I do?"

The little shadow turned in the chair to look at him. "You don't understand. She is Runda Nor. We have choices and freedom to do as we please. By deciding for her, you lose her."

Torn between saving her life or saving their relationship didn't change matters for him. "I'd rather her hate me than bury her."

"There is another option," Katar said, looking to Kieran.

"Katar can be her personal bodyguard while I return to the Runda Nor for my troops."

"You want to bring your military...here?" Aracaryn asked. "We should just welcome your army through the gates, and all will be well?"

Ettrian couldn't help but agree. Aracaryn had a point. There was no way to vet every member of Kieran's militia, and given that the Runda Nor hated High Elves, the king couldn't see that working. It smelled like disaster in the way the oceans smelled of salt.

"Not in the castle," Kieran said. "We can set up camps outside. If your people provide food and tents, we can reinforce the castle."

"Our enemy is a common one," Katar went on. "Their strategy is division. If we can work together, they will have no choice but to abandon their cause."

"And your militia is so loyal they will just do as you say?" Balqen's hands outstretched as he spoke. Clearly, the old elf found the proposition as curious as everyone else did.

"The elves who follow my command do so willingly, not because I was next in line. Those who do not wish to guard Radelia and the castle will remain in the village."

"I can't imagine the emperor will be pleased," Omaro said under his breath.

For the first time, Ettrian saw Kieran grin and found it deeply unsettling. It must have been how everyone else felt when he laughed at inappropriate times. "The emperor would torch the castle rather than see it in High Elf hands, but I imagine his daughter's life still holds some value to him. In any case, it doesn't matter. It's not his militia."

There was something there, a fracture between the emperor and general. He didn't know what it was, but one glance at Aracaryn suggested she saw it as well.

"It could give the clans a chance to get to know one another," Leaf piped in. Once again, she had taken up residence on his bed. She was worse than a cat, always claiming spaces that were not hers. But she had a point.

Ettrian nodded. "It's a way to reintroduce our clans with a safe, tall wall between us. We should expect some difficulties."

They spent the next several hours working through their plan despite the unknown variables. Much of their plan was placed on Kieran's shoulders. Too much for Omaro and Aracaryn's liking, but the general had a surety about him that even Aracaryn couldn't deny.

The way the general poured over the Leaf procured from the library downstairs fascinated Ettrian. He marked locations, explaining his strategy as he went. He had the quiet confidence of a male that had run security missions his whole short life.

With the night wearing on, Ettrian felt as though his input became less needed. Mostly, it was Balqen, Omaro, and Kieran who did the planning. Aracaryn kept a watchful eye on the deliberations from a chair, wrapped in a lace shawl. Leaf had curled up with a blanket on his bed. Evidently, she no longer considered the two Runda Nor a threat. That, or they'd worn her out with boredom.

So, Ettrian stood on his balcony and helped himself to the wine from the other night. High Elves were not accustomed to such rapid change. Last night he was confident that he and Radelia would overcome any obstacle and that the castle was on track to be saved. Tonight, he felt as if all was lost.

"Stranger tides have brought us together, it seems," Katar emerged from behind the drapes.

He swirled his wine in the cup and took another sip. "Your general has a captivated audience. Where did he receive his training?"

Katar tilted her head. "He trained in the Ruby Isles for several years with their military. Don't tell me you're jealous."

"They weren't always friends, were they?"

"That was a long time ago," the shadow explained. "For whatever reason, Kieran refuses to give Radelia the closure she needs. I tried to learn the reasoning for her sake, but I'm just as confused by his answers."

Ettrian nodded. He sensed something similar. Not desire or any special affection, more like there was something else in the room that sat there faceless, waiting for a name. Still, he was envious. The general had known Radelia intimately—something Ettrian desperately wanted but couldn't have unless she married him. He didn't see that happening any time soon.

So, there he was, drinking on the balcony he detested because it was better than spending another moment listening to Radelia's former lover talk about how to best protect his kingdom.

"I imagine the hardest part of being king is delegating responsibilities."

He smiled at her. She was rather considerate for an assassin. "You don't need to soothe my ego. My reign has always been guided by others."

"That's not a bad thing," she said, helping herself to his wine. "The only real leadership the Runda Nor have is Kieran. The emperor spends his days telling children old stories and warming himself by the fire."

Ettrian was aware that by freedom, the Runda Nor meant orderly chaos. When their people were hungry, they hunted and traded, sharing what they could. There was no plan on how they shared or how to prepare for next winter apart from preserving and rationing per household. All of this, he understood, but what he didn't understand was Katar.

"What is your story?" he asked. "How did you come by such skills?"

"For years, I've been waiting for Radelia to ask, but she never has."

He glanced downward at Katar. Was she so ashamed of her skillset? Leaf was trained to be his protector; it only made sense that Radelia had someone similar by her side.

"Since I'm betraying my emperor, I might as well commit to it," she said. "The emperor is a paranoid elf. From an early age, he had me doing little jobs here and there. I was too young to understand it then, but I was spying for him."

"You had a natural affinity for it, and the emperor saw that."

Katar nodded. "He spent what little gold the Runda Nor had to hire a mentor for me. Gold that should have gone to feeding our people. I trained in secret while Radelia was none the wiser."

There was much guilt in her confession. Ettrian understood why to some extent, but at the same time, having someone around with her skillset must have benefited the clan. There was no shame in that. "But you are a credit to your people with such talents."

She looked up at him and smiled in a way that made him feel I. "I helped my clan by being a healer. I spied on my friends and clan to pacify a paranoid emperor."

Ettrian instinctively glanced at Kieran, marking his map while others watched.

"Yes," Katar said. "Emperor Bellas was afraid that Kieran would unseat him. That Radelia would lead the people in a different direction. He's convinced the High Elves plot against him. It wasn't until I came here and saw...but now I know that isn't the case."

Ah, yes, the dismantling of everything she once thought to be true. He knew what that was like. "My father was everything to me," he said. "His word was truth in my ears, and his words were repeated by my lips. As I grew older, he revealed more of himself to me. While he was a wonderful father, he was perhaps the evilest being I've ever known."

She didn't ask what made him so evil. Perhaps Katar knew that it was a barrel best left sealed for the night. His shoulders sagged as he leaned against the doorway of the balcony. Ettrian wanted nothing more than to climb into bed, but everyone was still occupying his room, and he doubted Leaf would move even if he tried to climb into his own bed.

"My vassals are far too familiar," he mused.

"They're not afraid of you," Katar said as she watched Leaf sleep.

"No," he said with a smile. "Not at all."

Climbing out of the cellar, Radelia made her way back to her room. The guards posted outside her door asked no questions, but their noses crinkled as she approached. "What's wrong, never seen a bit of dirt before?"

They didn't respond, which was probably for the best. She had fire in her veins and was itching for a fight. If Leaf wasn't so preoccupied fighting with everyone else in Ettrian's room, she'd shoot an arrow near her head just to see what happened next.

"Tell the kitchens I want a bath," she said.

"Yes, princess," a guard grumbled.

The one she was truly angry with was Ettrian. How could someone propose and then send her away on the same night? She might not have been an expert on healthy relationships, but whatever she had with Ettrian wasn't it.

He was hiding stuff from her. Big stuff. Radelia didn't have an issue with that because she did much of the same. But to try and use his authority to send her away when things got a little hairy was not acceptable. She had everything to lose, including her life; the least he could do was consider what she wanted to do about it.

It was Yinren who knocked before hauling in a bucket. He did a double-take before asking, "What happened to you?"

While she soaked in the bath, her attendant remained in the room. His back was turned to her as Radelia told him about everything that ahd transpired. Judging by the amount of fidgeting he was doing, Yinren was deeply uncomfortable with learning of such events.

"You're not angry that someone attacked your home?"

Yinren shook his head. "I don't know how to feel about any of it. I didn't even know anything was wrong."

She raised one brow. He glanced at her from over his shoulder and sighed. "Okay, so I knew things weren't what they should be, but I assumed it was just a phase. Trees sometimes go through a dormant phase..."

Their troubles were no dormant phase. Radelia couldn't understand how so many could ignore so much. "And war...you never considered that?"

"It's not my job," his voice was tighter than strung leather. "That's their job. He can do all the research and the fretting, and his vassals can argue about what to do next. I just want to live my life."

Radelia shook her head. Couldn't he see that he was living a half-life? There were no children and no future. His home rotted from the inside, and enemies were closing in. She wanted to rage at him. To shake him awake from whatever delusion he suffered from, but in his own way, Yinren explained Ettrian's behavior.

"Do most High Elves feel as you do?"

"Well, yeah. It's their job, not ours. And their decisions make sense for the most part."

Ettrian and the vassals were making decisions because they were accustomed to the masses blindly following along. Their mentality was that the king knew best and that all his choices were some elaborate, long-running game that only they knew how to play.

She didn't know if that was something she could accept. If she did marry Ettrian, what would her role be in such a society?

"Thanks, Yinren," Radelia said. "I think you just helped me understand something important about Ettrian."

"You're welcome, I guess. Do you need anything else?"

The attendant practically fled the room while Radelia sat in the lukewarm water. Wiggling her toes, she watched the ripples they made in the copper tub. Once, she was left in awe of the beauty of the room, of the castle itself, but it had lost its luster.

Even in her room, there was a subtle draft that moved the curtains and chilled the bathtub. She hadn't spent much time in her room the last few days, and for the first time, Radelia could see the cracks along the walls glinting with blood sap.

The castle couldn't be saved, but she no longer wanted to fight it.

Seeing the future was a wicked curse. Like her father once told her, human lives are not destined. They could change their fates because their gods were long forgotten. Elves could not undo a millennium of deeds and actions that rooted their fate deeper than any tree.

Without the guiding hand of their god, the Runda Nor clan were changing. That should have meant they could determine their own fate, but who they once were was tied with the High Elves. Her people could no longer exist as they had. Radelia's only real option was to lead the Runda Nor from the forest and settle them near the humans. They would need to learn how to be human. How to adapt and till the earth. Their children with their human features would guide them. That was a happy thought, at least.

As for the High Elves, Radelia just didn't know what would become of them. They had another century, perhaps more. Once the barrier completely broke down and the walls crumbled around them, they would be paralyzed. Too old to change, too few to establish a settlement of their own. What would become of them?

Her thoughts went to Ettrian then. How awful it would be for him to endure. Radelia didn't know if she could tell him what she saw in the cellar. It might have been kinder to say nothing of it rather than to crush his soul with the truth.

The water wasn't getting any warmer.

She dried off and dressed in a simple ivory gown with a lace fringe. Heading downstairs, Radelia thought about what to say to Ettrian. Knowing what she did about the castle, it didn't seem right to continue courting him. It was like not warning her lover about the pack of wolves circling their meeting place.

But at the same time, if none of what they did would make a difference, why not just be together? He could abdicate and run away with her. The image of him tilling the earth and herding chickens made her snort with laughter, but no one was around to notice.

Where was everyone, anyway?

It was somewhere between breakfast and lunch, but typically there were people lingering in the great hall between services. She stepped into the gardens to find High Elves gravitating toward the center. Radelia joined them as they gathered around the fountain. They had finally taken notice.

Isilynor's crown was blooming. White petals curled outward to reveal their golden stymes. The vines that merely protruded were creating a firm tether atop her hair.

What did it all mean?

Oy, what's that one doing? What's he got in his hands?

Why is he putting that right there?

Ettrian ignored the spirits. It wasn't the time for their nonsense.

Isylinor had seen the future, and preordained fate could not be changed, yet Isilynor's crown bloomed with the long-lost flowers of Cardhon Nimloth. Was she trying to tell them to not give up? That was impossible; the star goddess couldn't reach them from up high.

That was when Radelia noticed something else about the crowd. Some of them were clasping pendants that hung about their necks. Ettrian had ordered necklaces to be made and handed out during the starless night.

She uttered a soft laugh. The High Elves were wearing symbols of Elpharae when the flowers bloomed. They were clutching the symbols of her god.

"Excuse me," she said to the nearest female holding her pendant. "What is that?"

"It was a gift from the king to any who wished to wear it. The jeweler said it's a symbol of fertility."

The High Elves didn't know what the symbol meant, but they didn't have to. Their collective desire for fertility had brought Elpharae to Cardhon Nimloth.

She started toward Ettrian's room. A dull pain snapped against her chest. It was wrong to give him false hope. Even Elpharae couldn't heal the castle in such a state. Still, she wanted to talk to him. Not for the fate of the castle or all elf-kind. They needed to discuss their future as a couple, or rather the lack thereof.

When she stepped into his room, it was still occupied. Did the vassals ever leave? When Radelia left, they were arguing, only now they were congratulating Ettrian. Kieran and Katar were gone; she didn't know where they went. But the vassals must have seen the crown and assumed the castle was healing.

The smug expression on Ettrian's face fell away when he saw her, replaced with sadness and longing. "If you'd all give us a moment."

"We've been in this room long enough," Aracaryn declared.

They were smiling at her on their way out, their eyes hopeful and wet. She had come to tell Ettrian what she saw and to end their relationship before it could truly begin. Radelia was going to take her people and build a settlement. All these things she had intended right up until she saw the statue and the looks of hope in their eyes.

She couldn't leave them.

Kieran could lead her people under her directive, but if Radelia left, the High Elves would be without hope. They thought she was the reason the flowers bloomed.

"We need to talk."

The king nodded and sat at the table, waiting for anything she had to say. It was as if he were steeling himself for the end the moment she walked in the door. It wasn't like that. She didn't want to break up with him. In her heart, she truly did not wish to leave.

"In order for this to work, we need to lay out all the cards."

He frowned and looked at the table. "This is a metaphor?"

She wasn't in the mood for his jokes. "Yes, Ettrian. I need you to disclose anything and everything pertaining to me and my people."

"That would take all day. You'd hate the sound of my voice by the time I finished. Perhaps you'd even hate me."

"Do you still want me to marry you?"

"Yes." He reached across the table and took her hands in his. "More than anything."

"Then I need to know how you became king."

He relented. "Okay, here it goes..."

Chapter 26

Ettrian always felt uneasy on horseback.

The saddle was too small, and his legs dangled too closely to the ground. Like a child who had grown out of a rocking pony but still insisted on riding their toy. His father emerged from the stables on a black mare, his long blond hair braided into a single rope tucked behind his crossbow.

"Come along, Ettrian."

The prince rode beside his father through the front gates. As was tradition, they raced to the forest, but he hadn't won that race since he was a child. His weight was too much for the horse, and he didn't wish to strain the beast.

The race was brought to a swift end as the horses crossed the first row of trees. "Do you think we'll actually find game this time?" he teased.

His father laughed. "Perhaps today is the day!"

Ettrian doubted it. They had been hunting in the forests for decades and never caught anything. That wasn't the purpose of the hunt. It was a time to get away from court and crown and be father and son. Sure, they saw animals, but his father never got his crossbow out in time. The crank was loud and scared off anything within range.

"What did you think of the coronation in the Ruby Isles?" his father asked, navigating his horse over an exposed root.

"It was," he struggled to find the words. "Extravagant."

"Rhys will make for a wonderful king and ally."

Ettrian had never seen so much red and gold in his life. Their fabrics were all silky, and there were so many performances and rituals. Ten days of celebrations followed. There was also the embarrassing incident with the ashes...

As if reading his mind, his father laughed. "You couldn't have known. I knew they wished to matchmake, but even I didn't know what that entailed."

"I don't think she likes me very much," Ettrian said as they waded deeper into the forest. "She's never shown interest in me before."

His father shrugged. "Aracaryn was first in line before she came to us. I think it's just protocol to make marriage offers in order of age."

Of course. One of Aracaryn's sisters wished to marry, so in order for that to happen, offers needed to be made for the firstborn out of politeness. Otherwise, she might take offense. And Aracaryn was easily offended.

The forest became too rocky for the horses. They dismounted and hiked. Ettrian frowned as his father took the crossbow off his back and pulled the lever back. "We made a bet, you see."

"Who?"

"Balqen and I. He said I couldn't catch anything even if I wanted to. I intend to prove him wrong."

Something soured in Ettrian's gut then. He had never killed any-thing before and had no desire to start. They had no need for hunting, and it felt wrong to take life over a single bet. He opened his mouth to say as much, but his father motioned for him to be silent. Ettrian did as he was told. Even if he didn't approve of what the king was doing, he still desperately wanted his father to like him.

"Seven elves miscarried over the last year," his father said as he aimed his crossbow. "The waters no longer run in the fountain unaided, and there are cracks along the walls. Meanwhile, our cousins have doubled in population."

There had been many closed-door meetings Ettrian hadn't been permitted to attend, and there was an air of conspiracy among the nobles at court. He assumed it had to do with the birth of Leaf. It was a horrid ordeal. What the prince did not understand was what any of that had to do with hunting.

"Balqen will never recover his immortality, will he?"

"I told him blood magic had consequences. Aracaryn urged him not to do it." The king shook his head. "Four lives for one babe."

Ettrian didn't know what else to say about it, but ever since then, it was like his father had shut him out. When the king asked Ettrian to hunt, he was filled with the hope that things would return to the way they once were.

"It won't happen again," the king vowed. "Our cousins are reduced to feral beasts in the forest. They breed like stray cats and gobble up Isilynor's power."

An overwhelming sense of dread came over Ettrian then. His father acted as though he meant to hunt Runda Nor and not an elk. Before he could debate the difference between defending oneself from an attack and actively pursuing unwitting victims with a crossbow, his father pulled the trigger.

A female cried in the distance. Ettrian's heart stopped. He stared at his father, hoping it was all just some elaborate prank.

There was a crashing noise in the distance. His father had actually shot someone. Ettrian took off running in the direction of the person. "I command you to come back!"

He ignored the command. Any loyalty he had for the king ended when he squeezed that trigger, and they both knew the king couldn't keep up with Ettrian's stride.

Stumbling into a clearing, he found her. An elf, but not any elf like him. Her eyes were large and further apart, and her ears were twice as large as his own. Her skin was deeply tanned with freckles. The frightened eyes that stared up at him were a mixture of greens and browns. Her hair was a burnt auburn that coiled beneath the ties.

Ettrian kneeled beside her. "Are you okay?"

She cried out and tried to get away, and that's when he saw it. Her right leg, along with both arms, was broken. They could mend the left arm, but without magic, there would be no saving the leg or right arm.

"Shh," he said. "I'm here to help."

But Ettrian couldn't help. There wasn't a single thing he could do for her. Carrying her back to Cardhon Nimloth would be agonizing. And his father...his father wanted to kill her.

He could take her back to her own people if he knew where they were. "Do your people have magic? Can they heal you?"

The elf opened her mouth to speak, but a pool of blood came trickling out. She was bleeding from the inside. He couldn't even hold her without hurting her.

"It's for the best, son," his father said as he approached. "They're like deer. If left unchecked, they starve in masses or get eaten by wolves. It's a mercy, really."

Mercy?

Ettrian glared at his father. "When you hunt alone...you do this?"

For a deranged murderer, the king wore sympathy well. "I hope she is the last."

He was putting another bolt into the crossbow. "But I should at least make it appear as though there was a fight. Otherwise, Balqen might think I found her by accident."

"You'll not touch her," Ettrian roared.

His father stepped back, annoyed at the defiance. "She's suffering, son."

The elf was suffering because he shot at her and made her fall from the tree. It was his doing. Cardhon Nimloth was forged by the four Elven gods, a place for all elf-kind. As king, his father was king to all. He was making sport of his own subjects.

"Fine. Get her on the horse," the king commanded. "We can heal her enough to keep her alive. Our healers wish to know about the changes they've made over the years."

The night before the hunt, the spirits were in a panic. They were so loud that he had to clamp his hands over his ears to block them out. Their ramblings seldom made sense, but at that moment, they did.

He's going to kill them. He's going to kill them all...

A poison pulled from their own veins...

Ettrian shook his head. No. He wasn't going to allow his father to shoot at the dying elf. And he was not about to allow his father to take her captive. Whatever the king intended to do, he wanted to use her for some larger purpose.

Unsheathing his dagger, the prince pointed it at the king with a trembling grip. The king shook his head. "If I don't cull their numbers, there will be no castle left for you to rule."

"There has to be another way!"

The king had lost his patience. He started toward Ettrian and the female he guarded. "You're not going to hurt me. I know you too well."

His father was right. Gods be damned, he was right. Ettrian couldn't kill him, but he wouldn't allow any more harm to come to the elf. With a split second to choose, the prince held the blade to her throat. Closing his eyes, he screamed as he drew it across her neck.

Things were never the same after that.

His father largely avoided him, which was fine by Ettrian. Whatever illusions he had about the king were gone. With new eyes, the prince became aware of the elves that joined his father's private councils.

"Rumor has it, there's talks of a trade fair," Aracaryn said as she joined his table. They both watched as cloaked elves garbed in greens and browns entered the king's room. Hunters or possibly trackers. They still couldn't find the settlement.

He shook his head. Something about what happened in the forest had made him mute. Unable to speak of the horrors the king had planned. He was frightened and without proof. A young prince without an ally. Who would believe him anyway?

"What is it, my prince?" Aracaryn asked, drawing his face toward her. "You barely eat, and you're beyond weary. Ever since the outing with the king—"

Food turned to soot in his mouth, and his nights were plagued with nightmares. He barely knew Aracaryn, but by all appearances, she worshiped his father. Ettrian often wondered if she was the king's mistress. Was she sent to prod him, to see what he'd say about the king, or was she just as in the dark as everyone else?

"It's not a trade fair," Ettrian said. "Nor an outpost. Nothing so prosperous."

The princess gave him a hard look. As if for a small instant, she too suspected something evil afoot. "The library is full of solace," she said. "Perhaps you might find something there to ease your mind."

Peace of mind would not come from a book. The only way he could sleep again was if he found a way to stop his father's plans. He was going to say as much, but Aracaryn was already gone.

If he could discover why magic was failing, perhaps the king would see reason. There had to be a way to show his father that the Runda Nor had nothing to do with Cardhon Nimloth. They didn't even worship the same god, from his understanding. How could they take power from Isilynor if they didn't even acknowledge her? He couldn't go into the room without reasons of his own other than morality. The princess's idea wasn't without merit.

For days, Ettrian dwelled in the library. Pouring over stories of gods and myths and the history of the castle itself. No doubt his father had searched with the same questions and found different answers. It wasn't until much later that he discovered the nature of the books. How could he have known the book's answers changed based on the reader?

Meanwhile, everyone doted on the infant squalling in the gardens. Oblivious to anything other than the pure innocence of Leaf's raspy cry. Her parents died bringing her into the world. As an orphan, she was everyone's and yet no one's. There was no shortage of arms to hold her, but only the noble families had the privilege of caring for her through the nights.

The cries were growing louder. Ettrian swore the baby was somehow migrating closer. It was becoming difficult to read.

"Can you take her?" A female said, standing in the doorway of the library. "She's been crying all morning."

He had barely set the book aside before the bundle was thrust into his arms. Ettrian held the little thing, squalling and angry. There were tears in her eyes. "Are you in pain, little one?"

The prince stood and bounced her around the library until the baby stopped crying. He suspected she disliked how loud it was in the gardens and all the times she had been handed from one person to the next. Resting against his chest, the baby slept while he continued his research.

Closing his aching eyes for just a moment, Ettrian woke to find a female attendant staring at him with smiling eyes.

"Am I relieved of duty?" he asked.

The room had brightened in the blink of an eye. It was midday. The most sleep he had in weeks. All because of the fussy little bundle sleeping on his chest. The female nodded and scooped the baby up to let him work unhindered.

Just when he opened up his book, the library shuttered, startling the prince so badly he knocked over a nearby stack of books. Thousands of whispers all cried out at once, so panicked and reaching for him all at once. The candles went out, and it felt as if daylight itself went dim.

No! He's found him. He's found them, and he will kill them all...

He bowed his head. Ettrian had run out of time.

Holding the book still clutched in his hand, words uncurled and took form. He read the contents and understood what needed to be done.

So sick with fear and grief, the prince paced the castle. He needed a place to think in silence. The northeast tower was always quieter than the rest, but that night, there were clicks and clacks echoing throughout the section. It was a communication of some kind. A distinct pattern was being followed, but he couldn't decipher it.

The hairs on his nape stood on end. So uncomfortable by the tension in the tower, Ettrian slowly backed out and sought refuge in the northwest tower. He had to come up with a plan to do the unthinkable, and it was hard to concentrate with all the clicking.

He didn't so much as step foot into the tower, and he was being bombarded by voices. Shrill and panicked, they manifested so intensely that his own thoughts were drowned out. The sheer thrumming buzz was unlike anything he'd ever experienced before.

Holding his hands against his ears, Ettrian winced as he was backed into a corner. The spirits were frantic. The dead clawed at the living to protect the future.

An unfortunate elf happened into the hallway at the same time. He was heading toward the tower, but something made him stop and bolt in the opposite direction. For the first time, Ettrian had confirmation that the voices did not solely exist in his head. They were so loud that any High Elf could sense something was amiss.

Watching the elf run in a blind panic to the thing he was subjected to his entire life, Ettrian laughed with relief. On one hand, it felt good to know that the voices were real and clearly spoke the truth. The king was plotting against the Runda Nor with some type of poison. Yet, knowing it to be true meant that Ettrian could not back out. Thousands of lives depended on him to stop that scheme before it was set in motion.

The southwestern tower was silent compared to the others, which was surprising as it usually required the last word. As the tower Aracaryn spent the most time in, he always assumed the spirits were mimicking her. Grateful for the silence, Ettrian still sensed a presence all around him. It bore down on him like a hovering mother guiding their child to the next tower.

He's asleep...

It was late in the night when he went to the king's tower. Dread turned his insides hard and heavy. He couldn't turn back. Ettrian tried fortifying himself with the images of what transpired during the hunt. The terror in the elf's eyes at the sight of him. His father's revelation and that crossbow that killed who knew how many.

Memories of that horrid day got him through the door. Ettrian sneered as the smell of wine overpowered him. On the table were dozens of bottles, and most were empty. The king had been drinking heavily as of late. At this, Ettrian's resolve wavered.

His father was drinking himself to death over his plan. The king didn't enjoy the prospect but felt he had no choice. Beneath his confidant façade, there was doubt. If Ettrian could just reach him and coax him to reason...

On the vanity sat a large tumbler full of clear liquid. Ettrian approached and read the letter beside it with trembling hands. The scouts had found the Runda Nor settlement. While they couldn't determine the numbers, they did manage to find a well.

The plan was to pour the contents of the tumbler into the well water before sunrise.

Ettrian looked out the open balcony. It was a few hours until dawn. There was no time to convince his father otherwise. He could dump out the poison, but the king would make sure the prince couldn't intervene a second time.

Drawing back the curtains, Ettrian stared at his sleeping father. Before he could draw on doubt or fully feel the weakness in his hands and arm. He pulled out the same hunting dagger and plunged it into his father's chest with both hands.

Ettrian fell to his knees then. He must have cried out. A commotion in the gardens was followed by the movement of lights. They were coming to see what had happened, what he had done. The prince didn't care. All he could think about was how easy it was to plunge the blade into the heart of his father and king. The wet gurgle as the body jolted and blood came trickling from his mouth.

An emptiness carved its way into Ettrian's heart after that. Everything was a blur. The guards that threatened him with shaking swords and the expression on Aracaryn's face when she held the scout's letter in her hand.

Balqen's head bowed as his lips moved in confession, but Ettrian didn't hear them. A loud slap broke the numbness for a moment. Aracaryn had struck Balqen. The guards were in total disarray, not knowing who to take away or what to do.

It never occurred to him, the prince, that he would be expected to lead in that dark hour, but the books had shown him the path forward.

"I demand a trial by my peers. Assemble the youngest, the oldest, the highest born and the lowest of our people, and make a demand of me. If I don't fulfill it, I will abdicate."

Chapter 27

Shock wasn't the word to describe the emotions rolling through Radelia. Ettrian's story was one of pain that entwined with her own. He had been the one to end her mother's life. There was no doubt of that in her mind, and she understood then why he went to great lengths to hide it.

"When did you realize she was my mother?"

Burying his face in his hands, Ettrian managed to look her in the eyes. "I was never certain. I just feared it to be true."

"And Balqen…" She couldn't finish the sentence without screaming.

Ettrian nodded. "He was one of the conspirators. The loss of his children gave him an appetite for revenge, but he wasn't aware of the full scope of my father's plans. He thought they were merely targeting the military faction."

That was utter bullshit if she'd ever heard it. Balqen must have known there was no way to pick and choose who drank the poison and just allowed himself to believe whatever the king said. "And he has the audacity to judge your reign?"

"He has vowed to never be fooled by a monarch again."

She had been pressing her thumbnail into her index finger so hard that she had punctured it, and the air stung the cut. Her stomach was thoroughly curdled, but her chest was so tight that Radelia couldn't have puked even if she tried.

"I need to be alone," she said, pulling away from the table. Fearing that another glance at him would stop her flight, Radelia didn't look back.

Ettrian made no attempt to stop her. He asked for no reassurance nor promises. Whatever feelings she had for him had changed, but in what way? Radelia didn't blame him for what he did. If she were put in that horrid scenario, she would have done the same. But she felt icky inside.

The gardens no longer appeared beautiful. Not even the crown on Isilynor's head held the same luster as it once had. Rubbing her arms, she felt a familiar biting chill. Staring up at the sky, Radelia saw white flakes floating in the night sky. The barrier melted the snow, and it came through as rain, soaking her hair and face.

"Radelia," a voice called through the rain. It was Miabelle, coming in a blur of gold and white. "Are you okay?"

She shook her head. "He told me." Her teeth were chattering so hard that she couldn't manage to say anything else.

Her friend nodded and wrapped an arm around her. "Let's get you inside."

They made it as far as the great hall before Radelia stopped. Betrayal seeped into her bones along with the wet. "Your grandfather tried to kill us."

"He what?"

She didn't know. Balqen kept the truth from his family and opted to paint Ettrian as something evil. "He was going to take his revenge by annihilating my entire clan!"

"Radelia, you're not making any sense. Let's go to your room and change your clothes."

She jerked away, not wanting to be touched by Miabelle. It wasn't her fault. Radelia knew it in her heart, but the rage within her couldn't be denied. If Ettrian didn't stop them, an entire clan would be gone, and they'd all be totally unaffected. They were all complicit in the former king's plot.

"We would have been blown out like a candle, and you wouldn't even have noticed."

"How can I notice things I can't see?"

"You choose not to see!" Radelia roared.

Miabelle swallowed and stepped back as if she expected Radelia to attack her. Her people cultivated ignorance while maintaining complete innocence. Once again, the Runda Nor beast was lashing out at the unassuming High Elf for no apparent reason.

She couldn't handle it anymore. Radelia turned and fled down the nearest corridor, not knowing where it led. The hallways were lit with candles, and the ceilings were lower. There were so many doors, but half were open, revealing vacant rooms.

There were footsteps coming her way. Rather than find herself face to face with another High Elf, Radelia stepped into an empty room and carefully shut the door behind her. It was unadorned with white linen sheets. Only a narrow little window gave any natural light, but there was a lit candle inside as if they expected someone to return at any moment.

Unlike her own extravagant room, this one didn't have its own private latrine and barely had enough space for the second small bed in the corner.

She sat on the edge of the bed and noted the carvings along the wooden frame. Tracing them with her finger. The triangles and curved bells were symbols of Elpharae. She was in a room that once belonged to a Runda Nor elf before they left the castle.

Her people were relegated to the bottom of the castle. She already knew this to be true, but seeing the room only rubbed salt in her wounds. Her father was right. If her people returned, crawling and begging, their pride would be forgotten. Their traditions and heritage would be suppressed.

What was the point of returning magic to people who had learned nothing from its departure?

As queen, she could ensure that didn't happen to some extent. There was also the matter of sheer survival. Her people needed help. They needed warmth and safety from the elements. Food and drink enough to fill their bellies regardless of the season.

Radelia couldn't make her people do what she thought to be right, but she could at least provide them the option. She shook her head, wincing at the recollection of his story. He had no better option, but still...he killed her mother and left the body to rot.

He claimed he cared for her people. Did he truly, or was he motivated to save his own hide? If Balqen could aid in the genocide of his own people, Ettrian could be capable of anything. The truth was that she had no proof that the king wanted to help her people, only that he wanted to save the castle.

She growled and scratched at a scab on her arm. Okay, Elpharae, I could really use a sign right about now.

Radelia was never great at praying. Katar would know what to do, and Kieran would tell her exactly what he thought of the king. Just thinking about them eased some of her tensions and made her smile. She wasn't alone in the forest, and it was high time she acted as a part of a team.

Leaving the little room, an unexpected noise halted her every movement. Was that a baby crying? The High Elves didn't have children. She followed the sound until Radelia stepped into what must have been the kitchens and was greeted by a surge of warmth from multiple ovens.

The kitchen was an expansive room that tunneled into several others. There were long, massive worktables piled high with food amid various stages of preparation. Herbs hung in thick bundles from the ceiling. Garlic and onion braided in wreaths mounted on the walls. Pots and pans befitting giants sat on top of metal plates as their contents bubbled over the flames.

It was beyond impressive. Her kitchenette back home was little more than a clay burner lit with a candle. To feed what was once an entire city, it made sense, but Radelia had just never thought about the sheer size required to feed so many. The other rooms were larders, she presumed.

The babe had since stopped crying, and Radelia was beginning to wonder if she was just imagining things when a goat trotted out. It was so random she burst into giggles. "What are you doing here, little one?"

Staring at her with its rectangular pupils, the goat stuck out its tongue and approached her for a pat. Kneeling down, Radelia gave its wide belly a pat. The High Elves seldom ate meat, but perhaps they used goat's milk and kept the animal around for that reason. She frowned at her own logic. It was still too much effort for the High

Elves for a single ingredient. One goat couldn't feed nearly a thousand elves.

An elf wearing an apron came out in a hurry, she stopped short at the sight of Radelia. "What are you doing here?"

She spoke as if Radelia didn't belong in the kitchens. "I heard a baby crying."

The elf's jaw formed a hard line. "We weren't supposed to tell you, but with all the troubles going on, it's no wonder you're here."

"You mean the castle?" Radelia stood. Her curiosity was piqued by the straightforward way the elf spoke.

"What else? The king didn't want you to know about the babes. He feared you'd get the wrong idea."

"So you have children after all." Lie after lie. She couldn't believe it.

"Not our babes. Yours."

The kitchen worker led her into a makeshift nursery. There her eyes fell on nine cribs. Seven babies in total, but it seemed they were expecting more. All round-eared and human in appearance. "The humans couldn't get a wet nurse and didn't know what to do. They were going to send them back to your people when the king intervened."

All along, the babes had been right under her feet.

"You're expecting more?"

"Two more in the next week or so and a dozen come spring. The king said that they're to be treated like elves even if they don't look like us. I'll need a few more goats come spring."

All this time, he'd kept them safe and cared for but said nothing to her. "Why didn't he tell me?"

"I can't speak for him, but I'd wager he didn't want you to think they were prisoners like your friends. Besides, we love babies. It's near impossible to get them all in their cradles. Lord Balqen tries to make off with one every chance he gets."

Nothing dampened her mood faster than the mention of that name. Fucking traitor. But still, something eased in her heart. All along, Ettrian was seeing to the children of the Runda Nor without thanks or accolades. He was preparing to take them all should it be necessary.

They left the nursery and returned to the main kitchen to find they were not alone. Several elves were taking the food away. "It's not dinner service yet?"

The kitchen worker gave her a wry grin. "Come and see."

Following the trail of elves out a back door, she waded through the snow already ankle-deep. The High Elves were placing food and medicine into Runda Nor baskets on the back of the old human merchant's cart. His horse was facing west. "You're going to my people," she said, stunned by the realization.

"Hello, Princess of the forest."

"How long have you been transporting these goods to them?"

"Oh, ever since you arrived, I should think," he said. "They think my village is sharing goods for the winter. Best they not know it comes from the High Elf king."

She doubted they believed such a story, but rather than waste perfectly good food, her people accepted it. "Does the emperor know?"

The old man shrugged his shoulders.

Radelia stepped back, allowing them to finish their task. Overwhelmed by the knowledge that her people's struggle would be eased, she blinked back the tears. All along, Ettrian had been doing this and chose not to tell her. He told her only the worst of himself and hid his generosity, not wanting it to be a part of some campaign to woo her.

"What's your name?" she asked the kitchen worker.

"It's Mavis," she said. There was no bow or formality to her like the elves who dined in the great hall. Radelia rather liked her.

"Well, Mavis, it seems I've spent too much time around the nobility."

The elf cringed and nodded. "That will wear on anyone. Any time you've had enough of them, come visit the rest of us. The king prefers us too, but don't tell the snobs that."

Radelia's smile was whole-hearted. Not all High Elves were blind to the struggles of others. They varied in what they knew and thought, just like the Runda Nor. She had been so focused on the landscape of their troubles, she hadn't considered the trees or the trail.

So what if magic couldn't be saved. The babes were healthy, and her people would have food despite the snow. Fewer would need to forage in the cold, and should their elderly get sick, the healers would have fever and pain reducers on hand.

Whether she realized it or not, she and Ettrian's fate were bound the day he encountered her mother. She would have demanded death rather than fall into the former king's designs. The deceased empress would have approved of Ettrian's subtle undermining of the cold war between their clans as well.

Radelia bowed to Mavis, who only laughed at the formality before racing to Katar and Kieran's room. Only Kieran had left, and she had totally forgotten. He was bringing his militia to Cardhon Nimloth. Those who would come, at least.

"Katar," she said, "You won't believe it!"

The healer tore her gaze from the window. She had a sad expression on her face but was trying to hide it. "What's wrong?"

She shook her head. "Nothing now. I was just beginning to feel lonely."

Katar needed to get out of that room. She wasn't a prisoner anymore, and it was time she understood that. Radelia took her friend's hand and led her out. "Come on. Let us walk the gardens," she said with her best High Elf impression.

The healer laughed and followed along. "Yes, let us stroll the gardens and watch the peasants work."

Radelia told her everything as they went. She had finished by the time they reached the summer garden, though Katar didn't appear surprised in the least. It always felt like she was the last to know. Like a little sister who was only privy to third-hand news when her older siblings were already wise to the world.

"It seems the king has kept you too occupied to notice."

Her face got all hot from the insinuation. Memories of the starless night came unbidden, and Radelia no longer wanted to fight it. "What do you think I should do?" she asked.

"Well, before I answer that, I need to ask your opinion on something."

She helped herself to the raspberries ripe on the vine. "You want my opinion?"

Katar shrugged and looked away. Radelia had never seen the healer appear so uncertain. "It's not your opinion so much as your blessing. If you're not comfortable with it, just say the word, and I—" She stopped short when Radelia cupped a hand over her mouth to keep from laughing.

Were the rivers running backward? She started laughing and couldn't stop. It was just too good. "Never in a thousand years could I imagine this!"

Katar growled and began shoveling raspberries into her mouth. "We were stuck in the same room for months. I got desperate."

"You're not locked away now, and yet you're asking for my blessing."

"It was actually something you said to him that softened his stubbornness. Evidently, he had no idea that all healers cheat the rite of passage."

The rite of passage was the final test for any healer to begin work. They locked themselves in Elpharae's hut for three days and three nights with no food or water. If they emerged before that time was up, they weren't ready.

"They shouldn't have had Kieran standing guard in the first place."

"When he caught me with the stash of food, he assumed that I was the only one who cheated."

Radelia rolled her eyes. The healers had that stash under the floorboards, and everyone knew it except Kieran. He thought her a cheating scoundrel up until Radelia told him otherwise. "So, the two of you are a couple then?"

"Only if you're okay with that," Katar said. "I know he hurt you."

He did, but she couldn't begrudge them for finding happiness. She'd always wanted them to reconcile; it was just surprising that they really went for it. "I don't feel that way for him anymore. I just wish I knew why he left the way he did."

Katar's gaze fell to the raspberries in her palm. "He should be the one to tell you, but he never will. He's too ashamed and angry over it."

"Then you need to tell me." Radelia couldn't deny she was a little miffed that Kieran revealed so much to Katar and not her, but more than anything, she just wanted to know.

"You know he uses henna to color his hair."

"Yeah?" That wasn't the direction she expected. What did his hair have to do with anything?

Katar dropped the raspberries and ground them into the lawn. "You share the same sire. When your father became aware of your relationship, he revealed the truth to Kieran. The emperor forbade him from telling you. Rather than lie to you, he left."

It was a sucker punch to the face. She knew her parents had struggled in their marriage, but she never imagined he was unfaithful. Kieran was her half-brother. The nausea was overwhelming. How did she not see it sooner? The hair and the eyes. Her father doted on Kieran, but she just didn't think...

"You should also know that I was trained to be a spy, employed by your father. The village gold was used in my training."

Radelia shook her head. She had enough revelations for one day. "I know," she said. "At least I had my suspicions. I remember the man that stayed in our village for a time. Father said you were getting more extensive training but left it at that."

The truth was that she didn't want to know. Radelia wanted a happy childhood, so she ignored her parents' stony silence and the quiet arguments from the other room. She ignored the dealings her father made when he thought she wasn't looking. By only seeing the good in her people, she shelved the bad on the High Elves. It was easier to blame those she didn't know for their troubles.

She had nearly forgotten it. Had Radelia not seen the babes and the food delivery, she might have rushed back home to pretend all was as it should be. In a way, she was no different than the High Elves who ignored their crumbling castle. Optimism had a funny way of turning into delusion.

"There's no bath strong enough to wash that off, but you have my unconditional blessing."

"Are you sure?" Katar's beautiful golden eyes were wide and watery.

"Yes!" Radelia said without doubt. She wished her friend all the happiness in the world and wanted nothing less for Kieran. Instead of saying as much, she responded with, "He's your problem now."

But the healer knew what she meant. Katar hugged her, and Radelia returned the embrace with all her might. Opening her eyes, the king's tower stood before her. A dark figure lurked in the doorway of the balcony, not daring to look directly over the edge.

Her sad and lonely king must have assumed the worst. Before she could go to him, unfamiliar sounds came from the gates. The High Elves were sounding an alarm.

Chapter Twenty-Eight

Chapter 28

Ettrian watched her tear from the room and flee from his sight, but he didn't spiral into darkness. Radelia had changed him forever in that regard.

It wasn't that he enjoyed the sight or that he was somehow pleased by the pain he caused. He was just relieved that she knew the full truth. The worry that he hurt her too profoundly waned as he watched her and Katar in the gardens. She could heal now that she understood how her mother died. More than ever, he was grateful for the day he first found the scouts and that Katar remained by Radelia's side.

Yes, he lost her, but at least she would be okay.

His attempts to manipulate her into marriage failed, but he was glad for it. If she returned to him, it would be because she wanted to, and it would be entirely on her terms.

Whatever conversation she and Katar were having below, it was a good one until they were interrupted by the sound of horns. Kieran had returned earlier than they anticipated. He watched as the messenger came running along the wall.

Panting and wheezing, the messenger stopped short of his doorway and said, "The Runda Nor have arrived."

"How many came?"

The messenger shook his head. "You have to see it for yourself."

He stood on the wall of the gate and looked out at the sea of people below. There were at least eight hundred, if not more. In one moment, the population of Cardhon Nimloth doubled. He had warned Mavis himself that they were to expect a sudden demand for more food.

The head of the kitchens was a no-nonsense High Elf who didn't have time for anyone—even the king. "Then they better volunteer some elves to cook, clean, and serve too. I don't have time for all your problems."

It was a good idea. If the Runda Nor had those within their group who would help make the food and serve it, the rest could be assured that the food wasn't tampered with. Not only that, but as he'd learned from the scouts, not everyone one in the clan shared Radelia's enthusiasm for different foods. He could feed her pond slime served on a piece of bark, and she'd still probably eat it.

"What are you smiling about?" Mavis said, armed with a long spoon. "All the new work you've given me?"

Between being chased out of his own kitchens and the loyalty of the Runda Nor clan, Ettrian's ego was feeling as bruised as the back of his legs from where Mavis had swatted him. Kieran said he would only take those who volunteered, and yet so many followed him. If he'd asked the High Elves to follow him to guard the wayward clan, less than five would follow.

Leaf was beside him, staring at the mass of elves below. She wore a hardened leather vest, and several swords and daggers were on her belt.

As if she were preparing for an invasion, not allies. "I'm beginning to see why the emperor spied on his own."

"Indeed," Ettrian agreed. "Having a military faction running separately from the emperor...it's only natural he expected dissent."

Balqen and Aracaryn joined them a short while later. The troops were already breaking off into groups and setting up camps along the walls.

"The way they just knew where to go," Balqen said. "So seamless and well-coordinated. I didn't expect that from a clan with little to no organization."

"See the colors on their vests?" Aracaryn pointed to an obscure dot of color blotted on each of their vests. "They're broken up by color and are told which camp is theirs in advance. The poll inside the tent will have a corresponding color in case they forget."

Ettrian and the two vassals looked at Aracaryn. She shrugged and said, "He studied in the Ruby Isles, remember?"

Radelia was already outside the gates with Kieran. The king noted the way the militia stopped setting up to stare at her. As if reading his mind, Leaf said, "It's like they assumed she was dead."

It was high time they learned just what the emperor told his people while Kieran was away. "Let's go out and greet them."

"Perhaps you should stay behind," Balqen said. "I don't know that it's safe—"

Ettrian waved off the concern. "I want to put a face to the name. To be seen with Kieran and Radelia so they know I am working with them and not commanding them."

He put on a determined face and marched with purpose, but the king's stomach flip-flopped when the Runda Nor all stared at him with their large eyes. Accompanied by Leaf, the other two stayed on the wall to watch in case things went wrong.

Even his brave little protector hesitated and inched closer to his side.

"I'm looking for General Kieran," he said to the nearest elf.

They pointed in the direction he already knew Kieran went, but Ettrian felt he had to ask for some reason. As if he'd stumbled into Runda Nor territory and needed to state his intentions.

He found the general and Radelia speaking with a small group. Radelia caught sight of him straight away and smiled as though she were happy to see him. Her merriment was unlikely on his account, though. She was thrilled to be reunited with her people. His chest spasmed as the king recalled their last conversation.

"Look at how many came!"

He joined their sides. There were a few curious stares from the elves he did not know, but their composure was steelier than the others. Kieran barely acknowledged him, but he suspected that was by design. "King Ettrian, these are my lieutenants."

"Thank you all for coming."

"We were just discussing the set up," the general said. "Everyone is preparing to camp for the night. Come tomorrow, we will begin patrol."

Ettrian nodded. The bruise on the back of his thigh throbbed as if reminding him of what Mavis said. "The head of the kitchens requests elves from your clan to help prepare and serve the food."

At this, he had the lieutenants attention. Kieran must have forgone telling his troops that they were to receive hot meals without a struggle. Clever to leave the good news for the king to tell. "I'll see to it," Kieran said. "One from each camp should be sufficient."

"I want to thank all of you for coming to our aid," Ettrian said with a bow of his head.

"We're here to protect Radelia and the castle," a lieutenant corrected.

There was tension in the moments that followed. He had to choose his words carefully. "I realize that," he said as gently as he could manage. "But both are very dear to me. You didn't have to come, and yet you did. I thank you for that."

The lieutenants eased in their hardened leathers, and the one that spoke went as far as to nod in understanding.

"Walk with me," Kieran said to him.

Leaf tried to follow, but he stopped her. "Stay with Radelia."

She openly pouted but did as he instructed. Likely being surrounded by unfamiliar faces kept Leaf's tongue in check. He cast a longing glance at Radelia before following. She gave him a nod, but her face was unreadable. Was she sad or hopeful? Perhaps a little of both.

They walked a few yards away from the others before saying, "Despite the emperor's best efforts, the militia remained intact."

"I would have thought he'd try to assume command rather than dismantle it."

Kieran shook his head. "No, it seems he made new allies. Bellas claimed he needed the barracks for an army of his own making and evicted us. When the blacksmiths were occupied with our contracts, he resorted to bribing them for priority."

"His own army?" Ettrian didn't like the sound of that.

"There was no sign of said army, but according to my people, the emperor has been issuing divine orders left and right. In Katar's absence, he sends his correspondence by some other means. The clan was also told that Radelia had been captured and killed by High Elves."

He couldn't understand the motives. Why lie to his people and try to destabilize the systems in place? Ettrian shook his head. "I can only imagine how shocked they were to learn otherwise."

Kieran turned to face him then. "Only the ones who agreed to come here know the truth. Everyone else in the Runda Nor thinks she's dead."

Being scapegoated wasn't Ettrian's idea of a good time. "Why not tell them?"

"Nothing I say will dissuade those who insist on remaining," the general explained. "They stay because they want to believe the emperor. To them, he's an example of Runda Nor pride and what it truly means to be an elf. Alive or not, Radelia wanted change just as I do. She might as well be dead as far as they're concerned."

There he was, a king, begging those around him to be more critical and aware of the dangers they faced while those who professed themselves free followed blindly. It was beyond ironic.

"How many of your militia came?" Ettrian asked.

"Half the militia came; half are civilians."

He looked around the grounds, trying to tell them apart. So many were not fighters, and with the talk of some secret army, Ettrian didn't like the idea of leaving so many exposed to danger. "Those who are not skilled in battle have no business on the front lines."

"I couldn't agree more," the general said, crossing his arms. "But I couldn't leave them behind."

"No, no, of course not. If they wish to remain in the castle, they're welcome to it."

Kieran shook his head. "I doubt they will do that any time soon."

He understood. It would take time, and it explained why so many stared at Radelia the way they did. They were told she was dead, and it was only when they came to Cardhon Nimloth did they learn otherwise. As frustrating as it was to be blamed for a murder he didn't commit, perhaps it was better to hold that information for the time being.

"I need to meet with my advisors," Ettrian said, glancing up at the wall. "

The moment he parted from the general, Leaf was by his side. She kept quiet until they were back inside the walls of the castle before saying, "They really don't like us."

"They don't have to like us. We have a common cause."

She frowned. No doubt Leaf shared a similar concern. What if not all of them had that common cause? There were nearly a thousand elves outside the walls, and it wasn't possible for Kieran to vet every single one of them. The rest of his vassals were coming down the stairs as he and Leaf reached the gardens.

"We will see to it that only Runda Nor permitted in the castle are the ones Kieran vets personally," he instructed his vassals. "If possible, we'll ask Katar to monitor them as well."

"That is most wise," Aracaryn said.

"Half of them are not militia—they just wanted to leave the forest. Any of them who wish to reside in the castle must speak with Kieran, Radelia, and Katar."

"And just how many of those elves want inside?" Omaro said, airing a note of skepticism he had only ever heard when someone debated giving alms to the poor.

"None," the king said. "But perhaps that will change. It is awfully cold out there."

"We might build homes for them outside the castle," Omaro suggested.

Ettrian whirled around to face the healer. "These people have just as much right to be here as we do. Their ancestors and their god helped forge Cardhon Nimloth."

Omaro shrunk under Ettrian's shadow until he was practically cowering. The king disliked using his size for intimidation, but sometimes it proved useful. There was too much to be seen to, and Ettrian did not wish to overlook it due to dissent among his own ranks.

"What will they do once they're inside?" Omaro asked.

"It's not as if they're lepers," Aracaryn said. "These are elves of great skill. They must be to survive in the forest."

Omaro stroked his chin and relented. "Do you think they have healers?"

"They do," Ettrian said. "Radelia said they have a whole community of them."

His eyes met with Balqen's. Ostracized by the High Elf healers, perhaps Omaro would find kinship in ways he didn't anticipate. With magic waning, they couldn't use the same techniques as they once did. The Runda Nor had more experience with wounds and illness. Both were things the High Elves would endure should the castle falter entirely.

The gods did not design elves to adapt, but if the Runda Nor could do it, so could the High Elves and the Dark Elves. If they didn't, they would meet the same fate as the Ice Elves.

CHAPTER TWENTY-NINE

Chapter 29

Radelia shifted her weight from one foot to another and re-minded herself yet again to stop gnawing on her lower lip, but everything about the situation was just awkward. And cold. She hadn't been outside the barrier in some time, and the winter air was a shock to her system. It was all she could do to keep her teeth from chattering as she accompanied her ex-lover and half-brother around the encampments while her people acted like she had risen from the dead.

Was this how Kieran felt whenever she was around? No wonder he was so stiff and uncomfortable toward her. Just looking at him made her feel like she was naked and covered in mud. No one knew other than the three of them. Her father too, she supposed, but Radelia was hyper-aware of her proximity to him and every gesture or word spoken between them. It was unbearable.

She gasped with relief when Ettrian and Leaf joined them and filled up the middling silence that threatened to give way to a conversation she and the general needed to have at a different time.

"I killed your mother" weirdness walked side by side with, "I hate your guts for no reason," yet it was still better than "So you're my brother…"

Why couldn't life just be normal?

Ettrian and Kieran went off on their own, leaving her with Leaf. The vassal glared at her. Folding her arms over her leathers, Leaf turned her back and did her best to ignore Radelia. That was fine by her. As if the lieutenants sensed the tension, they jumped at the nearest excuse and got away.

"He's risking everything for this. You know that, don't you?" Leaf said.

Radelia scowled at the back of Leaf's head. She had lost her father and ripped her clan apart to make things right. Her clan was losing the very thing that made them who they were. Ettrian wasn't the only one who stood to lose if the castle came under attack.

Her teeth couldn't chatter from the cold when her jaw was clenched. A lot of words came to mind, and not the flowery, High Elf kind. Instead of blurting them out, Radelia reeled it in. She wasn't about to be baited by Leaf.

"Correct me if I'm wrong," Radelia said. "But if Ettrian were to marry, the queen would be his council. Why would he need you?"

The expression of utter rage as the vassal looked over her shoulder was worth it. "He will require the vassals until he makes good on his promise."

"But there are flowers—"

"A few flowers isn't enough. The castle is still decaying."

"You expect one king to undo a century of damage overnight? Defining and redefining a promise to suit the needs of the now."

It was her best High Elf impression, and it was working. By insinuating the vassals had twisted their purpose for a firmer grip on power, Radelia had accused Leaf of an ulterior motive without quite coming out and saying it.

Leaf's face turned red and her lips trembled with anger. "I would never do that to him. I—"

The vassal stopped short, and Radelia nodded. She had always wondered if that was the case. Leaf was the closest to Ettrian's age and the famed child of magic. Raised to be the king's personal guard and likely brought up with the impression that she would one day marry him. She loved him, and Radelia couldn't blame her.

Before the conversation could get out of hand, a swarm of Runda Nor elves came their way. Radelia was busy talking to Jonik and a few others when Ettrian walked past her, taking Leaf with him. That was fine. As far as Radelia was concerned, there was nothing more to say.

"The emperor is telling everyone you're dead." Jonik's words were a slap, jarring her attention away from Leaf or Ettrian.

She shook her head, muted from shock. "He knew I was here. He even sent a letter to tell me I was banished."

"When Larriel came home, she told us where you went," Jonik explained. "We knew you were trying to save the others, but when the second scout came home, your father said you were dead. She tried to say otherwise, but he commanded her silence."

"I see." Her clan knew something was amiss right from the start. The emperor was quickly losing control of the Runda Nor and was using divine orders to keep a grip on his people. That didn't work well on a clan dedicated to free thinking.

It explained why so many came. They all knew they were being lied to, but only those who wanted to believe the lie stayed.

That gave Radelia a brilliant idea. "Jonik, the parents who had to give up their children, are they here as well?"

He nodded. "They were the first to pack up."

She didn't blame them. "Find them and bring them to the front gate; I have something to show them."

Of course, it wasn't as easy as all that.

Radelia found that in order to reunite the children with their parents, she first needed the vassals to approve. She needed Katar and Kieran to approve and vet them. Meanwhile, Jonik struggled to find them in the dozens of tents that circled the massive castle.

Between High Elf bureaucracy and the chaos of the small village assembling outside the wall, Radelia had to accept that it wasn't going to happen for another few days. Seething with built-up frustration and failure, Radelia nearly snapped when someone placed a hand on her shoulder.

"Oh," Ettrian's baritone voice sounded. "I didn't mean to startle you."

"I'm not startled," she said, kicking an apple that had fallen from the orchard. "I'm pissed off."

"Can I help with anything?"

She looked up at him and recalled that the king had been the one to keep the children safe in the first place. He had also been sending a steady supply of food to her clan in secret. Her shoulders relaxed as the tension in her chest uncoiled.

"When were you going to tell me about the babies and the food?"

"I knew I was forgetting something," he said with a grimace. His hand raked through his long hair. "So much has been going on, and things between us were evolving so quickly—"

Translation: he was too busy trying to get laid.

She grinned as his words stalled until he altogether gave up with a sigh. "That came out wrong."

He was so adorable when he was embarrassed. Radelia shook her head and stifled a laugh. "Yeah, but I know what you mean. The fate of elves and all that."

He gave a single nod as she gently let him off the hook.

"Everything is going to plan so far," Ettrian said. "Kieran's here with many of your people. Contact between the clans has been limited but respectful. There have been no signs of mercenaries. I doubt they will risk another attack."

They still didn't know who sent them, but given what they had learned when Kieran returned, there was only one obvious person. She snapped her eyes shut and forced a breath through her tightened ribs. It couldn't be him. "I just can't believe my father would try to have me killed."

"If it's any consolation, I don't think he issued the order either."

Ettrian's words were a lifeline in the storm. Before she could think better of it, Radelia wrapped her arms around his waist and rested her head on his chest. "He wasn't perfect, I know, but he wouldn't go this far."

"He has dedicated his life to maintaining the Runda Nor way. To hire mercenaries and reveal so much to outside forces... It's never been done. It took years for my father's scouts to find your village, and even then, they only found the well."

"Who else would gain by targeting me specifically? Who else would know my whereabouts in such detail?"

"Someone who stands to lose much if our clans are united."

Her father's opposition was one of pride, not of gain. He didn't want to bend to High Elf laws or rely on High Elf support due to principle. He believed Cardhon Nimloth belonged to the Runda Nor by right and would rather burn it down than see it in enemy hands. Spending precious resources to have her assassinated wasn't something they could even afford.

"I saw our gold pouch before I left," she said. "There wasn't nearly enough in it to hire an assassin, let alone six of them."

Squeezing Ettrian tighter, for the first time, she realized she was angry that someone wanted her dead. Furious that someone wanted to keep their clans apart. She wanted to succeed, but even more so, she wanted to win. Even if it was out of spite.

"Radelia," Ettrian whispered. "You astound me."

She looked up at his face, lined with troubles and worry. He must have thought she'd never forgive him for the past, but there was nothing to forgive. "You laugh at the wrong times and talk to people who aren't there, but your actions have always been the right ones. I don't hold any of them against you."

Cupping her head in his hands, he leaned down to kiss her. Radelia met him halfway, reaching from the tips of her toes. The hunger of his mouth pressing against hers sparked reminders of the starless night. She couldn't deny it anymore. She wanted him as much as he wanted her.

Breaking from his lips, Radelia had to catch her breath before saying, "Let's really piss our enemies off."

His wide mouth quirked into a smile. "What do you have in mind?"

"I want to marry you," she said, feeling like it should have been obvious. "The sooner, the better."

She felt him stagger as he clutched her for support. "You're certain?"

"And we'll have lots of giant children."

He broke into the happiest laugh and wiped a rogue tear from his eye. "Well, we can certainly try."

"So how does this work?" she asked. "Do we need to sign a paper or do some weird goblet exchange? Yell vows from the tower?"

"Well, for a royal wedding, there needs to be a public ceremony. Nobility requires at least the family to be present."

Something else struck her then. Miabelle's face flashed in her mind. "What happens if a noble marries in secret?"

"Well, I suppose they can marry in secret, but if it's not declared to the family within three years, it's considered annulled."

That was why Miabelle's secret husband was giving her such a hard time! He was pressuring her to declare their marriage, and poor Miabelle was trying to stop him from doing so. "How does one annul such a marriage before it's declared?"

It was like something dawned in Ettrian's face. "They must denounce their spouse publicly."

Radelia had to hurry. There was no telling how much time Miabelle had left before the marriage was set in stone. "I need to see to something," she explained, breaking away. "But go ahead and get the marriage ceremony arranged."

Before he could object, she was already heading to the great hall. He said something about needing her input, but she waved him off. "I don't care. Just do what you think I'd like."

She raced up the stairs and to the room Miabelle had moved into. Not bothering to knock, Radelia burst in to find Miabelle standing with an expression of shock. "Are we under attack?"

"No, silly," Radelia laughed. "I need to tell you something important."

Chapter 30

He sent for his vassals and waited in his room in a state of surrealness. She wanted to marry him. Radelia told him to get the ceremony arranged for as soon as possible. It was an astounding turn of events that left him wondering if it was more of a political gambit than anything. Only, he knew better than to believe Radelia gave a damn about politics.

"You wanted to see us, my king?" Balqen said. Ettrian found that all four vassals were in his room. He didn't hear them knock.

"Radelia wishes to get married."

"Right now?" the annoyance in Aracaryn's voice was palpable.

"My king," Omaro said, looking to the others for backup. "It is not the best time to be making such arrangements. We must see to security and—"

"As soon as possible," Ettrian interrupted. "It doesn't need to be as elaborate as a conventional wedding. In fact, I think Radelia would hate that. Something simple."

"Well, the Runda Nor are here," Balqen offered. "Both clans can bear witness."

"But does she know?" Aracaryn asked.

"Everything."

She nodded, apparently satisfied with the answer. The only one who remained quiet was Leaf, whose skin was a pale shade of green. He knew she wouldn't approve, but he didn't ask her to. Whatever tensions lay between Radelia and Leaf would resolve themselves in their own time. Radelia was to be her queen, after all.

"I think this is delightful," Balqen said. "A Runda Nor queen will make a strong statement to those who've recently joined our ranks."

"They haven't joined our ranks," Leaf said. "They're just here because they followed their general."

"Why are you so opposed?" Aracaryn asked. "They have come to support their princess, and to see her elevated to queen of Cardhon Nimloth would be undeniably important for everyone."

Leaf took a stance that reminded him a bit of a pouting toddler. Folding her arms, she faced away from them and refused to speak. She could be such a child when the mood struck her.

"In any case," Ettrian said. "We both wish to marry as soon as possible. It's imperative that we ferret out the spy within our ranks before any further damage is done."

"How do you propose we do that?" Balqen asked.

"I think the easiest way would be to employ Katar. Don't announce the wedding. Simply bring a few trusted Runda Nor to court and hold the ceremony. After that, we see who runs to send a message first."

Aracaryn was grinning. "Delightful."

The others were not nearly as comfortable with such a sleight of hand. They shifted and shrugged, Leaf gave a quick glance, but none argued. So deep in their own thoughts, when he clapped his hands together, the vassals jumped. "Excellent. Let's get to work. Leaf, if you could summon Katar. I think her input would be invaluable."

The vassal said nothing, but she presumably left to do as he commanded. Her absence also provided the opportunity to gain some insight. "I notice Leaf isn't enthused by the marriage."

Balqen chuckled. "You don't say."

"Yes, but why?"

Aracaryn arched her brows. "Isn't it obvious? She's always held a torch for you."

Ettrian made a face he hadn't intended to make. If he was honest with himself, the king had sensed the infatuation at some level. He always assumed it was her age and that she'd grow out of it. "She's very young."

"Radelia is half her age," Omaro reminded him with a teasing grin.

"Yes, but she is far more mature. Leaf still behaves like a child."

"The princess shares similar burdens as the king," Balqen said. "It's only natural that he be drawn to someone with the same fears and hopes as himself."

"There is another matter," Omaro said. "The Runda Nor are mortal. Radelia will age and die within the century, and you will become a widow in your youth."

A cannonball could have been shot point-blank at his chest, and it would have hurt less. Ettrian steadied himself with the back of Balqen's chair. He wanted to smash Omaro's smirking face in with the candelabra. As if it wasn't something that lingered in the back of his mind from the moment he'd learned Radelia was mortal.

"I am aware of that," he said through gritted teeth. "When the time comes, I will pay the price. For now, allow me to be happy for once in my life."

Omaro was a disgraced and nameless elf, elevated by the painful decision Ettrian committed to. Leaf was given purpose and Balqen redemption. Aracaryn was given the only thing she truly wanted, a word in edgewise. All those things were mere tokens in the face of saving all elfkind from his father's horrid plan. Yet Ettrian bore the brunt of it all. He was the sour bite in the wine. The creeping realization that something ugly was transpiring in their otherwise beautiful, eternal playground. The orphan no one wanted.

He was everything the High Elves loathed, and all because he made the choice no one in that room had the balls or moral compass to do themselves. How dare Omaro or anyone else try to cast a shadow on the only light in Ettrian's life.

The room went silent for a long while.

As if they knew the king's thoughts, his vassals lowered their heads in shame.

"My wife said the same thing," Balqen said at long last. "After Leaf's birth, when the age came on in waves and we realized what had transpired, I told her to leave me. Her family said the same, but she refused. It has a way of changing one's perspectives and priorities."

Ettrian couldn't agree more. Yes, Radelia would grow old and die. A fleeting and beautiful spark that would expire too soon. But he had seen the love between High Elf spouses lost in shorter periods of time. Not because of death but simply the lack of interest. Her mortality meant that he would savor every moment with her until the last.

Katar was in the doorway. She leaned against the frame as though she had been there for hours and was just waiting for someone to notice. Leaf wasn't with her.

His mood lightened the instant he saw her. "Thank you for coming. I'm afraid we need your help."

"I saw Radelia racing in the opposite direction. Is everything well?"

Was it well? It was wonderful. He smiled and said, "She's seeing to a matter that I neglected. Radelia also wishes to marry as soon as possible."

She didn't appear phased by that news, which was reassuring to Ettrian. It wasn't some spur of the moment decision. Radelia must have already discussed it with Katar.

The assassin strolled toward the table and had a look at the blank parchment. "And she left you to figure out all the details."

"Yes!"

He was grateful someone understood. High Elves planned their weddings together over the course of months. Their families waded in to relieve the burdens from the happy couple. Since he and Radelia had neither, Ettrian was at a total loss.

"The Runda Nor don't do weddings," Katar explained. "We don't marry until the end of our lives, and by then, we're too tired and old to invest that kind of energy in a ceremony. Also, you must remember our clan is poor. We don't have the financial capacity to do more than receive a blessing from the emperor."

He lowered his head. The one thing that would mean the most to her was something he couldn't provide. Perhaps he could at least try. "I want an invitation sent to the emperor," he declared. "He probably won't answer, but I must try."

The vassals looked at one another as if they wondered who would oppose first. It was their tradition that the emperor gave his blessing, and he knew it would mean everything to Radelia. His daughter might have been banished, but that did not mean the emperor wasn't allowed to attend his daughter's wedding.

"Well," Balqen said. "If we're certain he's not behind the mercenary attacks—"

"Invite the emperor who has hated us his whole life," Aracaryn interceded. "What could go wrong?"

Katar shrugged. "I doubt he will come, but Kieran is her next of kin as well as emperor in all but name. He will suffice if the emperor ignores the request."

Radelia's next of kin? Katar never let anything slip on accident.

"I wasn't aware they were related," Balqen said. "My family grows larger by the moment!"

"He's not Bellas, not directly, at least," Katar explained. "Radelia's mother was the Bellas heir, and the emperor only inherited her name when they married. The emperor's lineage is linked to Bellas, but his family was an offshoot from the main line."

Ettrian understood. The emperor was a distant relation looped back into the royal line to preserve their nobility. High Elves did much of the same. What Katar was truly saying was that Radelia and Kieran discovered they were too closely related for comfort, which severed their romantic relationship forever. It explained their awkwardness around one another.

"At the very least, we have a leader of the Runda Nor present. What else?" Ettrian asked. "How does the private ceremony work?"

"It's customary to gift a bride with a fur pelt. A strip of linen is placed on the folded fur and presented to the emperor by the couple, and he uses the sash to bind their hands and declare them married. All their wealth is then combined. Should one die, the other instantly inherits everything. Some families have more than others, and if they have anything of special value, it is declared before the emperor."

Aracaryn shifted in her seat. "So, it would be appropriate for Ettrian to declare his kingdom belongs to Radelia should he meet an early demise."

"That is correct. Since Radelia has been banished, she offers nothing. Not even her name."

None of that mattered to Ettrian. Dying before Radelia spared him grief and pain. He doubted he would care about it once he was dead, but he could see the concern growing in the eyes of the vassals.

"That's not entirely true," Omaro said. "Your clan still bears children. There's a good chance that Radelia will be able to provide an heir."

They all nodded at that. Nothing was more coveted than an heir, especially since the High Elves struggled in that regard. Though, Ettrian couldn't help but feel like the vassals were putting two prize horses in a stable in hopes that nature would take its course.

"Let's just start with the wedding," Ettrian said, eager to redirect the conversation.

"High Elves usually represent their house colors," Balqen said. "I'm aware the Runda Nor do not, but what color would best represent Radelia?"

"She does seem drawn to the color red," Ettrian mentioned.

"The royal color is red," Aracaryn said. "We don't want it to look like a massacre has taken place."

"Green?" Omaro proposed. "Like the forest."

Katar said nothing. She wasn't interested in tapestry colors either. "Why don't we go with black and white?" Ettrian said.

Black was his signature color, after all, and white was its opposite. Ettrian sketched out the room on a blank page. Black tapestries hung along the walls that contrasted a variety of white bouquets sat on pedestals and along the chairs.

There were nods from all around. At last, it seemed they were getting somewhere.

"But when would I have the opportunity to denounce him?" Miabelle was pacing the room. Her gown billowed in the winds that pushed through the window. Cracks formed along the curves of the sill and were reaching further than ever before.

The barrier was on a rapid decline. It wouldn't last another winter. Her clan could help teach the High Elves how to survive without it. They would need to cover the windows with furs and alter their farming techniques. Preserving and rationing food would be of the utmost importance, but if everyone worked together, they wouldn't suffer too much.

Cardhon Nimloth was going to die. Radelia had seen it with her third eye, and she worked toward accepting it. Ettrian and the other High Elves didn't know it, and she didn't have it in her to kill their hope. The king had so little of it to spare.

"At my wedding, of course," Radelia said, forcing a grin.

Miabelle spun around and squealed. "Oh, my goddess, Radelia!"

Her enthusiasm was contagious. They hugged, and Miabelle wiped the happy tears from her eyes. "What am I going to wear?"

"Whatever you want?"

"To a royal wedding? These things happen once in a lifetime! I'm so happy for you. What are you going to wear?"

She had put some thought into that, at least. "I was thinking of wearing the black gown that once belonged to Ettrian's mother."

Miabelle's eyes went wide. "That's perfect!"

It was hard to not get caught up in Miabelle's excitement. Soon, they were rushing around the room, talking about the most frivolous things. It was a nice change of pace from assassins and politics. Mia-belle had to tell her brother, Yinren, of course.

"Hang on," he said before darting out of the room.

The sounds of his footfalls down the stairs echoed. He must have been skipping steps all the way down because he returned not ten minutes later. His arms were full of cups and a bottle of wine. "I'm back," he panted. "I brought Radelia the smallest glass I could find."

Yinren poured while Miabelle caught him up on her own situation. The plan was that Miabelle would welcome everyone to the wedding, say a few words, and then use that platform to publicly denounce her husband.

"Well," he said. "Sounds like you two got everything figured out. A toast—to ending marriages and starting them!"

They drank a glass of wine and one more for good measure.

"Radelia, are you certain that you're okay with this?" Miabelle asked. "It's your special day."

She snorted. Marriages were nothing special; it was a formality and nothing more. "If I can right more than one wrong during this wedding, I'll gladly do it."

"Your people don't really do marriage, am I right?" Yinren said as he poured another round.

"Exactly." Radelia's tongue was already thick and clumsy from the wine. "We just do it to make sure assets are allocated correctly."

For a drunk tongue, big words were like a juggling act while in chains. She had to slow down to say them properly, but neither sibling seemed to notice.

Miabelle downed her goblet and slammed it on the table. "I can't wait to see the look on that bastard's face when I tell everyone how much I hate him."

"If only we had some way to make an instant portrait of his expression when you're up there. Something we can hang on the wall for all eternity."

"If I wanted to see his face for all eternity, I'd stay married to him, brother."

Radelia laughed. "How did you end up marrying him, anyway?"

"Like all terrible ideas, it started with this." Miabelle held up her goblet. "We'd been friends since childhood. Always joking that if neither of us were married by the time we turned five hundred, we'd just marry each other."

It was so hard to remember that those two were hundreds of years old. They acted like adolescents. The span of five-hundred years was staggering to Radelia. "So, you turned five hundred and got married."

"I didn't know it at the time, but he had been running the same game with three of our cousins! He didn't want to be married to me; he wanted to be married into the family. All he wanted was the nobility. But I only learned about that after we married in secret."

That really was terrible. Radelia's soured expression said it all.

"He's not the first lowborn to try that tactic," Yinren explained. "Our own grandfather married up, but it was different for them. Our grandparents are still madly in love."

The mood in the room dampened as tears rolled down Miabelle's face. "I always thought I'd fall in love and live happily ever after just like my parents and grandparents, but things just didn't work out that way."

That was a load of shit. Radelia shook her head, and the world swayed a bit. "It's not like you don't have time to find that person."

Miabelle had all the time in the world, in fact. Radelia once envied that trait once. Not so much for herself, but her people deserved immortality. Ettrian deserved a wife who could make him happy for a millennium.

"Here, here!" Yinren said, pouring another round.

"Not for me," Radelia said, pushing the cup aside. "I have a big day tomorrow."

Yinren nearly spit out his wine. "Tomorrow?"

"Or the next day," Radelia said. "I said as soon as possible."

"Yeah, but...wow."

Radelia stood and made her way to her room, fully concentrating on walking like she wasn't drunker than a worm in a fermented peach. "I got a seal to break."

Clearly, it wasn't an expression High Elves used. They stared at her in utter confusion but nodded as though they understood.

"Well, good night, your highness."

Radelia smiled. She could get used to that.

Chapter 31

A hand-selected team worked through the night to decorate the great hall in preparation. They rolled up the tapestries and tied them off so nothing would appear all that different during the breakfast service. Ettrian held court not too long after that. The flowers were kept in the kitchen corridors and would be brought out as breakfast concluded.

Balqen confirmed the time with Miabelle, who then relayed what gown Radelia would wear and the little speech that would take place before the wedding.

Ettrian had written the letter to the emperor himself and lent Katar a mount to hasten her return. More than anything, he wished to see Radelia, but it was considered bad luck to see the bride before the wedding night. That, and if she tried to seduce him, the king feared he would be unable to resist.

He whittled away at the hours by pacing his room. Tensing at every subtle noise, only to remind himself that Katar didn't make noise.

She insisted on going by herself. Ettrian was against it. What if the emperor tried to hold her hostage or even kill her? Katar only laughed. "Do you truly think that would happen?"

He supposed not. She knew the village too well, and given her skillset, it was unlikely. Brimming with anxiety, the last thing the king wanted was for Radelia's best friend to be detained or worse. It didn't help matters that Katar assured him it would take less than three hours when he had been brooding in his room for at least four. What was taking her so long?

There's nothing worse than feeling powerless. If Katar was in danger, he could do nothing. Employing Kieran to save the day yet again was his only option, and he had already asked too much of the general.

Turning to the suit that hung in the doorway of his wardrobe, at least some of Ettrian's worry dissolved. Marrying Radelia was the one choice he did have full confidence in. Aracaryn suggested he wear white since the princess was wearing black, but upon trying on a white tunic with matching white linen pants, her mind was quickly changed.

"Perhaps you should both wear black, and we will hang a white tapestry behind you."

Balqen agreed. "Black is the king's color. It should remain as such."

For once, they could all agree.

Want to place bets on how many times he'll stop to touch something?

He did it again!

At this rate, she'll never get him to the tower.

Ettrian spun around and raced toward the balcony. His fear of heights was eliminated as he placed his hands on the railing and saw what the spirits saw. Two cloaked figures were moving through the gardens. One with silent intent that could only be Katar and the other staggered with awe. His stomach plummeted, and for a moment,

Ettrian was convinced he made a terrible mistake. Never in a thousand lifetimes did he think the emperor would come.

Not willing to wait for the emperor to meet him, Ettrian went to them. Skipping steps along the circular staircase and sprinting out of the library, the king ran through the spring and fall gardens and only slowed when he reached the statue of Isilynor.

It would be an ideal place to meet. The emperor would see the flourishing crown on the goddess's head, and perhaps he would understand what it meant.

Katar spotted Ettrian standing by the fountain and grabbed the cloaked elf by the shoulder, practically dragging him forward. At least Ettrian wasn't the only one bone-rattling nervous and on the verge of bolting.

"King Ettrian," Katar hailed as she approached. "May I present the emperor of the Runda Nor."

Should he bow? No—they didn't do that. Ettrian shoved his hands in his pockets and ducked his head in a less formal greeting. "Welcome, Emperor."

"I never thought I'd see this place with my own eyes." The emperor pulled back his hood, revealing an older male with white hair and chapped skin. It was curious that even the emperor had the dry, weathered skin when Radelia did not.

"It's an honor to meet you."

The elf's eyes locked on the statue before him. His mouth agape, he stared at the crown, and Ettrian smiled. "So, you've noticed."

"I didn't think Katar would lie, but seeing it is something else, isn't it?"

"Some things we must see with our own eyes. Ever since Radelia came here," he explained, "she's changed hearts and minds alike. While I cannot prove she is responsible for this, we all believe it to be true."

"How is she?"

Ettrian laughed. "Feisty and headstrong as ever."

"She doesn't know I'm here?"

"I didn't know if you'd come. I didn't want to get her hopes up."

The emperor eyed him sharply. "Of course I'd come. Why wouldn't I?"

Something strange was amiss. Perhaps it was one of those Runda Nor rules where the clan could meet the banished but the exiled could never return. "In your letter. You claimed she was dead to you."

He shook his head. "I sent no such letter. It was your letter that informed me that she was dead. When Kieran returned with his story, I...I didn't dare hope it to be true. Then, Katar came and told me a very different story."

Something amiss indeed. "Do you have that letter, by chance?"

The old emperor shuffled through his pockets before producing a letter. Ettrian examined the seal to find it was indeed his own. "This can't be," he gasped. "It's my seal, but I never sent such a letter."

Plain as mid-day, the letter was addressed to the emperor. It stated that Radelia was caught trespassing and would be executed. He seethed at the signature; it even looked similar to his. Whoever wrote it had intimate knowledge and access to his room.

"Come," Ettrian said. "I wish to show you the letter I received."

They walked by his side through the library and up the stairs. Despite his age, the emperor had no difficulty with the steps. Ettrian dared to venture that the male was in better shape than some of the High Elves in the castle.

Extending the letter to the emperor, he too frowned at the seal. "It is my seal."

"You can see why I didn't question the contents of the letter," Katar said as she circled the room. Her eyes scanned the open balcony and all around as if she were searching for an unseen enemy.

"It even looks like my signature. Loops and all."

"Emperor Bellas, whoever forged your letter must be in league with the person who forged mine."

He slapped the letter on the table. "Someone has been taking advantage of our feud."

"But why?" Ettrian said, seating himself opposite the emperor. "Who has the most to gain from our separation?"

"Currently," Bellas said, "the Ruby Isles."

Ettrian frowned but said nothing, allowing the emperor to explain.

"When Radelia went missing, I sent a letter to them pleading for aid. They offered it gladly and without exchange. Their army marches this way and will arrive any day now."

Of course. How could he be so blind? "King Rhys passed away recently. Aracaryn's younger sister now rules. She must be attempting to capture Cardhon Nimloth."

"But why?" Bellas asked. "Why come all that way for a castle that isn't theirs?"

The emperor still believed the castle belonged to the Runda Nor. Ettrian would need to tread carefully on the topic. "There are many versions of how the castle came to be, and they often conflict. Some say the Runda Nor built it; others say High Elves did. Several say both clans built it together."

"Well, we know your clan doesn't build—"

"However," Ettrian interrupted, his patience drawn from the long day, "one thing is agreed upon, and that's that Cardhon Nimloth was the birthplace of all elves."

Bellas nodded. There was no denying that fact.

"I propose that history is altered and interpreted by the reader. I think all four clans had a hand in making Cardhon Nimloth since all four gods created the clans here."

"You mean to say that the Ruby Isles believes their claim is the right one."

"Correct."

The emperor looked away. "All they needed was a foothold. Proper justification to attack a longtime ally, and I provided it."

That was the part that did not add up for Ettrian. He understood the newly appointed queen had an agenda and the means, but the motivation was lacking. "All the remaining clans are struggling," Ettrian explained. "Perhaps not as harshly as the Runda Nor, but my own people can no longer conceive. Our healing powers are gone. The castle's strength wanes. According to my reports, the Dark Elves are losing their powers as well."

The emperor's eyes softened. Like Radelia, he had no idea that the High Elves had no more magic than they did. "They think as we do. That if they control the castle, they control the magic."

That was just it, though. "They know of our troubles. So, what good would attacking the castle serve other than hasten the demise of our race?"

Bellas grunted. "I hate it when Kieran is right."

"Me as well."

On that note, the leaders shared a laugh. He noted Katar grinning in the corner of the room, but it was temporary. "We need to find whoever is responsible," she reminded them. "Who has the ability to enter your rooms without question?"

"Just the vassals and Radelia."

"In your absence, another has taken your place," Bellas said. "A messenger from the Ruby Isles. Her hawk is trained to deliver letters. I thought it most useful."

As Katar and Bellas discussed the messenger, Ettrian fumed in silence. Someone who had his trust had betrayed him. Leaf had taken it upon herself to write to the emperor; perhaps she had taken more liberties than he knew. A response to unrequited love? It didn't feel right, though. Leaf might have been jealous, angry even, but to go as far as to establish contact with the Dark Elves, she wouldn't know where to begin.

Balqen wanted the clans to be reunited, so it couldn't be him. While it was true he once wished the Runda Nor dead after the death of his child, he openly acknowledged how wrong he was. The old elf's mission was one of grief, and when he lost his immortality, his priorities shifted.

Omaro had much fear and prejudice when it came to the Runda Nor. Ettrian couldn't tell if that fear extended to all others outside their own, but what motivation would he have to attack fellow High Elves?

The only one who had the connections and motivation was Aracaryn. Only Aracaryn could parlay so effectively with the Dark Elves. She was one of their princesses, after all. She stood to gain the most if he was unseated. Perhaps there was a bargain struck between sisters. Aracaryn would rule Cardhon Nimloth while her sister ruled the isles.

Yet, why would she be so invested in his wedding? When the other vassals urged more extreme measures, it was Aracaryn who argued for common sense.

Ettrian shook his head. "It can't be my vassals," he said. "Someone else must have access to my room."

"It wouldn't surprise me," Katar said. "Your security here is rather dismal."

All the while, Bellas quietly observed the way she spoke to the king. It was as if he were taking notes. If the emperor thought her criticism so blatant toward a king, just wait until he met the vassals.

"We don't exactly have the means, and up until recently, there was no need for such measures."

"You're not at all what I expected," the emperor said, eyeing him with curiosity. "I wanted to see the male that swept my daughter off her feet. I half expected that I'd need to rescue my daughter from a giant tyrant, but clearly, that isn't the case."

"I never live up to anyone's expectations," he said with a sigh.

Bellas didn't understand, but Katar said, "The king has a humor darker than his wardrobe."

"The day has worn on long enough. Perhaps it's time we retire."

Ettrian had never been so grateful for sleep in his life. "I suggest you stay with Katar in her room. No one is to know you're here, not even my vassals. If anyone asks, tell them you're Katar's father. We're going to figure out who's been coordinating these efforts against us."

After they departed, the king fell into bed. The last thing he saw before he closed his eyes were tiny saplings sprouting from the cracks.

Chapter 32

"Nervous?" Miabelle asked.

"No." Radelia wasn't the least bit anxious. There was no reason to be worried. It was just a day like any other, only there would be a brief ceremony. It wasn't like her life was changing forever or something like that.

Miabelle frowned. "You haven't touched your toast."

She eyed the slice of bread with as much enthusiasm as one would have for eating snails. "I'm just not hungry. What about you? Are you nervous?"

"About denouncing my secret husband in front of everyone I know along with many strangers? Oh no...not in the slightest." The sarcasm wasn't lost on her, but Radelia couldn't help but space off while her friend was talking.

Voices were increasing from downstairs, signaling that breakfast had started. Dread pooled in her belly and refused to be ignored. "Okay, maybe I am nervous."

Miabelle sat beside her and took her hand. "You're marrying young by your clan's standards."

"Yeah," she said with a sigh. "It's just that I didn't see myself here, getting married, becoming queen."

"It's a lot."

Months ago, Radelia came to Cardhon Nimloth to free her friends and kill the king, sparing her people from war. Her father wanted nothing to do with her, her friends were now lovers, and she was marrying the elf she'd tried to murder. She was beyond glad she didn't succeed, but still. This is what you get when you don't have any plans in life.

And where was Katar? She would have thought her best friend would be beside her, yet she wasn't anywhere to be seen. Knowing Ettrian, he probably had her helping with the wedding since Radelia didn't care about the clan colors or the ceremony. She just wanted to be with him. Baggage and all.

"We should get ready," Miabelle suggested. Radelia was already on her feet. Keeping busy would be a good distraction. That, and she loved wearing that gown. It was impractical and frivolous like the High Elves, but she had grown to love them regardless.

Miabelle laced up the dress as Radelia braided her hair into two rows, weaving the black and white ribbons Yinren had left on the vanity.

"The dress is a bit snugger than the last time."

That didn't surprise Radelia one bit. "I'm no longer hunting for weeks on end. I lay around drinking and eating."

Tilting the mirror downward, she noted the swell of her breasts underneath the sheer fabric and gave an approving nod. Those were a nice addition.

Miabelle applied perfumed oil to the hollows of her neck and behind her ears. There were boxes on the vanity she didn't recognize. "What are those?"

"The best part!"

Opening the boxes, Miabelle revealed a diamond-encrusted choker with matching earrings. They took the shapes of white flowers with yellow diamonds to denote the center. The flowers of Cardhon Nimloth.

"I think it's time," Miabelle said.

Radelia nodded, praying her feet would remain steady despite her wobbly knees. She knew the plan. Ettrian would hold court as he usually did until Miabelle spoke. When given the cue, she would go down the stairs and meet Kieran, who would escort her the rest of the way.

Blowing out a heavy breath, Miabelle let go of her hand and descended the stairs.

Ettrian's voice boomed as he regaled the latest news to the High Elves. "As many of you have noticed, we have guests. Please extend a warm welcome to our cousins, the Runda Nor. Our clans have struggled with our differences in the past, but we cannot carry on as we have. For the sake of Cardhon Nimloth, I beg you all to show one another the generosity and grace I know to be in your hearts."

Radelia couldn't resist peaking over the railing. He was wearing his crown. Someone must have found it. She noted the elves standing along the levels of the great hall. They were waiting for something.

"And now," Ettrian said as Miabelle made her way to the bottom steps. "I ask that you lend an ear to Mirabelle Bellas. Granddaughter to vassal Balqen Bellas. She has an important message she wishes to impart."

For someone who claimed they were nervous, Miabelle practically danced down the aisle before hopping up on the stand before Ettrian. She gave him a bow and said something Radelia couldn't quite hear before whirling around.

"I would like to make a dedication to my dear friend, Siveril."

A High Elf male stood among the crowd. He bowed as everyone clapped. The male had no idea what was going on. He must have assumed Miabelle was declaring their marriage, not the end of it. Radelia couldn't help but snicker. She was about to yank the hairs below the belt.

"Siveril," Miabelle said with feigned adoration. "One of my dearest friends. I have so many fond memories of growing up with you. We made a pact to marry if we were both single by our five-hundredth birthdays. Only, it turns out you made that pact with quite a few females."

The mood in the room shifted from joy to humor. High Elves loved drama and gossip. While the Runda Nor stared in confusion, the High Elves were practically salivating with what would come next. Miabelle looked up in her direction and nodded. That was her cue.

"Funny enough, you made that pact with every available Bellas. So, needless to say, the pact is withdrawn. I denounce you and any holdings you may think you have on me."

With that, Miabelle flashed a loveable smile before prancing away, leaving Siveril red-faced and shrinking back to his chair.

"And with that," Ettrian said with a gesture of his hand. "We have another important matter."

Radelia was already halfway down the stairs. Focusing entirely on her feet. The last thing she wanted to do was to trip and go hurtling down the stairs. If she was injured, it would make the honeymoon difficult.

With a triumphant grin, Radelia had conquered the last step. She looked up, fully expecting Kieran, but someone else was extending their arm.

She nearly fell backward at the sight. "Father?"

That mischievous twinkle in his eye...it could be no one else. She began to stammer and babble before embracing him. "It's all right, my dear. We can explain everything later."

How? She was banished. Dead to him. Radelia was trying her best to keep it together, but her face pulled and contorted as the tears streaked and the snot threatened to fall on her beautiful gown.

White tapestries were released and sent cascading along the great hall in time with their steps. In the crowd, she recognized so many elves. Jonik was there along with Katar's mentor and even some of her fellow trench diggers. Yinren and Mavis were there beside a Runda Nor female holding a baby in her arms.

When she reached Ettrian's throne, each of his vassals bowed, and Balqen embraced her. "I helped reunite those infants on your behalf," he whispered in her ear.

Katar and Kieran were sitting side by side in the front row. Everyone was there. "Thank you," she whispered. Looking around, she wasn't certain who else to thank.

Only then was she able to stare into her almost-husband's eyes. He was smiling. "Is everything to your liking?"

"It's perfect." She couldn't imagine anything better, and even if she could, she wouldn't want it. Her people were side by side with his. The families were reunited, and her friends were free to do as they pleased. Her father was welcomed through the threshold of the castle by invitation, not violence.

The vision wasn't what they thought. The Runda Nor was emptied not because her people had perished but because they were finally home. Perhaps the vision of the dead roots wasn't a bad omen either.

Ettrian took her hands in his as Katar handed her father a folded fur. He bound their hands with a strip of linen and said, "As emperor of the Runda Nor, I hereby declare Radelia and Ettrian are united under one household as equals and not guests."

Balqen stepped forward as her father moved to stand along the vassals. "Let Isilynor and Elpharae be your guides. Let the goddess's light see you through your darkest days, and may the gods' salt preserve you in hardship."

Balqen stepped back. With hands joined by the linen, she and Ettrian stepped forward as Aracaryn set a matching silver crown on Radelia's head. "Long live the king and queen!"

The room burst into cheers so loud it was deafening. Radelia flinched, but Ettrian pulled her in close and kissed the top of her head.

She laughed as Ettrian spirited her from the crowd and into the gardens. Wrapping her arms around his neck, he picked her up and swung her in a circle. "We did it!" she said. "We're hitched."

The party that followed was, of course, a revelry.

This time Radelia wasn't wading through a sea of strangers in the dark. She found herself toasting with her friends and family. High Elves were laughing at the faces Runda Nor made when taking their first sip of wine or eating cheese.

Balqen introduced himself to her father. "Hello there, young man."

She giggled. Side by side, they appeared to be the same age, but Balqen quickly explained their connection.

"I had no idea Runda Nor still resided here!"

"Not just Runda Nor," Aracaryn said. "Many Dark Elves remained as well."

"What of the Ice Elves?" her father asked.

"A curious bunch they were," Balqen said. "They spoke among themselves with a sort of clicking noise. Alas, they are long extinct."

Radelia was fascinated. What other tidbits of their culture could be found from one of the few elves that survived the first age?

"I've been receiving curious reports from the Isles," Aracaryn said. "Miners are reporting sightings of an unfamiliar race of people. Small and elusive, they emerge from the ground only to return when approached. I wonder if our long-lost cousins are not entirely lost."

Ettrian's ears perked at that. "What did they look like?"

"Hairy," Aracaryn said with a frown.

That wasn't a description ever used to describe elves. They all exchanged a confused glance before bursting into laughter.

"Ice Elves were not hairy," Balqen said. "Their skin was a bluish color, and their hair white and limp. They were small and elusive, however, so perhaps they evolved. Not unlike our Runda Nor friends."

That reminded her... Radelia searched the walls, hoping to catch a glimpse of her own friend. Katar had ducked out of the wedding before it ended. She was tasked with observing the crowd for any unusual activities. There was still the matter of the spy within the castle.

As if he could sense her worry, Ettrian pulled her in close and whispered in her ear. "Perhaps we can leave the party for a time."

She grinned. "We're going to check on Katar. We won't be long."

They made their way toward the library, unseen by the partygoers. At least, that was what she thought. But as they made their way inside, the Runda Nor all burst into song. Heat rushed to her face and prickled her skin.

Ettrian paused to look back, unsure of what was happening. She took his hand, "Come on."

"I don't know this song," Ettrian said.

"It's the song Elpharae sang to Isilynor at their wedding," Radelia explained.

His eyes went wide with the knowledge that all the Runda Nor knew what they were up to. "I see."

"It's customarily sung before a royal couple goes to bed. Supposedly, it assures fertility."

"Well," Ettrian said, whisking her off her feet. "It couldn't hurt to try."

She laughed as he picked her up. Walking in the gown was difficult but not that bad. It must have been a High Elf tradition for a wife to be carried to the marriage bed.

With the bedroom door locked behind them, Ettrian wasted no time in undressing. She had seen males many times before, but this was different. He was hers now. No ridiculous law could prohibit them any further.

She had been waiting for this moment since the first time they kissed, and now that it was finally here, Radelia hesitated. As if sensing her concern, Ettrian knelt before her. He took her hand and kissed it. "I'd wait forever if you wished."

Oh, no. She hadn't gone to all the trouble just to back down. "Don't tell me you're nervous."

His expression was awkward and made her giggle. "Well..."

Pulling him from his knees, she guided him until he was on top of her. His eyes scanned her body as she pulled the low-cut dress away, revealing her breasts. Ettrian hesitated for a few moments before pressing his body against hers. Her legs parted as far as they could to accommodate the thickness of his hips. His mouth crushed hers as his tongue slipped against her own.

He broke away from her mouth. It seemed the king was intent on exploring each curve and swell of her body. Working down her throat, his mouth clasped onto one nipple, and he nursed it while Radelia writhed with pleasure. The dress slipped away and fell to the floor. He stood and readjusted before climbing back on top of her where he belonged. The heat from his body warmed hers, smothering the goosebumps that emerged in the open air.

His body covered her. Braced in the safety of his broad shoulders, Radelia gripped his hips with her legs and urged him inside her. She was greedy and wanting. The ache between her thighs coiled so tight it allowed for no other thoughts. No other needs besides the one.

"Ettrian," she panted before his tongue forced its way into her mouth again.

Radelia bucked her hips upward, trying to help herself. Her mound rubbed against his person, and the king's moan resonated down her throat. Frustration boiled over, reducing her to a clawing fiend trying to take it from him before he finally reached his hand down to position himself at her opening.

Her eyes went wide as she realized why he hesitated. He wanted her to be as ready as she could be. She had often fantasized about what his proportions were like. They were nothing compared to what parted her lips and forced its way inside.

Radelia no longer clawed in frustration but in sheer pleasure as he penetrated her. He gave one final push that threatened to be too much before she fully enveloped him. Ettrian cried out, holding perfectly still for several breaths to regain his composure. He wanted this to last, and so did she, but her legs were convulsing on their own as that tight coil of frustration broke.

A slave to her body's needs, Radelia bucked and ground her mound against him as the climax took hold of her. Ettrian gave a frustrated roar as he thrusted into her with wanton abandon. She could feel his seed spilling into her before his body went slack.

They lay together and talked for a time. None of the conversation was important, and that was the point. They spoke as though it was the beginning of the rest of their lives.

"Hey," he whispered with more urgency than any whisper should hold. "Tell me about your childhood."

"I was a difficult baby. I cried whenever my parents put me down. I learned how to climb before I could walk. My father was so frightened by it he tied a blanket over the crib each night so I would not escape."

He held her tight and nipped her ear. "No one could control you, not even then."

"I got out anyway. They found me at Katar's house. That's how we became friends."

She rolled to her side and propped her head up with her hand. "What about you?"

"I'm told I was a calm child," he said. "I grew so quickly that my bones ached, and I'd be bedridden for days at a time."

"Did you do well in school?" She always got the impression he was a studious child.

Ettrian tilted his head as if he didn't know what she was saying. "School?"

"Yeah, you know, the place children learn while the adults work."

"There were no children other than myself at the time, but the elders raised me in the High Elf tradition. We let our children have free reign of the castle, show them how we weave tapestries, craft metal, farm. I learned as I pleased."

That was amazing! The Runda Nor had so much work to do, and much of it was dangerous. It was easier to keep children out of the way. "I love that."

He grinned, eyeing her lower belly, but caught himself as if he didn't dare wish for something so perfect. "The infants that remain in the castle will be walking and talking soon. It's only a matter of time before they trample the gardens and make their mark on the castle."

Radelia hadn't the chance to speak with the parents, but she had faith that Balqen and the others assured the parents that they were welcome to stay. Even if the others returned home with her father, she knew the pregnant elves would be encouraged to remain. The Runda Nor population within the castle would increase over time. Perhaps High Elves and Dark Elves would marry Runda Nor, and they could finally have children of their own.

It was more than they had hoped.

Radelia leaned in to kiss her husband to see if she could entice him with another round when a burst came from the gardens so loud, it sent shockwaves throughout the tower. Jerking upright, they froze in alarm. There was screaming, and the scent of blood intermingled with an unknown smell. Something terrible had happened.

Chapter 33

Smoke billowed upward. Unable to escape the barrier, it swelled and hovered over the disaster in the gardens. Bodies lay prone on the ground. Some were on fire, missing limbs, and countless others were fleeing in every direction. The air smelled of sulfur.

The statue of Isilynor was gone.

"No," Ettrian uttered as he threw on the clothes strewn about the floor.

Radelia was crying on the bed, uncertain of what happened and too sad and frightened to look. "Ettrian, the flowers."

He followed her gaze to the ceiling. The flowers once blooming over his bed were wilting. They'd targeted the statue for a reason. Its meaning was clear. Whoever attacked them was trying to keep their clans apart.

It wouldn't work. He wouldn't allow it.

"Radelia," he said, cupping her face in his hands. "We need to go help them."

"The roots," she muttered. "They knew to blow up the roots."

It took him several moments to understand. There was an old cellar beneath the statue. They thought the roots of Cardhon Nimloth were suffering from mold or some kind of fungus and dug out the cellar to inspect its health.

Someone knew of it and planted an explosive underground where no one would look. Radelia must have discovered it on her own at some point.

"We need to help our people right now."

His words had reached her through the panic. Her eyes sharpened with resolve, and Radelia nodded. "Let's go."

The gardens were a warzone. Elves were pushing and shoving, crying ove6r their dead. He could hardly see through the smoke, and Radelia was gasping for air. "We need to open the main gate," she said.

Of course! The barrier was designed to keep heat in and the elements out, but if the gate was opened, there would act as a flue, and some of the smoke would clear. It was already seeping from the weak spots, but it wasn't enough. They needed cold winter air to blow in.

Hand in hand, they waded through the chaos. Their vision was too distorted by the smoke; there was no telling who was who. A pair of frantic elves clipped his shoulder as they rushed past. "Balqen!" Ettrian called out. "Leaf!"

If he could get ahold of his vassals, a guard, someone to rally the others while he opened the gates, but the only response he got was screams of agony and fear. It was no use. Once the smoke was clear, at least some of the panic would subside.

Why hadn't the spirits said something? If anyone noticed a suspicious elf, it would be them, but they had been silent all day apart from the one that "always cries at weddings."

The smoke was dense in the great hall. They had to feel for the door with their hands as he and Radelia each pushed open a door. Smoke came streaming out. Once outside, their eyes began to clear, and the stinging subsided.

"What happened?" one of the militia asked.

"We don't know," Radelia said. "Where's Kieran?"

"Katar came and got him. They're somewhere inside."

"Gather your troops," Ettrian said, hoping the elf wouldn't balk at his command. "Find your general and help the survivors."

Thankfully, the Runda Nor didn't argue. He liked to think Kieran would have made a similar order. The male nodded and set off at once. Radelia was focused on the smoke pooling from the doorway. It made a steady stream upward as the winter air circulated.

"Let's find your vassals next."

Ettrian nodded. He had to duck to avoid the smoke, but he could already breathe easier. It was colder. He noted that the smoke was dispensing from the top as well. With the core of the castle gone, the barrier must have been fading.

What if the vassals were still lingering by the statue when it blew up? Her father was with them. They might have been disintegrated in the blast. Leaf wasn't with them. She had made herself scarce before the wedding. There was a good chance she still lived, but the others...

Radelia took his hand, and the turmoil in his heart eased. "Kieran and Katar are somewhere. If she brought him inside, it was because she found something or someone."

There was assurance in that. At least whoever was responsible would be caught. In the summer gardens, he spotted Omaro and a guard. They were tending to an elf on the ground amid the burning wheat.

"Over there, look!"

They rushed to Omaro, who was wrapping up a Runda Nor elf's injuries. "Where are the others?" Ettrian asked.

Clutching his chest with his hand, Omaro gasped. "Oh, thank the goddess you both are safe. I don't know where Aracaryn and Balqen are. Leaf was with Katar and Kieran. I saw them heading toward the southwestern tower.

Leaf accompanying Katar and Kieran only confirmed their theory. With the three of them combining their skills, no elf could stand in their way. Ettrian turned to face the guard. "I need you to rally the guards. The Runda Nor militia are coming to aid us. They have healers suited to situations like this. Anyone can come in, but no one is allowed to leave without my permission."

"Should we find Katar and the others?" Radelia asked.

"I'm sure they're fine. We need to help the injured."

She frowned as if she knew the truth of it. Ettrian didn't want her going anywhere alone since she was the primary target at one point. "I'm going to the site of the explosion."

At that, he relented. "Just don't go off on your own. We still don't know who the spy was."

Radelia sprinted off in the direction of the statue while Ettrian searched among the bodies. Far too many were dead. He checked each of the bodies, searching for any signs of life, but dozens were burned or maimed beyond life or even recognition.

He fell to his knees at the sight of Miabelle. Placing a shaky hand on her head, tears welled in his eyes with relief. She was still warm and breathing. The king carried her to the place where Omaro was seeing to a conscious Runda Nor.

"Did you see what happened?" he asked.

"No," Omaro said. "One moment everything was fine, and the next..."

Ettrian looked up to see a group of Runda Nor in white gowns and caps. There were fifteen of them in all. He flagged them with a wave, and they came running. "I'm trying to find the injured to bring them here," he explained, "but I can't cover enough ground on my own."

"Leave it to us," an older female said. They scattered like snowflakes in a blizzard across the garden.

They would be far more effective than he ever could be, so Ettrian went after Radelia. Knowing his wife, she wouldn't stay in one place for long. With the barrier sighing its last breath, the collected ash was breaking loose. It fell all around, turning black in the puddles of elf and tree blood.

A droning grown came from behind him. Ettrian turned just in time to see the northeast tower collapse in on itself. Onlookers watched with passive expressions. It was only the second worst thing to happen that day, after all.

In the place where the statue once stood was a crater. Kneeling, he peered in to find that the impact hadn't destroyed everything. A massive clump stood tall amid the broken fragments. Either too dense or too firmly entwined, the roots remained even when nothing else did.

"Radelia?" he called.

There was no answer.

Damn it all, she must have gone after Kieran and Katar. The king set off for the southwest tower, hoping that she hadn't gone too far or that the culprit was already dead.

Moving through the library, careful not to step on the broken panes of stained glass, Ettrian took the stairway opposite his rooms. Aracaryn's bedroom mirrored his own, and he would have to trespass through it, but given the circumstance, he didn't think she would mind.

"Hello?" The king pushed the door open. His heart sank at the sight.

The room was empty.

Aracaryn's trunks were gone, as were her fine silks and priceless artifacts. The only thing left was a letter from an unknown sender on the table. The room still smelled of wax, and the candle was warm. She must have read it and fled shortly after.

Right away, Ettrian knew the handwriting wasn't hers. Aracaryn was notorious for her terrible handwriting. This was a scrawling, lovely note with thick curves and gentle strokes.

Destruction gives way to creation. We must make sacrifices to regain what we lost.

She had help leaving the castle—that he knew. There was no way she could have packed all her things within hours and escaped without anyone seeing. He didn't want to believe Aracaryn was the spy, but it all made sense. She must have been packing in secret in the weeks leading up to the wedding.

The access to his seal stamp, all the information including the wedding... Ettrian slammed his fists on the table. How could he have been so blind? They knew she was a risk and ignored the threat. If he hadn't called for vassals, they wouldn't have had such a leak of information. Then again, there was a good chance the High Elves wouldn't let him sit on the throne otherwise.

Just as he was about to leave, the outward-facing door opened. Katar stepped in. Her eyes were watery as she shook her head. "I didn't catch her in time."

"Are we certain it was Aracaryn?"

"She had help," Katar explained. "I watched her leave the reception. She spoke with two High Elves and three Dark Elves. Outnumbered,

I fetched Kieran, and Leaf tagged along, but before we could confront them, they escaped on horseback."

He slumped against the wall.

"She was trailing after them with a sword in hand, and that's the last I saw of her."

"Radelia?"

"She's with Kieran and Leaf."

He nodded. The conspirators had fled the castle, so there was some consolation in that. "We need to send word to all the villages from here to the Ruby Isles. I will offer a trunk full of gold and gems to anyone who brings me their heads."

"I'll see to it personally."

Sensing he wished to be alone, Katar left. The moment the door shut, Ettrian broke down in sobs.

Radelia stood in what was once the cellar beside the roots. She pressed a hand against the gnarls and sensed no life. They were damaged and exposed. It was always an eventuality, but she thought they had more time.

"It's dead," Kieran said. "I'm so sorry."

She wanted to lash out at him for stating the obvious, but fatigue was coming over her like a wet blanket. Aracaryn did this? It didn't make sense. Leaf placed a hand on her shoulder. "We should go up top. It will give the people hope to see that the king and queen are safe."

"Hope." How could her presence be considered hopeful now? Cardhon Nimloth was dead on the day she wed the king. Things must have been bad indeed for Leaf to show her any kindness.

All she wanted to do was sit in the dark and cry. There was no sign of her father or of Balqen. Omaro and the Runda Nor healers were working as fast as they could, but the death toll climbed higher by the minute.

Kieran sat beside her, his arms wrapped around his knees. The cries of pain from above were a distant thing, but she winced at each scream. She was familiar with the sounds. The healers were amputating limbs to spare lives.

"If your father isn't found," he said at last, "you'll have the duty to carry on in his stead."

She knew that already. "You're full of the obvious truths."

"What I mean is that you'll be able to help both clans. The High Elves don't know how to survive outside their little bubble, and our people need their wealth. If we work together, all isn't lost. We can rebuild."

She wiped the tears from her ash-smudged face and sniffed. Her father and her half-brother were always in conflict. If he aligned with her, all the might of the militia would too. It didn't make her feel much better, though. It was like expecting a cake and getting snails instead.

How ungrateful her thoughts were. Radelia was fortunate that Kieran never did learn to read her mind.

"The day your father—our father—told me the truth," Kieran said. "It was the worst day of my life. I never could forgive him."

It was several years too late. She held no animosity for the end of their relationship. In light of the circumstances, she was glad. Looking back, Radelia could no longer see him in a romantic light. "I like you better as a brother anyway."

"And Ettrian... I couldn't ask for a better brother-in-law."

"I think he's a bit jealous of you."

Kieran's smile widened, exposing a missing tooth on the bottom row. She wondered when he'd lost that. "Why?"

She shrugged. "I think it's just the way you command others. He's had to fight for the respect of his people. It comes so naturally to you."

"That will change. The spell was broken on this magical village. They will be vulnerable and need leaders like never before."

Something squirmed in her lower abdomen. It wasn't uncomfortable, but it was unlike anything Radelia had ever felt before. And she was sleepy. She couldn't recall a time she had ever felt so tired. Leaning against the roots, she closed her eyes.

"Radelia?" Kieran called in the distance. Someone was shaking her by the shoulder, but she couldn't seem to wake up.

There were other voices then. She smiled at the sound of Ettrian's voice. "I'm just tired," she assured him, not knowing if her voice passed her lips.

"Is it growing?" an unfamiliar voice asked.

"Oh yeah, look at her."

"Finally!" another said.

There was a series of clicking noises, though she didn't know what it was. It reminded her of a grasshopper. Radelia didn't know who they were, but she was happy they were happy.

"What's growing?" she asked.

"You hear them too?" Ettrian asked.

Something cold and wet hit her face. Radelia spat and opened her eyes to find Katar standing over her with an empty goblet. "What just happened?"

Ettrian's face was warped with terror and ash. He was touching her face and pawing at her hair in desperation. "I'm fine," she assured him.

"You heard the spirits," he said. "They said something was growing. Radelia, what is growing?"

Instinctively, her eyes lowered to her belly. "I think I'm pregnant."

Katar blinked. "Well, so much for vows."

Ettrian scowled at her. "The first time we were together was hours ago."

"Radelia, you can't know you're with child hours after coupling," Katar said. "The headmistress taught you that much I trust."

Of course she knew! Radelia swatted at her friend, but her hand didn't reach. "It's not a child."

That made no more sense to her than it did to anyone else, but she knew it to be right. Still leaning against the roots, they seemed to whisper something to her, only Radelia didn't understand the language.

"They're not spirits of elves, Ettrian. The voices you hear, the voices I just heard, are the trees."

"Radelia was one of the few that could hear the trees speak," Kieran explained. "I heard the other hunters talk about it. She can track any beast, even if there's no trail."

Ettrian believed her. "But Cardhon Nimloth is one tree."

"Four Elven gods, four races, and four towers," she explained. "It would be impossible for a castle this size to be made entirely of one tree. It's four trees, shaped into a fortress."

"But the barrier," Kieran reminded.

"It was the gift of Isilynor. The strength of Cardhon Nimloth was weakening because our clans were fractured. We need all four races within the walls."

"But the Ice Elves are dead," Ettrian said.

She didn't think so. Balqen said that the Ice Elves spoke with clicks. Maybe that was what she heard coming from the roots. If their spirit was still alive, perhaps they were too.

Here it comes!

A strange, needling pain was coming from her stomach. Radelia sat up and pulled at the tunic she'd borrowed from Ettrian's room. Something was worming its way out of her belly button. Flailing, she pulled the tunic up, not caring who saw and screamed.

A sprout no bigger than a clover stem was growing out of her belly. It didn't hurt anymore, but it was wrong on every fucking level. She was spouting off every curse that she knew and a few she didn't. Ettrian refused to let her go, but he was moaning with fear.

Katar dropped to her knees and watched as the sprout grew. Kieran was vomiting. Had she eaten anything, she would have probably done the same.

"How?" Katar asked, poking it lightly with her finger.

"Don't touch it," Ettrian said. "What if it gets angry?"

The sprout coiled gently around Katar's finger like a garden snake and sprouted miniature leaves. "The spirits said it was growing," Radelia said, staring at the plant growing from her belly. "I didn't think they meant it literally."

The seed conceived of Elpharae and Isilynor's descendants' lives!

She and Ettrian locked eyes. Each of them had heard it even if no one else could. "You once said the royal line was thought to be a descendant of Isilynor."

The king nodded. "Your skin never reacts to the harsh environment. You can see the future and talk to trees."

All were said to be gifts passed through the Bellas line. It all made sense. Each god created a race of elves in their image. Each clan had a line descended from the gods themselves. By marrying their lines, Radelia and Ettrian had unwittingly reunited Elpharae and Isilynor. And...they conceived a plant?

"Isilynor is the goddess of stars," Ettrian said as if he understood where the logic ended for her. "She could only reach us with the aid of Elpharae. When they were knocked from the sky, Isilynor's connection was lost."

"And this is how they decided to forge a new connection?" Radelia thought she'd do anything to restore Elven magic, but the plant growing from her belly wasn't what she had in mind.

"It's coming out," Katar said. "Look, see the roots?"

White little ties were unlatching themselves from the small slit inside her belly button. A few more broke loose before the plant was completely removed. Extending her hand, Katar placed the sapling into the dirt beside the dead roots.

Radelia watched with a mixture of awe and horror as the little roots disappeared into the ground. The sapling uncurled itself from Katar's finger as it began scaling the dead roots. Already, it was sprouting leaves twice the original size. Even so, it would be years before it had the strength to restore the barrier.

"So, magic died, but now it's reborn?" At that point, Radelia just wanted a hot bath and sleep, but with all the chaos in the gardens, she would be needed.

"I...I think we did it," Ettrian said.

Had they? It was too soon to tell. With the barrier down, the sapling would face the harsh winter months unprotected. Her clan would have some ideas to help insulate it. Rebuilding the castle would be yet another hurdle they had to face.

Emerging from the cellar, the four of them observed the dire scene in the garden. The healers were carrying the injured into the great hall. At every turn, she saw a pair of healers with a stretcher. She watched a pair of healers move not toward the great hall but to the spring gardens. There, they laid the body of a High Elf beside a Runda Nor before covering them with a tapestry. Scarcely knowing one another, their bodies had no quarrel with who was beside them in the end.

She had to tear her gaze away. Up ahead, the northeast tower had collapsed in on itself. The cracks in the walls were so massive that she could see the Runda Nor camps on the other side. Ettrian rubbed her back with his hand. "Are you sure you feel well?"

Radelia was certain she was exhausted. She had birthed a plant and was standing in the aftermath of one of the worst disasters of their age. So, no, she wasn't feeling well. She wanted to fall to her knees screaming as she tore out her hair, but doing so benefited no one.

"I need to find my father."

She felt a pull toward the spring gardens. Toward the rows of the dead. If she found his remains first, it wouldn't be as traumatic as wading through the throngs of injured and living. If she searched the injured, it meant seeing his face in every single elf only to realize it wasn't him over and over again.

As if sensing her trepidation, Ettrian pulled her in close and said, "Don't give in to despair. I wallowed in it for decades. Trust me when I say it's no place to linger for long."

Radelia nodded. Though her heart ached, and her legs were jelly, she pushed onward toward the injured. What if he wasn't there? What if the elves looked upon their new queen and blamed her? There was no doubt in her mind that it was her fault. It was only natural they assumed the same.

#

What they saw in the great hall was beyond anything she could have imagined.

Countless elves were so badly injured that it was impossible to tell who hailed from which clan. Not that anyone cared at that moment. Not dying from their wounds took precedence over race. She searched the crowd, but it would be impossible to find anything in the mess of blood and bandages.

It was so loud. Moans and wails drowned out Ettrian's gentle assurances while the vacant stares were louder still. Radelia turned, ready to bolt, when Katar stopped her. "Look!"

Pointing her finger, Katar directed her attention to a healer. She knelt over the body of a High Elf. "No, not yet. Don't give up on me."

She was crying and pumping the elf's still chest with her hands. The High Elf twitched, and there was a distinct sound of ribs cracking. Radelia scowled at Katar. Why would she be so pleased by such a horrid scene?

Ettrian appeared equally confused and tried to smooth the situation before grief could get the better of her temper. "They are working side by side."

"No," Katar whispered. "Can't you see it? She's using magic."

Radelia and Ettrian both took a second look at the scene. The High Elf suddenly opened his eyes and gasped for air. The healer went slack before falling to the floor to kiss the ground. "How could you tell?" she asked Katar.

"The connection of her hands on his chest," the healer explained. "It was pulsing with magic."

Looking with a clearer head, Radelia focused on one healer at a time. The closest one to them was cauterizing a missing arm just by hovering her hand over the site. It was hard to tell through all the blood, but she was constantly moving her hand around a stump that was revealing more skin and less bone and muscle. The Runda Nor she tended to wasn't screaming in pain; they merely stared in awe at the process.

"Magic," Radelia uttered. She looked to Ettrian for confirmation. Was it really what she was seeing? Ettrian's eyes glistened. The knot at the base of his throat bobbed.

"It's real, all right," Kieran confirmed. "All the healers are using it."

Everything they had strived for had finally come true. Magic had returned to them. It was no doubt the sapling's doing. Their clans were united in blood and matrimony. The direct descendants of Isilynor and Elpharae reunited the gods torn apart by circumstance. Their marriage unified the stars and the earth creating a way for magic to return.

Yet, in that moment, she struggled to see it's worth. What was the point of magic if it couldn't save the ones she loved? Among the living, she knew without a doubt that her father was not one of them.

Radelia couldn't bear to lift the sheets. Kieran and Katar did it while Ettrian held her as though she would break apart at any moment. They knew the emperor better than she did, but when they lifted one tapestry, they both tilted their heads with confusion.

"The emperor only had one ring."

Kieran frowned and asked Ettrian, "Did anyone you know wear a pinky ring with a moss-green gem in the center?"

"Balqen," the king said with a nod. "An identical ring was gifted to his brother."

Radelia's legs went out from under her. She knew he was dead. His life was too much to hope for. They were next to the statue when it exploded, leaving nothing but a few pieces. Ettrian knelt to the ground with her as she came undone.

CHAPTER THIRTY-FOUR

Epilogue

In the months that followed the explosion, the death toll stopped rising, but the pain remained. Nearly two hundred were killed, and another hundred were detrimentally wounded. A string of suicides was counted among the casualties. Smiths and artisans that couldn't cope with the missing limbs. Others were simply unable to accept the loss of their spouses or children.

Ettrian saw to all of them himself.

She begged him not to. Each night he dragged himself to bed, weary with grief, but the king insisted that everyone received the highest honors in death.

Radelia had a plaque commissioned. The names of all they lost were cast into a bronze plate mounted on a smooth stone. Some she knew, but many she did not. Flowers and candles, along with various belongings, were left there by those who remembered them. The queen could be seen visiting them every day after breakfast.

But all was not lost.

The walls of Cardhon Nimloth were being stitched together by corded vines that grew from the dead wood. While the castle decayed faster than ever, new life could be seen flowering in its place soon after. The Runda Nor took up much of the empty space. Their reluctance died with the emperor.

Radelia stood on the balcony and reminded herself that joy would come and that the worst was behind them. The hole in the center of the garden was covered with a net moss blanket while the elves constantly returned to the cellar to examine and fuss over the sapling. It could no longer be described as a sapling, more like a massive vine plant that had wrapped around the dead roots. Every day it nearly doubled in size and was fighting against the covering.

At the rate it was growing, they'd have a full tree come summer. Whether or not it would restore the barrier was anyone's guess.

She couldn't help but smile at the fashion trends the High Elves were adapting.

With the barrier destroyed, winter snows occupied the gardens and the walls. Gone were the frilly lace gowns for more practical furs and leathers. They had enough food to survive the winter, but the lavish meals were replaced with more practical, simple fares. Hearty vegetable stews took the place of salads, and simple breads were issued instead of desserts.

She watched as a child hid behind a tree. No more than nine, he knelt to wad up a ball of snow and eyed his prey. A pair of High Elf women were walking by when he cranked his arm back and threw the snowball. It thwacked against the elf's fur before shattering into a mist of snow.

Oh, no. Radelia was about to go down there, fearing the High Elves would take offense. To her surprise, they made snowballs of their own and retaliated. She couldn't contain her laughter as an all-out snowball war ensued. Of course, the High Elves seldom played in the snow. This must have been something of a treat for them.

"Radelia," Ettrian called from inside the room. "What do you think of Kieran's proposal?"

A wave of nausea came on suddenly. She gripped the railing and steadied her breath. Kieran wanted to send scouts to find Aracaryn. To use his ties with the Ruby Isles to bring the traitor to justice. Radelia hated the idea.

As soon as it came, the queasiness was gone, and she joined Ettrian at the table. "I hate it."

The king nodded in agreement. "I worry that it sends the wrong message. Many of our Dark Elf residents are fearful that they will be associated with what happened."

Both made it clear that the Dark Elves who lived in Cardhon Nimloth were to be treated no differently. However, she did see the way they packed together, isolating themselves from the others. "There were complicit High Elves just as there were Dark Elves."

"Yet the Ruby Isles has refused to answer any of our messages."

She didn't know much of the Dark Elf stronghold other than what little Aracaryn described. The vassal had a reverence for her home, but she did not love it. It wasn't where her heart was. But why betray them?

"It's strange," Radelia said. "You'd think they would denounce Aracaryn's actions at the very least."

"Why remain silent and insinuate themselves with the explosion?" Ettrian agreed.

"When my father wanted to destroy the Runda Nor, Aracaryn was the only one who challenged him. I just don't understand. Why would she do this thing when she risked her life to oppose the other?"

The witnesses that saw her flee said Aracaryn had done so with sword in hand as she chased after them. For what was more, scouts found heavy cart tracks along the outside wall of the tower she stayed in. Multiple elves had packed the vassal's belongings and hoisted them down. The Runda Nor posted along that area made notes of it in their report, but everyone was so distracted by the wedding that it was overlooked.

"Do you think it possible that she was framed somehow?"

"From what I understand, she and the queen do not get along. I wouldn't be surprised. But we won't know unless we find her."

He had adjusted the bounty on Aracaryn's head. A chest of gold to anyone who brought her back alive and unharmed. The princess was the only one who could give them an explanation.

"We need Kieran to understand our feelings on this. Revenge isn't the—" Before she could finish that sentence, bile came spewing from her mouth. Grabbing the nearest vase, she vomited for the third time that week.

"That's it," Ettrian said, coming to a stand. "I'm getting Katar."

She had been putting off telling him. Not wanting to distract from their duties or give false hope. The king didn't see the symptoms for what they were because he'd never seen pregnancy before.

"Ettrian, wait."

"You're clearly sick," he argued. "What if it's an infection from the saplings or some ill-effect of magic returning or—"

There was no relieving his anxiety without the truth. "There's nothing Katar can do."

"We have magic—"

"I'm pregnant."

Her husband blanched, and his eyes went all distant as if he didn't understand what she said. "I'm with child," she said a bit more gently.

It was one thing for a female just over five feet tall to fall over, but for a male of Ettrian's size, it was like the felling of an old tree. He wobbled, still gripping the chair, before keeling to the right, taking the chair with him.

Folding her arms, Radelia stood over his body, shaking her head. Of all the things to make him faint... Just wait until he learned she wasn't alone in her condition. Not just the Runda Nor either.

It seemed they would need Katar's assistance after all.

About Author

S.M Fox is the author of the cozy fantasy series, Forgotten Gods.

Follow her on Amazon and Twitter

Subscribe to the mailing list here

Also By S.M Fox

The first in the Forgotten Gods Series...

For as long as Kate could remember, the Ghost King has stalked her
dreams and captured her imagination. But just what is he? Some
say he's Dominion's scourge. Evil incarnate. Cursed to wander the
continent in search of blood. His blight devours enemies, killing them
with unending cold. Others say the Ghost King is a gift. He only seeks

those who wish to harm the province. As a result, Kate's village has enjoyed a peaceful existence. When a prince disguised as a mercenary gets himself killed by the Ghost King, Kate fears it will lead to war. Rather than let it come to that, she uses her inventions to avoid the blight and forges an unlikely alliance with the Ghost King.